10651047

Don Juan in Paradise
and Other Amorous Fantasies

BY THE SAME AUTHOR

The Exigent Shadow
The Little Fays in the Air

Don Juan in Paradise
and Other Amorous Fantasies

by
Catulle Mendès

Translated, annotated and introduced by
Brian Stableford

A Black Coat Press Book

English adaptation and introduction Copyright © 2019 by Brian Stableford.

Cover illustration Copyright © 2019 illustration by Phil Cohen.

Visit our website at www.blackcoatpress.com

ISBN 978-1-61227-848-3. First Printing. April 2019. Published by Black Coat Press, an imprint of Hollywood Comics.com, LLC, P.O. Box 17270, Encino, CA 91416. All rights reserved. Except for review purposes, no part of this book may be reproduced or transmitted in any form or by any means, electronic or mechanical, including photocopying, recording, or by any information storage and retrieval system, without permission in writing from the publisher. The stories and characters depicted in this novel are entirely fictional. Printed in the United States of America.

TABLE OF CONTENTS

Introduction

This volume is one of a set of three collections assembling a substantial fraction of the short fantastic fiction of Catulle Mendès (1841-1909). It assembles more than eighty *contes*, fables and apologues employing supernatural motifs other than the apparatus of faerie, tales featuring *fées* having been separated out for publication in *The Little Fays in the Air and Other Tales of Faerie*, an addendum to the series of collections and anthologies produced in association with *Tales of Enchantment and Disenchantment: A History of Faerie, with an Exemplary Anthology of Tales*. Stories dealing with anomalous events and altered states of consciousness, which might or might not have supernatural causes, are also separately assembled in *The Exigent Shadow and Other Strange Obsessions*.

Mendès began writing short stories in 1860, and the works he produced during the next decade were aimed at periodicals that frequently used substantial articles and stories. He was the founder in 1861 of the *Revue fantaisiste*, which followed the then-standard practice of using relatively long feature articles and stories, but as the editor of the periodical, required to fill a fixed number of pages every month, he routinely had to supply "fillers" of various sorts. Most periodicals employed reviews and short items of non-fiction for that purpose, but Mendès immediately began deploying fictional "character sketches" of a kind that were later to supply the bulk of three collections entitled *Monstres parisiens* in the early 1880s.

That marketplace was devastated by the economic upheavals following France's catastrophic defeat in the Franco-Prussian War of 1870, and the bulk of Mendes' literary effort in the next decade went into poetry and work for the theater, but the situation changed drastically in the early 1880s when advances in the technologies of printing and paper production made newspapers and periodicals much cheaper to produce, resulting in a rapid and prodigal proliferation, and consequent fierce competition between them.

French newspapers already had a long tradition of "feuilleton fiction," by which a section of one page was ruled off, and the space below it used for serial fiction. Convention had established that the space below a standard feuilleton could accommodate between 1400 and 1700 words of text, and although much of the short fiction published by newspapers in the 1880s was not actually placed beneath the feuilleton, that remained a standard expectation of length, although Mendès frequently reduced the wordage even further, in order that his work could be more easily slotted into the limited space available in newspapers that were only four pages long, with the back page mostly taken up by advertisements. Writing stories of that brevity, with the variety that mass-production required, was an art that there had not previously been any incentive to cultivate, but Mendès mastered it quickly, and his work became an exemplar followed by many of the authors who subsequently adapted themselves to supplying such slots on a regular basis, including Jean Lorrain, Jean Richepin, Léon Bloy, Octave Mirbeau, Marcel Schwob and Jane de La Vaudère.

When the boom in periodical production began, Mendès was ready and prepared to take advantage of it. He soon became an editor again, for the short-lived geographical periodical *Le Monde Inconnu* and the longer-lasting bi-weekly *Revue Populaire*, both launched in 1882. The latter's chief stock-in-trade was reprinted serial novels, but in both periodicals Mendès employed his expertise in supplying fillers, initially under the pseudonyms Jean-qui-Passe and René Maugéant. Many were brief anecdotal sketches of contemporary Parisian life, often featuring Jean-qui-Passe's friend Valentin, who remained the hero of many of Mendès short stories long after he had abandoned the pseudonym. Mendès soon quit both periodicals, but continued supplying material in the same vein to other periodicals, broadening the narrative scope of his fiction considerably in an urgent quest for variation, distinction and originality.

It was in the context of that quest for variety, originality and ingenuity that Mendès began experimenting extensively with fantastic motifs. "Fays," modeled on English fairies rather than the fays of the French *contes de fées* developed by female writers in Parisian salons during the 1690s, provided him with his most abundant images, but he also made elaborate use of angels and other items borrowed from the Christian mythos, and figures borrowed from the lexicon of Classical mythology, especially the god Eros. Loquacious insects and flowers provided him with a useful series of voices for use in exotic dialogues, and stars provided him with a further set of symbolic images. The categories were by no means mutually exclusive, and overlaps were frequent, in the interests of constructing novel allegories

Two themes, in particular, provided him with the climactic motifs for his brief stories, many of which are more reminiscent of Baudelairean prose poems than stories, and are often formulated as wry jokes. The first and foremost of those themes was the wayward working of amour in relationships between young men and women, and the incessant battle between promiscuous natural impulse and moral restrictions imposed—always ineffectively—by religion and social prejudice. Mendès had his own liberal—or libertine—moral stance with regard to sexual relations, and his stories provided relentless witty propaganda for that opinion, while satirizing the opposing orthodoxy relentlessly. That preoccupation fueled his illustrative anecdotes of Parisian society abundantly, and his fantasies enabled him to add an extra dimension of exaggeration and irony to his fundamental argument.

The second major theme in his work—not unconnected with his libertine moral stance, and perhaps a corollary of it, is the difficulty of pursuing a quest for the ideal in a social and psychological situation that has ruled out *a priori* the orthodox routes mapped out by tradition and prejudice. Possessed of a poetic vocation, Mendès inevitable conceived his own ideal—characterized as almost impossible to achieve, but the only thing truly worth striving toward—in terms of literary vision.

The stories translated in this volume are arranged within each of its sections in the chronological order of the collections in which they were initially assembled, where they were usually mingled with anecdotal stories of contemporary Parisian life, on which they composed a wry commentary of sorts. The chronological order allows a rough perception of phases that Mendès passed through in the development of each set of images, during a productive period that lasted from about 1882 to 1904. The juxtaposition of the several parts also permits the perception and appreciation of certain general trends in his work, most obviously an inclination toward the increasing surrealization of his imagery.

Although not generally reputed as an important precursor of absurdism and surrealism, the later phases of the collection, especially the final group of stories, demonstrate that Mendès certainly took a hand in that particular evolution of the Symbolist movement—to which he made significant contributions, although, like many of his contemporaries, he refused to regard himself as a specialist and felt perfectly free to move back and forth between Symbolist and Naturalist narrative strategies, and to combine the two in his longer works. From the very beginning however, his sense of humor, ever quirky, tended toward the farcical, and his work in either mode was often possessed of a buoyancy that writers more earnestly committed to a narrower philosophy of procedure rarely showed.

That buoyancy, inevitably, reached its peak in work where he allowed his imagination to soar into the realms of fantasy, and it is on display in the present collection more prolifically and more colorfully than in the many collections where such stories provided imaginative spice for assemblies of Parisiana confined by the bounds of mundane possibility. In his younger days Mendès has been a close friend of Auguste Villiers de l'Isle-Adam, and he was a great admirer of the work assembled in that author's famous collection of *Contes cruels* (1883), which carried forward a kind of narrative strategy developed in the days of the Romantic Movement by such writers as Petrus Borel, S. Henry Berthoud and Jules Janin. Mendès frequently employed a similar narrative strategy, and he was capable, when he wished to be, of writing tales as cruel as anyone, but the vast majority of the stories in the present collection are not cruel, and staunch in their determined refusal not to be. Although the philosophy of life that they promote is cynical, thus lending an acidic edge to much of his humor, his cynicism is very often conscientiously mild, even gentle; it rarely sacrifices its compensating uplift to bleak dramatic effect, and there is a vein of nostalgic sentimentality that runs through all Mendès' work, persisting even when he grew old and more than a little jaded.

Throughout his career, Mendès tended to dole out the kind of extravagant fantasies represented in the present volume in relatively small doses. Only two of his collections, *Les Contes du rouet* [Spinning-Wheel Tales] (1885; revised in 1888 as *Les Oiseaux bleus*; tr. as *Bluebirds*), and *Pour lire au couvent* (1887) consisted entirely of fantastic materials, and only a further three or four—out of a total exceeding twenty—contain more fantastic material than naturalistic. That might not have been a deliberate policy, however, and he might simply have bundled up material as it accumulated in the many periodicals that he supplied with material, without any conspicuous attempt to sort material by thematic classification once he got into his stride. Even if the policy was deliberate, however, that does not mean that it is the only virtuous strategy of presentation, and there is definitely something to be said, not merely for aggregating so many brief fantastic works in a single volume, but also for aggregating the stories within the categories indicated in the list of contents.

Organizing the whole spectrum of Mendès' fantastic fiction in this way facilitates a kind of panoramic view of his literary cosmos, and splitting it into subcategories adds a few interesting features to the map. Bringing all the paradisal fantasies together, for instance, builds up a more complete image of the celestial realms as imagined by Mendès, and their aggregation encourages the rather striking observation that he is far more interested in setting stories in Heaven than in Hell—a rare choice among writers, who generally prefer to exploit of melodramatic potential of the realm of punishments. For such a markedly disenchanted writer, Mendès retained a stubborn a distinctive steak of amiable Romanticism and moral generosity that lends considerable impetus to the generally-upbeat manner of his work. Although violence and cruelty are by no means absent from his work, and there is a perennial threnody therein bewailing man's inhumanity to man, his literary universe is, on the whole, a relatively civilized and polite one—like Parisian society—where God can always find a justification for keeping the experiment going, and finding some delight in its continuation, even when disappointments pile up.

As the presiding deity of his own literary creativity, Mendès was by no means a vengeful spirit, certainly capable of indignant wrath, but almost always willing to err on the side of concession and forgiveness, at least in his brief and necessarily flippant works; his book-length fantasies, *Méphistophela* (1890), *Luscignole* (1892) and *Gog, roman contemporain* (1896) are much darker, employing their length to build up a rare degree of intensity, extending to stark horror. The prologue to the last-named novel, reproduced herein, forms an independent short story whose tone and content contrast sharply with the vignettes surrounding it, although some of the earlier ones contain faint foreshadowings to it, and those that followed it retained some of its acidity without its deliberate blasphemy, which was not something that could bear frequent repetition, although *Gog* first appeared as a feuilleton in the pages of the daily newspaper *Le Journal*, where it must have shocked many of its readers. The light-hearted flippancy of the vast majority of the short stories in the present collection has its own heroic dimension, however, in blithely sacrificing the copious resource of narrative energy to be found in the Devil's works in order to focus much more extensively on the kindly ministrations of angels, Eros and other benign figures; it is a testament of Mendès' ingenuity that the sacrifice in question was not a costly one, permitting him to maintain a level of productivity that few writers of his era could match.

Inevitably, given the volume of his production, it is not the case that Mendès' stories never fall flat or peter out, but such weakening is rare enough to be forgivable, and if he has a certain tendency to repeat himself, that too is forgivable in the context of the situation in which he was working and the pressure that was always upon him to find something new to write—and, if possible, something new to think. Whimsy might look easy to a reader, because it is so light-hearted and exuberant, but it is not nearly as easy for a creator as it appears to a casual glance; not many writers have ever been able to draw from that particular well as prolifically and consistently as Catulle Mendès, and there are only a precious few whose work could be assembled into a kaleidoscopic display of phantasmagorical materials as rich as this one—especially bearing in mind that, in its present format, it is only one volume in a set of three.

Translations of stories from *Les Petites fées en l'air* were made from a copy of the 1891 Dentu edition. The translation of the prologue to *Gog* was made from the feuilleton version published in *Le Journal* 20-22 Mars 1895, reproduced on the Bibliothèque Nationale's *gallica* website. All the other translations were made from scans of the relevant Mendès collections reproduced on *gallica* and the International Archive Digital Library at *archive.org*.

Brian Stableford

PART I: ANGELS AND DEVILS

Don Juan in Paradise

The balance swung in the direction of the pig.[1]
Victor Hugo.

When he was summoned—after the formalities, much simplified for him, of the throes of death—before the Judge who, selecting the good grain from the chaff, opens the gates of Paradise to the elect and casting the damned into the eternal Gehenna, Don Juan, according to what is written in the book by Charles Baudelaire,[2] did not deign to show any emotion, and, still young and handsome, his lips retained the smile that had made the Elviras and the Annas weep.

At the sight of that adolescent, whose had had the immortality of grace on earth, the virgins of Heaven dreamed of a paradise that they did not know, and sighed charmed; they said prayers, speaking to one another in low voices, for no serious charge to be laid against the accused, in order that he might be admitted into the imperishable joy, the salary of the innocent or the repentant, and that they might have the pleasure of strolling in his company in the road of stars that we call

---

[1] The line is from "Sultan Mourad" in *La Légende des siècles* (1862), the balance in question being the divine balance in which souls, taking on symbolic form, are weighed.

[2] The reference is to "Don Juan aux enfers" [Don Juan in Hell] in *Les Fleurs du Mal* (1857).

17

the Milky Way, and making music with him on the days of concerts before the Throne.

But they soon had to renounce those pleasant hopes. Don Juan had scarcely responded, nonchalantly, to the initial questions of the judge, when a groaning multitude of maidens and wives ran into the supreme tribunal, with their hair in disarray, their clothing disturbed, tears of rage in their eyes, and bloody wounds in their hearts.

They were the victims of the implacable lover.

He had pretended to love them all! He had deceived, tortured and forgotten them all! He had chosen the most beautiful in order to make them the most unhappy. Blushing children who were troubled behind the shutters at the sound of footsteps in the street, wives who feigned slumber, turning toward the wall behind the bed, listening with a delectable fear to the lover's serenade rising up to the above the husband's snores, and nuns awakened in the peace of cloisters, had all followed him recklessly, without listening to the imminent pursuit of maledictions, stepping over in their flight the cadavers of fathers or husbands, wrenching a scapular from the neck in order to strangle the opposed sister whose cries might have sounded the alarm.

His irresistible covetousness had not spared any living beauty; victoriously, it had raised him up as far as the most illustrious, and lowered him to the humblest; he had stolen queens from the alcoves of sovereigns and peasants from rustic beds of straw. And all of them—all of them—after rapid kisses, pleading and holding out their arms in vain, he had rejected with a mocking gesture and scornful laughter.

O cruelty of long abandonments after excessively brief delights! Dragging their shame and their mourning, simultaneously full of remorse and regret for the sin, they had searched for him for so long from one city to another and one country to another, guided by the despair that he left behind him, as one follows the trail of an assassin by means of the drops of blood on the road.

Now, at the feet of the infallible arbiter, displaying, innumerably, the betrayed beauty of their golden or ebon hair, their blue or night-dark eyes, their rosy mouths, their snowy breasts and their lacerated hearts, they demanded justice in their furious dolor; and around Don Juan there was something like the assault of an angry and plaintive sea against a rock.

A murmur of horror, because of so many cruel abandonments, ran through the celestial audience; the fearful virgins folded their wings over their faces.

However, as the accused, still smiling, disdained to respond, an angel, the official advocate, made a speech in his defense.

He did not deny Don Juan's crime. The evidence of the victims was irrefutable. Yes, undoubtedly, his client had brought to harm the most charming of the daughters of the earth, and, having seduced them, had left them without a word of consolation, without a farewell tear. He could be excused, because of the charm of the women, for having desired them excessively, but nothing could acquit him of such much ingratitude after so much joy. He seemed, therefore, to have merited eternal punishment. Nevertheless, was the admission of extenuating circumstances impossible?

Was it certain that the torturer had not been tortured? As the poets of the world below said, he carried within him an infinite need for the ideal; was it his fault if the insufficiency of terrestrial femininity had never permitted him to be fully satisfied, if he had been obliged to search, from one amour to the next, relentlessly and in vain, for the reality of his dream? How many sad experiments! And how he had undoubtedly suffered!

The advocate did not want, in any fashion, to speak ill of the honorable witnesses, whose legitimate chagrin was worthy of all respect; but, exquisite as the plaintiffs were, passionate as their tenderness had been, had they the wherewithal to fulfill the prayers of a soul always starved of impossible intoxications? Thus, the man who had made so many victims was also a victim; as much as the desperate women, he had known despair; and doubtless the tribunal, employing some indulgence...

But the angelic advocate did not have the leisure to finish. The plaints of the thousand and three abandoned women drowned out his voice with a redoubling of imprecations; at the same time, the increasing murmur of the assembly testified that the author of so much harm ought not expect any mercy; and a glint of menace was visible in the eye of the judge, like a flash of lightning before a storm, which was already a condemnation.

Don Juan was doomed.

But then an old woman approached.

Sordid and ragged, the skin of her cheeks and her neck hanging down like her other rags, her hair in dirty gray clumps, like islets of wool in the hide of a dromedary, swelling under a greasy headscarf, her bloodless face stained here and there by violent patches, her eyes jaundiced, a viscous tear trebling in her nasal hair, her tongue protruding over her sagging lip, she was so old and hideous to behold, tottering as if she were running after a crutch, that all the angels turned away, with a cry of revulsion; a nasty aroma of a rag-picker's basket emanated from her—a basket in which old clothes were mingled with other rubbish, the stockings of paupers and the chemises of whores: a stink of dank dives that would have withered flowers or moistened cosmetics.

In the midst of the desolate beauties who were similar, half-naked, to blooming flowers, she was like a muddy puddle fallen among roses.

In a hoarse voice, with a spitting cough, she said:

"Although I shall soon be a centenarian, and foul as I am, the enraged demon of lust has never ceased to stimulate my blood or heat my marrow. In order to buy young kisses for my aging lips, I had to sell my furniture, my clothes and my jewels. Now, like beggar-women, I haunt the crossroads and the narrow streets of the old city, eating things found on rubbish heaps before the rag-pickers pass by, sleeping under projecting roofs or in cellars open to the sky of buildings under construc-

20

tion. But hunger doesn't exhaust me sufficiently. I don't feel chilled by the wind or the rain.

"The ancient covetousness, surviving, was like an ever-burning stove within me, and it was neither sous not bread that I begged from nocturnal passers-by. O poor old woman, shaken like a rag in the wind by infernal desire! My hands, suddenly springing from a doorway, fell upon a shoulder, grabbed it, and held it hard. Alas, everyone fled me, snubbing me, hurling sniggers and insults at me, because of my ignoble face, my gray hair, my yellow eyes and my secular mouth, glimpsed in the darkness.

"No one wanted me, abject as I am—neither prowlers, nor thieves, nor drunkards for whom any kiss is good. Crouching behind some boundary-marker, my fists in my teeth, I wept tears of rage, or, standing up, I howled into the night like a mad beast. I was infamous, yes, but lamentable in that infamy, since, after all, I have not ignited the fire that was devouring me, and while scornful of myself, I thought myself worthy of pity.

"One evening when, with my ears pricked and my eyes wide, I was on the lookout for the hazard hoped for in vain. I saw an adolescent coming, under the stars, more charming than all the dreams of womankind. The extent to which he was handsome you know, you who are listening to me, since that passer-by was the young man who is here, since it was Don Juan. At the sight of him, I wanted to flee, fearing the torture of an unrealizable desire, the most absurd of all. That a camp-follower, some evening, starved and famished of caresses, as I was myself, might put his arms around my neck, I might have dreamed without being insane, but that ephebe with the golden hair, worthy of the bed of a queen, with what disgust he would reject me!

"Yes, I wanted to flee. But he approached, retained me with a gesture, and looked at me for a long time, compassionately, while I contemplated him, without saying a word, ecstatic, like a damned soul catching a glimpse of paradise. What was he thinking? What did he divine? It seemed to me that tears veiled his eyes, softer than the stars. Finally, he took me by the hand—him! me! him, so delectably adorable, whom everyone adored, me, filthy, scorned by drunkards and thieves!—and, having drawn me toward the darkness, tenderly, his mouth approaching mine, he put his arms around me, with all the dear words, for a long, long time, as a young husband embraces his young wife."

The menace was extinguished in the eyes of the judge, and the thousand and three amorous women lowered their plaintive heads, no longer daring to accuse the pitiless individual who had shown pity.

As Don Juan was absolved, the virgins of Heaven were able to stroll in his company along the road of stars that we call the Milky Way, and make music with him, on the days of concerts around the Throne.

Angelic Cuisine

The other evening, I had just finished climbing the cliff path when I perceived an angel who was perched on the slate roof of the chapel.

At first glance, one might have mistaken that vague pale form for a wisp of fog risen from the sea, which had clung on there, giving the impression of torn muslin, but it is not for nothing that the gaze of poets is accustomed to discover celestial realities under the vain appearance of illusions, and I saw clearly that it was an angel. He was sitting under one of the arms of the cross, motionless, his forehead inclined toward the valley. His white wings, brought around in front of him, gave the idea of a semi-naked young woman who had gathered her headscarf.

As it is rare to encounter a paradisal creature in this word, I thought that I ought to take advantage of the opportunity. In order to clarify certain doubts that I had always conserved with regard to the nature of angelic mores, I approached the child of light, resolved to interrogate him; but I was not without a certain anxiety. By what title should I address him? What rank had he acquired in the divine militias? To which of the three hierarchies did he belong, and to which of the nine choirs? Ought I to call him Archangel, Seraph, Domination, Cherub, Principality, Throne, Power, Intelligence or Virtue? In any case, at the noise of my footsteps or the sound of my voice, he might shiver, open his wings, and fly away, leaving in the air the wake of a white flight, quickly effaced, and in my soul, a dream.

Things went much better than I had dared to hope. Perhaps he knew that I had lived in familiarity with his peers for a long time in the heavens of Swedenborg, and felt inclined, because of that, to some condescension. What is certain is that he did not appear at all alarmed by my approach; it even seemed that, albeit without looking up, he had a slight golden tremor in his hair, as if making a sign.

Encouraged, I bent my knee , and, after a few trivial words in which I gave proof of the most courteous angelolatry, calling him, at hazard, Celestial Spirit—which could not compromise me or displease him—I prepared to question him. There was one point on which I was burning to be instructed. Do the angels nourish themselves, and, if they do, what do they eat? A capital problem, the object of many controversies.

Julius Sperberus, a little thoughtlessly, concludes affirmatively and mentions ambrosia mingled with manna, which appears to be a dish of his invention. Jacob Boehme, in his chapter on the seven astringent qualities of God, mocks Sperberus' cuisine very agreeably, and Jane Pordage, after having weights the fors and againsts, does not know what to resolve. [3]

Although there was a certain irreverence in importuning with such a question an undoubtedly immaterial creature, and I rather gave the impression, in speaking to one of the Elohim, of someone asking a parrot: "Have you dined, Jacquot?" the angel sitting on the chapel roof did not seem at all shocked by my audacity, and he deigned to respond to me, with a voice so delectably made of melody and clarity that there was, in the nocturnal silence, something akin to a flight of singing radiance.

"Yes, like birds and little children, like butterflies and women, my brothers and I do, in fact, eat, but our nourishment

---

[3] The name of the seventeenth century visionary and Cabalist Julius Sperber was appropriated for numerous apocryphal texts and accorded a significant role in the history of Rosicrucianism. "Jane Pordage" might be a misprint of "Jean Pordage," or might refer Jane Leade, the disciple and successor of John Pordage, himself a disciple of Sperber's contemporary, the mystic Jakob Böhme; the reference is probably to Pordage's posthumous *Theologica Mystica* (1683) which had a preface by Leade.

is not like those that please the vulgar appetite of humans and beasts; the painter who represented us preparing meat and peeling vegetables was much mistaken. Don't believe, however, that the stars are miraculous fruits with a golden rind, or that we compose our meals from the perfume of paradisal flowers, or that we drink the luminous milk of the Milky Way. Our nourishment—O sweetest of out eternal privileges—is the breath of earthly virgins. Did you think that it was not useful for anything, after having been exhaled, the breath of chaste lips that no mouth has ever kissed? That it disperses, along with all perfumes, in vain errant breezes? No, it rises up, intact and exquisite, distinct from other aromas, and every angel, who watches for it in passing, aspires the vaporized soul of a child. They are our delicious feasts, our incomparable agapes. The respiration of ephemeral young women enables us to live perpetually, and that precious smoke aliments our subtle substance. Sometimes it happens that a virginal breath, uncertain and too weak because it is so soft, cannot rise as far as paradise, which awaits it; then whichever of us it is destined for takes fight and descends to your world, to collect it closer to the lips from which it emanates, as a woman leans over to respire a flower."

After having thanked the angel for the complaisance he had shown me, I dared to ask him again: "Can any breath other than that of the immaculate serve as your nourishment?"

"None," he said.

"You can't satisfy yourselves with the scent, delightful as it is, that the mouths of our wives exhale, like more open roses?"

He had a disdainful, almost scornful, expression. I did not think it appropriate to insist further. I limited myself to insinuating, with a commencement of familiarity that had nothing wounding about it: "If I've understood what you've deigned to reveal to me, it might be that you've descended this evening, at meal time, to aspire the breath of some young woman?"

"You are not mistaken," he said, smiling. "While you are listening to me, I sense an ineffable freshness rising toward me, which penetrates me ecstatically. She has fallen asleep, whiter than her little white bed, under the sacred box-tree whose stem is steeped in the font; she is asleep, and not even dreaming, the one whose breath is my sweet nourishment: a breath that makes less noise, wandering over her lips, than the flight of a distant bee. She has never raised her eyes to the gallants passing by, and I hope that the hour will be long delayed in coming in which the kiss of a husband will dishonor her mouth. She is so chaste that she has never thought of asking why the other young girls consider with envious expressions, and also while blushing, the brides who emerge from the church on the arms of husbands. When she goes to bed she puts her doll between the sheets beside her, saying to it in a low voice: 'Good night, little heart!' O virginal bed, what snow made of the dust of lilies could be purer than your cold pallor? But purer still reposes the sleeping child, and in her breath—O dear immateriality!—I sate myself with all innocence and all modesty."

As he spoke in that fashion the angel appeared to experience an infinite pleasure; veritably, there was in his attitude—if one can compare divine delights with human satisfactions—a little of the visible wellbeing of a gastronome savoring a excellent morsel. Suddenly, however, the celestial gourmand made a grimace, which did not fail to astonish me. Had the adorable dish suffered some sudden adulteration? Cruel hypothesis: had an unexpected kiss—anything is possible, even in the cold bed or a virgin—intercepted the angel's supper?

I did not have the leisure to interrogate him on that point, for he opened his wings wide and disappeared into the somber azure.

I drew away, thinking that the alimentary regime of the celestial spirits is not without a few inconveniences. If they do not take care to assure themselves, in case of accidents, of more than one menu, they must often have to go to bed without having finished their supper.

Isamberte's Layette

The old wife of the mariner, going slowly down the cliff path, stopped for a moment, her two fists on her staff, in order to gaze at the Parisiennes sitting in groups on the beach; seen from a distance, in the billows of their skirts of all colors, with their broad-brimmed hats, they gave the impression of flowering bushes scattered on the shingle. I imagined that the poor woman, comparing her rags to so many beautiful dresses, must have a little melancholy jealousy in her soul

"Bah!" she said, responding to my thought. "One can follow one's path from this world to the next, from one end to the other, without those rich frills. A white rag suffices to live, to die and to reach Heaven."

With that, as we went down the grassy and stony slope together, she told me what her grandmother had told her about Isamberte's layette—a story good to tell on late evenings, of which the local fishermen have made a song that they sing when at sea, on mild nights when the sea is also singing.

The day when Isamberte came into the world, her father and mother felt singularly chagrined. It was not that it displeased them to have a beautiful little girl opening heavily eyes and flowery lips; they even had a great joy in hearing the first cry of the newborn, in which the astonishment of living is alarmed; there is in all men and all women a long mute echo that only awakens to that cry. But they had not been able to prepare the layette for the expected child, they were so poor.

They lived at the bottom, of the cliff in an old hut of worm-eaten plants, with a roof that was sagging, without a door, which had been abandoned to them out of charity, and in which the wind from the sea was engulfed by night, all the way to their meager bed, roiling them in a blanket of damp air and bitter droplets. When the man went fishing, he never

27

brought back fish, his nets being so old that their broken mesh always let the turbots and the soles escape; and the woman could not find employment in the village because her skin was visible though the holes of her rags, which scandalized the honest folk. When one is not well dressed, one cannot earn the wherewithal to dress oneself.

In truth, they would have died of hunger if the rich people did not have the custom of throwing kitchen scraps out of the window, into the back alley or the ditch. In consequence, it was necessary not to think of hemming swaddling clothes, making dainty vests, or pretty bonnets that so many fortune women ornament with ribbons and frills while smiling. What, then? Would little Isamberte have her first slumber on a stool, devoid of linen, stark naked, as she had been born? Fortunately, the mother espied a large scrap of muslin, embroidered with thin leaves, which she had once picked up on a rubbish heap, and of which she had made curtains for her unique window. Weak as she was, she set to work, washing, tearing, sewing and pleating, and Isamberte, as best she could contrive, had a layette in which she was so pretty, with her heavenly eyes and her flowery mouth.

When Isamberte had grown somewhat, she suddenly ceased to be joyful and laughing, playing with the other infants on the rolling shingle. She thought that she would not be able to make her first communion, on a beautiful sunny Sunday, in the midst of a crowd in fête, in the little church with the roof pointed like a mast, standing on the cliff. Certainly, she knew her catechism better than anyone, and Monsieur le curé had no more meritorious ewe among his flock of little girls. But for a communicant, a white robe is required. Alas, Isamberte's parents were not rich people who could go into shops, with pockets full of money, able to choose between twenty magnificent and dear fabrics.

More than once, she became desolate, dissolving in tears, before the beautiful shop windows. But her mother said to her: "Don't cry, darling." She took all the pieces of the layette, which had been a muslin curtain, out of an old chest, sewed them together, and made a robe as best she could, with the consequence that, on the day of the communion, Isamberte was dressed in white, as was befitting. The good God, who sees everything, pretended not to see the repairs to the bodice and the skirt, satisfied with the little intact soul; and, the little communicant being the prettiest, it even seemed to the people of the area that she had the prettiest clothes.

At eighteen years of age, she became smitten with a handsome young boy as poor as she was. They had a frank engagement, not hiding their love for one another, embracing in the evening on some doorstep whether people were passing by or not. They went fishing for crabs together, she bare-legged, leaping from rock to rock over the slippery wrack, he sustaining her by the waist, in order that she would not fall. If she turned round she found a mouth close to her mouth, which she did not flee; and, returning as the tide came in, they walked so close one another in the redness of the setting sun that one could only see one shadow on the wall of the cliff.

In the end, the healthy desire to possess one another gripped their hearts and their senses, and they declared that they intended to be united without delay. But Isamberte's mother was alarmed. "Do you think so, darling?" he said, in a low voice. "Can one marry when one is as poor as you are? Will you go to church in those brown rags, which give you the air of a beggar, and will you dare to sleep, next to the man you love, stark naked, after your rags fall away?"

This time it was the daughter who consoled the mother. "As regards being naked, she said, "there's no fear of that happening to me. I'll take the communion robe from the old chest, which had been my layette, and I'll make my wedding chemise out of it."

And she did as she had said. On the meager nuptial bed, she was all white in muslin. If the chemise had a few tears here and there, the husband did not complain.

It did not matter that they were poor; they were happy in the old hut where they lived alone after the death of the parents; the smile of being together, when people adore one another, consoles the most bitter sorrows, and there are no tears that kisses cannot dry up. They scarcely thought about earning any more than was necessary not to die of starvation; they only gave a few hours of their time, which their amour would have liked to have entirely, to indispensable labor, not worrying about the next day because, before the next day, there was the night. It was their joy, increasing every evening, to find one another on their return from their work, and, as their hut had no door, their mad laughter and ardent words were audible some distance away. Many rich people envied those poor people who loved one another.

It happened, however, that Isamberte fell ill; in poverty, the force of life is used up more rapidly than the force of love. Now she remained lying on the meager conjugal bed all day long, her lips pale and her eyes obscured; it was obvious that she would soon be going away, never to return. For long hours, they gazed at one another, not speaking for fear of confessing their thoughts. But each of them divined clearly what the other was thinking: that they would soon be separated, alas.

And in the soon-to-be-widowed husband the anguish of losing Isamberte was mingled with another anguish, which she also divined.

"Oh," she said, on the eve of the fatal day, "I know what you're thinking. There are no sheets on our bed, no linen in the entire hut, and you don't know what you'll bury me in. Beloved, quit that worry, at least. Take the wedding dress from the old wooden chest, which was my communion robe, and make a shroud of it.

The next day, buried as she had wanted to be, she was laid in the cemetery. Two angels descended from Heaven on a moonbeam in order to take her any carry her away. But they were two very small angels, newcomers to paradise, employed

30

for the first time in the function of going to collect the dead who were the elect. When they had removed the earth and lifted the lid of the coffin, they were very perplexed. Frail as they were, they would never have had the strength to lift the corpse and carry it all the way to the Lord's throne, for that throne is very high.

What could they do? What means could they imagine?

Discouraged, they were about to go back up again in order to ask the advice of a more experienced seraph, when they noticed the shroud of white muslin, which the evening breeze was causing to tremble, and they had the idea of making it into wings similar to their own. You can imagine that angels are adept at such work,

In less than an instant, the pale, torn fabric was adapted to the shoulders of the corpse in two mobile whitenesses, and Isamberte, half-resuscitated, rose up to Heaven very rapidly, winged by the shroud that had been her wedding dress.

The Tenderness of Justice

The just and terrible God who has lightning for a gaze and thunder for a gesture, the one who can precipitate suns and earths into eternal oblivion with a sign, without a single soul remaining to remember them, was listening pensively to the angels who were returning from our world one by one, bringing news.

The first messenger said: "I have visited the mysterious somber regions that mortals call Africa. There the men collect strange flowers, with arms as long as those of monkeys, in order to poison their arrows, and they drag their entrails painfully, heavy with human flesh. Black inside and out, their thought does not enlighten the darkness of their ignorance any more than the light bleaches that of their faces. They never raise their heads toward Heaven. Their divinities, fetishes of worm-eaten wood or crumbling clay, are so small, almost at ground level amid the stink of mud and the putrescence of dead beasts, that they do not rise to knee-height; when they worship them, they give the impression of invoking ordure.

"If they have wives and children, it is as dogs or wolves have bitches and pups. They live to kill, killing in order to eat, for every cadaver is a feast, killing to drink, for blood is the beverage they prefer, and killing to sleep, for their slumber is only good with the head upon a dead body, and if, during the night, hunger wakes them up, they feed on their fetid pillow.

"Filthy and ferocious, they have kings who are even more ferocious and even filthier, who are ecstasized by massacres. No less than a thousand executions are necessary for a celebration, and from the severed heads, the opened breasts, the eyeless orbits, the mouths devoid of teeth and the fingers without nails, the horrible red liquid flows so abundantly that it eventually forms a sea with red waves, in which I have seen

32

swimming princes bite the feet of little children and chew the breasts of women."

At those words, the just and terrible God had a frisson of wrath, of which the immensity trembled, and over all the clarity of space the shadow of his exterminating right hand was visibly raised.

The second messenger said:

"I have visited the lands of sunlight and gold were all birds sing and all roses flourish. There, the plains are so vast, beneath the enormous azure, and the forests of bandhiras and evergreen oaks so profound, that the distant roaring of tigers arrives at the ear as softly as the cooing of doves. Crushing the bamboos in which corallines and madhavis enlace—serpent-flowers and flower-serpents—the royal elephants come to drink from the great rivers starred by the flowers of lilies and nelumbos.

"O paradisal splendor of horizons! Snows of the Himalaya, which melt in torrents of light! Valleys blooming in clouds of perfumes! India is the whole of ancient Eden, dispersed. But the cowardly Adams no longer have the strength even to pluck the fruit of forbidden trees, wallow innumerably and yawn stupidly under the most beautiful of skies In the ardent life that surrounds them, they have a horror of living; their ennui, aspiring to slumber, to the eternal slumber, does not see the horizons, the snows, or the valleys in which the gallop of antelopes resounds in the mornings; their idleness disdains the kiss, and, emaciated and withered, their skin reddened over fleshless bones, they have Famine for a hostess and the Plague for a bed-companion.

"Meanwhile, in halls decorated with precious stones, under the glare of diamantine chandeliers where light is illuminated among all the enchantments of opium, the triumphant masters lie on the hides of dead lions and the hides of living women. A measureless fête smiles on high, not even touching with a foot the measureless misery below. All pride, all glory, and the pale nudity of dancing girls in flying muslins, puts a kind of apotheosis around the princes; to make their joy perfect, or to divinize their damnation, every night the virtue of wives, the modesty of virgins and the flower of soiled children are spilled over their august couches like odorous petals, with the consequence that the vague noise that rises from the sunlit continent where the lords are awake in joy and the people asleep in ignominy, is made of a few songs of celebration over an immense snore."

At those words, the just and terrible God, frowning, lowered his right hand, ready to make the formidable sign.

The third messenger said:

"I have seen the obscure islands, even more mysterious than Africa, and more hideous, where the carnivorous native offers his guest, on feast days, the left eye of his new-born son. I have seen the rich Americas, shaken by the rumble of machinery, where souls have no other reverie than the smoke emerging from factory chimneys. I have seen Europe, abominable and charming; if it became similar to its double desire, it would be all gold and blood, but an odor of flowers rises up therefrom, because of the young women.

"There the men no longer know that you exist. O powerful God who judges them; and along with the faith that created you, they have lost all fine beliefs. They have thrown on the rubbish heap modesty, charity and tenderness, which only poets sometimes collect, rag-pickers under the stars. The hope-bird no longer nests in the branches of dream. They are astonished by heroes and they smile at lovers. They have heard mention of amity, and of fidelity to oaths, but they have no personal knowledge of them. They might say of the sacrifice: 'That's someone I don't know,' They are recklessly covetous of gold in heaps, of banknotes in wads; their hearts are soon empty, but their coffers are full, full to the brim with a fortune honestly or dishonesty acquired—which is to say, of luxuries, of satisfied pride, realized ambition—full of the misery of others, who envy them!

"And, the supreme decadence, they no longer love amour. In spite of so many beautiful wives and delicate virgins, in spite of so many triumphant courtesans, it is henceforth forbidden for them to know what pure joy blossoms, like a divine flower, from the hymen of two souls; and if they were able to pluck that flower, they would not want it, having other concerns. They kiss red mouths, embrace snowy bodies, swoon upon panting bosoms, but there is not one of them who conserves between the pages of a book a violet picked together. They go into a boudoir as they go into a restaurant, because they are hungry, and the majority are clients of fixed-price alcoves.

"Then, suddenly, these men clinging to their base joys are seized by rage and shaken; they can no longer love but they can hate! They attack one another, frantic and frightful, with cries of death that rejoice the echoes of cemeteries; and on battlefields or public squares, amid the din and the conflagration, even more blood flows than around the monstrous charnel-houses of the black princes of Africa."

At these words, the terrible God stood up. He was about to complete the sign punishing the culpable world; the earth, justly chastised, was about to disappear forever into the immeasurable abyss.

But a fourth messenger arrived, saying:

"As I was returning to the blue paradise, I cast one last glance at the abode of humans. In a path lined by eglantines, near a village of low thatched cottages, two children were walking, he sixteen years old, she fifteen, both blond, hand in hand, not talking, but gazing at one another, at a slight distance, with eyes moistened by tender tears..."

Hearing that, the just God did not complete the sign that punishes worlds, and the earth was not destroyed, because two children there loved one another.

An Angel Seeks a Wife

Stuck to the walls of the city, suspended from the poplars of the road, hanging from the branches of florid woodland paths, posters announced that an angel desired to take a wife among the daughters of the earth. Damsels and widows disposed to contract such a union were requested to render, the day after tomorrow, to a large meadow on the edge of the river, and there, all the desirable information would be furnished to them regarding the conditions to be met in order to merit the celestial husband.

You can imagine the surprise and interest that notice stimulated. To marry an angel is a glory for which one rarely has the opportunity, even if one is very pretty, and no matter how angelic one is oneself. The most ambitious schoolgirls, under the dormitory lamp, in slow sleepless nights, would not dare to think of such a fine suitor.

The posters added a few details appropriate to charm the mind and heart of a demanding young woman. The angel in search of a wife was not one of those unimportant spirits whom God employs in minor tasks such as carrying messages to prophets in the desert or going in search of the souls of Ursulines who die in an odor of sanctity, or playing the viol on days of concert near the Throne. No, more beautiful and more luminous than any human words can express, he occupied a very high rank among the paradisal aristocracy, being the first Choir of the second hierarchy. In addition, far from resembling the little cherubim of paintings, composed solely of a face with inflated cheeks and wings, he had a body whose perfection left nothing to be desired from any point of view— which did not fail to interest the whim of the majority of widows, and young women too. How many feminine hearts beat faster, full of hope!

There was no question now of the lovers one had had before, of fiancés chosen by families, of going to pick violets in the woods with young men who neglected to dress in diamond armor and would have had great difficulty rising up into the heavens on a sunbeam or a moonbeam, no question of marrying businessmen, engineers or rentiers. Away with all that! And, as every woman in a state to be married flattered herself, even though she was not unaware of the conditions required for the glorious hymen, that she might succeed, it would be difficult to estimate the number of dismissals that were issued, with the advice to seek elsewhere, to many poor devils who were seen weeping in the streets under the cruel windows, as piteously as anything in the world.

Even the daughter of the king was no less troubled than her father's subjects. She declared flatly that she held the Emperor of Golconda, to whom she was promised, in very mediocre esteem, and that, if he found himself embarrassed by his pearl and his precious stones, it was only up to him to make a present of them, in rings and necklaces, to some scullion who might, perhaps, want to adorn herself like an empress.

In sum, because of the tempting posters, there was, throughout the land an emotion, a hubbub, a delirium of which it is necessary to renounce conveying any idea. Shiny fragments of glass were encountered here and there, which were the debris of mirrors that anxious ugly women had broken.

Only Etiennette was unmoved; but no one was astonished by the calmness that she retained. She was a poor beggar, not pretty, clad in rags, who went along the streets and roads without looking at people, often neglecting to pick up the alms that were thrown to her. It would have been too funny for her to aspire to marry an angel, all the more so as she was a little bit mad, lingering by day, with the appearance of not thinking about anything, watching ladybirds climb the stems of bedstraws, and in the evening considering the first star rising in the distant blue mist.

The day finally arrived. Anyone who saw, at dusk that day, the vast meadow on the river's edge, while the first star vacillated far away in the heavens, could say that he had admired an incomparable spectacle. Never had so many beauties come together in the same place; and all of them were pompously adorned, imagining that the angel might come in person in order to select his wife himself. How many trees, the color of gold and the color of ebony, quivering in curls over the brocade of garments or the satin of shoulders!

The king's daughter, on a white elephant, was enthroned among tremors of pearls, which were the fringes of the baldaquin; and many little negroes, following groups of marquises, lifted up the trains of dresses a little higher, in case the angel had the idea of arriving slyly, coming up behind people. And there was an adorable stir, everywhere, of impatient golden muslin, lace and silk.

A drop of light, falling from the azure, stopped near the river, on the tip of a red. It trembled, inflated, and took on life; it was a little fay clad in radiance and verdure.

"Good day, ladies, good day, damsels," said the fay, with a curtsey. "You would like to marry the angel, then? I will tell you, without delay, the condition on which one can become his wife. Ugly or pretty, old or young, it does not matter; he has in his own eyes all the beauty and all the youth that might be offered to him. But what he demands of his bride is that she go to join him where he is. He will be the husband of the first person he sees."

"Good," said the king's daughter. "That condition has nothing to discourage me; for I can, if it pleases me, climb into a carriage borne away by horses more rapid than the wind."

All the damsels and all the ladies thought that they could find some means of getting ahead of the princess.

"But where does he live," they asked, "and what road is it necessary to take to reach him?"

"Oh, his dwelling isn't as distant as one might imagine, and it won't take long to arrive there." Then the fay burst out laughing. "Let's go, ladies and damsels, set forth without delay, and see who will arrive first in the star that is trembling in the distance in the occident!"

As she finished speaking the fay took the prudent precaution of disappearing, for it is probable that, furious at having been mocked, so many damsels and so many lades might have put her in a very bad state. So, a trick had been played on them! In order to marry the angel, it was necessary to go to a star. That was the requisite condition. As if it were easy to go to the stars! The proudest eagles that one might mount would stop half way, and the lightest balloons did not rise high enough to feel the radiant warmth of the Evening Star. You cannot have any idea of the anger that stirred all the silk, the lace and the muslin.

Sharing the irritation of its mistress, the white elephant carrying the king's daughter seized with its trunk one of the little negroes following the group of marquises and hurled him toward the star; but the boy fell to earth a hundred paces away, an example of the impossible ascension.

Only Etiennette was unmoved.

She had come, the poor little beggar, who was not pretty, clad in rags. Why? For no reason; by chance. She drew away, not thinking about anything, raising her eyes, occupied in considering the rising, in the distant blue mist, of the first star.

Disappointed, the widows and the damsels consoled themselves rapidly. In sum, would it have been very agreeable to be the wife of a spirit? First Choir of the second hierarchy, so be it; but, in spite of the posters, it was not very certain that the angel in search of a wife would differ sensibly from the little cherubim of paintings, solely composed of a face with inflated cheeks and wings. Nothing would have been more afflicting than a disappointment in the nuptial paradise—an eternal disappointment!

They returned, without too much chagrin, to their previous tenderness. It is quite unnecessary for a young man with whom one picks violets in the woods to dress in diamond armor, and one can marry with pleasure bankers, engineers, and even businessmen. The king's daughter let the Emperor of Golconda know that she would gladly accept, as wedding presents, diadems or rings, and a sufficient quantity of precious stones and pearls. And the ordinary course of things recommenced placidly and honestly throughout the country that had been troubled momentarily by the posters stuck to the walls of the city, suspended from the poplars of the road, hanging from the branches of florid woodland paths.

A month later, in the little cemetery outside the walls of the city, an event of no importance occurred. Etiennette the beggar, not pretty, who had gone along the streets and roads in rags, was buried. She had been found dead on the edge of a wood in the evening, her face smiling toward the sky. Alive, she had been a little bit mad, lingering by day, with the appearance of not thinking about anything, watching ladybirds climb the stems of bedstraws, and in the evening considering the Evening Star rising in the blue mist, and no one took it into her head to think that she had gone to join the handsome angel, her husband, in the distance, in a star.

Paradise Refused

Once, when I was dreaming, a white form appeared to me; as it resembled a young woman dressed for a ball—his wings imitated deployed muslin—I recognized immediately that it was an angel.

"Handsome angel," I said, "What have I done to merit the joy of receiving you at such a nocturnal hour in this chamber, where the perfume of amorous tresses still lingers, near a bed where I cannot remember ever having done anything that might be worth the favor of Celestial Spirits—for they are generally reputed to be a little prudish. Don't you sense here a troubling odor of sin, which must offend your nostrils, accustomed to censers swung in the immaterial azure by the hands of the eleven thousand virgins? For God's sake, don't approach my table, where you might perhaps see the portrait of some pretty girl clad only in the memory of a dress and the regret of a chemise. As for what is on my bookshelf, refrain from wanting to choose a book therefrom; you won't find anything but bitter and somber poems, which I read while smiling, and crazy tales, which I read with melancholy.

The angel replied:

"Spare yourself the care of giving me advice. When my peers and I enter people's homes we know what it's necessary to do there. And don't embarrass yourself either on enquiring by what virtue you merited my visit. Omnipotent as we are, we frequently permit ourselves the caprice of favoring those who seem the least worthy of our mercy; and omnipotence can't exist without a little whimsy.

I took that as read, and didn't breathe another word, no longer sensing the strength to argue with an apparition who resembled a young woman so perfectly.

"I've come," said the angel, "to ask you if you would care to come up to Paradise right away, without passing through the vain formalities of death and a funeral."

As you can imagine, that proposition was as agreeable to me as possible; I had always had a fervent desire to contemplate the august splendors of Heaven.

"Let's depart right away!" I cried

Scarcely had I finished speaking than a pink cloud, in the form of a balloon, descended into my room by way of the open ceiling; the nacelle, large enough for two people to take their places there, was made of a trellis of radiance.

As soon as the angel and I were seated there, he said: "Release all!" to invisible servants, and we rose up hectically into the blue and somber solitude of the night.

While the dwellings of men dwindled into a tenebrous distance and even the mountains became confused shallows, I asked: "Is Paradise really as magnificent, as our reveries imagine, handsome Angel? Speak to me, my divine guide. Tell me about the marvels that are promised to my gaze, the joys that are offered to my soul."

The angel deigned to respond: "No words in human language—the only kind you can comprehend, imbued with humanity as you still are—can express the perpetual prodigy of the paradisal abode. Even if you were to succeed in imagining the miracle of a garden in which the soil has the color and transparency of the summer sunlight, in which all the flowers are virgins more ingenuous than lilies, where the air is made of vaporized pearls, your chimera would still be as far from the exquisite reality as a black winter midnight differs from a April morning. And what is even more impossible for you to appreciate is the is the infinite, eternal, immutable joy with which you will be enveloped and penetrated as soon as you have crossed the august threshold, as soon as you are one of the pure flames of the incorruptible conflagration."

That speech was well designed to redouble my impatience. "Let's hurry! Let's hurry!" I said.

But I perceived that the balloon—we had already surpassed the first stars—was no longer rising, immobile in the immensity. "Oh! What's happening?" I cried.

"I see what it is," said the angel. "You're too heavy."

As I had not taken the trouble to get dressed for the voyage through the heavens, I did not have the resource of throwing my garments over the side of the nacelle.

"In any case," said the angel, reading my thought, "that wouldn't do any good. The weight that is interrupting our ascent isn't a material weight. If you want to rise further, it would be helpful for you to rid yourself of ambitions, dreams of glory and opulence, which are dragging you down toward the inferior world."

Certainly, it cost me a great deal to accede to my guide's advice. What poet does not have those chimeras: capital cities full of acclamations; crowds tamed by the pompous rhythm of verses; and in palaces of gold and stone, choirs of young poetesses singing the praises of the triumphant rhapsody? But the desire for Paradise prevailed in me over all other desires. Resolutely, I launched into the darkness, toward the disdained earth, my pride and my hopes of renown and wealth; and as soon as the balloon made of a pink cloud was deballasted of those vain weights, it recommenced rising, furiously, beyond all the stars.

Although we were still very far from the sublime goal, a soft white light bathed me and charmed me. We emerged from terrestrial darkness; it was here that the true heavens commenced. In a light that seemed to be made of liquid silver, great pale flocks went by silently, and the wind of those wings put exquisite caresses in my forehead and in my hair; the air that I was breathing flowed into my mouth, into my lungs and into my heart like a warm tide of enchantment. Oh, by what intoxication would I soon be invaded in Paradise itself, since such a distant proximity already filled me with such delight?

But I perceived, anxiously, that the balloon had ceased rising.

"I see what it is," said the angel. "You're still too heavy."

"Have I not repudiated ambitions, and dreams of glory and opulence?"

"Yes, but you have in the depths of yourself memories of human amours; you have not forgotten the laughter and the kisses of beautiful sinners; they are tender regrets that are dragging you down toward the inferior world."

What! You too, reminiscences of subtle flirtations and slow embraces; you too, odorous memories of open corsages and unbound hair; you too, vibrant echoes of the whispers of the alcove in languorous midnights; it's necessary to lose you, alas?

Oh well, in order to render me worthy of Paradise, I consented to that cruel sacrifice; I threw through the glimmers, toward the obscurities below, the memory of your complaisance, rosy lips, pale breasts, smooth loins of warm satin; and the balloon resumed rising, as if with a surge of joy, into the ever more resplendent light.

O spectacle! I saw, I finally saw the diamond gates of the incomparable abode. Paradise was there, above me, so close; I had all the celestial dazzle of it in my human eyes. Who would dare to describe that flamboyance, more terrible than an immense flash of lightning, softer than the blossoming of a white rose? And further away than the open gates, I contemplated, under the leaves of diaphanous snow in which the stars flowered, the mysterious passage, in couples, of beautiful male angels and even more beautiful female angels. O ecstasies of seraphic hymens, perpetual kiss of lips forever pure, I too could know you; I was about to enter the august gulf of eternal joy!

But suddenly, I perceived that the balloon, almost on the divine threshold, was no longer rising. I was seized by a bitter despair.

"However," I cried, "have I not thrown everything over the edge of the nacelle, like ballast? Nothing any longer remains to me of ambitions, vanities and culpable lusts."

"You're still too heavy," said the angel, "For you still have..."

"What, then?" I said, anxiously.

"There still remains in the depths of your heart, down there, down there, more profoundly than the ambitions and concupiscence that haunted you, the memory of a little child, not beautiful, scarcely pretty, who turned her mouth away from yours in a grove of aspens, on the evening of your sixteenth birthday. Come on, throw that weight away, like the others. See how radiant Paradise is!"

But I said: "No,"

Then, at an angry gesture from the angel, I sank through the light and the darkness toward the inferior world, and I fell on to the black and hard earth—so far from paradisal splendors!—frightened, broken, perhaps dying, but glad to have retained the memory of the pale darling, very small, so timid, who refused me her lips, on the evening when I was sixteen, in the grove of aspens, where the eglantine of my first amour did not finish blossoming.

The Worst Torture

Once, a soul so frightfully criminal arrived in Hell—it was, as you might well suppose, the soul of a man—that King Satan found himself in a great embarrassment, not knowing what new torture he could invent in order to punish him. For there could be no question of using, in the present case, cauldrons of molten lead, red-hot forks, white-hot metal parquets, beds of nails, vats full of vipers, or the other means of meager tortures commonly employed with regard to vulgar sacrileges or simple parricides.

What strange sins, then, had the man whose soul it was committed on earth? Had he been one of those ferocious kings who only took pleasure, in a victory, in the odor of the fields of carnage; a traitor who did not refuse on principle to deliver the honor of his father and the life of his dearest companion, and did, in fact, deliver them if the price was paid; or a seducer of virgins to whom the memory of their kisses was only sweet when it was mingled with the memory of their tears? Had he, in particularly horrible circumstances, lied, stolen, cheated, murdered, or—a sin more abominable still—had he lived for long years without liking verses or music, without taking pleasure in the perfume of roses?

History tells us nothing precise about that; it is necessary to resign oneself to admitting, without any other explanation, that he was unimaginably criminal. And because of that, Satan was, as I said, in a great perplexity. At the time, he had good reasons for believing that the good God had suspected him for a long time of nonchalance and lack of ardor. He was not unaware that a few seraphim charged with the inspection of infernal tortures had insinuated in their reports that the executor of celestial justice ought to be an angel of proven austerity and not a demon, always suspect of indulgence in the punishment

46

of the sins that he suggested; an accomplice can only be an excessively merciful executioner.

It was, therefore, urgent that the Devil, this time, gave proof of the most irreproachable zeal, and make a terrible example.

Yes, but in what fashion? He had racked his brains, but he had not found any truly excessive and bizarre torture, not outdated but curious—in a word, amusing—such he would require to reconquer the confidence of the Lord.

In order to stimulate his imagination he decided to reread Dante Alighieri's poem and that of Alexandre Soumet.[4] Right! What good was that? Those makers of verses did not understand anything. To be entombed in ice; to wear leaden copes; to swim in a lake of blood; to be enclosed in the bark of a tree; to climb, step by step, the entire ladder of one's sins; to see, as a mother, one's newborn grow old, faded and wrinkled, becoming a centenarian, while remaining very small—pleasant tortures! Why not lay the damned right away on silken beds strewn with roses, amid kneeling slaves waving perfumed fans, while offering them, in crystal chocolate-boxes, candied lemon-peel and pearl jam?

As King Satan was lamenting, with cries and gnashing his teeth at being unable to imagine any truly extraordinary inconvenience, a voice groaned: "Sire!"

It was coming from a flaming vat. It was the voice of a poet recently arrived in the somber empire, who was expiating in uncomfortable heat his excessive fervor in singing the praises of the living gold of tresses and the snow of breasts in which roses blossom.

"Who is talking to me?" asked the Devil.

"Someone who can get you out of trouble, if you deign to grant him a moment of respite in his suffering."

"Only a moment? So be it. I wish it."

---

[4] Alexandre Soumet's *La Divine épopée* (1841).

The poet, outside the vat, stretched himself delightedly in the cool air, and, enrapture after a *lied* by Heinrich Heine, hastened to sing a sonnet by Ronsard.

"Go on talk," cried Satan.

"This is it, Master. In a city called Paris..."

"I know it," said the Devil.

"...Under the oleanders, almost not yet in bloom, a young woman, blonde with blue eyes, is embroidering, or holding in her hand a book that she is not reading. Go to her, Sire. She will reveal to you the most frightful of tortures."

As the moment had passed, the poet was suddenly plunged back into the vat, but for quite a long time, he did not feel the bite of the flames because, ecstasized by rhythms, he was thinking about the poems he had sung.

The Devil, however, was scarcely satisfied with the advice he had received. What means was there of believing that an inhabitant of earth would have more ingenuity, in making torments, than him, the prince of the eternal Gehenna? However, as he had the leisure and it would not cost him anything to attempt the adventure, he decided to depart for the earth.

His black wings open, he traversed the tenebrous spaces, soared in the sunlit azure, rapidly got his bearings, turned his flight toward Paris, and did not take long to discover the verdant balcony on which the young woman was sitting, with a book on her knees, amid the oleanders. Then he was gripped by a great anger, and promised himself to put a few thousand extra faggots underneath the poet's vat, for the latter was obviously making fun of him. The Devil had only had to see, even from a distance, the child dreaming among the branches to be certain that there could be no thought of wickedness in her; and when he considered her at closer range, he was even more convinced of it.

Under light golden hair, so pale that it trebled like a vaporized nimbus, she had an infinite softness in her eyes, more limped than virgin lakes; the snow of her incomparably white forehead was only explicable by the candor of her flowering dream; and on her mouth, hardly a bud—for the damsel was a little girl—in the slenderness of her arms, her spare hands and her breasts, which did not admit to adolescence; in her entire bearing of a schoolgirl whom nothing has yet troubled, even in the tightly-bunched pleats of her narrow dress, there was the charming ingenuousness that astonishes everyone, not even aware that evil exists, and weeping warm tears for a ladybird crushed by carelessness in the sand of the garden.

Satan, who knew innocence by virtue of having enlightened more than one, recognized that he had never encountered one similar to this one; the idea of tempting her did not even occur to him, moved by so much purity and mildness, even though he was not generally vulnerable to such emotions. And, discontented because he had made a wasted journey, he burst out laughing at the idea that he had come to ask that child, that angel, to invent a torture.

However, at all hazard, he confessed the motive for his visit, apologizing—for he is very courteous—with a great deal of respect and humility.

She opened her ingenuous eyes very wide.

"What? A torture more terrible than all the tortures of Hell?"

"Precisely. Forgive my folly."

"Oh," she said, with her little girl's smile, "but I think that you couldn't address yourself better."

"What?" cried the Devil. "You know a torment?"

"My God, yes."

"Frightful?"

"At least, it is considered to be."

"And endless?"

"Certainly, because of the memory."

The Devil looked at her, stupefied by surprise.

"This is it," she said, following with her eyes a white butterfly that was fluttering over the bushes in the sunlight. "Bring the person you want to punish here, to this balcony, by the oleanders. I'll show him the embroidery that I'm finishing, the book of tales of fays that I'm reading. I won't look at him, I won't smile at him, and when he has desired my lips..."

"He'll desire them?"

"Yes. When he has desired them..."

"Then?"

"Then I'll refuse them to him," she said, in a voice so soft that all the flowers on the balcony blossomed with ease.

The Judgment of the Angel[5]

The diabolical tribunal has just entered into session.

For want of seeking information with due care, however, so many lies have been told about the fashion in which souls are judged after their flight outside the body that it does not seem inappropriate to give some precise information about that mysterious procedure.

It is first necessary to set aside the ludicrous idea—too generally admitted, like many other errors—that God takes the trouble to integrate spirits recently arrived from our world personally. He has many other concerns! Occupied with regulating the movement of the spheres, respiring the perfumes that emanate toward him from the constellations—for every star is a golden censer—listening to the seraphic concerts, of which he has made an agreeable habit throughout eternity, you can imagine that he does not care to waste time absolving or considering persons newly derived of their terrestrial envelopes, all the more so as he only has a rather mediocre interest in their loquacity.

All of them protest their innocence with an energy certain to inspire doubt. The young women who, according to the charge sheet, spent five or six nights of seven in beds to which they were not summoned by conjugal duties, claim that their entire nocturnal life was employed in listening, even admiring, the snoring of their husbands. Old men swear, with great oaths, that they have always omitted to pinch, in the gloom of corridors, the fat behinds of chambermaids; other husbands, younger, believe themselves to be in a situation to affirm that they have never gone home slightly intoxicated after midnight with rice powder on the collar of their frock-coats. Oh, if they

---

[5] This story first appeared under this title in *Gil Blas* 11 July 1886 before being reprinted in *Pour lire au convent* (1887) as "Le Mauvais passant" [The Evil Passer-by].

still had them, those frock-coats, it would be clearly visible that there is no rice powder on them.

As for thieves, they cry: "Search me!"—which would not require skill, since they no longer have any pockets. Infidel employees recount ingenuously that, far from having taken, in any circumstance, the smallest sum from the cash-box of their employer, on the contrary, they added to it every morning before the office opened, in anticipation of difficult reckonings, from the small sums they earned breaking stones on the road.

Once, a ferocious and cowardly murderer, while passing one of the eleven thousand virgins, who had descended from the Milky Way in order to look for a pearl from her necklace that had fallen into one of the Great Bear's ears, murmured on seeing the lily in her hand: "That's what I resemble!"

In truth, God could not be asked to listen to such nonsense; and one would be ill-advised to reproach him for employing a substitute in his functions as a judge.

Henceforth, it is in Hell that the supreme tribunal assembles, but it is necessary not to believe that Minos, Aeacus and Rhadamanthus are seen sitting there; those are forgotten names. It is a long time since the divine and infernal Constitution has been revised, in the wake of circumstances that are still present in the minds of the majority of people. No, the present judges are chosen, according to circumstances, from among the most competent of the damned, into whom the Lord, for the occasion, and reserving the right to reverse the judgment, puts a little of his equity.

If it is a matter of appreciating the sins of a lady who made the mistake of not contenting herself, at the price of her nights, with the memory of kisses, Laïs, illustrious in Corinth, and Rhodope, famous in Memphis—not omitting Blanche d'Antigny[6]—are asked to don the red robe of justice, although

---

[6] Blanche d'Antigny (1840-1874) was an opera singer with a colorful past, lavish with her lovers' money, who found it politic to go to Egypt when one of them committed suicide after having ruined himself for her, came back with typhoid,

they can remain naked underneath it, and give their advice on the case that is presented. It is by Cartouche and Mandrin, and also the great Collé, under the honorary presidency of Fal-va-Zou,[7] who robbed traveling kshatryas in the forests in India, and Kakos, son of Hephaestus, the terror of Italian roads, that pickpockets and burglars are interrogated.

If one hesitates to let into paradise poets who sing with overly vivid tenderness of the flowery breasts of shepherdesses and beautiful courtesans, they are summoned to appear before Theocritus or Moschus, or before the divine Amaru, who, for having passed through the bodies of a hundred women, retained such perfumes in his hair and lips that people said, when he passed beneath a window: "What! Is it spring already?"

That fashion of having criminals judged by their peers has produced better results; it is true that those magistrates, who have often been culpable themselves, are inclined to extreme severities—it is from the former impure that the most prudish are made—but in order to avoid too great a frequency of severe sentences. God does not fail to send to Hell, on the days of the assizes, an archangel with a tender heart, endowed with a certain faculty of elocution, who is charged with representing divine clemency.

That day, Avinain. Papavoine and the pale Lacenaire were sitting behind the table of justice, for it was a matter of interrogating, and doubtless sending to the worst convict prisons of Gehenna, a man and a woman who had rendered themselves culpable of a frightful murder.

The accused were introduced.

---

and died penniless. She was employed by Émile Zola as he model for the eponymous heroine of his novel *Nana* (1880)

[7] This name produces no hits with the aid of the *gallica* search facility except for the present story; Collé is equally enigmatic in context.

Although they were deprived, in reality, of their mortal flesh, they conserved the appearance of it, as is customary, and there was no sorrier sight than those two individuals. Old, very old, with dirty gray hair, noses florid with red warts, lips hanging down, they were objects of horror even among the diabolical assembly, which is however, well accustomed to considering ugliness; and as they had humps in front and behind, were lame and one-eyed—he the left eye and she the right—it could be divined that in the days of their adolescence they had been as ugly as possible. Oh, what vile children they must have been, fit for the terrorizing of bees and the frightening of butterflies on the roads, on the edge of woods, and in clearings!

But of what were they accused? Of having beaten, bruised and murdered a farmer who was passing along the road, and of having mauled the cadaver thereafter, with the fury of enraged beasts; it was not certain that they had not devoured a few fragments of their victim with avid teeth. The farmer, naturally, was bringing a civil suit; he was hoping for a considerable indemnity—three or four thousand years of purgatory deducted from the punishment to which he had been condemned for various misdeeds whose listing would have nothing in common with this story.

The hideous old man and woman admitted their crime. However, they indicated, very humbly and tremulously, that they had something to say in their defense.

"What's the point?" said Avinain.

"What excuse could they invoke?" said Papavoine.

"The case is open and shut!" said Lacenaire.

But the angel of the Lord, the messenger of clemency, extended his hand. "I believe that it is necessary to listen to what they want to tell us."

It was the old man who spoke.

"When we met one another for the first time, Madeleine and I—it was an April morning seventy years ago, behind a clump of trees at the bottom of the hill—we were dazzled, she was such a beautiful girl and I was such a handsome young man."

There was a sharp astonishment in the assembly, and a great desire to laugh, for it was evident that, even in the time of their youth, the two wretches had been horror and ugliness personified.

But the angel said: "Silence! Listen."

The old man continued: "No, never had I seen anything as pink as the rose of her mouth, or anything as blue as her cornflower eyes; and since then, I've often admitted to myself that in looking at me that day, she believed she was seeing a man different from all other men, more handsome than all other men. We went back to the village together and we married a month later. What it would be impossible to express is how happy we were. The idea that we possessed one another, and that we would possess one another forever, filled us with such joy that we had almost as much pleasure hoping for kisses than actually giving them. Our happiness made people jealous, we were well aware of that. People came to laugh around our cottage and threw stones at our windows, and when we went to church we heard mockery behind us. But the wickedness of people didn't both us. My wife said to me: 'They're furious because I've married the handsomest man in the region,' and I said: 'What makes them angry is that I've taken for a wife the most beautiful woman in the world.' And we stopped behind the trees to kiss."

"These are facts," said Lacenaire, "that have absolutely nothing to do with the case."

But the angel said: "Let's listen."

The old man continued: "What was extraordinary is that, in spite of the flight of days, we didn't cease to be young and beautiful. Others grew old. We were as rosy and fresh as flowers moistened by dew. Counting on my fingers, I was obliged to recognize that we were older than before. Forty years! Then fifty, fifty-five, sixty, and even more, But Madeleine always had spring in the rose of her lips, in the cornflowers of her eyes, and I could see clearly, by the delight in her gaze when she embraced me that I hadn't ceased to be the handsomest of all men. In any case," the old murderer went on, "consider us,

Messieurs Judges. Isn't it true that there's nothing to see as charming as us? Oh, my wife is pretty! But don't look at her for too long, I beg you, for you'll become amorous, and I'll be jealous."

After having bitten his lips in order not to burst out laughing—for he had the sentiment of his dignity as a judge, Lacenaire interrupted again.

"I repeat that this whole story has no connection with the murder."

"Listen anyway," said the angel.

The old man continued: "With the murder of the farmer on the road? I beg your pardon, Monsieur. One day, when my wife and I were taking the air outside the door, we saw a passer-by who seemed to be a little drunk, begging your pardon. But we soon stopped worrying about him. We were looking at one another; we were talking; we were kissing one another on the mouth. Never had my wife, with her blonde hair and her flowery youth, appeared so desirable, and she was hugging me with a passion so tender that my heart nearly failed with intoxication, and she murmured close to my ear: 'Oh, how handsome you are. my love!'

"We heard a great burst of laughter. The passer-by had stopped, and was looking at us, writhing with laughter. 'Oh! Oh! The horrible old woman!'

"You'll divine my anger. 'Oh! Oh! The horrible old man!'

"Madeleine uttered a cry of rage. But the man was still laughing. 'No, no, I've never seen such monsters! Aren't they frightful, with their dirty gray hair and their noses red with warts, and their pale slack mouths!'

"Messieurs Judges, on hearing such lies we were no longer masters of ourselves, and we murdered on the road the madman who couldn't see that we were young and beautiful."

"The crime is admitted. To the prison of Phlegeton!" cried Lacenaire.

Avinain said: "Yes, certainly, let them be plunged into the worst of penal colonies."

And Papavoine approved the sentence of his colleagues.

But the angel said to the old husband: "Rise toward paradise, gentle souls, toward the paradise where you will become as you think you are. You did well to murder the man on the road, the evil passer-by who nearly killed in you the most precious thing in life: the illusion of amour and beauty."

White Snow and Pink Snow

The angel who was entrusted with the mission of making snow fall on our earth was troubled last week by a very serious chagrin. "Oh," he said, "it was a very sad adventure, and even in eternal paradisal delights, I don't believe I shall ever console myself. Until this winter I had believed, proudly, that nothing equaled in whiteness the whiteness that descends from the clouds—no, nothing: not the august lilies of estival gardens; not glorious ivory; not the wings of swans on the azure of lakes or the azure of skies. My snow was whiter than everything that is white; and I was proud.

"A little while ago, however, when parting a curtain of mist in order to follow the slow fall of snowflakes by eye, I saw in the distance, far away, yes, I saw, behind the pane of a window, a young woman named Marion, who was removing her corset, and I was forced to recognize that her breasts, the envy of swans, ivory and lilies, are more delectably white— yes, a little more—than the celestial snow!"

Because of his defeat, he angel was tormented.

And idea occurred to him. Could he not, in order to avoid the comparison that humiliated him, change the color of the flakes that fall languidly to the roofs and the fields?

Certainly he could. He decided that henceforth, snow would be pink. You still remember the astonishment that we all experienced the other day when we saw flakes falling from the clouds similar in color to the blushing eglantines of the bushes, new artemisias and wild strawberries. The snow was pinker than anything pink, and the angel was proud.

But soon, having parted a curtain of mist in order to follow the descent of the flakes by eye he saw, in the distance, far away, yes he saw, out there, a young woman named Marion, who was removing her corset, and he was obliged to recognize that the vivid nipples of the breasts blossoming behind the pane of a window, of a pinkness envied by the wild strawberries, artemisias and eglantines of the hedge, were more exquisitely pink—yes, a little more—than the celestial snow!

One cannot have any idea of the jealous melancholy to which the angel abandoned himself. He swore that he could not endure such a humiliation; it would not have taken much for him to resign his meteoric functions—to which, however, he was very attached.

But the reverie of a poet who was wandering beyond the clouds was moved by that sadness and, alighting on the angel's wing, he said: "Oh, beautiful angel, it's wrong of you to be desolate. You ought, on the contrary, to rejoice in a legitimate pride. For is it not a supreme glory, for your white snow that triumphs over lilies, ivory and swans, and for your pink snow, victorious over eglantines, new artemisias and wild strawberries, to be almost as white and almost as pink as the roses of Marion's breasts?"

The Fortunate Star

Far away and very high, further away and higher, in the incorruptible azure, a star was pensively upset, and she resembled the eye of a slightly melancholy woman who is about to weep.

An angel who was passing by said to the sad star: "Why are you dreaming so dolorously, gentle star?"

She replied: "It's because, having seen her by night, when I radiate over the cities, I envy one of my sisters, who is scintillating and darkening down there in one of the black gutters of Paris. I'd like to be in her place. I'd like, myself or my reflection, to tremble in the obscure water near the sidewalk where the crowds pass by."

The angel was very surprised. "What!" he said. "You contemplate the miraculous distances of the nocturnal azure; you are the neighbor of the paradise that opens porticos of opal and lapis lazuli; you mingle with the prodigious enflamed round dance of the constellations; you are, in infinite space, like one of the purest pearls of an immense necklace of gleams; you see glorious sunsets when you rise; you admire the roseate pallor of dawns when you set; and you are jealous, celestial jewel, of a star fallen in the mud like a faded flower?"

"Yes I'm jealous of her," said the star, "And, radiating so far from the earth, I feel ready to weep tears of pale gold. For my sister who is in the gutter—she or her reflection, the star fallen on to the pavement where the water flows—can see the furtive ankle-boots and a little of the legs, of the Parisiennes who are passing by."

The Guardian Angel

It would be difficult to imagine a person as perplexed as Marquise Lise de Belvélize was that morning, and one can affirm that, having emerged from her home into a December fog, she had no idea what she would decide to do. No, truly, she did not know. There was also a fog within her, a fog in which the will could not find its way.

Let's see, what was she going she do? She had promised to take to a poor family—the grandmother very ill, the children in the cradle—the consolation of alms, and those poor folk were waiting for her with an anxious hope. But she had also promised Monsieur de Marciac to have lunch with him in the bachelor apartment that he had leased and furnished expressly for her on the first floor of a house in the Rue d'Aboukir, above a toyshop; for it is prudent to put the solitudes of amour in the noisy business districts; how can they be suspected there? And in the room where the odors of Havana cigars and ylang-ylang perfumes mingled, she was desired even more ardently than in the mansard where the exhalations of rancid tisane lurked.

How she cursed her stupidity! It would have been so easy for her to space out her duties, to fix one time for the unfortunate household, and another for Monsieur de Marciac. But the harm was done now. It was necessary to choose between the charitable visit and the tender tête-à-tête. A difficult alternative!

She had not climbed into her coupé, and she had not taken a fiacre, because it would have been necessary to give the coachman an address. And alongside the shops, enveloped in otter-fur, with a veil over her eyes and her mouth muffled, she walked hesitantly, utterly tormented.

Certainly, it is very good to give alms; the resuscitated smiles of the poor people one helps are a precious recompense for the staircases climbed in seamstresses' houses and long sojourns in fetid hovels. But it the end, it cannot be contested that there is some pleasure in being embraced, as soon as one crosses the threshold, by a lover full of fervor; and over dessert, when the second bottle is empty, on the table placed between the bed and the fireplace, it is not at all annoying, while the already-bare feet are offering their pink transparency to the redness of the embers and the shoulders toward the bed-head—where is the bodice, then?—while caressed by a hand that doesn't stop at that, to grant a kiss to very dear lips in which the warmth moistened by pleasure is already mingled with a little champagne froth.

Oh, how charming Monsieur de Marciac was! No man ever showed himself, in the company of a woman, exquisite as she might be, breathless to the point that he was with her. He had a fashion of gazing at his lover, of caressing with his breath her half-closed eyelids or the hairs on the nape of her neck, of putting into her ear, without words, a warmth counseling all follies, all fashions of enlacement, of abduction, of extinction that were capable of causing a pleasant disturbance to the most virtuous person. And it was with a sighing retreat that she remembered hopes previously realized.

But, abruptly, she was heroic. No, she would not go to Monsieur de Marciac's apartment, since she had sworn to go to the home of the grandmother and the children in the cradle. She would sacrifice herself; in order to make others happy, she would renounce being happy herself. Yes, she would be sublime in her abnegation.

She made a sign to a coachman, climbed into the vehicle, and gave the address of the indigent family.

A few minutes later, she entered the mansard, placid, almost proud—for it is necessary not actually to be proud—with the serenity that only the consciousness of a duty accomplished gives to souls and faces.

The person who was content was Madame de Belvélize's guardian angel.

Don't hasten to smile! There are still guardian angels, veritably. The legitimate horror of being rendered banal by the insipidity of romances has not convinced them to fly away. As before, they descend toward young women and watch over them tenderly, opening the whiteness of their protective wings.

It is not only between the curtains of convent dormitories or toward the couchettes of ingenuous schoolgirls that those celestial spies lean; they incline toward socialites too, scarcely quitting them, following them to the Bois in the morning if they mount a horse, accompanying them invisibly to the dressmaker, the patisserie at four o'clock, and early evening tea-parties, to official diners and balls where their mission obliges them to twirl in the slowness of waltzes around the naked breasts of the soul of which they have the guard; it is perhaps a little of their vaporized ethereal candor, an exquisite cloud of perfumes, that one sees trembling over the shoulders of dancers, which one assumes—mistakenly—for an escape of fine veloutine.

Even by night, obstinate in their beauty they do not rise back up to paradise; whether their charges sleep alone or are accepted in the mysteries of the alcove into the vicinity of a friend who rejected their austere virtue years ago, the guardian angels find, in the fall of white muslin or Malines at the foot of the bed, an ingenious pretext for the presence of their pale furled wings.

So, the seraph charged with noting the meritorious actions of the marquise was as satisfied as possible. As he entered behind her the home of the unfortunates that she had come to help, he promised himself to recommend her to the attention of the providences that dispense just recompenses; and he kept his word, as we shall see in due course.

Madame de Belvélize showed herself to be charitable beyond all expression. It goes without saying that she put on the corner of the mantelpiece the gold coins from her purse, and that she asked whether there was the Bordeaux for the old woman and the flannelette for the girl who was always coughing that the visits of a physician had promised. She did even better; she sat down on a wicker chair, installing herself, having taken of her hat, as if she were at home, and listened, without apparent ennui, to the lamentations of the grandmother. Finally, beside a cradle—oh, how wretched that cradle was, devoid of batiste and a silk coverlet—she leaned toward the poor, suffering, unclad boy who was like a chick devoid of feathers in a nest devoid of moss.

She was no longer thinking about Monsieur de Marciac—not, she was not thinking about Monsieur de Marciac at all! Oh, how much reason the guardian angel had to be content. She asked the sick child whether he desired anything; anything he wanted, she would give him; he only had to ask.

"Oh," he said, "What I'd like is a large polchinelle, with gold and satin everywhere."

He was asking too little. All the polchinelles, the puppets, the clowns with little bells, she would send to him. And don't think that an hour later, when she had gone down the stairs of the sad house, she had forgotten her promise. No, no, she told the coachman to stop outside the first toyshop that he saw on the road.

The joy of having done a good deed, and the hope of doing even better, put a delightful innocence into her heart. She was so perfectly pure that no beautiful young man named Monsieur de Marciac existed on earth. In the fiacre she formed more honest projects. She had a husband? Well, she would love that husband; at least, she would try to love him. She would renounce the vain pleasures of the world; she would devote herself entirely to charitable works. Oh, the beautiful and noble life! What joy is worth as much as that of being thanked by widows and orphans?

The guardian angel was so charmed that he wept tears of tenderness. The carriage stopped outside a toyshop.

Immediately, the marquise went into the shop. She bought four polchinelles. Japanese babies and shepherdesses, and kitchens with a hundred saucepans, and order all those beautiful things to be delivered to the poor boy without a chemise in the cradle like a nest without moss.

But as she went out of the house she turned and looked at the façade, instinctively. She was astonished, and blushed slightly. It was curious; that house resembled the one...and in fact, it was, in the commercial district, the house where Monsieur de Marciac had leased and furnished the bachelor apartment.

What a strange freak of chance!

Chance? Not at all. The providences, just dispensers of due recompenses, had watched, directing the coachman.

As can easily be imagined, Madame de Belvélize could not contain the curiosity of knowing whether, three hours having passed, her friend was still waiting. She went upstairs very quickly. Doubtless he was no longer waiting.

He would have waited for her until the end of time! And as soon as she crossed the threshold, he embraced her. Oh, how exquisite it was, the sweetness of the first kiss! The thousandth caress was no less adorable.

Hidden under the transparent pretext of muslins at the foot of the bed, the guardian angel, although a trifle scandalized, did not begrudge the marquise the long and multiple sin whose delights she had merited so well.

Lost Stars

While I was searching for the fifth feminine rhyme of a rondeau, my valet de chambre said to me: "Monsieur, there are two angels here who desire to speak to Monsieur."

Have they given you their cards?" I asked.

"Here they are."

On one of them I read: *Helial*, and the other, *Japhiel*. Two angels, indeed.

"Have them come in," I said.

It was not without pleasure that I received those visitors of quality. They were clad in great wings, each made of seven plumes that combined, beneath a down of auroral mist, the seven colors of the rainbow. What could be seen of their bodies seemed to be diaphanous snow, slightly pink. With a gesture, I invited them to sit down and enquired politely as to the motive that had earned me the honor of making their acquaintance.

"We shall be brief," said Helial. "Sixteen years ago, one beautiful July night, Japhiel and I were playing billiards on the green baize of the sky..."

"Pardon me," I objected. "I thought the sky was blue."

"It's blue in certain parts of its immensity, but in others, particularly those that float over the cities and countryside of Persia, it's a green that is very agreeable to the eyes."

I made no reply.

Helial continued: "Now, we were using stars for billiard balls, the most beautiful that we could find..."

"And for cues?" I put in.

"The tails of comets, naturally.[8] The game interested us greatly; I was on the point of wining when, with an excessively violent shot, I caused two balls to jump over the edge."

"Over the edge?"

"Yes, the horizon. It was a great disaster, for two stars fewer in the sky is quite an affair. It was signified to us by the One who remains eternally seated on a throne of cloud and lightning that we would not be admitted to listen to the paradisal concerts until we had recovered and replaced the lost stars. We can say that we have been traveling for sixteen years over the earth, where, according to all appearances, the two stars fell. Our research, alas, has been vain. We were about to resign ourselves to eternal exile when we heard talk of the incomparable eyes of a young woman, who is your friend, if current rumor can be believed. Everything seems to indicate that, instead of human irises, she has the celestial gleams for which we are searching, and we hope that she will be kind enough to return them to us."

I felt strangely perplexed. The mere idea that someone might take the eyes of my dearest caused me a frightful anxiety. However, what means was there of not aiding two exiled angels to recover their divine fatherland? I therefore sent for Mademoiselle Mésange and explained to her in a few words what it was about.

She did not seem surprised or troubled. After having reflected for a few seconds she turned to the visitors and then, raising her eyelids as far as she could, she said: "Look, handsome angels, and tell me whether you recognize your stars."

They drew nearer. They considered with the utmost attention Mésange's bright eyes. At times they spoke to one another in whispers, like judges communicating their opinions.

Finally, Helial said: "No, those aren't the clarities that disappeared sixteen years ago. Ours, although they were the

---

[8] The pun that links *queue* meaning a billiard cue, and *queue*, meaning a tail [of a comet] does not translate.

most admirable of the July night, weren't as gilded or as radiant as those."

With that, they left, crestfallen. I felt sorry for them, with all my heart, although I was very content that my friend's eyes would not be taken from me.

And Mésange? She roared with laughter.

"Didn't I fool them?" she said. "Certainly, my mother told me a hundred times over that, shortly after my birth, two stars fell through the open window between my little eyelids. But while the angels were observing me I thought about the moment when you kissed my lips amorously for the first time, and I was sure that the memory of that delight would be sufficient for my eyes, former stars, to become more divinely luminous that the most beautiful stars in the sky!"

Baptistine; Or, The Three Beds

Baptistine's guardian angel, the whiteness of his wings furled in the night, was leaning on the iron head of the little virginal bed.

"Baptistine! Baptistine!"

"Eh? Who's there? Who's speaking to me?"

"It's me, your guardian angel."

"Oh, you frightened me! There's nothing as troubling as being woken up with a start. I thought that a thief had got in, and that he was about to steal the golden cross that grandfather gave me for Christmas. But since it's you, I'm reassured. What can I do for you, my good angel?"

"Baptistine, I'm not content with you. First of all, you've just lied, because you weren't asleep at all, in any fashion, and, while not asleep, you were thinking about that young man you met the day before yesterday under the linden trees of the promenade. If you had stayed awake in order to examine your conscience or to say a prayer, I wouldn't hold that against you, but it's impossible for me to tolerate that a young woman whose soul has been entrusted to me should occupy the hours of the night in very reprehensible thoughts, from which a memory of a dark moustache is not nearly absent enough,"

"You're severe, my guardian angel! Since I'm of an age to be married, I don't see why it should be forbidden to me to think about the man who might be my husband; for the young man who was introduced to me under the linden trees of the promenade has asked for my hand, and he's been accepted, I announce to you, by my family."

"Baptistine! I had formed other dreams for you. What? You, who are more charming than the most beautiful angels of Paradise—you, who would have merited, after spending your mortal life in a cloister, being married in Heaven to some spirit of the highest hierarchy, want to enter into society and know its vain pleasures? You want to become the wife of a man—you, who might be, from now on, the bride of a divine fiancé? Resist, I advise you, temptations down here, and reserve yourself entirely for the celestial wedding."

"My good angel, I have nothing to say against you; you have always acquitted with an abundant zeal—perhaps too much zeal—the duties that you had to fulfill around my virginal bed. In truth, however, I imagine that the matters in hand at present are not within your competence. I beg you not to take offense if I prefer to everything on earth and in Heaven the man whose loving and faithful wife I shall be."

"Alas," said the guardian angel.

And he flew away, his wings open wide, into the night, where the stars were blinking like subtly mocking little golden eyes.

Baptistine's guardian angel, the pallor of his saddened wings scarcely visible in the gloom, was leaning against the head of the nuptial bed.

"Baptistine! Baptistine!"

"Eh? Who's there? Who's speaking to me?"

"It's me, your guardian angel."

"Oh, you're wrong to be there, and I advise you to fly away as quickly as possible! It's necessary to tell you, my good angel, that my husband is very much in love with me; he loves me as much as I love him! And any moment, he's going to come into this room, to which my mother has brought me, weeping and smiling. Your presence, immaterial as it is, might be displeasing, I'm sure of it, to the man whose name I shall bear henceforth. You only just have time to flee to your paradise, leaving us in ours."

"Baptistine, I'm not content with you. It's true, then, that you're about to become a wife like other wives, and that you've repudiated forever the sacred desire to be a nun behind the grilles of the cloister and the choir of the chapel. Oh, what a magnificent future was offered to you! After days and nights sanctified by prayer and the rude observances of the rule, you would have risen up directly, like an arrow toward a target, all the way to the eternal joy of the elect, and there, in the ineffable paradisal rapture, you would have been beloved by an angel with snowy wings, a magnificent angel with wings of flame!"

"I don't disdain the future that awaits me down here. I'll have an excellent husband, whom I will love with all my heart and all the rest of me; and soon, the laughter and cries of children playing will be heard in the house, not rich but visibly cheerful, where I shall be a good housekeeper. A happy wife, a joyful mother, that's what I shall be. Don't feel sorry for me, my guardian angel. No, no, I'm a good Christian, I'm not renouncing my place in paradise, eventually; but in the meantime, I love and adore the man who loves and adores me. Now, go away quickly, with your pale wings, for I can hear him coming upstairs, and he's quite capable, the jealous fellow, of ripping out a few of your feathers!"

"Alas," said the guardian angel.

And he flew away, his wings open very wide, into the dark azure sky in which a few little stars, blinking like golden eyes, were mocking impertinently.

Baptistine's guardian angel, his wan wings partly deployed in a moonbeam, was leaning on the tombstone of the white marble mortuary bed.

"Baptistine! Baptistine!"

"Eh? Who's there? Who's speaking to me?"

"It's me, your guardian angel. I think that this time, you'd do well to pay some attention to what I have to say. Now you're dead, young woman! And certainly, you're bored in that narrow and somber hollow in which your body has been placed. How you must regret not having followed my advice! If, insensible to worldly temptations, you had gone into the convent, you would have risen the day after your death, to the divine Paradise; you wouldn't have stayed so long in this place of desolation. But you preferred to live a common life, with a husband and children, and now you're being punished for it."

"Punished? Why? What is certain is that I can't repent of doing what I did, of having lived as I've lived. With all the strength of my life I've loved the man who loved me; I've seen my children with beautiful rosy cheeks laughing around me, like a bunch of living flowers. I've been a wife, I've been a mother, and I've been happy. Oh how charming it was, in the evening, to put the teapot and the cups on the table, in the room full of honest peace, and to see my husband smile at my sleeping son. It's true that I regret having died so young, still having so much happiness to give to those who gave me so much joy, but God's will be done!"

"Baptistine! Baptistine! Leave, I beg you all these human chimeras. I've obtained from the Almighty that he won't take too much account of your overly keen attachment to temporal things, and the moment has come for you to quit your sepulchral container to come with me to the marvelous Paradise."

"To tell you the truth, I ask for nothing better, my good angel, for I'm beginning to get bored in the gloom in which I've been placed."

"Come, come then! Get up, come! Take flight with my wings! You'll see the dazzling and perpetual prodigy of infinite skies! You'll hear the universal harmony, you'll blossom, better than a rose in the sun, in the incorruptible light! And to culminate your glory, it will be given to you to be married to a spouse worthy of your perfections, in a diamond church where God himself officiates. Oh, what delights will be yours!"

"Certainly, my joy will know no bounds, for I shall have for a husband in Heaven, will I not, the man who as my husband on earth?"

"Baptistine, it's a base thought that persists in you. A very considerable angel is promised to you, an angel will be your husband; as for the man who turned you away from celestial hopes, learn that he isn't dead, and that many days will pass before he descends into the death from which one rises again to immortal life."

Baptistine, awakened in the tomb, was thoughtful as she listened to those words.

"Well, aren't you coning with me?" said the angel.

"No," she cried, "no. Since my husband isn't yet in Heaven, what would I do there? Go, go away, leave me; I'll wait to live again until he lives again too; even sublime, even celestial, even celebrated by God, I refuse the glorious joys of infidel marriage. To the seraphim who would love me I prefer the man that I love. I'll wait for him here, resigned and confident. It's together that we'll rise to Paradise! And if the gates of Heaven are refused to us, the eternal sleep of the two of us, together, in this grave, will be sweeter to me than eternal wakefulness with another in the splendors of Paradise."

"Adieu, then!" said the guardian angel.

And he flew away, full of fury, his wings open very wide, toward the melancholy azure. But the little stars, who had seen so many things, who know everything and are never mistaken, blinking like golden eyes, seemed to be saying: "She's right, right, Baptistine, Baptistine!"

The Faithful Soul

Prompt, brisk and innumerable, words are exchanged amid sonorous impacts and pale scattered sparks:

"Pass me the soap, please."

"Look down there at that starveling leaning over; it's indecent."

"Her cleavage isn't so beautiful that she should want to show it!"

"There are uglier ones who have less modesty, my dear."

"Do you have any azure, neighbor? Lend me some."

"My arms are beginning to feel a little weary."

"Aiee! My beater!"

"What, don't you have it?"

"It slipped from my hands, and look, it's going down, down, disappearing."

"Bah! Clumsy!"

Then all the women laugh, their hands on their hips, because of the scatterbrain who does not know her métier and has dropped the instrument of her labor.

But anyone who, deceived by appearances, might think that I am reporting the speech and laughter of laundresses beating laundry on the planks and beneath the awning of some boat at Sèvres or Villeneuve-Saint-Georges, would be singularly mistaken. The women saying these things are high in the sky, several million leagues from our earth.

Who are these garrulous laundresses then? The eleven thousand virgins.

In what river are they doing the washing? The Milky Way.

What are they washing? Souls stained by sin.

For scholars do not know what they are writing—and what is more, they write it badly!—and human memory would only be populated with absurd errors if poets were not there—

the poets who know everything, and write it well!—to maintain the eternal verities.

It really has flowed from your radiant bosom, Hera, the marvelous pallor that divine Arethusa traverses, without ever mingling with it the blue immensity of nights. When the new gods were installed in the Empyrean, they did not know at first what to do with the long white stream. Saint James risked himself as far as to paddle in it, in order that a new name might be substituted for the ancient appellation,[9] but the change did not appear tolerable, for how could the feet of a man, even a sacred one, be admitted into the milky candor spread by an immortal?

As for giving their approval to the hypotheses of astronomers, the gods could never consent to that, recent as they might be, but knowing nevertheless what goes on in the universe. With the consequence that the Milky Way might have remained without employment if a strange circumstance had not been produced in the vicinity of the heavens.

A soul presented itself there one day too scantly laden with sins to be precipitated into Hell or cast into Purgatory, but not sufficiently immaculate to be admitted into Paradise. It was necessary to cleanse it of the little sin that was attached to it, and the Lord decided that it would be washed in the pale purity that an austere goddess had poured into the heavens.

That celestial laundering was so successful, the first time, that it was perpetuated in custom. The eleven thousand virgins, who did not have a great deal to do on the steps of the Throne, because they did not know music, were designated to

---

[9] The popular twelfth-century romance *Historia Caroli Magni* [History of Charlemagne], sometimes known as the *Chronicle of Turpin*, mistaken by some readers as an authentic history, relates how St. James appeared to Charlemagne and told him to go along the Milky Way, by which the emperor understood that he was to use it as a directional indicator for the pilgrims' path now known as the Camino de Santiago [Way of Saint James].

be the laundresses of souls not entirely worthy of being accepted to celestial delights. They clean them, as one removes stains, of persistent errors and insufficient repentances; and the noise of beaters, amid their cheerful chatter, and the scattered pale sparks, soon provoke the opening of the lapis-lazuli gate encrusted with stars, behind which the garden of paradisal enchantments expands eternally.

Once—thousands of years have passed since this adventure—it happened that a young soul, whose body had been a deaconess in a community of the new church, rose up, borne by a angel-dove in which her modesties and fervors were realized, all the way to the threshold of imperishable joy.

Knock knock!

"Come in," said the apostle Peter. But, having seen her, he said: "No, don't come in!"—for the great saint, in consequence of the functions that have devolved to him, has acquired a remarkable perspicacity; a single glance suffices for him to disentangle, among deceptive appearances, the slightest flaw in a spirit that wants to participate unduly in the rapture of the elect.

He saw immediately what the problem was. Yes, this soul, when she was a young girl. had been as chaste as a missal whose pages have never been turned; she had, without any regret for living persons or things, devoted her thought, her amour and her entire life to the altar on which the gold of the monstrance shines. In addition, for love of the jealous Spouse, she had practiced mortification, driving thorns into her frail flesh, and also fasting, even in the orchards offered to the appetite of children; one morning in July she had even thrown away, before putting it to her lips, a mulberry picked from a hedge. And, being charitable, she could not encounter a beggar without dissolving in tears, the good girl, and without giving him everything she had: money, things, even garments, so that she often returned to the community barely dressed because of the gifts she had made to the poor.

One summer evening, however in a wood where there were nymphs, and which was frequented by nuns, she encountered a young deacon, as chaste and virtuous as her, who was troubled, as she was troubled, by the languid warmth of the commencing night. On her knees in the warm grass, which tickled her skin, under the caressant tenderness of the willows, they put their hands together to pray. Alas, the hands of the deacon touched those of the deaconess and they fainted, those children. The eternal tempter, who was hidden in the willow grove, was able to rejoice in seeing that, in their common fall, their breath had mingled momentarily.

Certainly, the little deaconess stood up before any other friction, and fled, and returned very rapidly to the chaste habitation of fervent Christian women. But throughout her life, the warmth of a breath, amid the prayers, mortifications and fasts, had remained on her lips; and the good apostle Peter saw the memory of the kiss on the semblance of a mouth that souls retain beyond the tomb.

When he had conferred regarding that special case with the One in whom all justice and all clemency resides, the Saint who guards the door declared that before entering Paradise the solicitous soul had to be washed clean of the sin that still soiled it, in the Milky Way. As soon as it was clean, it would be elect. And the beaters of the eleven thousand virgins were raised for a very facile task.

They had purified souls much more stained by sins. In between the words and sparks they had cleansed adulteresses, courtesans and many other criminal women. Nothing would be easier, thanks to the candor of the Milky Way, than to render the almost-elect worthy of Paradise.

And they set to work, passing the young soul from one to another, from beater to beater, in the divine milk. The celestial laundresses were soon astonished, however, for the sin, amid the foam of the clouds, was not effaced, and persisted, not wanting to be effaced.

But whatever they did, asking for more soap, and requesting azure, they did not succeed, finally becoming weary and letting their beaters fall, in cleansing the rebel soul, which clung to its petty stain.

It is time to say that the young deacon, in the wood where there were nymphs, which the nuns frequented, a thousand years ago, was me. I remember very clearly having been, in that wood, the Christian man kneeling next to a Christian woman in the grass that tickles the knees, under the caressant tenderness of the willows. I have lived many other existences since, but I shall never forget the hour when my breath mingled with the breath of the young deaconess, when our two mouths, so chaste, touched so briefly. And often, leaning on my elbows at my window on summer nights, I consider the long, pale divine milky light that traverses the sky.

So many souls, which the eleven thousand virgins have washed, scintillate there delectably, but above all, I admire one tiny patch that is slightly dark—oh, how quickly I find it with my eyes!—a little stain that, beneath the divine beaters, does not want to become entirely white, and which retains, even at the price of Paradise, in order that I might love her and adore her forever, the memory of my kiss.

The Devil's Last-Born

One day, the Devil thought:

"It's time to be mediocre. For too long, in matters of evil, I've been formidable or delectable, heroic or refined—in a word, Romantic. Let's be modern; which is to say, pitiful. Since Victor Hugo and Emile Zola, those prodigious exaggerators of human life, have fallen into desuetude, let my enormity finally resign itself to median stature; let's create a being—a woman, it goes without saying, since I'm the Devil!—who is abject but banal, detestable but paltry.

"Once, female Lovers—those of legend, history and fiction, and also those of dreams, took pleasure in being excessive. Since Primawada[10] with the pointed teeth, who ate the sex organs of the tiger she had killed in a lotus, like a triple fruit in a cup; and Rhodope, marching with one of her feet bare, since the eagle had carried away the slipper, between the tall flowers of terraces or through the blood of crushed hearts; and Cleopatra, who accepted in the morning as an almost amusing aubade, the howling convulsions of the handsome black slaves poisoned between four lips, but rendered them in a smile the intoxication of nocturnal amour, and then intoxicated herself on pearls in order to forget them, or to remember the; and the prowler of the strands of the Cytherean isle who, raising them up and letting them fall stiffly upon her, in the depression in the sand, prostituted herself furiously with the cadavers of sailors rolled to the shore by the tempest; and Laïs—not the one of Corinth—the pursuer of herds of wild hogs through meadows, stark naked and tearing at her breasts; since you, Aspasia, accomplice of complaisant Alcibiades;

---

[10] Primawada is a character in Schubert's opera *Sakuntala* (1820), based on the fifth-century poem by Kalidasa.

since you, Thestylis,[11] who, on your threshold by night, drunk on nepenthes, tucking up your robe toward the stars, as if to challenge all the golden stars with a single black star, struck your belly with clenched fists in accordance with the rhythm of frantic couplings; and since Flora, who had for an heiress the city that had been her spouse; and since Messalina, who did not waste time in choosing but who had the grandeur of being eternally unsatisfied; all the way to Manon Lescaut, who chose took frequently but who was amorous, the darling; all the way to Madame Marneffe,[12] who could have eaten gold but deprived herself of dinner in order to buy flowers, all the great culpable women have redeemed the ugliness of their souls by something grandiose or charming, a charitable gift of tradition or poets. There was in their infamy some unknown beauty or grace that attenuated the horror.

"Well, I, the Devil, will once again create a woman of monstrous appetite, avid for broken hearts, content with ruins; but to the one I engender, I will refuse everything that might render her less detestable. She will not be a queen, for her moral hideousness would be scarcely visible to eyes dazzled by the radiance of gold and the glitter of satins embroidered with blazons. Not will she be the errant prostitute who offers herself on libertine street corners in the evenings, for she might perhaps borrow something ideal and dreamlike from the hazards of Bohemian amour. She will not have regal opulence or picturesque rags. I intend that she will be commonplace, anyone, and, the definitive baseness, almost similar, in sum, to the honest women who would have the right to despise her.

"Being evil incarnate, since she is my daughter, rolled in all the mud of amours devoid of amour, she will have at the same time as the restrictions and refusals of daring that characterize conventional and bourgeois virtue. And she will not be called Lesbia, or Faustina, or Theodora, or Marozia, or

---

[11] Thestylis is featured in the idylls of Theocritus.

[12] Madame Marneffe is a character in Honoré de Balzac's *Comédie humaine*, introduced in *La Cousine Bette* (1846).

Marion Delorme, or even Marguerite Gauthier; the name that concierges most frequently give to their daughters is the name that she will obtain; I do not want men to obtain any glory in repeating her name. However, she will not be correct in society; between her malfeasance and the honest simplicity that seems to imply the regularity of existence, there will be a discord a contradiction, by which she will be singularized, but it isn't necessary that she be an original.

"Painter, port or ballerina, devoid of genius—for she must not be sublime—but not without talent—for she must not be ridiculous—she will exercise a function thanks to which what she will manifest or affect of eccentricity will appear to be normal and seem necessary. Perfect vulgarity: she will be extraordinary by profession, or by imitation of those who, in similar circumstances, would be; she will not even have the strangeness of not being strange.

"Beautiful? Scarcely. Ugly, then? No; in truth rather beautiful, but not to excess, in order that she does not have the rarity of refining to the extent of charm the disgraces of ugliness. Anyway, ugly or beautiful, she will be terrible, an inexorable and evil soul. Later, when she looks around, she will see, with satisfaction, eyes burned by tears and dishonored foreheads. But for fear that, if she does harm for the pleasure of doing harm, she might owe to that species of disinterest some semblance of elevation, I shall give her cruelty three causes, the vilest of all: hatred of amour; envy of the good fortune of others; and rancor of accepted joys; and in order to refuse her even the pride of difficult triumphs, those that I give her to despair or kill will not be illustrious heads or great rebel hearts; I shall save for her the shame of victims that there is no glory in striking, prey that is poorly defended.

"The man who will incline before her, whom she will damn for the greater joy of my avid Hell, will be some ingenuous child with a heart inflamed by the reverberation of ardors that emanate from him alone, or some imbecile poet with paltry, manic and inveterate illusions, a poor fellow to whom one can do anything one wants, and who—as mediocre, alas, as

81

her—will not have sufficient imagination to recreate her perfect and sublime, nor sufficient genius to adore her and exe-
crate her in verses that will make her immortal."

Thus thought the Devil—and you appeared, my love!

The Prologue to Gog

> And the word of the Lord came unto me, saying:
> Son of Man, set thy face against Gog...
> and prophesy against him.
> (*Ezekiel* 38: 1-2)

In a very ancient olden time, in the vast evening, so vast in solitude and silence, the Tower, which the snow cloaked with ermine, elevated its mitered[13] crenellations facing the unfinished Castle, already colossal, which, above the white earth, resembled the black formless calyx of an enormous lily.

The Castle belonged, but not freehold, to the windowed Comte de Larmont en Cervaisis, the sixth son of a very august king,[14] for he had acquired it by marriage to Mahaut, the daughter of Isabelle and Gaston, the Dame de Haubour.

As for the Tower, that was the Devil's. It was constructed from blocks of stone transported here after the ruination of Babel, one by one, on his back, by a giant named Gog, later reduced to servitude by the mage Metatron. In addition to that,

---

[13] The French term *mitre* [miter] in French can refer to a chimney cowl as well as a bishop's hat but the use of the term here is eccentric, improvised in order to support a double meaning that appears a little further on in the text; I have retained the American word miter for both those meanings, even though the present one is not licensed by Webster.

[14] This character is fictitious, but his surname echoes that of Robert de Clermont-en-Beauvaisis (1256-1317), the sixth son of Louis IX (Saint Louis), who married Béatrice de Bourgogne, Dame de Bourbon, and became the founder of the house of Bourbon. Their eldest son, Louis, became Louis I, Duc de Bourbon, known as Louis le Boiteux [Louis the Lame], and was the direct ancestor of Henri IV.

it was believed that Sabbats were held there, and that, on the rainy nights of the equinox, mud rushed torrentially from is only gargoyle, formed like the maw of a tarasque, mingled with stones, which, having fallen, formed signs in which the sorcerers read the future; and because hoarse noises emerged from it on silent evenings, it was known as the Groaning Tower.

Riding between the Castle and the Tower, across the plain of snow, accompanied by a single servant, was Robert, Comte de La Harche et de Vastres, Seigneur de Valadon, the son of Pierre, Comte de Larmont, and Mahaut, Dame de Haubour. A good son, he was coming to visit the later, having been summoned because she was ill.

As he went around a bend in the road that climbed in zigzags toward the seigneurial dwelling, Robert de La Harche cried: "Curses! God wants my soul!" and fell from his horse; for the beast had slipped on the icy snow, and the rider, during the journey, had emptied not merely the bronze water-bottle that he wore, sonorously beating his armored hip, but two small barrels that the servant had placed in front of and behind the saddle.

In fact, Robert was a drunkard and a glutton; although he was not yet very old he had a very heavy belly, which he agitated gladly hunting wild boar and chamois but which, in sum, rendered inapt for warrior enterprises that son of a once-royal race, always aristocratic and bellicose. On the other hand, he had an amiable heart and a noble spirit; he was just to everyone, more affable to poor folk; a rather learned theologian, he liked nothing better than to spend his time in pious reading after rendering justice, doing charity and swallowing a good meal greedily. He raised a face that was mildly proud, with child-like eyes, very blue and very pure.

The servant leapt to the ground.

"I think," said Robert, "that I've broken the femur of the left thigh."

"Seigneur, I'll put you in the saddle and you can reach the castle.

But an avalanche of crows descended from the Tower, compact at first, and then scattering like black snowflakes, brushed the horses from all directions; frightened, they ran away across the field of snow, bucking and whinnying.

"Can you walk?" the servant asked."

"I don't know; I drank too much while riding, and the bone is stabbing me."

"I'll carry you, then."

"You couldn't, given the belly I have."

"What can we do, then?"

"Go and fetch people from the castle; don't tell my mother, for fear that she might be anxious, but just in case, bring a splint for my leg and the chaplain for my soul. Also, tell the cook to prepare supper."

When the squire had gone, Robert felt his leg, thinking: *What happened was bad luck...*

"There is no bad luck, there is only ill will..."

"Whose?"

"The Evil One! And it presages..."

"What?"

"Evil!"

Then Robert, although he was a very pious seigneur, an exact observer of the Commandments, swore. What was that? Although he had thought without speaking, someone had replied to him! He turned his head and he saw, very close to him, a short and thickset form, scarcely human, a black toga under a black hat, between which a white beard and white hair emerged; the whole was somewhat reminiscent of the stunted trunk of a willow devoid of branches and foliage, from which snow was spilling. Accommodated to prodigies by the imaginations of wine, however, Robert was not excessively astonished, even when the form spoke, saying:

"Be welcome in your domain."

"You know me, then?"

"You are Robert I, Duc de Haubour."

"No,"

"You are Robert I, Duc de Haubour.

"My mother, the Dame de Haubour, is alive, and Haubour isn't a duchy."

"You are Robert I, Duc de Haubour."

Robert laughed, shrugging his shoulders. "And you, who are you?"

"Your master."

"Eh?"

"You have the Castle, I have the Tower. We are face to face, but the Tower is higher than the Castle, by virtue of the miter. When you are King, I will be Pope."

"King! Me!"

"And me Pope."

Laughing more loudly, Robert asked: "What is your name?"

"Metatron."[15]

"The angel who informed Moses of the veritable meaning of the signs engraved n the bronze of the Tablets?"

"No, learned responder. His great-grandson—for the angels engender."

"You're an Egregore, then?"

---

[15] The name Metatron is mentioned in the Talmud, but the mythical invididual only elaborated in apocryphal documents associated with the Kabbalah, where he becomes the Recording Angel, and sometimes as the angelic transfiguration of the prophet Enoch, the supposed author of the apocryphal *Book of Enoch*, whose first part refers to the War in Heaven and the fall of the angelic Egregores [Watchers], some of whom fathered the Nephilim, a word translated in the Authorized Version of *Genesis* as "giants." The word "egregore" was co-opted into French by Victor Hugo in *La Légende des siècles* (1859) and taken up by Éliphas Lévi in *Le Grand Arcane* (1868), becoming a significant reference-point of the French Occult Revival, adapted by various litterateurs in different fashions, employed by Jean Lorrain to refer to a kind of psychic vampire.

"Indeed."

"How small you are!"

"It isn't the time of my veritable height. But we've arrived in the Tower."

"What?"

"Look."

In fact, Robert saw around him the high walls of a narrow round room.

"Curses! Who carried me, then?"

"Don't worry about mysteries that aren't worth being explained, at the price of those of which you'll be instructed. Lie on this bench; I'll rub your thigh with these herbs. It's necessary for you to remain lame, but you'll cease to suffer."

"Why is it necessary for me to remain lame?"

"In order that there be an interim."

"Between what, or between whom?"

"Between the first and the last." And the Egregore sang: "Who commences lame/Will end up the same." He added: "You'll be cured. One leg a little shorter than the other is no great affair. Now, the supper will be served."

In the middle of the narrow round room there was a table, and on it victuals and wines.

"But how can it be," said Robert, leaning over the dishes, which he sniffed greedily, "that Our Lord suffers your magic and your diabolical miracles?"

Metatron sniggered. "You don't know much, although you've been instructed by the Benedictines of Louvignolles. It's necessary for me to inform you that *Genesis* is not, as is taught, the first of the sacred books; it was preceded by another bible, entitled *The Wars of Jehovah*. If that bible were rediscovered, there would be a great change in human opinions. It's scarcely to be feared that anyone will get their hands on it. It was hidden in the hut of a Northern barbarian, under the icy ground, by the last mage to whom it was given to read it. At the present moment, bestial men clad in walrus skins and smeared with seal-oil are eating the entrails of fish with their backsides above the only Scripture that can reveal the veritable destiny of God and human beings."

"The veritable destiny of God?" said Robert, his mouth full of half a swan-wing spiced with pistachio nuts. "But you know that Scripture?"

"Well enough to reveal to you what you need to be told. Know, then, that in the immemorial wars in which the most beautiful and the strongest of the Angels fought the Lord, it was not the latter that won the victory."

Robert nearly choked on the bone of the wing.

"God was defeated...?"

"By Iblis, also known as Lucifer. And if he does not cease to be, it will be because nothing can last except eternity. But he was precipitated into sealed darkness, from which escape is nevertheless difficult."

"Heaven! That's a strange lie and an abominable blasphemy. Enjoy your wine, which is excellent..."

"It's from Saint-Pourçain."

"I would have sworn it...I would have inclined my soul to the passion, if not, Noël aid me! But who, then, created the world, as it is related in *Genesis*?"

"The leader of the victorious Angels, the one you call the Devil."

"The Devil created the world?"

"Undoubtedly, and it's singular that, in view of the fashion in which it is made and in which humans govern it, no living being, without being informed of it, has suspected as much."

"But it's written that God, in six days..."

"Not God! The one who took his place and his name. For it would have been maladroit to confess to the initial races, and later to successive humankinds, that they had for a dominator, not the true lord but the triumphant rebel, the fortunate usurper. That would have harmed his prestige. He understood that, and made those who had fought and vanquished with him understand it; the evil Angels agreed to pass for the good Angels buried in eternal darkness, while Lucifer took the place of the fallen Jehovah: hence the world in which we are, and life."

"So that it's the Evil One who is in Heaven?"

"And whom you invoke in saying your *Pater*."

"In consequence, what we think of as the Truth, Virtue, Modesty, Righteousness, Honor..."

"Has much chance of being nothing less than that—if one supposes, to be sure, that one word has no more significance than another, and that it is unnecessary to believe that the inverse is the exact opposite. In any case, no one is very well-informed regarding the personal ideas that the original Lord had on the various questions that preoccupy the human consciousness."

Robert said: "I would gladly have taken more of this blancmange powdered with scraped deer-horn, but the plate has vanished."

"Let that not remain so!" said the Egregore.

A deep dish reappeared, full to the brim with a milky whiteness dotted with a red powder.

"These," said Robert, "are strange revelations. But what if the Lord, in spite of the sealed darkness, surged forth and seized power again?"

"He has attempted that many a time; having not succeeded, it's probable that he will work quietly henceforth. Thus, we were not without anxiety when Cain, inspired by the spirit..."

"Of the Devil?"

"Eh? No."

"Oh, yes. It's not easy to get used to that change.

"...When Cain struck Abel, in whom lived..."

"God?"

"Eh? No."

"Oh, yes. That's not recognized."

"And our anxiety was even greater when an entire people demanded the torture of Jesus, who was in harmony with Lucifer, in order to accomplish his own prophecies; fortunately,

Lucifer was able to gain an advantage, as you know, from that misunderstanding."

"I think that I would go mad, if I weren't drunk..."

"Now," the Egregore continued, "We're more tranquil; but even though immemoriality has legitimated the usurpation, so to speak, and perhaps the Devil himself, misnamed the Fallen, had finally come to believe himself, having become accustomed to it, to be the one he precipitated, certain indications reveal that the vanquished has not lost all hope of reprisals. These Sabbats and Black Masses, in which dolorous multitudes mock the rites of our holy authority, in which the misery and despair of humans blaspheme and deny us, are perhaps the conspiracies of the eternal Justice and the eternal Good.[16]

"Vainly, full of industry, we have been ingenious in obviating them by mingling in them, hideously, under the feigned resemblance of our true figure; passing through these mobs is a hurricane sublime anger that does not come from the diabolical Heaven any more than the human world. That is why we are pursuing those troops of hypochondriac fanatics like enraged beasts. That is why we are employing in pyres twisted brushwood that bristles with sheaves of menace, and forests of strangely prophetic oaks.

"But who knows whether we will have enough judges, enough tortures? Who knows whether God, in accord with Humankind, which he perhaps loves although he did not create it, uttering his victory cry in all the sobs of all the desperate, all the howls of all the starving, all the dying gasps of all the martyrs, might finally establish the invincible revenge of we know not what order of things, originally desired by a

---

[16] Mendès was undoubtedly familiar with the thesis put forward by the historian Jules Michelet in his scholarly fantasy *La Sorcière* (1862), which asserts that the witches ardently persecuted by the Church as instruments of Satan in the sixteenth century were heroic feminist rebels against the ideological tyranny of the Church, who founded a virtuous secret religion for that purpose.

goodness and an equity the conception of which has remained latent within him, and in Him alone? And that the poor, mysteriously, foresee them?"

"Damn!"

"Now, the advent of another Destiny would not be without inconvenience..."

"For you, as Pope."

"And for you, as King."

"Damn!"

The Egregore thought aloud. "In any case, there is no reason to conceive immediate anxieties. Our faith and our laws are robust, and will not totter for a long time, and you will still have time..."

"To empty," said Robert, his lips moist, "this goblet of..." He did not finish speaking or drinking. "Eh! What's the noise rising through the flagstones, which seems to be coming from subterranean depths?"

"Or from the depths of the Tower. It's not the tumult of Elohim in ascension, but one of ours becoming impatient, whom we were obliged momentarily—no more than three thousand five hundred and eighty years, in fact—to reduce to inaction, while awaiting the Sign."

"What Sign?"

"The one that has finally been given."

"When?"

"This evening."

"By whom?"

"By you."

"How?"

"By falling off your horse."

"What! My broken bone..."

"Is the Notch on the tree of destiny."

"The Notch?"

"And will be the Defect."

"I don't understand..."

"It doesn't matter."

"Good," said Robert, taking up the goblet again. "But the noise is increasing and persisting, damn it! One might think that an armored troop were writhing and howling in chains."

"You have passably perspicacious hearing, for the one who is struggling and shaking his irons is the giant Gog, who, by virtue of his own strength is equivalent to the numbers of a large army."

"Gog?"

"Your knowledge is mediocre. Don't you know what Ezekiel, son of Buzzi, of the sacerdotal race, said about Gog in the thirty-eighth chapter of his book?"

Pretending incompetence in hermeneutics, not without winking maliciously at the little pink star laughing in the red depths of the goblet, Robert asked: "And what does Ezekiel say?"

"The Lord came unto me..."

"Which is to say, the Devil."

"Exactly."

"I'm beginning to recognize your intrigues quite well."

"So, Ezekiel:[17] 'The word of the Lord came unto me and said: Son of man, set thy face against Gog, the land of Magog, the chief prince of Meshech and Tubal, and prophecy against him. And say: Thus saith the Lord God:

"'Behold, I am against thee, O Gog, chief prince of Meshech and Tubal; and I...will bring thee forth, and all thine army, horses and horsemen, all of them clothed with all sorts of armor, even a great company with bucklers and shields, all of them handling swords, Persia, Ethiopia and Libya with them, and all of them with shield and helmet, Gomer and all his bands, the house of Togarmah of the north quarters, and

---

[17] The passage from *Ezekiel* cited by Metatron is abridged from the Biblical version, as Robert subsequently points out, but is equivalent to verses 2-13 of chapter 38. I have employed the English text of the Authorized Version rather than back-translating from the French, but I have marked the cuts with ellipses.

all his bands, and many people with thee. Be thou prepared, and prepare for thyself, thou, and all thy company that are assembled unto thee, and be thou a guard unto them.

"'After many days thou shalt be visited; in the latter years thou shalt come into the land that is brought back from the sword, and is gathered out of many people... Thou shall ascend and come like a storm, thou shall be like a cloud to cover the land, thou, and all thy bands, and many people with thee...

"'And thou shalt say: I will go up to the land of unwalled villages; I will say to them that are at rest, that swell safely, all of them swelling without walls, and having neither bars nor gates, to rake a spoil and to take a prey; to turn they hand against the desolate places that are now inhabited, and upon the people that are gathered, out of the nations which have gotten cattle and gods, that dwell in the midst of the land.

"'Sheba and Dedan, and the merchants of Tarshish, with all the young lions thereof, shall say unto three: Art thou come to take a spoil? hast thou gathered thy company to take a prey? to carry away silver and gold, to take away cattle and goods, to take a great spoil?'

"You see," added the Egregore, "that Gog is not an individual without importance, and that he has no complaint to make of the destiny that was assigned to him."

"Good, good," said Robert, "there is doubtless some advantage in dominating the nations and possessing gold, silver, and the larder too, to which the wine-cellar is adjoined, I assume. But this seventh draught of Saint-Pourçain has returned my memory, and it seems to me that you are omitting more than one point of the prophecy of Ezekiel. Eh? Wily citer, is it not said in the fourth verse of that thirty-eighth chapter: 'I will turn thee back, and put hooks into thy jaws?'"

"Perhaps."

"Surely. That makes poor Gog less triumphant than the spirit of the Lord appears to prophesy."

"Is there some baseness in bending under the breath of the Almighty, in having His will as a bit between the teeth?"

"I shall refrain from thinking it, although it is frequently represented by apostles as capable of forcing you to dance with a strange vigor, and that a tug of the bridle might make the bars bleed cruelly. But I agree that the Church cannot be wrong. What I would criticize more forcefully is your not having reported the end of the prophecy, which is no less unfortunate for Gog, chief prince of Meshech and Tuba. It is this, for once swig more has made me as knowledgeable as a priest:

"'And I will call for a sword against him throughout all my mountains, saith the Lord God; every man's sword shall be against his brother. And I will plead against him with pestilence and with blood; and I will rain upon him, and upon his bands, and upon the many people that are with him, an overflowing rain, and great hailstones, fire, and brimstone.'[18]

"And further on," Robert continued, "in the thirty-ninth chapter, it is written:

"'And I will smite thy bow out of thy left hand, and will cause thy arrows to fall out of thy right hand...

"'And they that dwell in the cities...shall go forth, and shall burn the weapons, both the shields and the bucklers, the bows and the arrows, and the handstaves and the spears, and they shall burn them with fire seven years. So that they shall take no wood out of the field, neither cut down any out of the forests; for they shall burn the weapons with fire; and they shall spoil those who spoiled them, and rob those that robbed them, saith the Lord God.

"'And it shall come to pass in that day that I will give unto Gog a place there of graves in...the valley of the passengers on the east of the sea; and it shall stop the noses of the passengers; and there shall they bury Gog and all his multitudes, and they shall call it the valley of Hamongog.'[19]

"Damn it!" Robert concluded, "I think that Gog will finish, as they say, in virile fashion, and he will be scalped for

---

[18] *Ezekiel* 38: 21-22.
[19] *Ezekiel* 39 2; 9-11.

having possessed and tortured the people assembled from the nations. It's necessary not to forget that passage."

Metatron said: "The Saint-Pourçain isn't as good as the wine made from the vines of the region of Saumur; you can drink two or three lots of that, I suppose?"

"Four," said Robert.

"And here's a pâté of wild boar in quince jelly tinted with redcurrant juice. As for the verses you've remembered, I omitted them deliberately, because I believe that they were interpolated in Ezekiel's prophecy."

"By whom would they have been interpolated?"

"Perhaps by the inspiration of the vanquished, who provoked Cain and the enemies of Jesus. He cannot remain at peace in the shadow to which we have relegated him, still conceiving vengeances and meditating their accomplishment in the nation that is the navel of the world. In addition, another reason counseled me not to recite those menacing verses; as a courteous host, I did not want to sadden my guest."

"Me?"

"Of course."

"And what have I to do with all this, being a good horseman and hunter, eating well, drinking well and sleeping well, but not at mass, unless having drunk and eaten too much."

"You have to do with this what was announced by the spirit of the Lord."

"Of the Devil!"

"For Gog, of the land of Magog, Gog who, in the Tower standing facing the Castle, like the Pope above the King, was to remain in slumber until the hour of the Sign, Gog, who was to be brought out, and to be powerful, superb and numerous, through the multitude of days and men, is you, and your race, Duc de Haubour."

"That is not my name."

"Robert I, Duc de Haubour, known as the Lame, I, the miter, recognize you and crown you; and let destinies be accomplished, even if they end for us in the valley of sepulchers, and for the peoples in deliverance in Life, alas, in accordance with the will of the Other."

In order to clarify his ideas, Robert had extended his hand toward a large goblet, which contained no less than two lots of Saumur wine, but he did not have the leisure to take possession of it, for darkness suddenly fell around him: darkness, solitude and silence.

He no longer knew where he was, but he had the idea that he was no longer in a room, that the space round him was immeasurably enlarged, that he was seated, alone, on something very high, in the middle of an immense abyss.

And a voice, which no longer resembled that of the Egregore, said, in thunderous rumbles: "Robert I, Duc de Haubour, known as the Lame, contemplate yourself, multiplied in centuries of centuries!"

And then, out of a noise of chains that sprang forth like a thunder of menacing hope and fell back into a silence of accomplishment, a colossal form loomed up made of splendor and darkness. It was like the emergence of a mountain, with peaks reaching up into infinite space and black overhanging rocks that overwhelmed valleys, and holes full of blackness and azure lakes and wells into which torrential avalanches fell, and green slopes, pink with little flowers, and a chaos of colliding landslides, and meager altars at which pilgrims knelt, and towers and huts, and stars in the embrasures of crenellations of granite, and the lamentations of the wind in the unknown of abysms.

However, the form had a vague human resemblance; by dint of considering it, Robert discerned therein tresses of hair, a face with terrible eyes, arms that were making gestures of order, feet that were marching impetuously through a mud of darkness from which lava of flame and blood emerged. And he gazed at the face of that being, the face of Gog. He recognized himself in it, vertiginously magnified, as if in a mirror equal to the immensity, in which the moment expanded to the end of duration, or the minute became almost eternal. He recognized, however, that he was different from himself, not so much by virtue of the enormity of the image as by the adjunction of he knew not what features, which completed him in a type, in which he became, while still himself, another self.

Then, whether because he took better account of what he was looking at, or because the object of his attention really had varied, the colossal figure became that of a hero fully armored in white, who was lifting into the dawn the sword of a victorious archangel, like the luminous pistil of a grim silver lily; and that gigantic, very pure hero was the precise and supreme accomplishment, in Hope, of all the will-power of the chaotic apparition.

Darkness fell again, more intense, and the form vanished into it. Soon, however, similar to what it had just been, but smaller—more proximate to humanity, to tell the truth—it was recomposed and multiplied, sometimes in momentarily motionless groups, sometimes in tumultuous processions of warrior figures, riding and brandishing weapons along a strange living wall, a swarming cliff made of writhing human bodies, bristling with hair and clenched fists, against which a howling sea of drowned men and wrecks in the ebb and flow of disaster came to beat horribly. And the beings succeeded one another, their feet in that sea, along that cliff.

In a din of cannon-fire there was a knight, his armor shattered under a hail of cannonballs; and another, with a red cross on his breast; and another, charged with chains; and another, who, behind a young woman in a silver breastplate, resembling a celestial warrior, was lifting a white oriflamme.

Ecstatic, Robert made the sign of the cross.

Soon, surrounded by hymns and howls, a formidable leader of armies charged, whose hand, red with the generous blood of his own wounds, was kissed recklessly by an old queen walking in her knees, and which he withdrew in disgust from the mud. And several more passed, in clusters or separately, and in the costume of a mountain man, like a bear-hunter, a king! And, bold, radiant, joyous, with oaths and laughter, his armor scintillating in an innumerable reflection of swords, a proud battler followed by men and women in a tumult of glory and amour, and, all their wings open toward their white-plumed leader, a flock of cawing crows and singing victories.

It seemed, while he passed, that the sea precipitated less disaster toward the cliff of hatred and desolation; and Robert smiled, content.

Then there was a pale figure with a bowed head, melancholy and sighing, reminiscent of a debilitated and docile Prometheus under the scarlet wingspan of a enormous red vulture.

Now, along the cliff, howling louder, but so dazzled by an incomparable flamboyance that it ceased to extend all its fists to shield its eyes, a sumptuous crown-bearer proceeded, illuminated by glory, joy and sunlight, in a marvelous apotheosis. From the four corners of the sky, trumpets sounded victory toward him alone, and an infinite procession ran to kiss the hem of the august mantle with which he covered all the red foam of the sea, swollen in great waves with more numerous cadavers and debris. An immeasurable triumph! A radiance unequaled down here! The expansion of the greatest of lilies in a solar calyx!

No less innumerable than the crowd of his servants, a litany of men and women, some carrying poorly-closed coffers in the haste of flight, from which coins tumbled, others holding wailing children in their arms, exiled themselves from all that splendor, hurling the maledictions of despair and hunger at him on the foreign roads. But with the slow grace of a ceremonial dance, seemingly accompanied by the organ of a luminous basilica in which black-clad priests and red-clad cardinals officiated in great pomp, beautiful women in silk, gold and precious sons surrounded the pompous monarch, to whom grave and gentle men bowed, removing the imperishable laurels from their pensive and meditative foreheads, which they offered as crowns to his splendid head.

And Robert swelled with pride.

After an open coffin in which a young man was lying, another coffin passed by, also containing a young man, with the mild appearance of a sleeping child, followed by a bishop throwing flowers, and, amid the momentary silence of the frightful tumultuous décor, these words fell toward the white corpse syllable by syllable, like teardrops: "Your Marcellus."[20] But he was dead, and Robert wept, his soul unquiet.

Then, among coins streaming from split bags and the sound of kisses and clamors of revelry, a handsome gilded child advanced, led by a hand; he grew, still golden, became a man, and an old man; but relentlessly, a hand held him and guided him, between semi-naked women who, enveloping him with caressant flesh, prevented him from seeing the arm and the face of the man guiding him at will. He no longer sought to see them. Sometimes, men ran to him who spoke to him in whispers, with expressions of sorrow or anguish, doubtless warning him of perils, messengers of defeat and disaster. He did not listen, turning his head toward the beautiful women with laughing teeth and beautiful offered breasts. And amid the laughter and the songs and the fortunate cleavages of favorites, he pleased himself, while not listening to the lamentable noise, the ferocious noise, of the furiously-exasperated dolor of the living wall alongside which he was marching, and the sea in which entrails, eyes and brains were splashing; he crushed the dead and the ruins under resounding golden soles.

Robert was afraid because of the eternal human mourning that was becoming frightfully wrathful.

And there was no longer a sea beating the cliff of anguish, not a cliff beaten by a tide of corpses; but the former, swirling in a cyclone and the latter, collapsing in a cataract, formed an immense and turbulent multitude of ferocious eyes,

---

[20] The reference is to the nephew of the Roman emperor Augustus, who was his intended successor before dying young, when the Empire fell to Tiberius—a circumstance lamented in Virgil's Aeneid. Some French writers lamented the death of Louis XIV's grandson and designated successor, the Duc de Bourbon, in a similar fashion, and the consequent succession of Louis XV.

menacing fists and hateful teeth: a frantic populace of furies and vengeances; and before

The formidable riot of maledictions, princes clad in gold and ornamented with gemstones fled, with violet priests and scarlet priests, and, with fragments of a scepter in hand, a heavy and staggering form that no longer had a head bore a crown upon its shoulders. Many others also had no head, and howled and danced in frightful celebration, like the hurly-burly of a chaotic infernal ocean, around the decapitated red necks; and women and children took the heads of the tortured by the hair and held them up in the air, swallowing the flowing blood with their wide open mouths.

Everyone was gone except, down below, in a somber hole in the wall, a frail child, whom Robert recognized, in which he saw again the resemblance of all those who had already passed before him. But the child paled, becoming weaker and weaker; he tottered, and died. Then, it seemed to Robert that he no longer recognized him.

And everything was extinguished. Before the visionary there was, implacably, a curtain of opaque darkness, as if everything had finished in shadow with the little being who had just rendered his soul. The sounds of battle, cannonades and fusillades, crumbling ramparts, cries of victory and blasphemies of defeat, sounded behind the wall for a long, long time; but Robert felt that he was absent from that enormous and long tumult, which he heard but did not see; he thought that it was over, that the night would have no dawn.

A first light rose, however, like an evening twilight, and the ancient sea was visible, but devoid of motion, as if the junction of cadavers and wreckage had paved it with disasters; and the cliff also reappeared, but, as if the immemorial martyrdom was immobilized there in solid masonry, it was no longer anything but a long bas-relief of torsions and grimaces.

Under a daylight that no longer resembled the bright radiation of old, a man, crowned, but not by honest solarity, was walking at a hesitant pace, with anxious eyes, conversing without raising his voice with men with fearful and sly faces, who responded in whispers. Another man, also crowned, followed him without looking either forward or back, reading a book; under the pressure of a crowd that threw cobblestones asked him, ripped up from the street, he drew away and vanished. Robert was scornful of those princes, obscure laggards of a dazzling cortege; and he thought that they were the last, and sighed.

After a long time, however, another man, alone, not on the sea before the cliff but by a wide pale gray road, went past at an uncertain pace, limping toward a distant house. And because of that solitude, because of that mild face with very blue eyes, as pure as the eyes of a child—a melancholy resemblance of the end of races to their commencement—Robert liked that supreme passer-by, whose limping gait of exile he saw entering the distant house. It closed; the sound of the door audible, like the fall of a tumulary slab. And the house did, indeed, resemble a pale sepulcher, with a cross on the fronton, which trembled, unstable, about to fall.

The exile did not come out again, doubtless defunct. Robert thought that he was dying himself, for the last time.

He was lying on the snow between servants who had come running. He remembered, and was frightened; but he thought that he had fallen asleep because of the weakness caused by his wound, and because above all, he had been drunk when he fell from his horse. Someone tried to help him to stand up, and to sustain him—needlessly. He was marching awkwardly, limping a little, that was all.

He had not been dreaming, then, since he was healed? He looked toward the Tower. It was black, bleak and sinister beneath its mantle of snow, and dominating with its high miter. It seemed to him that noises were emerging from it. He dared not go in that direction, He walked toward the Castle, resembling, in the midst of all the snow, the formless pistil of an immeasurable lily. He was thoughtful. The servants, with one urgent voice, a voice that gives news, were talking to him; he did not hear them; he was still thinking.

What! Had the future of his race really been revealed to him by magic? He wanted that, and he feared it; having a calm soul and a gentle heart, most of all, he feared it; he would have liked to persuade himself that he really had slept, and dreamed.

When he arrived at the castle he found his mother entering her death-throes; she only had time to embrace Robert and to tell him that Haubour was now his. A good son, he wept tenderly, and did not only bear mourning in his attire. In the midst of his trouble, however, he could not help thinking that Metatron had prophesied accurately, at least in part; and he was frightened by that.

He had further reason to be disturbed when, sometime later, on the occasion of his imminent marriage to Agnès de Brabant,[21] the daughter of Louis II, Comte de Brabant, the barony of Haubour, by the grace of the King, was elevated to a duchy.

A peer, then, as the Egregore had said, he was Robert I, Duc de Haubour. Henceforth, he walked curbed, as if he had the weight of enormous destinies on his shoulders.

On the evening of his wedding, after the feast, while his companions were still drinking in the hall on the ground floor, Robert, unhurriedly, followed by two squires carrying torches, went up the narrow spiral stairway toward the chamber where Agnès de Brabant, Duchesse de Haubour, was already in bed.

Once he had had a very tender desire, not for her but for a sister she had; with her, it seemed to him, he might have had a good life of affection and calm, the life that he wanted; on returning from hunting he would have saluted a dear affable face, and she would not have made grimaces if, in the evenings, after the communal prayer, he without his morion and she already in her night-cap, he had kissed her with a mouth still scented with the wine and meat of supper.

---

[21] Louis the Lame married Marie de Hainaut, the fourth daughter of Jean II d'Avesnes, Comte de Hanaut; they had eight children.

Instead of the one he desired, so pretty, with such a benevolent air, he had been given the other, not beautiful, whom he did not love, but accepted by virtue of courtesy not to disdain. He went up the stairway without haste however, and before the door, having sent the squires away, he hesitated in the darkness.

Through an embrasure, he could see the plain from above, beneath a night with rare stars. The dominating Tower loomed up opposite the Castle, even higher. And suddenly, as if fires of joy had been lit on the summit, flames that resembled a blossoming of furious triumph sprang forth from the crenellations of the miter throughout the darkness. He shivered. But that splendor was extinguished, and disappeared like an eruption swallowed by a black crater, barely having been belched forth.

He went into the nuptial chamber, from which, on seeing him, the women who had put the bride to bed emerged. She was waiting for him, docile but unsmiling—almost ugly, in fact. And he shuddered again. She had never appeared to him exactly as he saw her now. He seemed to recognize in that face the features that that were lacking in him to compose the prolifically multiplied face of his long descendancy; and, fused in a single mirror-image he and she would have been the same vision, ever renewed, which had passed before the living and howling cliff. He was afraid, because of his race; but he was too good a Christian to spare himself the duty that the holy sacrament of marriage commands.

He undressed, got into bed, made the sign of the cross and, lying on top of Agnès, he engendered five centuries of triumphs, disasters, glory, infamy, splendor and mourning.

How The Devil Went Bald

Everyone knows that the Devil is bald, and logically, it is necessary that he is; for the worst of ugliness—ha ha, I'm a silversmith!—would not be spared the abominable author of all human evil.

What is less generally known, however, is how Lucifer—whom some call Iblis and others Beelzebub, which is like saying Lord of the Flies—lost his hair.

I shall tell the tale as it as told to me by a barber in Pamplona, a great bilboquet player, tradition has it, between the beard and the curls, who had for a sign: *Satan's Wig*.

Blond as the morning star, red as the Inferno, black as the eternal night, the hair of the rebel angel was so prodigiously bushy and bristling that when he was precipitated, it emerged over the entire earth and all the seas like an immeasurable umbrella of tufts and locks. And Our Lord was very chagrined because, even by putting on his spectacles—which are made, as everyone knows, from the last star in the south and the last in the north, connected by the tail of a comet—he could not distinguish the world he had created, which was so beautiful, through the enormity of that flamboyant shock. When one has invented roses, at least one ought to have the pleasure of seeing them. Besides which, according to the most authentic portraits that we have of him, the Lord has more beard than hair, and perhaps he experienced some jealousy.

Doubtless nothing would have been easier for him than to set fire to the Devil's hair with the Lightning, but he had already split his forehead with it, and, a demiurge seized by the scruple of an honest dramaturge, he was reluctant to employ the same means twice.; with the result that he would have remained perplexed for quite a long time if the Holy Spirit, always clear-sighted, had not said to him:

"How embarrassed you are, Cousin, by such a little thing! Simply decree that for every murder that is committed on earth, Lucifer will lose a hair. To judge by the way that humans kill one another, he'll soon have a head as bald as a rock on the strand worn away by twenty centuries of tides."

"What!" sighed the good Lord. "Do those I made like unmaking one another as much as that? But so be it, let's try that means."

Then, having said: "Let Lucifer lose a hair for each of the murders committed on the earth," he fell silent, waiting amid the splendor, the azure and the music of eternity.

And crime depilated the Devil! No blow was struck with a dagger, a sword, a club, a spear, a rifle or a cutlass that did not extract a hair of shadow or flame, and battles pulled out entire clumps. However, so marvelously numerous were the Devil's hairs that, some time having passed—it was a day in April—the Lord, leaning over, could not perceive through it, even vaguely, the lilac branches in which the hedge-sparrows built their nests of amour and song.

But the Holy Spirit said: "Don't lose hope. By virtue of some strange anomaly they're killing one another less than usual down there. Merely decree that at every theft committed on earth, Lucifer will lose a hair. As, all things considered, humans only possess what they have stolen from one another, his head will soon be as naked as the buttock of a baby angel."

"Cousin," sighed the good God, "I can hardly believe that mortals are all thieves. What do they have to take, since I've given them the beauty of the sky and women, flowers, birds, the waves of the sea and the profundity of green forests where they can take siestas in the shade? However, I'll try that new means.

And he said: "Let Lucifer lose a hair for each of the thefts committed on the earth." And while waiting, he took pleasure in the concerts of the seraphim.

The infernal cranium was strangely shaken. If a gamin filched a ball, a highwayman robbed a passer-by, Alexander the Great conquered India or Caesar took Gaul, if a prostitute emptied the pockets of a sleeping old gentleman or a pick-pocket unfastened the watch of a provincial, there was a hair, a hair, a hair and yet another hair extracted by every act of larceny. There were coups on the Bourse that cost him enormous hanks. But the miraculous hair only had a few stripes here and there, as an immense forest has paths, and Our Lord still could not see his beloved earth. Most of all, he would have liked to follow, through his starry spectacles, loving couples strolling among the hawthorns, which he had made so perfumed in order that they might be drawn hopefully toward the moss, which he had made soft expressly for them.

The Holy Spirit, worried, said: "They steal so little, then? Let's make a great decision. Order, Cousin, that for every stupid thing said upon the earth, Lucifer will lose one of his hairs.

"Now, now, Cousin," said the good God, "you're losing respect. Do you think that those made in my image, and whose souls are born of my breath, are utter imbeciles? Nevertheless, I'll try your proof. Let Lucifer lose one of his hairs for every stupid thing that is said on earth."

Oh, Beelzebub's poor head. It was denuded like a field of loose sheaves by a storm wind. Puns, cafe-concert songs, and reflections before paintings in salons ravaged it. The premières of vaudevilles and Monsieur Brunetière's speeches grabbed his temples and the nape of his neck and pulled out masses.[22] But the innumerable and invincible tresses persisted, in spite of all the efforts of human stupidity, and it still emerged, like a vast umbel of tufts and locks, even hiding the paths of flowering may-blossom where loving couples strolled.

---

[22] Fredinand Brunetière (1849-1906) was the professor of French literature at the École Normale and editor of the *Revue des Deux Mondes* when the present story was written; he presided over numerous conferences at the Sorbonne, and promoted a theory of the evolution of literary genres based on the Darwinian theory of natural selection, which Mendès was not alone in thinking a trifle silly.

Furious, the Holy Spirit said: "Let's employ the supreme means. Order, Cousin, that for every adulterous kiss given in Paris, Lucifer will lose a hair."

The good Lord became very angry. "Oh, truly, Holy Spirit, you're going too far! What! Do you have such a low opinion of the young women into whom I put all my care in order to perfect them, so pretty and so honest—and in particular the Parisienne, who is *the* woman, as the rose is *the* flower. The wives down there, happy to be the grace and charm of the hearth, conversing in the evening with their husbands and children under the familial lamp, refrain from running around. Certainly, they're amorous, for I wanted them to be, but their virtuous tenderness doesn't contradict their tender virtues.

"Try anyway," said the Holy Spirit.

"To show you how naïve you are, yes, " said the Lord, and added: "Let Lucifer lose a hair for every adulter..."

He had no need to finish. The Devil was bald.

Burned Tears

That poets, even the most mediocre, are provided, in regard to their estate—which is to say, Dreams, Amour and Pity for the poor—with a very particular understanding, and also with a science refused to popes, emperor, kings rabbis, doctors and other omnipotent or omniscient individuals, is a truth that, if contested, would emerge from the contest even more evident; and, if they can be refused the art of politics or war, theologies or scientific inventions—in my opinion, they are refused wrongly, for the mere possibility of a beautiful sonnet or pleasing rondeau implies, in effect, the knowledge of power of Everything—it cannot be denied that, by nature, poets excel in the divination of sublime chimeras, in the adoration of splendid dreams and in the tears that console human dolors.

Engineers pretend to be unaware that the means of locomotion commonly known as the railway was imagined by the Persian poet Firdausi, as one can be convinced by reading in the Book of Kings the description of the steam elephants that King Iskander sent forth against the army of King Phur, but they are obliged to recognize that the good news of the hope of the Beautiful and of Mercy were brought to humans by those who make verses; with the consequence that you will not experience any astonishment on learning from me (I obtained the certainty of it from a legend engraved on a palm leaf by a beggar-poet of the time of Saint Mary of Egypt[23]) that, for many centuries, the infernal punishments with which devout souls are so justly preoccupied, have been abolished in fact, if not in law.

There is no more Gehenna; there are no more eternal tortures; and, to tell the truth, paradise is accorded to the worst sinners on earth as easily as to simple girls who died in inno-

---

[23] i.e. the fourth century A.D.

cence before even putting on the short skirt that is the commencement of damnable perversity.

That is a fine encouragement to persons inclined to the seven deadly sins, notably that of lust, which is the most frequent, being the sweetest to commit and the most similar to Good because of the beauty of the arms than breasts that invite you to it. In any case, it is as I say; and, precisely by virtue of an excess of antithesis explained by the infinity of mercy, it is to Our Lady Mary, the paragon of celestial virtues, that we owe the sure hope of not being chastised for our crimes on earth. But it is necessary to tell the tale of that fortunate change; and I shall do so by translating for you, in French prose, the poem invented by the beggar-poet at the very moment when the repentant Egyptian was traversing the Nile without her bare feet, which the crocodiles adored, sinking beneath the surface.

It is averred in all times and confirmed by the most authentic sacred texts that, as at the gates of our cities, there is a tollbooth at the fates of Heaven.

At the beginning of time, angelic tax-collectors with partially deployed wings asked souls arrived from earth after corporeal death: "Have you anything to declare?" and, in accordance with what they declared or did not declare, they were permitted or refused entry. But there were abuses. Sinful spirits dissimulated their sins, just as it happens every day that clever smugglers do not admit to the bottles of alcohol concealed under their clothing or, in their vehicles, under vegetables being transported to market. And fraud populated paradise with scarcely commendable souls, entirely appropriate to adulterate the purity of the recent Elect and the ancient Elect.

As pure as a ring-dove but as wily as a monkey, the Holy Spirit found a means to ward off such a great inconvenience. There were balances henceforth at the door to the Blissful Abode, which Saint Peter held in the air and in which, the sins on one pan and the virtues on the other, the merits and demerits of the soul that wanted to enter into Eternal Joy were weighed. Whichever pan, being heavier, descended, decided the fate of the candidates. They rose up or were engulfed, in accordance with the proof, toward Heaven or Hell.

That was well imagined! But it was not long before it was perceived in Heaven that the Devil, desirous of increasing the population of his empire, and who, as was only just, had obtained permission to witness the proof of the Balance, had found a mean of taking possession of a large number of souls that were not his due. He quibbled over the equality of the balance-pans, and affirmed that dead humanity was being saved at false weight; to hear him, the sole venial sun of a nun who had sighed while watching a young curate pass by should have outweighed a heap of innocences, prayers, fasts and penitences accumulated on the other pan. In addition, he cheated. Slyly, half turned away, seemingly thinking about something else, he hooked the pan with the tip of a claw in the direction of Hell.

Saint Peter, a good fellow, whose sight was slightly troubled by the serenity disturbed by the third crow of the cock, did not see any of these underhand practices, and the tenebrous empire filed up immeasurably to the detriment of the celestial Eden.

Oh, how chagrined Our Lady Mary was by that! For she is the Mother of elect souls, and the more children she has the more content she is. As God the Father could refuse her nothing—he certainly owed her that compensation—she easily obtained permission from him to witness the proof of the Balance, on the sole condition that she would be completely hidden under a veil: a veil of cloud and a veil of stars; a veil which, by virtue of dazzling, did not allow either her virginal visage or the divinely material bosom to be seen—for it is inappropriate for Evil to contemplate Beauty, and one is no less jealous for being God.

At first, matters regarding the two pans passed rather equitably; Lucifer would not have dared to stoop to sly pettifogging before the radiant simplicity of Mary, and he even renounced subterfuge, not risking the trickery of the claw that made the balance lean, because of the eyes behind the veils, which he sensed to be so pure and so perspicacious—and equity presided over Judgment for a long time.

But how troubled the saintly Virgin Mary was by so many souls whose sins, by weight, prevailed over the weight of their virtues! She had so much compassion that it cost her to have justice. Alas, Hell lasts so long, and so, in spite of the hope of an end, does Purgatory! Was it truly necessary that, for a little too much Anger or Envy, Sloth or Pride, so many souls should descend into the formidable tortures of punishment? And she, the Virgin of virgins, would even have liked to spare the culpable souls issued from libertine bodies those tortures. Heaven is amour too! And she did not know what sin there could be in the kiss, not having known the pleasure of it.

Always thickly concealed by celestial veils, and so beautiful beneath them, clemency led her to attempt to enter into an accommodation with the Devil. She tried to persuade him that it was not just to be so just, and that, in sum, no great wrong would be done if a few souls that ought to have been his went to her, a little unduly. Above all, being so pure, she felt sad because of chastised courtesans, and she had for the unknown mud the condescension of snow.

But the Devil persisted in his strict rights, and dragged souls that were too heavy on the evil pan to Hell, feet first.

Then, it came about that, Lucifer no longer cheating, it was Our Lady Mary who cheated in her turn.

Oh, how much cunning she put into it, without any appearance of it! Standing alongside the pan of merits, when all hope that it might prevail was lost, she pretended, beneath her long veils, to be almost disinterested, turning away as if indifferently—for this time, needless to say, the Devil was in the right—but, with the adroit abandonment of the flap of her sleeve, she weighed the pan whose inclination would have decided the election of a soul; or, with the nail or her little finger, she tried to hook on to and bring down the excessively light elevation of Christian merits.

Lucifer is not one of those who can be mocked; in addition, he had noticed that, not content with the weight of the flap of her sleeve or the heavy subtlety of her little finger, Madame God—as the evil tongues of Hell, where there are journalists, call Mary—risked the impudence of her clemency to the extent of dropping into the pan of salvation, sometimes a ring, one of those that the Eternal had put on her fingers, and sometimes one of the diamonds of the pendant earrings that she had in the pink lobes of her ears, or, one after another, the pearl-stars of the Milky Way, which she had around her neck under her veils.

And the Devil was annoyed.

Accustomed to talking to the Lord since the prologue in Heaven of Goethe's *Faust*, he demanded—and the Almighty, who is also Absolute Justice, had to comply—that Our Lady Mary should only witness the operations of the paradisal toll-booth deprived of luminous gems capable of weighing down one or other pan of the balance.

The ever-compassionate mother of the tender Jesus no longer had any jewels under her veils. Now what would she do? How could she cheat? By means of what ruse could she weigh down the decisive pan of Salvation?

And, because of a poor girl who, for having loved to much down here, was about to suffer eternally, she wept. She wept tears: so many tears that they weighed down the pan and saved the amorous woman.

And from that moment on, she only longer employed, in order to save souls from Hell, the single stratagem, so sincere, of pity.

At every proof, in the pan that threatened to be insufficiently heavy, her love for the disinherited, the abandoned and the culpable wept.

Now, the Devil had nothing to say. He did not have the right, in sum, to prevent the Virgin from weeping.

But who knows whether, finally tortured by his eternal hatred, he too did not come to know pity for those he would torture? Either by virtue of natural clemency, the memory of former divinity, or supreme subterfuge—I incline to the last hypothesis—he began shedding abundant, and heavier tears—oh, how much heavier!—in the pan that inclined toward Hell.

In response to trickery—trickery and a half!—Evil prevailed, by means of tears, or the simulation of tears.

And all souls fell toward Gehenna, and there was no longer, even for repentant souls, the joy of Heaven.

Our Lady Mary foresaw her defeat, and a Paradise without Elect, and the supplication of joined hands hammering at the closed doors of Justice. And Mary looked at Lucifer. He was still handsome, for having been an angel; it was impossible that there did not subsist, in his vanquished pride, from his ancient felicity, a little tenderness.

Sublimized by the habitude of Heaven, a memory of the triumph of her charms awoke in her pure soul of a young girl once regarded complaisantly by young men when she brought the midday meal to the good blacksmith who smiled at his beautiful wife, and she thought that one could tempt the Devil, since the Devil had tempted God...

While the clever damnatory tears fell on the pan of Hell, she suddenly took off all her veils of clouds and stats, and, with her face and breasts naked, she looked at Lucifer. He looked at her too, forgetting to be frightful, radiant for having been dazzled.

Softly, she continued weeping into the divine pan of the Balance; but he, looking at her, contemplating her, possessing her with his eyes, in which the ardent aurora of ancient mornings revived, was no longer able to weep, his tears burned by the radiant apparition of virginal Glory...

...And for a long time they have been standing thus, facing one another; and that is why all souls are now saved.

The Story of the Good Wolf and God's Justice
A Russian tale

To Louis Léger[24]

"No," said the valetudinarian old man, when he was drunk on vodka, like a priest who has been invited to a boyar's wedding, "I won't tell you the story of the fellow whom nurses call the Little Finger, because he was born behind the stove of the thumb that his mother cut off while chopping red cabbages; nor the tale of the city lady saved from going to Hell by the grace of the Panagia, who gave her as a golden doll to the cherubim of paradise; nor the tale of the soldier who made soup by putting the ax in the saucepan, instead of cutting of the head of the evil hostess. And it's necessary to send the young women away from the room where we're drinking. Let them go for a walk along the road, holding one another by the waist and singing songs. Me, I'll tell, not as others tell it, but as I know it, a story that makes lads who have courage when they're drunk get up from the bench after thumping the table."

There was a wolf who was hungry. He had a mouth to catch and teeth to bite, but he didn't dare to catch and if he had caught he wouldn't have dared to bite, because he was good. And he was very thin. He went to find God, who is the Tsar of Heaven, and when he was before him, he said:

"Almighty and very equitable eternal Tsar of Heaven and all the worlds, I'll die before long if you don't give me something to eat."

---

[24] The writer Louis Léger (1843-1923) was a significant pioneer of Slavic studies, who published a collection of *Contes populaires slaves* (1882).

God replied: "It's only just that I give you something to eat, since I created your hunger. You can see from here a meadow bathed by a great river; go to that meadow and eat the ewe that is grazing the grass."

"Thank you, God."

"Bon appétit, wolf."

Tropp, tropp, tropp, the wolf gallops. Here he is in the meadow. He sees the ewe.

"Good day, ewe," he says. "Say your prayers; I've come to eat you, with God's permission."

"Eat me? Who are you, then?"

"I'm the hungry wolf."

"You look more like a dog. But, wolf or dog, would you have the heart to devour me when I have little lambs who are still suckling, and who won't fail to die if the milk from my teat is lacking. Look how gracious they are and how lightly they leap over the flowers with little *baa baas!*

He wolf was moved to compassion.

He went back to see God.

"Eternal Tsar of Heaven and all the worlds," he said, "I didn't make a meal of the ewe because of her little ones, who were playing in the grass. I'm going to die soon if you don't give me something to eat."

God replied:

"You're right not to harm the ewe, the mother of lambs, who never did any harm to anyone. You can see from here, close to the church, the pasture where the priest's two white bulls are grazing. Go that way. Don't touch the white beasts, because they pull the ploughs by means of which the poor folk sometimes have bread, but go into the church. You'll find the priest there. He's very fat. You can eat him. He deserves to be overtaken by some misfortune, since he lies and blasphemes and takes the broth from the mouths of beggars to inflate his belly."

"Thank you, God."

"Bon appétit, wolf."

Tropp, tropp, tropp, the wolf gallops. He traverses the pasture. He doesn't touch the bulls. He goes into the church and he sees the priest.

"Greetings, priest," he says, "say your prayers. I've come to eat you, with God's permission."

"Eat me? Who are you?"

"I'm the hungry wolf."

"You look more like a dog. But, wolf or dog, would you have the heart to devour me when I have so many souls to console on earth and guide toward celestial joys? Don't you know that it's me who baptizes them, me who marries them, me who gives the dying supreme hope? If you devour me, there'll no longer be anything but despair in life and annihilation in death. Then again, consider my robe shining with sacred ornaments, and the little golden images handing around my neck, and look at this chalice. That would be a strange tablecloth, place-setting and an unexpected glass for the dinner of a beast."

The wolf was very disconcerted.

He went back up to see God.

"Almighty and very equitable Lord, I haven't made a meal of the priest in the church, because of his sacred garments and the golden images hanging around his neck. I'll die before much longer, if you don't give me something to eat."

God replied:

"You're very compassionate, truly, and very religious, for a ferocious animal. However, I'll try to satisfy you. You see that palace with radiant windows, as if they were made of diamond glass? A carpet of all the colors covers the perron. Go into the palace. You'll find the local boyar in the middle of dinner. He's even fatter than the priest. You can eat him. It's time that the bad master was punished for the harm he does his servants, his peasants and everyone else. The crack of his bones between your teeth will be a sound very agreeable to my justice."

"Thank you, God."

"Bon appétit, wolf."

116

Tropp, tropp, tropp, the wolf gallops. He goes up the perron, and he sees the boyar at table in the palace.

"I lick your feet, Boyar," he said. "Swallow that grouse wing quickly. I've come to eat you, with God's permission."

"Eat me? Who are you?"

"I'm the hungry wolf."

"Ha ha ha!" said the boyar, roaring with laughter and holding his sides. "You're a stupid animal and I never heard mention of such an adventure, or such an imbecile. Look, idiot, I'm surrounded by my servants, who, if you took it into your head to show your teeth, would beat you with sticks or disembowel you with their big knives. Come on, come on, don't be nasty. Instead of being a wolf, be a dog. You look like one, anyway. And I'll put a fine brass collar around your neck, with little bells.

The wolf marveled at the collar that was put around his neck.

He went back to see God.

"Ha ha!" said the Lord. "I expect that you're well content now. There's nothing more succulent, is there, than the flesh of masters?"

"Alas, because of this collar..."

"In truth," cried God, "this is a very difficult wolf to nourish. However, it's only just that I give him something to eat, since I created his hunger. Come here, then, come closer, closer. Since my eternity commenced, I've been the misfortune of all men and all women. Because of me, they've endured miseries, treasons, remorse and the frightful gasps of death-throes. The time has come when my own equity ought to condemn me to expiation. Open your mouth, wolf, and eat me. Are you afraid of not finding me to your liking?"

But the wolf shivered, and said: "Eternal Tsar of Heaven, I'm too well aware of the respect that I owe you. Lord, to make you my meal."

"Are you going to die of hunger, then?"

"It's necessary," said the wolf, resigned.

With that, he went away, his head down, and his tail between his legs, and he died in the forest.

Now, since that time, the Lord has reflected a great deal. What has happened under heaven, then, for the wolves, to whom he gave ferocity, to be so hesitant, so timid and so cowardly, even when they are hungry? Is it dogs that have courage henceforth? Is it necessary for the work of wolves to be done by dogs? Is it by dogs that the priest, the boyar and God ought to be devoured?

The Lord thinks about that. He thinks about it often, all the time. There will be something new in the world.

"And God told me that personally," concluded the valetudinarian old man, "once when I was visiting him. I was drinking hydromel and beer, but it ran down my beard, and didn't go into my mouth."

Premières in Paradise

In his box radiant with suns and lightning, the Almighty, the eternal spectator of the human comedy, yawned, and having yawned, said: "Someone summon Chance for me."

Poet, and also the impresario of the Universal Theater, Chance advanced, prostrated himself and then, not without some anxiety, said: "What does Your Sublimity desire?"

The Almighty, still yawning, said: "Chance, you're deteriorating."

"Lord!"

"You're deteriorating, I tell you."

"Lord!"

"You're absolutely lacking in imagination. What is the play you've put on for me today? Another repeat?"

"Oh, Eternal, how could you think that I would dare...before you? It's a completely new drama, I assure you. It's true that it isn't perfect with regard to the stage-set and the interpretation, having been put on in haste, but I hope that the subject will interest you nevertheless, since it's a matter of a brave little people fighting to sustain your glory and avenge your martyrs against a nation that shows itself very hostile to the laws established by your Bible, your Evangelists, and, in a word, your preferred religion."[25]

"Truly, old Chance, in spite of your white beard, so long that it can make a tour of infinity three times," said the Almighty, "you make speeches that would hardly befit, being to ingenuous, your little sister Providence or your aged brother Destiny, fallen into senility. Do you think that at the point in

---

[25] The reference is to the Russo-Japanese War, which began in February 1904, the same year as the publication of *Le Carnaval fleuri*, the collection in which the present story appeared.

119

Everything, and the moment in Always, at which I've arrived, I still care about the fashion in which I'm adored or blasphemed? But let's leave that aside. It's theology, which isn't your department. Your play, repeat or not, was utterly tedious."

"I offered you, however, enough frightful battlefields."

"You've already shown me too much carnage."

"You've seen a prince flee over the cadavers of his people."

"I've seen so many flights of emperors or leaders of free races above heaps of corpses."

"You've seen warrior women charging along the ramparts of their city..."

"Like Jeanne Hachette."

"And a young woman dressed as a soldier marching at the head of an ardent multitude.

"Like Jeanne d'Arc."

"My soldier isn't a virgin."

"A facile novelty. An unimportant concession to naturalist theater. Chance, either you're collaborating with deplorable melodramatists who have leaned genius in the feuilletons of Francisque Sarcey,[26] or you're your own plagiarist."

"It seems to me, however, that I presented to you, no longer ago than yesterday, a spectacle sufficiently new and gripping. I was so certain of the effect that I didn't hesitate to print on the posters: *Great Attraction*, and I've received compliments from the most enlightened theater-lovers, by which I mean the Thrones, Principalities and Dominations. Even the

---

[26] Francisque Sarcey (1827-1899) was the highly influential drama critic of *Le Temps* for many years, where his "feuilleton"—a regular column—to which reference is made appeared. He was loathed by the Symbolists and mercilessly parodied by the humorist Alphonse Allais. Although cantankerous, Mendès' drama criticism for *Le Journal* was definitely not following in his footsteps.

Virtues, who are judges very difficult to satisfy, have admitted that they were entirely moved and surprised.

"You mean the disaster of an equipage divided in four vessels, dying of hunger, dying of thirst, and dying of everything except the excessively slow death to come and the rage of my tempests battering the reefs of my oceans?"

"No, Eternal. I confess that in that tragic intermediary I was a little too reminiscent of my *Raft of the Medusa*."

You mean, then, the little child martyr torn apart, quartered, devoured and exposed in a deserted place by a sinister brute, under the gaze of a helpful and faithful dog?"

"No, Eternal. I admit that, for that representation I borrowed a great deal from my repertoire; it was merely, with reminiscences of young Oedipus, Astyanax and the dog of Montargis, an anecdotal reduction of the frightful and eternal Moloch."

"Do you mean that conflagration, in a palace of planks, of so much youth, beauty, joy and glory?"[27]

"Yes, Eternal, in truth, I thought, in inventing that drama, that I was making my masterpiece."

"You've invented nothing at all! What! Like the most ancestral rentier of the Society of Dramatic Authors, who, having reached the age of Methuselah or Enoch, would recommence the *Grace of God*, ingenuously, and offer it to new races with the simper of a little flower-girl selling eglantines not yet in bloom, you no longer remember your own glories? You've forgotten your auto-da-fés? You've forgotten imprisoned ships ablaze in the open sea? You've forgotten the Albigensian women and children burned alive in locked barns? You've forgotten your churches collapsing in flames on your faithful also in flames and your theaters crumbling into embers, with the leader of the claque as the sole survivor, because he is eternal, like me? And the bodies soaked in naph-

---

[27] Probably the Iroquois Theatre Fire in Chicago on 30 December 1903, in which some 600 people died.

tha that blazed over the ruins of the ice-palaces of Catherine the Great?

"Oh, poor, poor, poor imbecile Chance! You don't put on anything before my box that you haven't put on a hundred times before. Not one of your trap-doors through which fire and flame emerge does anything but imitate the geysers and eruptions of Vesuvius. You tragedy of Ischia,[28] with a picturesque figuration, isn't bad, but it pastiches your Lisbon earthquake terribly, where there were also pretty costumes. In Java you were malign;[29] that had never been seen, that end of a world, but all the same, you only had to put on stage the prophetic imaginations of the Apocalypses that even my own Saint John had imitated!

"Let's admit it, Chance, you ceased to be ingenious a long time ago, and the other day, the Holy Spirit, who knows the substance of theatrical literature, said to me: "If this goes on, I'll cancel my subscription." As for me, I'm not far from withdrawing your subsidy.

Chance fought back.

"Truly, Eternal," he said, "you've become singularly difficult to satisfy. I only know one dramatic critic as exigent as you, and no one takes account of his ill humor because, only being a mediocre poet, he's scarcely a god. Oh, how long ago it was that you never wearied of seeing the mystery of an apple picked from a tree played every day! You need the unexpected. Don't blame me if I don't give you any, tragically. The fault is in your humankind, whose forces toward evil you've limited, and who reached the limits you marked out immediately. Render it capable of more new and ever renewed horror, and you won't have anything to complain of the Shakespeare I give you.

"In the meantime, you're unjust, Almighty, not to admit that, if I can't make you shiver and weep any longer, I'm still able to make you laugh. I can't any longer, because of the ba-

---

[28] Presumably the earthquake of 1881.
[29] The eruption of Krakatoa in 1883.

122

nality of the subjects, be a Corneille but I pride myself on being a Regnard.[30] I've let Aeschylus go, because Prometheus is always the same, but I'm hanging on to Aristophanes, because the fashions of making fun of Socrates are infinitely diverse, and if I'm an outmoded dramatist, I'm still an amusing vaudevillian. You can't deny that you guffawed, Eternal, the other day when I made you hear Monsieur Brunetière, in a country distant from France, proclaiming that the French novel is a school of filth and shame, and that Baudelaire was admitted as a 'dancer' at nocturnal fêtes at the Moulin Rouge, which would dedicate a statue to him alongside that of Valentin, the teacher of La Goulue."[31]

"Undoubtedly, that was funny; but Aeschines, in exile or traveling—sheltered from blows—mocked Demosthenes, in spite of the excuse: *Monstron Boonta*."

"You can't deny that I made you roar with laughter in making you see that it was precisely the humble merchants of the Rue du Sentier, having never gone to the Rue Cambacérès, who were reproached for going there, while two senators who went there every day proved that they had never seen it! You alone had seen them, Eternal, because you see everything. And they were charming little celebrations."

"Yes, Chance, but I'm inclined to think that you have read Petronius."

"And did you not have a real diversion when, in the little scene at the end, I revealed, with active marionettes, that an emperor, the murderer of a race, premeditated coming, in the city of that race, to see whether the blood had dried on the pavements he had turned red? But he dared not come!"

---

[30] The prolific writer of comedies Jean-François Regard (1655-1709)

[31] The star dancers of the Moulin Rouge in the 1890s were Valentin le Désossé (Jacques Renaudin) and La Goulue [The Glutton] (Louise Weber). The lecture by Brunetière to which reference is made was presumably one delivered during his lecture tour of the United States in 1897.

"I laughed, Chance, but you haven't invented anything. Remember that the glorious ham Nero, resembling simultaneously a mime and an executioner, loving musical instruments—flutes—that dream and musical instruments—trumpets—that kill, also wanted to go to Greece, and he went to Greece, and brought back all the prizes at all the Olympic Games that neither Corneille nor Pindar any longer remember. But suddenly, seized by a strange anxiety—honorable, though—and a need to go home, and a fear of not being at home in a city where there had been a Pericles, returned to Rome without entering Athens. Because of what? Because of whom? For no reason. Because of Gavroche, who, from the other side of the great entrance gate, amid the ceremonies of the chiefs of the city reduced not speaking, would suddenly have shouted, in Greek, while slapping his thigh: 'Oh, that head! Zut!'"

"You're confusing the epochs, Eternal. But since you don't take any more pleasure in vaudevilles than in tragedies, what is it that you need?"

"The New," said the Lord.

And from all the points of infinite space, at that moment, stars, nebulae, innumerable galaxies, vermilion suns, and suns that were thought to be dead but revived—in sum, everything that had been created by the first word ordering light emerged, anxiously, that word innumerably multiplied in all the echoes of the immensity:

"The New!"

"The New!"

"The New!"

Pensively, Chance said: "Them too."

"Well?" said God.

"Well?"

"Well?"

"Well?" said the Immensities. "The New! The New! Give us the New, Chance!"

Chance said: "There isn't anything new any longer." He added. "The best thing would be to close down."

From all points of infinite space: "Close down! Close down! Close down! Close down. Yes, nothing, nothing, nothing. Chose down!"

Then the Eternal: "Undoubtedly, undoubtedly. Close down. That would be best."

Chance, the director, said: "Should we put up posters: *Closing down*."

"Wait. Isn't there a little piece in which a girl, with her amorous friend, goes to collect strawberries, and allows her lips to be collected?"

"Curtain up, then?" asked Chance.

"Yes," said God. "Recommence."

The Golden Clarion and the Ebony Olifant

It is a question always controversial among scholars as to whether, in Paradise, days and nights are submissive, as on our earth, to changing hours, or whether the celestial abode is incessantly resplendent with the beauty of light. Fortunately, it is one of the functions of poets—the others are rhyming rondeaux or ballads and making, with the wives of the bourgeois of the city, children as beautiful as the morning, who will, in their turn, rhyme poems and make children with loving bourgeois wives—to reveal what all other men do not know, and, without wasting any more time, I will tell you in honest faith that a sun in the sky up above, like that in the sky down here, rises and climbs, and descends and sets. But how much more radiant it is than the obscure sun, adapted by a clement God to suit the weakness of human eyes!

Perhaps you feel some curiosity to learn by whom I am so well-informed. Know that it was by an angel. Oh? What species of angel? A guardian angel. Very well, the guardian of whom? Not me, certainly. Who, then, if you please? My friend Alcyonne—you know, the one who travels the roads saying to good looking young men: "I'll never finish unfastening my girdle if you don't help me."

That's a fine occupation for an angel, to be the guardian of a person like that! So, having once been her guardian, he wasn't any longer, and if he came in the evenings to lean with folded wings over the white little bed where she gave the impression of a bunch of jasmines on a bed of lilies, it was uniquely for the pleasure of seeing her in a chemise.

So, to return to my subject, there really are days and nights in the divine abode; it's even the custom for an archangel, chosen from among the most handsome, to sound a golden clarion to announce the dawn, and to sound an ebony olifant to announce the dusk, while a very old saint summons the Elect of both sexes.

Now, in a pathway in a cloud, in which eglantines flourish that are tiny stars, one of the Elect recently arrived from earth said to one of the Blessed who had been celestial for a long time: "My sister, I confess that I can to longer stand it here. It's absolutely necessary that I go back down there, at least for a few hours."

"Oh, my sister! What temptation is troubling you in the paradisal enchantment?"

"My God! My sister, I don't want to speak ill of the pleasures that are offered to us in this place of eternal recompense; I grant that the choirs of harps have a peerless sweetness, and that there is a real satisfaction in wandering, the toes brushing pink mists, amid the infinite forbearance and caress of the skies, perhaps when I've been in Paradise for thousands of years like you, I won't be able to conceive of any other joy than that of listening to your music and strolling along the Milky Way, which is undoubtedly a pleasant promenade; but I'm not yet entirely liberated from the regret of human delights, and I've resolved to escape today."

"Mercy! Think of the danger that threatens you. If anyone learns that you've fled the heavens, you'll be precipitated into the worst Gehennas of the fuliginous Inferno."

"Yes, but no one will find out, thanks to you, dear sister. As soon as the ebony olifant has sounded, as soon as I've responded to the evening roll-call, I'll pretend to reenter, as usual, the azure dormitory where billions of little clouds serve us as beds, and slyly, adroitly, I'll take flight toward the earth—it's an imprudence to give wings to the newly Elect—but I'll be careful not to linger for too long. I'll return before the golden clarion sounds the awakening call, and as you'll take care to leave the door of diamond encrusted with chrysoprase ajar, I'll regain my bed without anyone having perceived my absence. As soon as the morning appeal sounds, you'll see me rubbing my eyes and yawning, giving a perfect impression of a little soul who has slept sagely on my dark blue and starry pillow."

"Wretch, what are you asking of me? Although I love you tenderly, I could never resolve to be the accomplice of such a grave escapade. Fie, my sister! You're in Heaven and you want to play truant!"

"I tried it more than once, on earth, and never had reason to repent of it. In any case, all your objections will only make my more determined, and if you won't consent to leave the door to the dormitory open, well, someone will catch sight of my return and I'll be precipitated into Hell, that's all."

The Blessed, a long time celestial, was so good that she did not want to expose her companion to such a terrible adventure. She did what she was asked to do; and after the evening appeal, the young Elect slipped away toward the terrestrial abode.

Where, then, was she going? I am not far from thinking that she remembered some tender bed of which, when alive, she had not had to complain; and, like a moonbeam insinuating itself between the curtains, perhaps she caressed with immortal lips amorous eyes that were weeping for her. Perhaps even, in the arms of the slumbering lover, she became—for amour is omnipotent—the real lover that she had once been; what her kiss had of the paradisal would not have astonished the mouth of the sleeper, so divine had it already been before.

What is certain is that she was not bored on earth, for she remained there much longer that ought to have been necessary, and up above, in the celestial dormitory, the Blessed who had left the diamond door encrusted with chrysoprases ajar was alarmed to see day about to break. Alas, what would happen if the absentee delayed any longer in reappearing?

It was not to be feared that the dawn would awaken the Elect; dreams are so beautiful n Paradise that slumber is prolonged here willingly; but the Archangel who sounds the ebony olifant in the evening and the golden clarion in the morning was very faithful to his duty; he usually slept with one eye open in order to catch the first light of dawn. Surely, he was about to sit up on his couch, seize the clarion and fill the twilight with a violent fanfare. Everyone would get up, there would be a roll-call, the disappearance of the new Elect would be observed, and nothing would be able o save her from the eternal punishment.

The charitable Blessed gazed with anguish at the shadow, still starry but soon matinal, through which the imprudent voyager had not returned. Oh, my God, what could she do? How could she prevent the announcer from sounding the awakening?

Bewildered, she quit the dormitory, ran toward the Archangel's tent and parted the curtains. Fortunately, he was still asleep, with both eyes closed. She considered him, full of fear and also admiration. How handsome he was, lying there in his silver armor! But the light was already penetrating the tent.

Oh, it was terrible! He was about to raise his eyelids and put the clarion to his mouth. Instinctively, she put herself between the light and him. A futile precaution: he awoke. But as she had deployed her wings in order to intercept the daylight, it was not the dawn that he saw but an adorable body, of a saint, certainly, but a woman, and that body, so lilial, was completely naked, for the Blessed have no other garment than their wings.

He extended his arms, ecstatically. Alas, how she was trembling, how she feared being obliged—oh, in Heaven!—to a sin that would be all the more frightful for being so sweet! Undoubtedly, she could have fled, but if she had stood aside, he would have seen the daylight. It was necessary that he did not see it. She had to give the absentee the time to return from the base world, to regain her couchette of azure and starry cloud. She had to have the magnanimity, in order to save her companion, to expose herself to the worst of perils.

He put his arms around her; she did not pull away, and even, resigned and heroic, kissed him, on his eyelids, in order that he would not perceive the dawn.

For a long, long time she consented to that sublime sacrifice, so long that the clarion finally sounded, shaking the entire sky.

But who, then, had sounded the awakening call? It was not the Archangel, whose lips, at that moment scarcely cared about the mouthpiece of a clarion.

It was the young Elect herself, finally returned from earth, and between the clear blasts, she giggled, saying: "Oh, if I had known in what fashion I was awaited in Heaven, I would have refrained, my sister, from coming back up so soon!"

PART II: NYMPHS AND KINDRED SPIRITS

Flowers in the Water

There was a very small lake in the valley, with the pallor of opal, so small that a single tree, a birch, sufficed to cast tremors of bright shadow all over it, and what was reflected therein of the sky, when the wind inclined it in the other direction, could have be continued in a slightly widened eye.

One morning, the king's daughter—the one who watches from her window the pretty drummer-boys retiring from the war pass by, in the songs of my homeland—was standing on the edge of the lake, very occupied with a dragonfly that was striping the water with swift zigzags. In order to give all her attention to the quivering comings and goings of the insect, she had put down her doll, clad in brocade and gold, on the bank, where it gave the impression of a maid of honor lying in the grass.

The princess, whose fifteen years had flowered the month before with the first primroses, was still a very ingenuous girl, running after butterflies, content from dawn to dusk with a sparrow fallen from the nest. Although she was pretty, she only suspected it slightly, and what gave her pleasure when she looked into her mirror, was a dainty pink face beneath hair the color of the sun. She had never wondered what purpose it might serve to be pretty, nor what blue eyes and lips in flower might accomplish.

There was no shadow, not even that of a dream, over her little white soul. She did not have the slightest comprehension why the princes that were welcomed at her father's court gazed at her with ecstatic expressions, uttering deep sighs. When the drummer-boys returning from the war went past the palace singing: "Daughter of the king, would you like to be my wife?" they had all the difficulty in the world preventing her from going with them, so ignorant was she of what it was to be someone's wife. You could have asked her, on the pretext of teaching her a game, to come and lie down next to you, without a chemise, and she would not have felt any alarm, and would even have taken off her dress immediately, and everything else, if you had promised her, on oath, not to tickle her.

Suddenly, she uttered a cry. What was it? In leaning over the lake in order to see the dragonfly at closer range, had she nearly fallen in, her foot having slipped on the damp grass?

No, but she had seen, and could still see, something very extraordinary. In the depths of the lake there was a lily whiter than ivory and snow! And she remained thoughtful for a long time, considering it—for, after all, it is not customary for the lilies of gardens to blossom under water.

Sometime after that a young man arrived at the court, who played the guitar and whose profession, like that of the birds, was singing songs. He knew such beautiful ones that a fay had doubtless taught them to him, but his voice alone was sufficient to delight the soul, so sweet and pleasant was it. Everyone—even the princess, who did not care for virelays or ballads, and men-at-arms accustomed to delight in the hoarse cry of clarions—had to agree that there was an infinite pleasure to be found in listening to the musician; when he made a tour of the company after having narrated amorous legends, many gold coins fell into his bowl. Only the king's daughter gave him nothing, remaining mute, her eyes half-closed, lost in a dream.

She had become quite different, because of the songs, and it was her heart of which she would have liked to make a gift. She no longer amused herself in watching the quiver of dragonfly wings or taking sparrows from nests. She understood why so many princes at her father's court gazed at her uttering deep sighs, and what the pretty drummer-boys said as they passed under her window.

Like the damsels whose adventures the guitar-player celebrated, she would have liked to follow through forests and over mountains some gallant knight who had carried her away on the rump of his horse until night fell softly—to such an extent that she shivered, frightened and charmed, wanting to say no but nodding yes, once when the singer, passing close to her, dared to whisper in her ear that he would wait for her, at nightfall, on the edge of the little lake, under the birch tree.

She came to the rendezvous, trembling. There, under the branches, also musicians, he sang for her all the beautiful poems that the new; he invented some more beautiful still; and she listened, moved, very closely—so closely that she finally felt the song kiss her lips. Then he fell silent. The murmurous silence of the night was their only epithalamium. Their arms entwined, their mouths united, in the soft grass where she had once laid down her doll, they embraced delectably, the shadows putting curtains around their conjugal bed and the moon, like a discreet lamp, veiling herself with a cloud.

But suddenly—it was the pale hour when the last stars were going out—the king's daughter uttered a cry. What was it? Had she been frightened by the sound of approaching footsteps, or because of someone watching through the branches?

No, but, inclining her head, she had seen, and could still see, something very extraordinary. In the depths of the lake, there was a rose redder than coral and rubies. And she remained thoughtful for a long time, considering it, because, after all, it is not customary for the roses of gardens to blossom under water.

The king experienced a great wrath when his daughter declared to him, that she intended to marry the guitar player, all the more so as, a long time ago, he had resolved to give her in marriage to the nephew of the Emperor of Trebizond. He agitated his scepter in a very formidable manner. He declared that he would never accept for a son-in-law a reciter of non-sense, a minstrel good for playing for dancers at village weddings.

All of that only made her go pale. The princess begged, wept, cried, and it was necessary to resolve to content her, to the great scandal of the courters and princes, when she had confessed the mystery of the nuptial grass by night on the edge of the lake.

But a new surprise was reserved for the monarch. Far from showing the slightest joy at the news of the glorious marriage that as offered to him, the singer of ballads protested that he did not want to be married, giving for a unique reason that certain birds were unable to sing in cages. And he took advantage of the amazement into which all the witnesses were lunged by that response to run away with a burst of laughter before anyone thought to chastise him for his insolence.

Alas, what sadness for the king's daughter! She was not angry, having too much chagrin. Thus, it was all over; she would no longer know the sweetness of music, and of kisses after the music, and such a long bitterness followed such brief joys. People tried in vain to console her; she fled and remained shut away in her apartment, looking out of the window at the road by which the ingrate had fled, unable to believe that he would not come back, on the lookout in the silence or the noises of the road for the song that might return; or she stationed herself alone for long hours on the edge of the small lake, contemplating the dear trampled grass, which had not yet sprung up again, with eyes moistened by tears.

Once, as she lowered her head, heavy with sad thoughts, she uttered a scream. What was it? Had a new dolor bitter that heart already lacerated?

No, still a single dolor; but she had seen, and could still see, something extraordinary. In the depths of the lake there was a marigold, a pale, faded marigold, like a discolored ray of sunlight. And she remained pensive for a long time, considering it; for, after all, it is not customary for the marigolds of gardens to blossom under water.

But then the trunk of the tree split, and a little dryad emerged, or a little fay, who said to the king's daughter: "They are not veritable flowers that one sees in the depths of that water. Know, my dainty princess, once pure as the lilies, who bloomed recently like a red rose, and are more melancholy now than pale marigolds, that you have come to the edge of the lake that reflects souls."

The Sorrow of the Sirens[32]

One day, when I was going along the sea shore, I heard the sirens lamenting in the blue solitude, in the melancholy moonlight.

"Alas! Alas!" they said, "The times are no more when the handsome young men of the land, lulled by our appeals, bewildered by our whiteness, glimpsed beneath the diaphanous mystery of the water, followed us into the depths and died of our kisses on floating beds of seaweed. It is in vain that, risking ourselves near the shores, we sing in the dusk, enlacing our raised arms; no one listens or stops, and our disdained sighs mingle until dawn with the vague plaint of the waves."

As I listened attentively, I distinguished among the voices one voice more sorrowful, which said:

"Every evening, out there, between the two rocks, a window is illuminated, and I see, through the shadow and the curtains, a form with head inclined over a book. I recover hope, I glide through the waves, I approach the light, hoisting myself over the sand, tearing my pale flanks and my breasts on the shingle.

"'Hear me, solitary worker, who is consuming the nocturnal hour of kisses in sterile efforts! There is no human reality that is worth as much as the chimera of my amour! Quit deceptive books! Scorn vain science! It is in my glaucous eyes that you will read the sweetest of secrets; my mouth will reveal to you the mystery of joy. Oh, come! I will teach you the languor in which bitter thought becomes somnolent; the cradle of my arms is one of waves of delectable forgetfulness.'

---

[32] This story, initially reprinted in *Rose et noir* (1885), was reprinted again, with very slight modifications, as "La Plainte des belles-de-l'eau" [The Lament of the Water-Beauties] in the collection *Les Petite fays dans l'air* (1891).

136

"But the one I summon remains motionless, with his elbows on his table; disdainful, he pays no more heed to my supplicant tenderness than the moans of the squall or the beating of the wings of a dazzled seagull against his window."

The voice fell silent. Another rose up, even sadder, saying:

"One night in summer, I saw in the bow of a ship a man leaning over the side, watching the tremor of the sky in the sea. As he was very young, with a softness in his gaze, I thought that his heart would not be cruel, and, floating on my back, with my arms behind my neck, displaying the enchantments of my luminous torso, I spoke to him amid the smooth sounds of the foam and the water.

"'Are you contemplating me, you who are dreaming? Am I not more beautiful than your dreams? Is there a star in the azure that you prefer to the double roseate star illuminated in the whiteness of my breasts, and what sky reflected in the sea is worth the infinite space of my green eyes? In the distant lands to which your ship is carrying you, there is no fruit more flavorsome than my kissed lips; no siesta is as sweet, in the sunlit forests, amid the arm perfumes and chirping nests, than slumbering beneath my hair, to the sound of my giggles and whispers. Oh, come, you who are exiling yourself, into an exile more charming than any fatherland, in the unknown world of ineffable delights!'

"But the one I was summoning did not interrupt his reverie; he continued leaning over the bow of the ship, with the immensity before him and bales of merchandise behind him, stacked on the deck. And then I realized that he was not watching the sky trembling in the sea, but counting, by the light of the stars, gold coins clinking in an open bag."

Another voice made itself heard in the desolate silence of the moonlight.

"Full of the sound of a host and resounding with the clash of weapons, a ship greater than any other ship was traversing the tumultuous sea; the light of dawn, amid the clinking of bronze, was scattered over the helmets and the sabers in a thousand flashes of steel; and we, like a flock of seagulls, beating the air with our arms, to which the foam lent wings, enveloped the moving ship with our enlaced games and our laughter, which rang joyously in the din of the waves.

"Oh, the madmen! Where were they going? Toward a battle? Toward hideous death? 'What! For the vain chimeras that men call honor, glory and the fatherland, so many young hearts will cease to beat, and so many mouths will know no other kiss than that of pale death? Is there no couch more pleasant than fields of carnage, soaked in mud and blood?

"'But you don't believe us young men! Far from wars, fatigues, and sterile triumphs, you could come with us, so blonde and so tender; you could prefer to rude hand-to-hand combats the caresses of our unarmed nudities. Oh, come! We are beauty, amour and joy. O killers, we are life. Is not the blood of our mouths more beautiful than the blood of wounds? If you require combats, accept those in which victory is certain—certain and so delectable. Triumph over us, warriors! There is no booty worth as much as our bare breasts and our open arms, and after our fortunate defeats, it is in kisses that we, as prisoners, will pay our ransom!'

"But the armed men considered us without tenderness, rejecting us with a scornful gesture. As I clung on to the side of the ship, I felt the cold bite of a steel blade in my arm raised for an embrace, and I fell back into the waves, whose foam was red."

Having heard these things, I said to the sad sirens:

"Don't hope for me to feel compassion for you, dangerous temptresses. Men, having become serious, assiduously occupied with their duties or their business affairs, turn away from you with reason; they are not unaware that you have what is required to trouble the most resolute souls, to disrupt the most useful plans; neither the scholar, nor the merchant, nor the soldier, no one, if he listened to you, would follow his path. We also know, and know above all, how brief the intoxication is that you promise us. O cruel liars, death is the aftermath of your kisses."

The sirens replied:

"It is true that we are redoubtable. It is our dearest game to wear away with our caresses the virile pride of energies. It is true that we are perfidious. Our lovers die in our first embrace. But what mad and despicable race are you, then, new men, who prefer the imbecile vanity of human tasks, and judge that a kiss is not worth dying for?"

The Last Sylph

In the bed of my most dear, one evening when I was not sleeping there—oh, what an indistinct indication of time, for sleeping in that adorable bed was what never happened to me!—my mind was carried away (she had closed her eyes, the darling being a trifle weary) to the forest of Broceliande and the vague isles of Avalon.

Thinking about the lands that the fays inhabit, the little fays themselves who dance rounds on the grass at the forest's edge, pallid in the moonlight or rosy in the dawn, is a customary reverie for me. I am one of the last men who worries about Oriane, Viviane and the merciful Abonde. My pillow is not unaware of how much I love to recount, in nights of insomnia, beautiful stories in which the Good Ladies come to the aid of princesses captive in cruel keeps, where knights are the prisoners of living lianas beneath bewitching flowers, and if they escape therefrom, I feel sorry for them.

That evening, I was thinking of you, Holda, Urganda, Urgèle, and Mélusine, with a very particular emotion, even more tender than usual; perhaps it was because my most dear, before being weary and in order to merit being, had cradled me better than ever in enchantments, and maddened me better than ever with magical perfumes. With my eyelids half-closed, I saw you amid the chimerical décor that the perforated rapprochement of eyelashes creates in the penumbra, as beautiful as you were, as you are, allowing your robes to trail over the flowers. I even distinguished the shimmer around your slow dance like that of a scarf borne away by a thousand little sylphs who were beating the moonlight with light thrusts of transparent wings; one might have thought it pink air within the blue air.

Then, having turned away from the dream for a moment, I had a bitter sadness.

Certainly, I knew that the exquisite fays had not ceased to exist, in spite of the railways that traverses the wood near Athens; sometimes I encountered them, sometimes here and sometimes there, sometimes clad in diamonds and dawn, sometimes dressed in rags the quickly transform into regal costumes dazzling with gold and precious stones. If I were not the most discreet of lovers I could say that two or three times it has been given to me to linger in the depths of the mystery of grottoes in the company of Morgane, who has slightly red hair because she often has the whim of tinting it with the dew of red roses, or with Alcine, who has green eyes because she is the cousin of a siren. But I confess that I had never encountered sylphs—in real life, at least! No, never, in any place, in any circumstances; neither in wooded pathways starred by glow-worms, nor in the fêtes to which the confidence of gnomes and goblins invited me.

I was saddened. I said: "What, do the sylphs no longer exist, in fact? Do they no longer sleep in the roses, their dearest alcoves? Has the night ceased to be populated with their furtive quivers, scarcely alighting on foliage or tresses, like presentiments of vague kisses? Who, then, if they have disappeared, knocks at midnight with the tips of feathers on the windows of enamored little girls?"

And I was saddened more and more when an exceedingly faint and soft voice, so faint and so soft that I mistook it at first for the mysterious song of the breath asleep on your lips, my dearest, replied to me in the dying light of the alcove:

"Oh, you can, indeed, weep for us, poet full of compassion for defunct graces; for now we exist so slightly that it might well be said that we will soon no longer exist at all. More numerous once than the fecundating perfumes transmitted by the wind from one palm tree to another, and one peach tree to another; once present in a tumult of diaphanous butterflies at fêtes that were celebrated in paths and clearings for the hymen of eglantines, sylphs have disappeared without return, tumbled, terrified and broken by violet machines that traverse the silence and mists of the woods with whistles and fumes.

Science, the killer of dreams, has killed the sylphs, who were also dreams, and of all my brothers, I am the only one who survives, so close to dying and so desirous of death."

I heard, but I did not see. "O last of the sylphs," I said, "Are you so close to vanishment that you already have the invisibility of immaterial beings?"

"I can still be discerned," he replied.

Indeed, on widening my eyes, I did not take long to distinguish him, fluttering and trumpeting over the slumber of my dearest: a mosquito! Yes, a mosquito! That is what had become, after how many traverses, of the survivor of all the sylphs. From the wings that he had once had to those which he had, what a decadence! My first thought was to seize him and crush him between two fingernails, for was the cruel individual not about to bite the pale pink flesh of a breast that, her chemise having slipped and her arms being parted, my sleeping darling was innocently offering to the imminent awakening of my desire?

He foresaw the attempt. "Oh, mercy! Since my last hour is so close, since, fallen from ancient glories and pretty flights over early-blooming roses, I desire a kinder death than that of an obscure insect with gray wings; let me at least," he said, "die the death that I have chosen, and permit me to choose my tomb!"

What did he mean by that? I observed him, astonished and moved, but almost anxious. He was still fluttering, with scarcely a susurrus over the dear body of the somnolent young woman; the threatened her eyes, he approached her lips, he almost alighted on one of the flowery tips of the moving breasts. If he had settled there, I would have killed him pitilessly, in my furious jealousy; but he remained in the air, still uncertain; and I watched him.

Suddenly, as if in the decision of a definitive choice, he precipitated himself under my friend's shoulder, toward the mysterious tuft of the red curls of the armpit. Perhaps bitten, but without waking up, my most dear extended her arm along her upper body, and the little creature was trapped in the re-closed odorous prison.

Certainly, I had a surge of anger, but a pity came to me, and I did not have the courage to conserve any rancor against the last of the sylphs, nostalgic for calices, who had wanted to die—his gauzy cadaver was discovered the next day—in the most perfumed of blonde roses.

The Grateful Hamadryad

In the very ancient times when I was a shepherd of lambs and goats for a miserly farmer by profession, and a flute-player for my pleasure, and I wandered along the banks of the Eurotas, scratched by oleanders, I loved with a grand amour a virgin with a face as flowery as a clump of blushing eglantines, hair more golden than the wheat heaped up in sheaves in the reapers' cart, and a bloody mouth, a scarlet alveolus where my kiss would have made such sweet honey. But how disinclined Naïs was to grant me her lips!

It was not that she was naturally rebellious to caresses, as the nymphs of Artemis are said to be. More than once she put up little resistance to the covetousness of pastors in the selvage that was the pasturage of her goats, and she sometimes returned undisturbed from the depths of woods into which she had been taken by the hairy violation of fauns or sylvans, although they have the wherewithal to reduce even the most blossomed young women to alarm and tears by the enormity of their amour. It was toward me alone that she showed herself cruel, and with what atrocious barbarity!

In vain, in order to soften her, I offered her the first milk of my youngest ewe in a cup rubbed with odorous herbs. In vain, I went to collect, on the slopes where the descent is perilous, the rare flowers of which bouquets are made that are pretty between the gold of tresses. In vain I brought her, in their nests of leaves and moss, little turtle-doves that, as yet devoid of feathers, already gave a good example of cooing. None of my offerings succeeded in counseling her to any gratitude. She accepted the presents, and ordered me to give her others, but never recompensed the obstinacy of my zeal with a kiss or a smile. And I lamented incessantly because of the refusal of Naïs, mingling my tears with those droplets fallen

144

from the stars, perhaps also rendered dolorous by a disdained amour.

Once, I had composed a poem in which I praised the charms of the person who was causing me to die; I decided to inscribe it in the bark of a birch tree, hoping that she would read it that evening or the next day, and I began to engrave the tree with a metal point.

How it began to groan, alas, at the first wound! A woman whose heart was being torn by the beak of a vulture or bitten by the teeth of a wolf would not have uttered more heart-rending sobs, and one day after the death of Adonis, the unkempt widows of the young man with the handsome profile did not utter such desperate clamors. It was suffering, the poor tree! I was doing it harm; it was me who was hurting it!

But, in order that Naïs could read them—Naïs, the easy prey of shepherds and satyrs, malicious to me alone—in order that she might know with what humble meekness I implored her inexorable scorn, I continued to engrave my verses in the living and weeping bark.

It seemed to me that I was torturing a plaintive young creature, that I was the executioner of an amorous and soft flesh; it seemed to me that I was killing a soul. It did not matter; I did not have the leisure to experience long remorse, so long as I belonged to my desire for the young shepherdess, and I finished engraving the poem in the bark, amid the increasingly bitter moans and gasping reproaches of the frail, agonizing tree.

When I had finished, I saw Naïs nearby.

"Oh, at least," I said—the birch was still moaning—"will you read these verses?"

But without even glancing at the bark, she said to me: "Listen. I'm finally bored of being dressed in coarse fabrics and living in a sordid hut roofed with dried plants and earth. Tonight, you must murder the farmer whose service you're in. He keeps numerous gold and silver coins in the straw and ferns of his bed. You must carry away those treasures after killing the man, and we'll meet under the stars at the bend in the road that leads to the cities where beautiful hetairae triumph.

"But will you love me after the man is murdered and robbed?" I asked.

She burst out laughing. When she laughed, her teeth were more visible. I understood that it would be impossible for me to disobey her.

"So be it," I said.

When night fell I slipped into the bedroom of the sleeping farmer, and I fled, my hands bloody, laden with coins. We met, Naïs and I, at the corner of the road. She was lying down, a little weary, and slept well. She did not permit me to approach her. She had demanded that I put between us, as a chaste barrier, the heap of silver and gold red with murder.

Rich, thanks to my crime, she was seen at the Ceramicus in a chariot harnessed to Thessalian horses. She wore tunics that the crimson of Tyrian mollusks had bloodied—a frightful resemblance to the wounds under my fingers. Flute-players who ran before her celebrated her recent glory, and young men were smitten with her flowery cheeks, her golden hair and her scarlet mouth. Old men could not remember having seen such a beautiful courtesan. Oh, how she triumphed, because I had murdered the poor man in his house!

But she did not testify any gratitude to me for the crime committed for love of her. She never permitted me to kiss the pink nail of her little finger, the nail similar to the petal of a very small rose. While she opened her door to the fortunate lovers who threw supplicatory garlands on her threshold or hung them on her wall, I wept, my fists in my teeth, outside the dwelling closed to me alone.

One day, she said to me: "Leave me alone, murderer!" But I did not revolt, so soft were her eyes. I thought that she had good reason to be scornful of a cowardly assassin. She might have loved me if I had conquered some sublime glory in her honor.

The archons had just instituted a competition in which the genius of the greatest poets of Hellas wound contend. The one who prevailed over such rivals would be famous throughout the world; the crown on his forehead would make the diadem of light resplendent on the head if the god who bore the lyre jealous.

I sang, in strophes that Corinna of Tanagra had once invented, about the beautiful face and the cruel heart—cruel to me alone—of Naïs, and I triumphed easily, so accustomed had I become, on the banks of the Eurotas, to composing noble verses, and so inspiring was the love that I had for the young woman who refused me her mouth. But when, followed by people who were celebrating my name, with laurels on my head and laurels under my feet, I approached the house in which my Naïs lived, I found the door closed. The next day I knew that the slut had kept in her ingrate arms until daybreak—because he had solicited her at a street corner with an impudent gaze—the most unworthy of the rivals that my genius had vanquished.

I was sad, not angry. She did not attribute any value, that was all, to the renown that one merits in poetic games.

It happened that a war broke out between two republics. By means of my ardent speeches and promises of victory, I contrived to be put at the head of a troop of combatants, and I deployed so much bravery that the enemy, defeated and dispersed, not stopping, carried to the most distant lands the illustrious fear of my sword. But when I returned to the saved city, I learned that Naïs, made famous by my triumph in poetic combats, to whom I now brought bellicose palms, had departed immediately after my victory to join, in the retreat, the most cowardly of those that my courage had put to flight.

Then, without the hope of ever being loved by her and without even dreaming of seeing her again, I returned to the banks of the Eurotas, where I had once been a shepherd of goats and lambs in the employment of a miserly farmer, and a flute-player for my pleasure.

I suffered strangely because of the vain memory of Naïs. For her, I had killed; for her I had vanquished the most illustrious singers; for her I had put to flight the most formidable enemies; not once had she delighted to permit my mouth to inhale the breath that rose from her dear breast. Oh, the cruel, barbaric woman! In exchange for all the good that I had wanted to do her, all the good that I had done her, how much pain she had given me! Unable to forget, I wandered, full of melancholy, along the banks of the little river, scratched by oleanders.

One evening, passing not far from a sickly tree—a birch, it seemed to me—that was swaying in the wind, I heard a very soft voice...

Yes, a voice, emerging from between the leaves, caressed me with tender words, while tresses unfurled from the branches caressed me with a tender enlacement; it was as if something very good enveloped me completely and loved me.

"Oh!" I said, marveling. "What's happening?"

The voice beneath the tresses murmured:

"I am the Hamadryad of the tree in which you engraved your poem, of the tree that you tortured. You tore me with a metal point, you reduced me to tears and plaints, and then you fled with the woman who did not love you, and you gave to her without recompense all honors and all glories. Wounded and suffering and weeping, I have retained your memory. Oh, I know that you never belonged to the fortunate, to the ingrate, but with my voice and hair I will console you, and I will love you forever, since you have done me harm."

On the Banks of Lethe

That day, the good Consolatrix, the dear Muse with the tender eyes, who always loves me and always advises me like a guardian angel, looked at me for a long time, moved by my tears, and made me a sign to follow her.

For many hours, many hours, far from cities, far from plains, far from mountains and everything that is the mortal earth, we walked through pale mists, under a cloudy sky in which the increasingly aerial fluidity of vague, scattered, disappearing forms seems to the weary traveler to be the tatters of his soul flying away.

Finally, we reached the tremulous bank of a river—a shore in the clouds!—and the calm and bleak water, pale, scarcely visible, that fled silently under slender, melancholy, dangling plants was like a phantom of a river between the ghosts of reeds.

The Consolatrix said to me: "You see the divine Lethe. Since the reminiscence of lost amours is devouring your heart pitilessly, and you cannot even laugh any longer like other men or sing like other poets, because of the implacable Past, drink until intoxication the water of the bleak and calm river, and be liberated from memory."

The she drew away, mist through the mist, after having given me a diaphanous cup of snow, so light and so pale that it was reminiscent of the calyx of a lily whose flesh is made of moonlight. Like Tantalus finally about to calm his devouring thirst, I leaned toward the river.

But no, I did not fill the cup, and the chalice of snow at the end of my enfeebled arm, which was hanging down, did not even brush the water between the vague reeds.

It was in a little house in an outlying district, up which clematis climbed, that Denise lived. I was sixteen years old,

149

not even that, fifteen. What astonished me was that so many people, market gardeners going to market in the town, poor early-rising clerks hastening because of their cantankerous supervisors, peasants walking with their pick-axes on their shoulders to the nearby field, or carters climbing the hill, shouting "Giddy up!" amid a fusillade of whip-cracks, could go past that house, indifferently, without seeming to suspect that the most adorable of young women was asleep there, behind the closed gray shutters.

For myself, I knew full well that Denise was there, so delectably exquisite, and that she was sleeping in her narrow little bed, dreaming about the quarrel that her two favorite birds had had the day before, in their cage, prior to hiding their heads under their wings. And I also knew what it was necessary to do to wake the idler up. Going along the wall, as if distracted, my hands in my pockets, and passing under the closed shutters, I sang a song that she had taught me, the old song of our young amours. Then, very quickly, I hid in the alleyway alongside the house.

I did not have to wait for long. Very gently, in order not to wake her father and her mother, she opened the door, and put out her pretty pink face, laughing prettily, her gray eyes, under her flyaway hair, sunlit and marvelous in the bright abruptness of the day. And we went along the paths beside the gardens behind the houses, toward the wood moist with dew.

Do you remember too, old elms, so many little flowers picked beneath your jovial shade, which stirred and parted here and there with smiles of light? We marched further on in the green profundity of branches, through long grass, and abruptly, semi-wild cats, hunters of little rabbits, bounded through a scattering of campanulas, fresh broken pearls. Hand in hand, she sometimes leaned her head on my shoulder, and we said tender things to one another, with sighs already and laughter again, while the birds in the trees awoke, babbling like us, and loving one another like us.

Like us? No. Our hearts were so ingenuous that when she asked me, astonished, why that finch over there was fluttering like that, with its feather ruffled, on top of its female, beating the dust with its wings, I didn't know what to reply. Oh, the sweet, the dear hours!

But one morning I sang the old song in vain outside the gray shutter, sadly closed, and three days later, Denise finally came out of the house on the outskirts of town, under a white sheet, in a coffin followed her father and her mother, and peasants with bowed heads, and me too, a little further behind, in tears.

My heart constricted by that funereal memory, I plunged the cup into the river, but I did not draw it out, and the calm and bleak water made a little splashing eddy around the chalice the color of snow and moonlight...

Beautiful, no, but very blonde and very white and very plump, all refrains on her lips and all follies in her eyes; a thirty-nine franc dress without a corset underneath, inflated by healthy plenitudes of flesh; a diabolical vivacity, which, lit up by champagne at three francs a bottle bought at the grocery on the corner and crayfish at ten centimes apiece taken away in paper from the food shop, hat and cape thrown on the bed, and the sole supper candle extinguished with the toe of an ankle-boot; Rose-Rosa-Rosette astonished, dazzled and enchanted my student youth. Not a sou the next day? Bah! We'll eat this evening; and late mornings have nothing unpleasant about them when the mistress isn't thin.

I almost came to love her, and when she was taken away by some infamous traveling salesman come from Belgium to repopulate the public harems of Brussels or Antwerp, I remained very morose in the little room in the Rue de Fleurus, where she had laughed her laugh and sung her song.

I withdrew the cup, full. But I did not put it to my mouth; and I gazed with staring eyes at the dying water asleep in the wan lunar light...

You were perfect, O Lucienne! Tall, slim, so tenderly grave in your long dress, the train of which—when you got down, rarely, from your coupé—gave the impression of being scornful of the pavement of the road, you appeared, your mouth always open, eyes half-veiled under the reserve of lashes that lowered like Aristocracy personified, almost a goddess, scarcely a woman. All the charms that are neither consents not promises, with all the perfumes that are not odors, emanated from you, haughtily.

In the evening, you had a fashion of leaning on your elbows on the velvet of your box at the Opéra that disdained all men, singers or spectators, only paying heed to vague and pure tenderness of the music; and when you were kneeling in church, in the morning, there was something in your simultaneously humble and proud attitude that made God notice that you were there, and ordered him to grant your prayer. Alas, you, so elevated, so distant, I, a poor man, loved.

When you went out at midday I followed you, unknown, running in order to see you cross the sidewalk outside some humbler home to which had gone in order to give a consolation of gold with your gloved hand. I dreamed of being old and wretched, lying on a meager bed and dying, for perhaps you would come into my mansard, and with what ineffable delight I would have kissed the dear coins of my alms, but not too close to your fingers!

In the Bois, that man who threw himself between carriages in order to get closer to yours, at the risk of being crushed; the man who mingled with the braided crowd of domestics under the coaching entrances of town houses in order to watch you descending the carpeted steps in the lights, between rare plants—that was me! And I didn't lament being so far away from you.

I knew that you were, simultaneously, the greatest, the most beautiful and the purest; that, even if I were admitted into your society, into your intimacy, I would not have been able to conceive any hope; that the severity of your smile extinguishes desires in all hearts and stops pleas on all lips. I accepted the melancholy of being, for you, someone who does not exist. You were the divinity, I the devotee. Does God know all his faithful? The happiness of adoring you consoled me for the sadness of not being able to tell you so.

And that happiness lasted for three years, until the day when I learned that your husband had applied for a legal separation because, one evening, as he returned from hunting, he had found you in the arms of his palfreyman in the loft above the stables.

Resolute this time, I lifted the cup to me lips; but I did not drink a drop of the bleak and calm liquid it contained, which fell back, like tears, into the river, between the reeds...

Then the one who had guided me to Lethe came, and cried: "What! You didn't want to forget, you who are suffering?"

"Cruel consolatrix," I replied, "there is no fatal or abject amour the memory of which is as frightful as the despair of not having loved! And if you know a river whose blessed and accursed water revives and exasperates memory, guide me to its banks, in order that I can intoxicate myself with anguish and delights!"

Larceny in the Woods

When she was quite certain, beneath the quivering undersides of the leaves, that Clitandre, Parisian poet, was no longer in a state henceforth to offer the opportunity of a resistance or a fall, Comtesse Clymene said:

"Alas, it is no longer a time to want to conceal it. The interruption of our walk has had nothing that could leave me a painful memory. It is very evident, virtuous as you know me to be, that in accepting to go into the wood of Meudon on your arm, to watch the play of the sunlight through the tangle of the branches, I had no other thought that, in fact, to see between the tangle of the branches the play of the sunlight. I would have considered as a very impertinent prophet anyone who had told me that, after the twelfth tree, a little before the clearing, you would put a kiss on my mouth to which I would acquiesce with so little timidity.

"No, I scarcely expected to pick today, amid the gilded mosses and the already-reddening heather, the flower of an amiable remorse. But since the harm is done, since you have triumphed, with the aid of the sun, over my intimate snows, and that you have strangely scandalized, as well as mine, the modesty of these solitudes, I do not see any inconvenience in recognizing that the fault into which I let myself fall, under the pressure of our desire, did not fail to offer me some pleasure, which my treacherous sighs revealed, alas, and I only hold it against you in moderation, even though you have rendered yourself, three times, worthy of all rancor.

"I will go further; I confess that you are not solely culpable; I was undoubtedly wrong, on this summer morning, yes, I was, to be much prettier than usual; it must be very difficult for lips not to covet my lips, and I accord that I myself, on seeing them in a mirror, would have kissed them. However, it is necessary to be reasonable, as they say. Supposing that you are still capable of further outrages—which must be rather dubious—the time has come not to commit any more, and to return to the inn, where they ought to have finished preparing our lunch.

"Come on, Monsieur, don't pretend to sulk, I beg you; return the skirt and bodice that you removed from me with such perverse intentions, which are, I think, hanging on some branch. You don't hope, perhaps, that I will return to the civilized world in a costume whose insufficiency would have the wherewithal to surprise the persons least inclined to austerity?"

"As you please, Clymene," he said—for two things were impossible for that poet lover: to tolerate a bad rhyme and to disobey his friend.

But what a strange adventure! The bodice and the skirt, previously suspended from a branch, were no longer there; not even the shadow of the vanished items remained.

"Oh!" said Clitandre. "Who has stolen them?"

The wrinkled face of a sniggering human beast, a faun, emerged from the tall ferns.

"The thief," he said, "is me."

The apparition of a sylvan demigod had nothing that could surprise Clymene or Clitandre; a sufficiently long familiarity with Parisian boscages had permitted them both to know that it is sufficient to make love there for them to be populated with divinities like the woods of Attica, and when two lovers mirror themselves by bending over the river where the washerwomen of Sévres beat the linen, it is immediately the Cephise.

"Faun," said the lover, "we won't waste time reproaching you for the larceny from which your leisure has drawn amusement, but remember that there are rural policemen! It is not permitted to young women to walk in chemises on the roads. Return the skirt and the bodice, since honesty invites you to do so, and they are of no use to you."

"Oh, I no longer have them," said the faun. "A dryad with whom I was playing in the thicket beyond the twelfth tree beyond the clearing, while you were embracing, demanded that, having stolen them, I make her a gift of them. She's the only one who can return them to you now."

"But I won't return them!" said the nymph, in her turn.

It was an amusing thing to see her half-dressed, the girdles poorly joined and the clasps poorly hooked, in a worldly costume; she evoked the idea, although she was a goddess and as pretty as the Amaryllis of eclogues, of a monkey that has dressed in haste in a Parisienne's wardrobe.

"No, I won't return them," she said, "unless..."

She looked at Comtesse Clymene's friend.

"Unless what?" asked Clymene.

"Unless the young mortal with whom you're smitten consents to prove to me, in private, far away from everyone, in the amorous profundity of the wood, their perfect inutility. For goddesses sometimes desire human amours."

"Comtesse," exclaimed Clitandre, "it's urgent for you to be dressed again. I'll devote myself, if necessary!"

But Clymene, her teeth malicious behind her curled lip, not without admiration for the resolute lover full of resources, said: "I shall return to the abode of men without a dress. You don't think that I'm going to permit you to undress this hamadryad, who appears to me to be a very profligate nymph?"

Having said that, she went back to the road, in her chemise.

He followed her, not without anxiety; and they encountered a rural policeman, who arrested them formally. They were taken to a commissaire, who interrogated them severely, and they were kept at the police station all day, because no one wanted to believe, plausible as it was, that the skirt and the bodice had been stolen by a faun and a dryad in the wood of Meudon.

The Sprite of the Swirling Water

To Jocelyne, a little woodcutter's daughter who went barefoot, Grandmother had made a present of a cake.

"You can eat as much as you like," the old woman had said, "and there will always be some left, but dread giving it away or allowing it to be taken."

The cake was made with a flour called wealth and a honey called good fortune; as for the powdered sugar with which it was sprinkled, that was all the small contentments of life. You can imagine how she was looking forward to biting into that cake! It sufficed to sink one's teeth into it to be dressed in a golden robe, with coins of all lands clinking in the pockets, to be the most beautiful and the most powerful woman in the world; merely by licking it with the tip of one's tongue, you had horses, carriages, a castle on a hill, good meals, soft beds, musicians who sang to send you to sleep or to wake you up and pages dressed in satin and lace who carried the train of your golden robe.

As soon as she had the cake, Jocelyne, who was very greedy by nature, opened her mouth wide in order to eat it in one go. In that fashion, she would have all the joys at once. But she did not swallow it, because of a pool of clear water near the path beside her, swirling around and around, gilded by the sunlight; one might have though, the sun's rays breaking up there into a thousand prompt crumbs, that it was a small whirlpool of precious stones.

Then, without biting the cake she had in her hand, Jocelyne said: "Oh, pretty water, pretty water, how pleasant it is to see you swirl! There isn't, I think, any prettier water on earth, nor any that swirls so rapidly."

"What would you say, then," cried a water-sprite, sticking his little head, like a pink lotus not yet in bloom, between the reeds, "if you saw what there is beneath my pretty swirling water? Come, little woodcutter's daughter who goes barefoot, let yourself fall in the luminous vertigo, and you'll enter the land of unparalleled beauty and infinite delight."

"I have Grandmother's cake," said Jocelyne.

"You'll only eat terrestrial pleasures there, but it's all the superhuman enchantments that await you in the mysterious abode that is the reflection of the sky."

"I'd have golden robes."

"You'll dress yourself in a costume of azure and aurora."

"I'd have coins of every currency in my pocket."

"Under this water, to which the sunlight is given to pay for paradise, a money of stars is minted."

"I'd marry a very powerful and very handsome prince."

"The god of the delectable abysms will take you for a wife and sit you beside him on a throne of flowering madrepores and radiant coral."

"I'd have horses..."

"Supple tritons will carry you through the green-tinted spaces."

"Carriages..."

"You'll be cradled, amid the languor of the waves of dream, in a seashell the color of chrysoprase, amethyst and daylight!"

"A castle on a hill..."

"What a joy to inhabit a palace that has mystery for a threshold, the ideal for banqueting halls and the infinite for a window!"

"I'd eat good meals..."

"You'll know the dishes that the angels cook.

"I'd lie down in a soft bed..."

"There no couch lovelier than the mattress of clouds woven by the seraphim."

"Musicians would play for me..."

"In addition to the fact that there's no better musician that Saint Cecilia, you'll hear the little cherubim—for a poet has said so—playing the ecstaseon."

"And will pages carry the train of my golden robe?"

"And stars, with their fingers of radiance will carry the train of your comet-skirt!"

But Jocelyne did not allow herself to be deceived by the malicious tempter, and, being able to limit herself to the present that Grandmother had made her, she was about to swallow the nourishing and flavorsome cake when the sprite of the swirling water said:

"Good, good! Do as you please! But be careful that you don't choke."

It's true, Jocelyne thought, *that it's not light, terrestrial happiness*.

"In your place, do you know what I'd do?"

"Go on, what would you do?"

"Since you don't want to descend into the luminous whirlpool—how wrong you are, alas, how wrong you are!—at least dip that indigestible cake in it. Moist, it will go down more easily, and it will also take from the mysterious water a chimerical taste that will make it more agreeable."

"That," said Jocelyne, "is advice that one can follow, since there's nothing perilous in it. When someone speaks reasonably, I gladly accord with the advice I'm given. And I'd like to dip the cake in the pretty swirling water."

She leaned over toward the bright whirlpool, Oh, how bright and radiant it was! She dipped the cake...and she uttered a scream, for the water had swallowed it like a greedy mouth.

Jocelyne wept.

"Alas, that's a very perfidious whirlpool and a very treacherous adviser!"

But the sprite, who was laughing, said: "Well, the harm isn't great. The water isn't as deep as it seems, and it will suffice for you to plunge your hand in to get the cake back. Try!"

"Let's try," she said.

She uttered another scream, more fearful. The whirlpool had torn off her hand; her arm was a stump: plump and pink, but a stump.

"Alas, what an adventure! I've certainly been punished for not having obeyed Grandmother's will."

"Well, the damage isn't without remedy. Plunge your whole arm into the water. You'll recover your hand and the cake it's searching for. Go on, try."

"Let's try," she said.

She screamed desperately. The whirlpool had seized the entire am; she still had the right shoulder, but she no longer had an arm."

"Alas, what will I do in order to hug the prince who will be my husband?"

"It's true that the accident is troublesome, but I can see the cause of it. The cake isn't made for the hand or the arm; it's for the mouth that it's destined. That's why you haven't been able to get it back. Plunge your head into the swirling water, and you'll recover your arm, the hand and the cake. Go on, little woodcutter's daughter, try."

"Let's try," she said.

And this time, she did not scream, for scarcely had she put her forehead in the whirlpool of gems that, seized, she entered into it entirely, and the threshing of her vanished feet hastened the swirl of the mysterious water.

However, Grandmother, as old as Cybele and as eternal as Erdu, has not ceased to make, as she has since the first of days, cakes that she gives to barefoot little woodcutters' daughters, and many other little girls. She knows full well that all the Jocelynes, and the others too, will see the whirlpool of precious stones in which a reflection of infinity quivers, and that the malicious sprite will give them strange advice, but she always prepares her terrestrial cakes of riches, good fortune and contentment. And that is the way of the world. No one knows which ones are right, of those who eat the heavy and good cake, such as it is given to them, and those who precipitate themselves into the water that swirls, swirls and swirls— into the water that is perhaps the vertigo toward the heavens.

The Fortunate End of a Dream

It is before dawn on a day that will be beautiful. As I was unable sleep because of a poem that is haunting me—the poem in which a very beautiful person, like the demigoddesses of woods of oleanders, will end up, I know, swooning in the arms of the poet, but as a consequence of what events I don't yet know—I have leapt out of bed...or rather, I thought I leapt out of bed. I have opened the window very wide and, my elbows on the sill, I am gazing, ecstasized by the freshness blowing from the thousand invisible mouths of nature, scarcely yawning, the quiver of tall trees, waves of soft mist and the less bright frisson, the smooth frisson, almost black, of the lawn, and the rosy light of dawn, veiled by the azure of the night, between the blinking of leaves, and, on high, in the sky, the last star, a silver spark, the star that ought to be called the shepherdess's star, for the evening one is male but the morning one is female.

And all of the imminent awakening of life—flowers, gleams, moist branches, with the progress toward human dwellings from the mysterious distance of other lives unknown but certainly delightful and virginal—smells good, smells young, smells new, shines, so slightly, with the blossoming of I know not what, of childhood, of hope, and also of a promise, so similar to the reignited reflection of a memory, that one wonders whether the Archangel, yesterday, before closing his eyelids, might have forgotten to close the gates of the terrestrial paradise.

And suddenly, a blackbird sings.

The blackbird sings well, but has pauses in its song, reticences that resemble irony; it is tender and malign; it is harmonious and dissonant; its song, while it charms, mocks; it is the Heinrich Heine of birds. Doubtless it is suffering.

I listen to the blackbird singing in my garden. I would have preferred the supreme swoon of the plaint of a nocturnal nightingale, but it is necessary to be content with what one has. I listen to the blackbird.

Now, its chirping speaks.

"Go away! Go away! Go away!" it says.

"Eh, blackbird!" I say. "Why would I go away? I'm at home, I think. I certainly have the right to lean on my window sill."

"Go away! Go away!"

"Don't count on my obedience! Why are you telling me to go away, pray?"

"Because She won't dare to come out so long as you're there."

"Come out?"

"Yes."

"She?"

"Yes."

"Who is She?"

"The woman who is in the trunk of the tree in which I'm singing."

"There's a woman in the trunk of your tree?"

"A woman, yes—or, to be more precise, a nymph."

"Don't try to play with my credulity, Blackbird. This is the wood of Saint-Germain, neighbor of a famous restaurant from which mail-coaches depart, and everyone knows, pertinently, that dryads, hamadryads and even wood-nymphs, which are more familiar, disdain forests traversed by bicycles."

"Poet! Don't try to make me believe that you're unaware of your power over mythological beings. As soon as they learned that you were living in this area, the demigoddesses who take pleasure in the murmur of branches migrated to it, delightedly; all the way from Saint-Germain to Marly the trees are haunted by forest nymphs, like the boscages of Attica."

"I'm delighted to hear it; my odelets will be prouder for it henceforth. However, since the dryad in your tree has come because of me, why is she afraid to come out, because of me?"

"Because..."

"Because?"

"Because..."

"Because?"

"...she's naked."

"I should think that she is naked, since she's a goddess—which is to say, infinitely beautiful. But you can tell her that she's quite wrong to be embarrassed on my account. My modesty adapts very well to female immodesty, even when it isn't divine, and I have ideas accustomed to the ideal and the unreal. Let her come out of her tree! Let her come! Let her be resplendent!

"Doubtless, bored with the narrow sheath of bark in which he's hiding, the caprice is amusing her to run barefoot over the lawn, to mingle her chatter with the susurrus of awakening nests and to make her morning toilette with the dew of flowers that open in the form of beautiful vases? I wouldn't be at all offended to see the auroral garden serve as her dressing-table.

"Certainly, I understand her hesitations and I would refrain from dissuading her if the notary who lodges in the next villa, behind that curtain of willows with parted branches like torn chemises, a worthy man, with observant spectacles, or the vaudevillian with the ancestral beard who, with an Agnes of the subsidized theater whose little cat died of old age twenty-five years ago, who is renting the house with the turrets surrounded by four cedars of Lebanon, had already opened their casements; but the notary, the vaudevillian and the immemorial ingénue are still asleep in their opaque futility of being, their serene annihilation—what an opium stupidity is!—and the dryad of your tree, loquacious blackbird, has no reason to fear that, the only one awake is me, for whom her two arms, which she should not hide from him, would be a glorious distich, her breasts and her abdomen a lyrical swelling of an ode, her hips metaphors that would alarm twin snowy hills, and all her whiteness dreamlike!"

I have spoken. The blackbird remains silent.

Then a voice—the voice of a lily that might have a bee in its calyx—ventures: "Do I dare?"

I cried: "Amaryllis! Noppea! Leuconoe! Thetis! Aglaé! Myrtho! Naiss! Eumymone! Dare, Nymph!"

She dares.

It is miraculous, outside the tree, so much beauty. It is light, it is softness, it is perfume, it is enchantment, with little feet that are afraid of the grass; and I have seen, on the lawn, a toenail, which is indeed a toenail or a buttercup; but I am quite sure that that dream of a heel is not the fallen roundness of the petal of a poppy, but a veritable heel, like those of Aphrodite steeped in the blood of the Adonis-rose. And the end of the night becomes the commencement of the day! The light makes the resolution to blossom, to expand in desire; it tints that mouth rose, that hair gold, that flesh white, becoming sunlight because of its beauty!

"You to whom I gave the names of so many names, nymph," I said, "what is your name?"

"Alphesibea," she says.[33]

Alphesibea, going back and forth, kisses the roses on the mouth, twitters in the nests between the parted branches, informs, by the movement of her dancing legs, the sway of the long grass of the rhythm of grace, laughs scornfully at the defeat of a yellow iris that reared up while she ran in a temerity of confrontation with the smiling rose and the unique golden lily! She is resplendent, so luminously nude that I believe that the daylight that illuminates her is coming from her! And it seems to me that that goddess is not sorry to be nude before a poet.

But suddenly: "Ah!"

And she flees.

---

[33] According to Hesiod, the mother of Adonis was named Alphesibea (his father being Phoenix).

For, at the open casement behind the row of willows, the face of the notary has loomed up, with observant spectacles.

Alphesibea has taken refuge behind the cedars of Lebanon that surround the house with turrets.

"Ah!"

She hurls herself away again.

For the old vaudevillian and the centenarian ingénue have just opened the window.

Bewildered, the dryad implores me.

Full of pity, and jealousy too, I say: "Come! Come! Climb up!"

Alphesibea hurtles toward my window, and bumps into the stone. "No, no," I tell her, "the branches..."

She takes hold of the thin sinuous trunks of the ivy and the aristolochia. She hoists herself up. She puts her leg—Gods! Her legs!—over the sill of the window and allows herself to fall into my arms, with uh a pretty: "Oh, how frightened I was!"

But she will still be frightened, because the ingenue, the vaudevillian and the notary, dazzled and famished by so much beauty, have come out of their houses and followed the dryad, and have climbed up behind her, and their heads, hideously lubricious, are about to appear.

"Where can I hide?" she says.

Sagaciously, I propose: "In the bed."

"Yours?"

"Ours!"

"Oh, I consent to that," says the nymph.

And, the windows firmly closed, I embrace her under the sheets, swooning. She is so beautiful, so perfumed, and so white, that I think that she has brought with her, in order to put them in my arms, all the flowers, all the odors and all the dawn...

And I also think that perhaps I have not got up from my bed, and that I am dreaming, and that I am embracing—oh, really awake, this time—all of the delightful ending of my poem.

PART III: EROS AND COMPANY

The Danger of Charity

In order to make young women fall into his traps, the terrible child-demon Amour not only employs any weaknesses they might have, but even the virtues that they have. It is of no use to them, for example, to be decent or faithful, since he is able to draw opportunities for sin from those very merits, with which to compensate forcefully for fidelity and decency. He resembles a magician thief who only sees in a doubly locked door the facility of passing through the keyhole.

That is so true that many pretty young women—what is the point of worrying about those who are not pretty?—renouncing their natural virtues deliberately, of their own accord, can only delay the inevitable defeat momentarily, with no other effect that adding to it the humiliation of a vain preparation for defense.

For those of my female readers who still doubt—how I congratulate their husbands and lovers?—the cleverness of the demon Amour in giving birth to evil via good, I will tell them a story appropriate to convince them. It was told to me in a cameo boudoir, with pictures above the door of nymphs and shepherds, by a cheerful grandmother, dainty and very thin, her wrinkles rejuvenated by make-up, her curls whitened perhaps with powder, who remembered confusedly once having been, on an isle of old, beneath the flight of turtle-doves and amid oleanders, a loquacious and mild ancestor, happy to teach amorous legends to the little girls and young boys of Cythera—with the consequence that she blithely confused the location and the time, not really knowing whether she was

166

speaking Ionian Greek or Parisian French, signing herself, when she was in a devout mood, in the name of Cypris, Eros and the Dove; and if she put her nose to one of the windows of her château, she sometimes mistook for a faun smitten with a dryad the bare-armed woodcutter kissing a farm-girl on the sunlit edge of the wood.

There was in times past a shepherdess who was definitely the prettiest shepherdess imaginable. A grandmother, in the days of Greece, would not have failed to name her Naïs. She added that the story had happened near a sacred wood, on the banks of the Cephine, but I have good reason to believe that the heroine of the tale was named Michelette, and grazed her flock in the meadows browsed by the ewes of Madame Deshoulières.

Michelette, then, was the daintiest creature in the world. Anyone who might have been comparable for freshness with a rose, and for the lightness of her step to a gamboling lamb, would have proved that he had good judgment. And she combined goodness with beauty; her heart was as soft as her face was charming. She was moved to tears merely by seeing old men returning from the forest pass by under their heavy bundles of wood.

"Would you like me to carry half your wood, my worthy man?"

She broke open the money-box into which she put the money of her wages very rapidly, in order to give alms to the poor women of the hamlet. She also took pity on animals, crumbling three quarters of her bread for the birds and let her dog drink all the milk in her pitcher.

Once, she remained sad until dusk—she normally sang all day long—and when people expressed surprise she said: "It's because I trod on a beetle this morning as I went along the path."

But if she had a tender heart for the poor, she was very cruel to the amorous. Although she was already sixteen years old, she never gave rendezvous under the willows, near the laundry, in the wheat or among the vines. To anyone who asked her for a kiss she replied with mocking laughter; she had even rejected the tenderness of a young ox-drover who was the handsomest fellow in the region.

What distanced her most of all from amour was having heard it said that married couples, and lovers too, had the custom of taking off their clothes in order to kiss one another more easily. Take her clothes off! She could not bear that idea. Not that she would have had great difficulty or wasted a great deal of time in taking off her clothes: clogs, a fustian skirt, and a chemise of coarse cloth were her entire costume. But she could not conceive, so ingenuously modest was she, that one could resolve to uncover one's skin, no matter how white and soft it might be; to show it to a man seemed to her a terrible thing, more criminal than any crime: impossible.

One morning, when she was thinking about such things, she swore a great oath never to remove the fabrics that hid her pretty little body, except to slide into bed very rapidly, with the light out. But that oath had for an echo a burst of laughter in the branches.

The person who was laughing like that was Amour, the child-demon. He decided, wickedly, that the little shepherdess would not take long to break her promise, and you shall see how he obtained that end. What, you might think, he seduced Michelette, who had so many virtues? Well, it was one of those virtues of which he made use, in order to triumph over the others.

As she passed through a flowery pathway under a beautiful bright sunlight that gilded the green leaves, she saw poor little birds—eight or ten, perhaps more—drawing themselves along awkwardly, wings devoid of feathers, almost naked, among the pebbles and the brambles, cheeping in a heart-breaking fashion. Doubtless, in a gust of wind, they had fallen from their nests. Michelette, good as she was, felt very moved.

She picked the chicks up, one by one, kissed them, warmed them with her breath, and thought that they were be very comfortable in her two cupped hands. But they were still cheeping, opening their little yellow breaks wide. Doubtless they regretted the flowery bush where they had emerged from the egg and the shade of the foliage over the frail beating of their little wings. Then the shepherdess searched for empty nests, from branch to branch, here, there, and everywhere. She did not find any; the wind had carried them away, or some naughty child had taken them as a game.

What was she to do? There was plenty of moss there, and threads of spidersilk traversing the path, but she did not know how to construct nests, not being a linnet or a warbler, and the dear little things did not cease complaining. She had an idea. Putting the birds down in the grass momentarily, she took off both her clogs—they were so small that one of them would not have been sufficient—garnished them with smooth leaves, put the poor fatherless creatures into them, five in one and four in the other, and the clogs, placed on nearby branches, were two nests in which the chicks, no longer complaining, seemed completely at ease when their mothers returned, fluttering above them with cries of joy.

Michelette went away content, albeit slightly chagrined by her bare feet, at which the half-closed eyes of violets gazed through the grass.

Following her route, she traversed a clearing, where she was astonished to see an old woman she did not know sitting at the foot of a tree. She looked like the wife of a poor wood-cutter or some beggar woman. The woman seemed so old, with her short gray hair, her extinct eyes and her tremulous chin, that she must have been a centenarian at least. At times she shivered from head to toe and said: "Oh, my God! Oh, my God!"

Michelette approached.

"What's the matter, Madame? Are you ill?"

"I'm cold," the old woman replied, her teeth chattering.

"Cold in this beautiful sunlight?"

"Cold because I have a fever. I walked so much yester-day that fatigue has worn me out. The wind, which seems warm to you, chills me through my rags, and I believe that I'll die in this wood"

"Come with me, poor woman. I have a good fire of vine-stocks in my cottage, and you can arm yourself in my bed."

"I don't ask as much. I need to go on my way. Only give me your fustian skirt, in order that I can be covered on the road."

The little shepherdess only hesitated for a moment. She unfastened her skirt and made a present of it to the pauper, and the latter, having got up, went away, no longer shivering under the thick fabric, of which she had made a cloak.

Michelette was glad to have obliged the old woman, but she was very ashamed, because she was in her chemise.

She hid in the deepest part of the wood. She decided to stay there until nightfall and only return to the village at an hour when no one would be abroad on the obscure roads. But how she trembled in the meantime! If anyone came, she would die of fright!

She was thinking about nestling in the hollow of some oak, when she heard a faint, soft plaint, like that of a dying child. Guiding herself by the sound, she took a few steps, parted the heather, and found a little fawn lying there, mouth open, eyes vague, in which a tear shone, and bleeding from three wounds.

Oh, how sad it was to see it thus, pretty and desolate. The first thought she had was to carry it away; she would care for it, and cure it. But, light as it was, she tried in vain to lift it; it was so heavy. If she had only been able to staunch the blood of the wounds! Full of pity, she tried, with moss and leaves; the red tide overcame the obstacles and flowed more abundantly.

Well, she took off her chemise, tore it up, made dressings and bandages, blocked, closed and covered the three scarlet wounds. And certainly, there was some magic in that whole adventure, for the fawn, suddenly healed, got up with a pretty bound and disappeared through the heather.

Now Michelette was naked. Naked! In broad daylight!

She uttered a cry of fright, and began to weep, with all the more reason because the head of the young ox-drover who has the handsomest fellow in the region suddenly appeared out of a hawthorn bush, while the child-demon Amour laughed triumphantly in the branches.

The Pawnbroker

In the Rue Grenéta, on the second floor above the entre-sol, the god Eros has established himself as a pawnbroker. Enveloped in a dressing-gown with a floral pattern that is fraying in the sleeves, with a Greek bonnet like an acorn over his solar hair and a pair of spectacles on his nose, he has the appearance of an old man who might be very young, so bright are his golden eyes—stars that have put on spectacles—and so fresh is his red mouth with snow-white teeth, like a pearly flower; he takes snuff with pink fingers.

All day long he sits in a large green leather armchair in front of a register in which the names of borrowers—all female—are inscribed. For he never lends to men! His clientele are the young and the beautiful: good girls without a care for tomorrow who go put on poorly fastened satin dresses to buy two sous' worth of milk on credit from the fruiters opposite; socialites having too rarely refused to pay the gambling gloss-es of some clubman who pushes delicacy to the point of not wanting to be attached; little seamstresses for whom the coins in the money-box are not sufficient to buy hats in the Passage du Saumon; and all the Jos and Los.

Furthermore, refrain from believing that he accepts as pledges, like some vulgar clerk at the Mont-de-Piété, earrings, watches, or pieces of cloth with silver thread. He sometimes lends on curtains—Holland linen, batiste garnished with lace—when they owe a surplus value to special circumstances, of which he is a good judge. But the pledges that please him most of all and make him open his cash-box, always full of banknotes and streaming gold, are love letters, cherished miniatures and withered flowers: all the frail things that divinize the memory of a kiss or the memory of a tear.

He excels in evaluating these inappreciable trivia. It is not him that one should try to deceive regarding the value of an eglantine conserved between the pages of a book for a long time—a value that depends, it goes without saying, on the more or less sincere joy with which the eglantine was once received. As others know the tariff of diamonds or cashmeres, he knows the current prices of violets picked at Meudon on a spring morning by amorous ingénues. In exchange for a gardenia detached, one evening in a private booth from the buttonhole of a black coat, he will not give a very large sum, but he offers louis in piles and bills in wads to anyone who can bring him the perfume that she had on her lips on the evening of her first virginal kiss. And the room in which he heaps up the adorable pledges is like a store of caresses and smiles, an odorant bazaar of tender reminiscences.

Once, it happened that Colette Hoguet—the most foolish of the young women who, in these pragmatic times, still consent to be foolish—was obliged to perceive that the various sellers of things have the bad taste of wanting to trade their merchandise for hard cash. It is in vain that one says to a couturier: "Make me the most beautiful of dresses, in order that I shall be the prettiest of women," if one cannot support the reasoning with a more solid argument; and if one does not show them considerable sums in a partly open purse, the most devoted Potels and Chabots limit themselves to admitting theoretically the urgency of filling breakfasts after laborious nights of amour.

What had Colette done with her town house? She had sold it in order to buy a house in the country for a baritone who sings Tyrolean songs at La Scala. And her coupé harnessed to two large Russian high-steppers? She had ceded them to a sportsman, one of her friends, to pay for the fiacres in which she had rendezvous with an alto at the Folies-Dramatiques, who, full of scruples, would never have consented to climb into a carriage supplied by a rival. Then, because of a thousand eccentric caprices, the diamonds had disappeared like dewdrops in the sun; nothing could any longer be seen in her jewel-cases but the empty cavities of amethyst bracelets and pearl necklaces; and Colette, who, like Rotrou[34] behind the vine-branches of his loft, had the habit of scattering her riches among the clothes in drawers, now searched for hours without discovering the smallest gold coin—with the consequence that it was necessary for her to have recourse to the pawnbroker of the Rue Grenéta.

What troubled her somewhat was that, many times already, she had gone to see the god Eros on the second floor above the entresol, and she was not very sure that she still had anything to offer him.

As she was one of his most faithful and dearest clients, the divine usurer welcomed her with a very particular consideration; he even complimented her on her pretty eyes, which were a trifle weary, for Eros' commerce was not exclusive of some gallantry. Soon, however, with the seriousness that it is appropriate to have in business, he said, while readjusting his spectacles: "I hope, Madame, that you have not taken the trouble of rendering me a visit in order to offer me a mediocre operation, and without a doubt, you have there some object of considerable value?

"Considerable, indeed," said Colette, audaciously, determined to sell her merchandise "Look."

Alas, he laughed disdainfully on seeing the pledge that she took out of her muff.

"Ah!" he said. "What's that? A glove?

"The most precious of gloves. It received the first kiss— the kiss of avowal—of a very handsome young man for whom I nourished sentiments of an incredible tenderness."

"Hmm! Hmm!" said the god Eros, in a well-simulated cough. "That's a pledge that can't be acceptable to me. You're a person who scarcely lingers over the bagatelles of flirtations; a kiss, the courtesy of which doubtless has a part of the tenderness, is not likely to have left you with a very precious regret. And then, give it to me, your glove, so that I can sniff it. Ah! Bah! You're making fun of me, I think? This Swedish

---

[34] The tragedian Jean Rotrou (1609-1650).

174

leather does not have the exquisite perfume of a scarcely-odorous rose that ordinarily emanates from your lovely person, and this is the relic of a long-forgotten caprice—a valueless relic, in consequence—unless you've had the bad taste to bring me the glove of your former chambermaid.

"If you have nothing else to offer me...," the money-lender added, rising to his feet with a cold, dismissive amenity.

Colette uttered a little sigh, and said, full of cunning: "Well, I see that it's necessary for me to separate myself from the object that I treasure more than my own existence! The sacrifice is so cruel that tears are burning the borders of my eyes."

"My condolences," said Eros, in a tone of polite commiseration.

"At least, before giving you the pledge—in exchange for which I would only accept with regret all the treasures of Faerie—let me touch it again, let me rediscover the memory, alas, of the indescribable joy of which it was the caressant witness and accomplice."

"Let's see the object, Madame. What! It's only a chemise?"

"The chemise of my dearest coupling! The chemise in which I shivered in an evening of unforgettable delight! You'll remark that it is torn near the top, which testifies to the fervor of my initial enthusiasm."

"I don't deny it, I don't deny it. The rip gives a certain price to this batiste rag. Nevertheless, to my great regret, I can't be content with this pledge."

"Eh! Why?"

"It isn't crumpled," said the expert. "Furthermore, you've acquired too much experience not to agree with me that mere fact of having kept a chemise on at the moment of supreme abandonment implies, on your part or that of your friend, a very regrettable reserve."

Desperate—for she had resolved to buy a fifty thousand franc diamond necklace admired in the establishment of a jeweler in the Avenue de l'Opéra—Colette offered successively the lorgnette with which she had gazed for a entire evening at the baritone of La Scala, the viola that the musician of the Folies-Dramatiques played "A Burning Fever" for her so often, and portraits, letters, and leaves from a climbing rosebush bought during a morning idyll at the market of the Madeleine.

The usurer refused them all, pitilessly, saying at times: "I wouldn't lend a louis on such trivia."

She felt so sad that it would not have taken much for her to weep authentically.

"Oh," said Eros, finally softening, "don't be so desolate; there might be a means of reaching an accommodation. Reflect, seek, find. Let's see, can you not think of some other pledge—what do I know?—less banal, with a more intimate charm, to which memories and hopes of a veritably serious nature are attached?"

She thought. Suddenly, she had cheeks as red as the poppies of the wheat-fields.

"Wait!" she exclaimed.

She disappeared into the next room, and came back very quickly, her cheeks even more crimson, offering the miserly god Eros, between two of her slender fingers, a tiny cluster of curly hairs, similar to a pinch of golden saffron, extracted with the aid of the teeth of a tortoiseshell comb.

And the delighted pawnbroker opened his cash-box wide.

"Take the gold and the banknotes in exchange for this, all the gold and all the notes! And I'll give you checks drawn on all the banks of the two worlds; and if you don't have enough, I'll sell the houses of porphyry and lapis lazuli that I possess in Paphos by the sea shore, and my Cytherean woods full of cooing doves."

The Futility of Examples

At the time when I was still so infantile that I was scarcely as old as an aged pigeon, I set forth for the future in the company of a magnificently clad young lord whom I didn't know, but who was none other, as I learned later, than King Eros, son of Kypris.

We saw a sorry fellow, resembling a vagabond or a malefactor, ragged, hirsute and horrible, whom policemen were handling roughly and shoving, abusing him verbally. I approached the poor devil. It seemed to me that there was still something in his obscure eyes like a memory of joy. I asked him what he had done to merit being reduced to such a pitiful state.

"I have loved," he told me.

A little further on, on the same road, we encountered a crippled beggar. With a crutch under each armpit, he was dragging himself along painfully, in sordid rags. He no longer had any hair, or any teeth; his eyes were dead, like those of a centenarian, although he might not have been very old.

I approached the beggar. It seemed to me that there was still the residue of a smile on his pale lips. I asked him what he had done to merit falling to that degree of ruination and abjection.

"I have loved," he told me.

At a bend in the road we saw a man with a rope around his neck who was hanging from the branches. He was frightful in the beautiful morning; his face was violet-tinted; a swollen tongue protruded from his mouth; and although he was not quite dead, he was more frightful than a cadaver.

I approached the hanged man. It seemed to me that he still had a gleam of triumph on his forehead. I asked him what adventure had invited him to desire to seek death.

"I have loved," he told me.

Then the young lord with whom I as traveling toward the future turned to me and interrogated me.

"You who are sixteen, child, who will be entering into mysterious life tomorrow, what will you do in life?"

"I shall love," I told him.

The Enchanted Chemises

In the miraculous abode where, far from out world, the young king Amour lives eternally among the immortalized choir of illustrious lovers of both sexes, who only cease kissing one another's lips to sing the praises of the august Kiss, very bad news circulated one day. Voyagers recently arrived from human habitations affirmed that the women of the earth, in their appetite for Gold or perverse Pleasure, had mostly renounced the delights of pure tenderness; even the maidens, those people said, formed evil designs in their solitary white beds.

The chagrin that a magnanimous prince would feel on learning that that plague or leprosy was ravaging his people, Amour felt as soon as he heard that news, and throughout that paradisal country there was such a desolation that Juliet drew apart from Romeo in order to shed bitter tears, Chimène ceased momentarily to mirror herself in Rodrigue's proud eyes, and a cloud, the sudden panic of Petrarch, veiled the double sky that Laure had beneath her eyelids.

However the young king said: "No, I cannot believe that such a calamity is afflicting and dishonoring tender humanity; the most subtle observers can be deceived by appearances. I shall go and see things for myself."

And with that, he departed for the earth. By what route? Along a ray of sunlight that descended toward a garden down here; and Amour reached the ground between a bush, lilies and roses, with flowers still closed, which recognized him, were stirred, and bloomed.

Sometime after that, a stranger in marvelous apparel arrived in the largest square of the largest city in the world. Although he was easy to recognize as a charlatan, since he was standing up with broad gestures amid the sound of big drums and trumpets on the balcony of a carriage he scarcely resembled the Mangins and Fontanaroses that one is accustomed to see;[35] it was not a plumed bronze helmet that he had on his head, not a scrap of vulgar crimson cloth that he wore on his shoulder; luminously coiffed in the aurora of his own golden hair, with a breastplate of precious stones, he was sparkling, charming and sumptuous.

On seeing his arrogant young face, as terrible as lightning and as beautiful as a flower, the idea came of some god become a merchant of quack medicines. As for the vehicle on which he was perched, and which a flock of snowy doves surrounded with palpitations, it seemed to be made of a gigantic sapphire encrusted with diamonds and stars; and the musicians beating the drums and blowing into trumpets in front of three coffers doubtless full of merchandise, had wings on their backs, and were so sumptuously adorned in frivolous fabrics and multicolored ribbons, that they might have been mistaken, at a slightly greater distance, for pages who, in order to amuse some capricious queen, had been dressed as birds of paradise.

It goes without saying that such an arrival caused a great curiosity in the city. All the women emerged from all the houses, shopkeepers from shops, courtesans from boudoirs and princesses from palaces. The doors of convents, opened as if by magic, allowed flocks of bewildered nuns to escape, and there were no more schoolgirls in the schools because they were all in the square, mouths and eyes wide, staring at the handsome charlatan.

Then, dominating the exquisite multitude, he said:

"Gazes of stars, smiles of flowers, graces, charms, beauties, O women, listen to me. The mediocre hope of lucre is not

---

[35] "Monsieur Mangin," who sold pencils on the Parisian streets in the late nineteenth century with the aid of an elaborate patter, attracted the admiration of Phineas T. Barnum, who devoted a chapter of *Humbugs if the World* to him. Doctor Fontanarose is a seller of patent medicines featured in a play by Eugène Scribe, *Le Philtre* (1831).

what brings me to this place. I am not selling, I am giving. And I am not giving ointments or cosmetics, of which, being fresher than April meadows, you have no need, nor hats, nor jewels, nor dresses. What is it that I am offering you, then? Chemises! But chemises that cannot be found in the city's shops: talismanic chemises, enchanted chemises. Thanks to them, Ladies, your dearest wishes will be realized, and Damsels, your sweetest dreams.

"I have three sorts. Some, although light, are the color of ingots that you see at the money-changers; others are as pink as offended modesty; and others are whiter than lilies glimpsed in diaphanous morning mist. And before making your choice, learn what privilege is attached to each of the sorts.

"Those of you who, in the evenings, at the hour when the expected lover is due, put on the gilded chemises, will henceforth have a share in all luxury and all opulence; nothing that pride or cupidity desires will be lacking; and always, in the morning, on waking up after the departure of the man who loves them, they will see with eyes still somnolent, on the table, on the shelves and on the mantelpiece, piles of gold coins or wads of banknotes."

Thousands of hands avid to take, snatch and carry away were raised toward the seller of talismans.

He went on: "Those of you who put on the pink chemises will know other joys, alas. There are mysterious caresses that the malice of overly subtle lovers invent, strange sins that tempting demons advise in whispers, kisses that are the purest of enchantments, perhaps the most infamous of pleasures. No diabolical delights, no infernal paradises, will be spared the bold individuals who choose the pink chemises; and in the morning, in the bedroom full of excessively warm perfumes and alarming memories, they will be afraid to open their eyes because of the innocence of the daylight that passes through the blinds."

Ardent breath burned his face, so many women were pressing toward him, tumultuous and unkempt, their eyelids fluttering.

He continued: "How preferable the white chemises are! Refrain from not choosing them. Thanks to them you will know the ingenuous rapture of loving and being loved in a perfect peace in which the soul is ecstatic. No troubling ambition! No desolate repentance! You will be the faithful lovers of faithful lovers. To merit possessing you, to be worthy of not losing you, they will be reserved, good, loyal, honest and heroic. They will not lavish you with princely offerings; their kisses will not ignite devouring flames in your mouth, but you will have everywhere, on the lips, on the forehead and throughout your being, the freshness left by the glide of an angelic wing moistened by the dew of Heaven. Gazes of stars, smiles of flowers, graces, charms, beauties, O women, accept the chemises whiter than lilies glimpsed in a diaphanous morning mist!"

But he was scarcely given time to finish his speech; from all parts of the square innumerable women rushed forward, crying:

"Gilded!"

"Pink!"

"Gilded!"

"Gilded!"

"Pink!"

"Gilded!"

"Pink!"

"Pink!"

"Gilded!"

The charlatan did not know which to heed; although he was aided by his musicians, he would not satisfy, at the whim of their haste, all the furious covetousness of those who grabbed the talismans almost tearing them. The distribution lasted until nightfall, and the women, shopkeepers, courtesans, princesses, nuns and schoolgirls, would not consent to withdraw until the coffers were empty. All three? No—only two.

There was one that there had not even been any need to open:
the one that contained the honest white chemises.

When the young king Amour had renewed the proof in
all the cities of the earth, and at the crossroads of the humblest
villages, he felt full of an infinite sadness. They had not lied,
the bearers of bad news. It was the end of his glory. Luxury or
lust, such was the goal—the unique goal, now—of feminine
desire; and after having been the prince of healthy ardors, innocent joys, devotions and fine heroisms, he, Amour, was no
longer anything but the lord of avarice and dirty concupiscence.

Alas, it must be a cruel adventure for a god to be debased
by those who serve him; and he would have preferred his altars to be deserted than to be soiled.

One evening, when he was sitting on the edge of a ditch,
lost in a melancholy dream, after having distributed so many
gilded chemises and so many pink chemises all day long, he
heard the sound of footsteps in the silent shadows nearby. He
turned round. He saw a thin little girl, a pauper in rags, so
pale, but pretty in a moonbeam.

Timidly, in a tremulous voice she said: "Oh, don't be annoyed, I beg you; I'm so frightened. You're going to find me
very audacious. A little while ago, around your cart, many
women were crying: 'Gilded! Gilded! Pink! Pink! Gilded!' I
didn't dare say anything, but I have a great desire to have a
chemise of my own too."

"You, little girl?" he said.

"Yes. You see that hovel at the corner of the road?
That's where I live with my uncle and my aunt. They have a
son a little older than me, who works in the field; personally, I
look after the sheep. We love one another. We're going to be
married. It would give me great pleasure to be happy with him
for a long time, forever. So, you understand, if it's no inconvenience to you, please give me a white chemise."

King Amour raised his forehead proudly toward the
stars. There was on earth, then, in a woman's heart, an honest

183

and simple tenderness! That was sufficient for his glory not to be entirely extinct. It seemed to him that he had reconquered his divinity. Certainly, he gave it to her, the chemise the color of lilies and snow, and in addition, he resolved to do great honor to the little pauper, so paltry and so pale.

"When are you to be married?" he asked.

"Next Monday, early in the morning, I think," she said. "But it won't be a beautiful ceremony, because we're so poor."

"It will be a ceremony so beautiful, by the number and the fine apparel of the witnesses, that there will never have been anything similar at the wedding of a princess!"

And, climbing the length of a moonbeam, he rose up joyfully to the paradisal country where he made his abode. What was his design? He had decided that he would be a witness to the marriage of the shepherdess, and that he would not go alone.

When the day came, he came back down here, followed by the cortege of illustrious lovers of both sexes who only ever ceased kissing one another on the lips to sing the praises of the august Kiss: Juliet was there with Romeo, Chimène with Rodrigue, and Laure with Petrarch, and so many other amorous women immortalized by renown, with as many amorous men. It would certainly have been a fine company at the wedding of the pale little shepherdess!

But as that crowd set foot on the road, not far from the hovel, King Amour saw that there was a white funereal curtain over the door. Astonished, he interrogated a peasant who was passing by

"It's because a child died who was lodged there," the man said.

Then the fallen god wept, for the poor little bride had ceased to live before the wedding, and there was no longer a woman on earth who wanted the white chemise.

The Way to the Heart

It is an ancient custom well known to all poets—for poets are not unaware of anything, that before receiving the Bow and Arrows with which he enchants and desolates humans—before, as it were, being armed as a Knight of tender Tourneys and libertine Quests, every young Amour must emerge triumphant in which his subtlety and skill in the exercise of his employment are measured. And who is the judge of whether he triumphs or not? The royal ancestor Eros, sated on victims and glories, drunk on sobs and hymens, who, in the maternal island, amid the bittersweet myrrh made of all despairs and all ecstasies, dreams on a throne of golden Paros marble, his hair the color of white roses slowly stirred by the air eaten by the wings of doves.

Very magnificent and very august, he is nevertheless languishing, and if gods could die, he would die, even though the host of Desires surrounds him with praise, and even though hasty maidservants, who are goddesses, rub his entire body every morning with the exquisite sweat of recent nuptial beds, and put beneath his chilly feet, like good cushion, the hearts of virgins broken yesterday. But beside him, half-flowered on a frail branch, he has a wild eglantine, not pink and scarcely odorous; and on seeing that absence of color, and respiring that lack of perfume, he smiles and is comforted.

The other day, a very young child, the son of a faun of the Sèvres thickets and a nymph of the Meudon woods—they had bumped into one another by chance on the forest edge and rolled into the ditch—appeared before the golden Paros throne in order to undergo the proof.

"Infantile Amour," said the ancient Eros, "I shall not be too exacting a Eurystheus; in order to merit the Bow and Arrows, it is sufficient to insinuate yourself into the heart of a young woman who, as I speak, in a city called Paris, is riffling

185

pensively through a novel by André Theuriet[36] among the oleanders of a balcony."

Such a proof did not seem very difficult. The son of the
faun and the wood nymph, certain of soon being armed as a
Knight of tender Tourneys and libertine Quests, flew away
with his slender wings of pink snow toward the city named
Paris. But, undoubtedly, the task imposed in him, in spite of
appearances, must have had some difficulty, for, two days
having gone by, he returned to the Cytherean isle, not with the
air of a victor, but with the timid gestures and a distraught
expression of someone ashamed.

Not without a smile, Eros asked: "You haven't succeeded, then, infantile Amour?"

"Alas!" he said.

"Doubtless you slipped up?"

"I did everything that it was necessary o do."

"What went wrong, then?"

"This," said the child. "Wings scarcely furled, like a
swallow settling on the edge of a roof, I advanced cautiously. I
saw the demoiselle reading a novel by André Theuriet among
the oleanders of the balcony. Soon I was very close to her, and
with one of my feathers brushing the place where the heart
was beating, I murmured very softly, in accordance with the
lesson I was taught:

"'Oh, what are you doing in your solitude, desert heart,
closed heart, like a cold lily without a bee? Quiver, warm up,
blossom, virginal heart, in order that I can penetrate into you
and cheer you up delightfully. Don't believe, Mademoiselle,
that your sole destiny is to dream, on a balcony, with your
chaste eyes attentive to a chaste book. There are fiancés, evenings, the embrasures of windows, while the grandparents are

---

[36] The poet and novelist André Theuriet (1833-1907) was celebrated for elaborate descriptions of rustic and sylvan life. He
was elected to he Académie française in 1896. The novel in
question might well be *Reine des bois* [Queen of the Woods]
(1890)

playing whist under green paper eyeshades. A young man will talk to you about a beautiful honeymoon voyage to Italy and Spain, and you will be so infinitely moved by his voice that you will think you bear within you all the vast quivering azure of an April morning.'

"Speaking thus, I continued, like someone striking rather than knocking, to caress beneath the demoiselle's corsage the dear place where the heart beats. But she did not pay any heed to me, still reading, and I did not get in."

As soon as he had finished that story, utterly crestfallen, the Desires burst out laughing, and the maidservants of Eros, the goddesses, had to bite their lips in order not to roar with laughter. Ordinarily, it was not to their own teeth that they confided the care of making their coralline mouths redder.

Although august the ancient Eros was jovial himself. "Child," he said, "you're truly very innocent and not up to date, for an Amour born of a faun of the thickets of Sèvres and a nymph of the Meudon wood. Come on, it's an education to remake, as they say. Nymph Erato, cease for a moment gazing at the slender golden play of a furtive sunbeam in the russet nape of your friend and instruct this little Amour, if you please."

It was very willingly that Erato obeyed; she took the child behind an oleander. There, very humiliated, he sighed: "Have I committed some grave fault, then, Nymph?"

"Know," she said, that the path to the heart of a woman is not as direct as it seems to you."

"What! In order to insinuate myself into the heart of the demoiselle, I should not have addressed myself to it right away?"

"Certainly not."

"What! No?"

"No, I tell you."

"Perhaps it was necessary to slip in through...the ear?"

"In no way."

"By the eyes?"

"Not that."

187

"Via the nose?"

"Bah! Ignoramus!" she said.

Then, leaning toward him, she spoke so quietly that the faint song of her voice did not go as far as disrupting the hymeneal flight of two white butterflies almost settled in her hair.

The young Amour trembled, suddenly lowering his eyes, a poppy in each cheek

"Oh!" he said.

"Yes," she said.

"But there, nymph Erato..."

"Well?"

"There, one is...?"

"One is what?"

"A long way from the heart, I imagine?"

"Oh, no, little fool," she said, "Not if one stands up a little."

That overheard comment amused the Cytherean court greatly. What means is there of being severe when one is in a good mood? Although he had not triumphed in the proof, the child received the Bow and the Arrows.

In any case, he acquired in very little time, by the example of other Amours, all the necessary science, and he was the delight and disaster of souls, just as well as any other.

PART IV: INSECTS AND FLOWERS

The Firefly Wedding

As I was coming back from the fairground, I saw a child in a ray of moonlight who was asleep standing against a tree by the roadside, beside a plaster cathedral with narrow red glass windows, much smaller than him. Who buys those hideous miniature basilicas, square and low, from which a long perforated steeple rises, illuminated by a candle-stub placed on the altar?

I felt sorry for the poor little merchant, who must have tried to sell his church all evening, had not found a buyer, and had fallen asleep there, perhaps dreaming about the blows that were awaiting him at home, Ragged and dusty, as sunburned as a young *lazzarone* beneath the shock of his hair, he was dirty and pretty.

I woke him up, gave him some small change, and, in order not to mortify him with alms, I accepted the plaster cathedral. It was very inconvenient, under my arm. I walked more rapidly, in haste to be rid of it; I would put it in a pathway in the orchard, where it would serve to frighten the sparrows that came to peck the cherries. I must have given the impression of one of those people carrying, in devout paintings, the minuscule resemblance of the chapel that they have dedicated to Saint Timoleon or Saint Idlevert in expiation of their sins.

Midnight chimed. I was lying on my bed, not yet asleep, my eyes half-closed; but it was an insomnia devoid of fever, vague and delectable, refreshed by the lunar light coming in through the open window, and putting into the winding garden pathway, close at hand, over the bushes with open flowers and the grass of the flower-beds, the enchantment of its pale magic.

Without thought, but not without joy, not feeling alive, and yet ecstatic with life, rather than a human being, I was a fortunate, blooming thing. And the vast silence, the immense scattered calm, made of solitary distances, sleeping nests and motionless leaves in the still air, was also made of the almost arrested beats of my heart, the dispersion in a dreamless sleep of all my dead desires.

A small noise astonished me

One might have thought it the scarcely sensible impact of a very light object against an unresistant surface, and it sounded in accordance with a rhythm, at equal intervals, awakening the idea of a very distant bell heard through muffling clouds.

The noise did not cease, importuning me in my quietude, soft and so nearly imperceptible as it was.

I got up and went to the window; it is so low that the highest rose on a Bengal rose-bush surpassed the sill, on which it had shed petals.

I had a great surprise.

The cathedral, which I had placed in a narrow path near the door as I came back, like a church at the end of an avenue, in which the candle-stub was long extinct, was radiating an interior conflagration through all its red windows. As I leaned out, attracted by the closer sound, I realized that the inclination of a convolvulus had coiffed the tip of the steeple with a tremulous bell-tower in which a bee moving back and forth was performing the office of clanger.

What was happening in my garden, then, under the magician moon?

I climbed over the window-sill, silently, and knelt down in the shadow of an acacia. In the wall of the little basilica, behind the choir, there was a crack to which I was able to put my eyes.

More than a hundred fireflies, like illuminated chrysoprases, were hanging in candelabra to the summits of colonnettes, suspending chandeliers in the aerostyles, and taking the place of candles in front of the main altar. And at the tip of the bell-tower the bee was still ringing in the convolvulus, summoning the faithful to some ceremony.

The crowd did not take long to appear, innumerable and processional. There were crickets coming from the grass and grasshoppers from the wheat; the aphids had quit the roses and the whirligig beetles the water-lilies; elegant rhipiptera,[37] seemingly gossiping together, were opening and closing the fans of their wings; a ladybird, in order not to be ruffled in the populace, had perched on the wing of a dragonfly; white-clad beadles and praying mantises formed a cortege for a cochineal adorned with cardinalesque crimson. Without overmuch tumult, with the compunction befitting a sacred place, there was a flutter of wings and a patter of tiny feet, in which, amid the blackness of ants in formal dress, busy and dignified, the sapphire of flea-beetles and the emerald of cantharides scintillated here and there.

When all the members of the congregation had taken their places, methodically, to the right and the left, a bumble-bee, with a flap of its wing, leapt on to the balcony of the organ, and a humming music, religious and yet joyous filled the basilica illuminated by fireflies. The ceremony was about to commence.

On seeing two of the good God's creatures heading for the choir, one in a victorious manner, beating its elytra, and the other timid, hardly daring to advance, I supposed that it was a matter of a marriage; and it was no longer possible for me to doubt it when a magnificent scarab beetle, chasubled in green gold, assisted by two necklace ground-beetles, officiated before the main altar, sometimes turning, with a gesture of blessing, toward the two ladybirds.

With my eye to the crack, I did not miss a single detail of the august ceremony. But I pushed curiosity even further. As

---

[37] Rhipiptera was the name given in the nineteenth century to a group of flying insects whose larvae are parasites of wasps.

soon as the crowd began to flood away, when it was all over, and the glow-worms began to go out, one by one, I turned round without making a sound, almost without a gesture, waiting on the sand of the bright alley for the two spouses, who parted the multitude and the tumult.

Where were they going? Would they fly away on their honeymoon voyage, to a warmer azure beneath more ardent stars? Or would they content themselves with the first corolla that came along, appropriately open, under the discreet curtain of a leaf?

"No matter where desire leads you, may the ephemeral and fast-fading primroses be clement, gentle insect couple! May there be much joy in the few hours of your only spring; may no peasant's clog or the slipper of a woman dreaming under the branches ever frighten you while you are fluttering so close to one another over the strawberry bushes or the moss; may the pearl of dew that you drink together always be perfumed to your taste; may the preferred calyx never refuse you an odorous refuge; and if you have to serve as the plaything of a cruel child, may it at least be the same little hand that takes you both, in order that you can suffer and die together!"

While I was making those prayers for their happiness, the two creatures of the good God had not flown away. They climbed up the Bengal rose-bush, the highest rose of which, surpasses my window-sill. And I saw them disappear into the flower that had shed some of its petals, which closed its remaining petals over them, gently.

Not for a moment did I have the idea of going back inside through the window, as I had come out; a movement of the leaves would have troubled the delighted newlyweds in their primal intimacy. I was about to draw away in the direction of the door when I noticed another ladybird on the stone sill, which I had not perceived previously, which had doubtless also followed the married couple.

What was it doing there? Why had it come? Was it a relative of the bride, or—who knows?—a rival of the husband?

There are few humans who have not suffered under the windows of a nuptial chamber, and perhaps, among the insects as among us, it is of the misfortune of some that the happiness of others is made.

The poor creature remained immobile, near the rose-bush. I touched it lightly with my fingertip. It did not budge. I think that it was dead.

Azaleas

In a path in the garden, the poet-lover considered with delight a basket of blooming azaleas.

"O flowers," he said, "the rose is more beautiful than you and the lily prouder, but you are prettier than the lilies and the roses. The illustrious corollas have a certain pomposity in their smile; their triumph is careful of etiquette; queens in ceremonial garb, they always retain, even wide open, a little of the stiffness of the bud, that corset; but you, mingled and casually adorned, with your petals that give the impression of not doing anything and the no-matter-what of your crumpled grace, are flowers in peignoirs. And you have the tender charm of being neither entirely pink nor entirely white, showing the indecisive color, scarcely a color at all, that is reborn in the cheeks of a convalescent child. Where did you get that uncertain, exquisite nuance, O delicate azaleas, of paling redness and reddening pallor, lips slightly moistened by milk, snow slightly tinted with blood?"

A voice responded to the poet-lover, so soft and faint, almost inaudible—a sound that was not a sound—and, as no one was passing along the path, he was obliged to admit that the individual responding was a butterfly posed on a leaf.

"We, the yellow butterflies, were once red butterflies, when those flowers, white in those days, did not yet have the tint that pleases you. Now it happened that, one warm afternoon, we went to sleep in the nascent blooms, and while we were asleep, a storm broke, with heavy rain. When we awoke, our wings, wet and discolored, had ceased to be similar to crimson petals, but because of the water in which our ardent color had dissolved, the azaleas, still white, blossomed almost pink."

The poet-lover would not have failed to believe that explanation—plausible, after all—if a black-headed warbler that was flapping its wings not far away over the balsam flowers had not testified by little angry cries that it did not accept the legend imagined by the discolored butterfly; and warblers, ever since one of them alighted on the divine Thorn, are hardly unaware of anything that happens on earth and in Heaven.

This one twittered:

"Once, in paradise—it's my custom when I go there to perch on the highest key of a seraph's viol—there was a great fête in preparation for the marriage of a soul recently arrived from earth with its sister soul, which had been waiting for three billion centuries in an alley of clouds where they had arranged a rendezvous. The most beautiful music had been ordered from angel musicians who were able to sing as agreeably as nightingales and almost as well as warblers. Nine were sent to a vast hall with walls of light and ceilings of suns. In order to ornament the thrones of the Dominations and the stools of the Blessed, Cherubim were collecting the prettiest of the stars and weaving them into garlands.

"The ten thousand virgins, in order to fête the spouses, had decided to host a ball, but they were not without anxiety on the subject of their costumes. As they had quit the world below a long time ago, they had no idea of present fashions, and while knowing that nothing could compare with their eternal adornment of youth and sanctity, they had a slight fear of seeming ridiculous to the newly elect soul, whose body might previously have been dressed by very famous couturiers. There were long discussions.

"Saint Chloe proposed putting on linen tunics dyed with the blood of Tyrian mollusks. Saint Catulla expressed the opinion that crowns of roses would have the best effect amid the gold of unbound hair. The objection was justly raised that they would be too evidently reminiscent of the costume and coiffure of the Roman beauties of old, and that since that time women must have invented many other means of embellishing their beauty.

"After a thousand arguments, it was agreed that they would not seek in any way—given, as well, that it was impos-

195

sible—to imitate human adornments, but that, being saints, they would dress in the fashion of paradise. Nothing is more delightful than the pale redness of dawn mists; it was with those diaphanous mists—formed, it is said, from a roseate pearl dissolved in winged foam—that they would make ball gowns and sashes; and they believed that they were quite certain, when they entered the ballroom, of not having to fear any comparison.

"They were mistaken, alas. Not one of the ten thousand virgins was invited to dance, while all the ecstatic seraphim pressed around the bride, who had taken the precaution of bringing with her from down here a chest full of clothes in the latest fashion. Needles to say, they were singularly humiliated. So great was their chagrin that, in spite of their reluctance, very natural in young elect, to undress in front of everyone, they took off, tore away and rendered into pieces the twilight bodices and dawn skirts. In their fury they even threw the adorable shreds over the walls of paradise, which flew and floated, rags of roseate gleam and tatters of white glitter, and finally fell, like scattered feathers; encountering the branches of azaleas, previously devoid of flowers, they clung there and blossomed."

The poet-lover refrained from making any reply to that, and he drew away convinced that azalea flowers had been made with the torn-up muslins of the dawn, unless they owed their tender color to discolored wings.

That evening, however, the woman he adored said to him, shrugging her shoulders:

"The butterfly is boasting and the warbler doesn't know what it's twittering about. It's me who can tell you the truth. One day, in the time when I was Eve in the marvelous Eden, I went to sleep in the shade of a large tree, among smaller trees, very tint, on which white corollas opened; but I didn't take long to wake up, because of a dream I had, and that dream didn't quit me when I awoke.

"The tempting serpent hadn't yet spoken to me under the fruits of the apple tree, but I often had tender anxieties regard-

196

less; the instinct of the adorable sin was within me, like a rosebud that wants to blossom. I had never felt as troubled as I was at that moment, though. Although Adam was far away, occupied in contemplating the work of the six days, it seemed to me that he had been lying on the moss beside me, that he had taken my hands, and put his arms around me, and that I had his breath in my hair, on my neck and on my lips.

"Those caresses—which made me shiver in delight, giving me I know not what shame and I know not what joy—I would have liked to return, but I dared not. In the end, though, the tenderness was more powerful than the dread. I seized him, I embraced him, seeking his eyes with mine, his mouth with mine. Alas, I was alone among the flowery branches; what I was clasping against my heart, with all the dread and all the intoxication, were the stems of azaleas; it was their flowers that I was kissing; and after that, they were so delectably pale and pink, for having touched the modesty of my cheek and the fearful desire of my lips."

The Emperor and the Butterflies

The chimerical country in which our dreams play truant was once governed by a very cruel and very charming young emperor, the Heliogabalus of the land of the fays. He was amiable and sinister, gracious and ferocious; the amusing originality of his caprices went as far as barbarity, and beyond.

One day, when he felt weary of the whiteness of lilies, he had a great many young women killed in the flower-beds of his garden, with thrusts of a golden knife, in order to kiss the red roses.

As he was very curious to admire the quivering clarity of the stars, one evening, he put out the dear eyes of his favorite mistress with his fingernail, because they were dazzling him and preventing him from seeing the beauty of the stars.

He imagined the most delicate enormities. In order to go to war he had an innumerable army of little blonde girls, very well disciplined, who attacked the rudest soldiers without weakness and violated them after the victory, gently. The fathers and mothers of those children had not seen them constrained to military service without a painful surprise.

In the end, by the ingenuity of his despotism, which made new demands every day, he alienated the hearts of his subjects progressively. With regard to his female subjects, although he maltreated them harshly, he did not displease them as much as one might think, because of a custom that he had. Twice every summer, all the men in the country having received orders to remain shut in their houses, he bathed naked in a pool of water in front of the imperial palace, under the gaze of the assembled women, and he was so pretty in the nude that they forgave him many things.

The fathers, lovers and husbands were less accommodating, however, when they were quite certain that their subtle and terrible master would never cease stealing their savings in order to put diamond buckles on the shoes of his pages, and emptying their beds into his with the indifferent gesture of someone pouring himself a drink; when it was no longer permissible for them to believe that the emperor might return to honest sentiments, they began to think that the time had come to shrug off such an intolerable yoke.

Their irritation no longer knew any bounds on the July morning when an imperial decree ordered all the male inhabitants of the country, without distinction of rank or age, to devote themselves to hunting butterflies from dawn to dusk without repose, until there as not a single meadow brown on the hawthorn hedges or a fritillary in the fields of lucerne.

That was too much. Hunt butterflies! Renounce honorable labor to follow frivolous winged creatures, which palpitated and never settled through the woods and plains, as little girls do in the courtyard of a convent! That was the value he placed on them! What, they would have the extraordinary sight of magistrates quitting the halls of justice, bankers fleeing their counters and shopkeepers emerging from their shops with the sole aim of imprisoning in a silken net the melicerta that kisses the roses or the parpaillot that draws nectar from the thistles? What did he take them for?

True, they had supported very humiliating adventures. Unable to do otherwise, they had tolerated him taking their money, and their wives, almost as precious. They had consented, with gritted teeth behind their smiles, to dress entirely in black one evening for a ball at the court, in order that the whiteness of the naked dancing girls should be even whiter against a dark background. But when it was a matter of chasing butterflies, it was necessary not to expect them ever to be resigned to it.

One notary, especially, showed himself proudly rebellious. Two or three times, he said things that would have been the envy of the citizens of ancient republics. "Die rather than hunt butterflies!" was the slogan of the revolutionaries. And the tocsin sounded, and the insurgents rushed the palace where the young emperor, without listening to their vain noises, was playing chess with a beautiful semi-naked courtesan, who, every time she lifted her arm to move a pawn, showed the golden tuft of her russet armpit.

The halberdiers and musketeers did their duty valiantly. They did their best to resist the assault of the bourgeois multitude, but it was necessary for them, alas, to succumb under the weight of numbers. Even the valiant army of little blonde girls did not take long to run away, because the sight of so many magistrates and bankers took away any desire for the species of victory to which discipline obliged them. Finally, a triumphant and tumultuous crowd flooded the vestibules and the staircases, and went on to break down the doors.

That racket did not frighten the young emperor, who was playing chess, smiling. For a long time he had foreseen the probable end of his joys and his pride; he had two means within reach of escaping from the fury of the populace: in the pocket of his silk coat he had a phial full of a delicate poison that kills in beautiful dreams; and on the other side of the open window there was a courtyard paved with precious stones where he could break his bones and shed his blood over rubies and amethysts—with the consequence that he was utterly tranquil.

But the semi-naked courtesan, falling at her imperial lover's knees said: "Sire! Sire! Don't persist in a perilous resistance! Renounce a vain caprice. What do the butterflies of the gardens and the meadows mater to you? Do you not have anything that the most reckless desire could envy? Are not the most ardent and the most tender young women yours? Who has ever resisted you? What mouth, as soon as you have wanted it, was not a kiss beneath your lips? Give in, just this once! Let me tell those furious men that you have retracted the decree that irritates them, and, as before, you will know triumphs and delights without peril or bitterness. Oh, sire, what motive of hatred do you have against the white or yellow butterflies that flutter two by two in a sunbeam?"

The emperor had ceased smiling.

"What motive for hatred?" he said, grinding his teeth, while the menacing noise around them grew around them. "Listen!

"The other day, I was walking on the edge of a flowery wood. I was happy and joyful; the night before, in a fête, among all the intoxications that the eye can owe to the whiteness of flesh and the mouth to the redness of lips, I had enlaced, embraced and possessed the most beautiful and proudest of mortal women. Princesses had come from unknown countries to smile at my desire, perhaps at my disdain— princesses, and peasant women too—and I had had the joy of seeing a queen on her knees, removing, in order to please my lassitude, the shoes of a blushing servant girl.

"I was thinking about that pleasant night. Never had I known so perfectly the pride of omnipotence. I bore within me, like the expansion of a dream, the certainty that all terrestrial beauty belonged to me alone. But I saw, on the branch of a bush, a very paltry eglantine in bud that, even blossoming, would scarcely have give the impression of being open, a poor flower hesitant to be born, fearful that, once born, it would not be pretty.

"I suddenly experienced, furiously, a passion to see it open, that sad eglantine that no one would have wanted. 'Unhealthy floret of an almost-dead branch, flower for me,' I begged. 'Smile, poor little thing, and the kiss of your pale mouth will be softer than any other!' Alas, I begged in vain. It was in vain also that, seized by anger, I gave the stupid thing an order to open immediately. It pretended not to hear me.

"O rage! At a sign from one of my chamberlains, so many wives and so many virgins had grouped before me their offered pink whitenesses, and that eglantine resisted me, in its delicate modesty! But a worse humiliation was in store for me. Yes, while I remained still and silent, stupefied by that resistance to my caprice, a white butterfly alighted on the frail floret, and I saw it blossom, in a delectable separation of petals, under the palpitation of wings.

"That is why, you see, I have sworn to have the insolent butterflies in all the gardens and all the woods of my empire, captured and exterminated..."

But the young emperor did not have the leisure to say any more. The doors gave way under the pressure of the crowd. He was about to be enveloped and become the plaything of bourgeois fury. After a shrug of the shoulders he launched himself out of the window toward the courtyard paved with precious stones, where his limbs would be broken and his blood was shed over rubies and amethysts. And he fell very rapidly.

He did not even have time to seize in passing—oh, how joyfully he would have crushed it!—a butterfly that was fluttering there, in the sunlit air: one of the butterflies that roses prefer to emperors.

The Ashes of the Rose

That morning I was in a very sentimental humor, because the day before, I had heard a young woman about to be married singing a very tender ballad at the piano, in which butterflies, during the final organ note, lingered over the heart of roses. And the garden that attracted my stroll was well designed to maintain me in that amiable state of mind; it had nothing wild or busy about it, with its flower bed in which blue, red and yellow balsams were arranged in good order, like Sèvres cups and Saxe figurines on a provincial dresser; with the sand of its pathways, where the rake had left stripes as even and parallel as the lines of a musical score; and with its correct, uniform, borders, like the pleats of a dress that had never been crumpled, it was suggestive of the ambition of an agreeable ideal in good taste, devoid of violence, narrow and elegant, appropriate to form the subjects of water-colors. The July sun, prodigal with its golden dream, put into that garden everything that infinity can contain in a bouquet.

A butterfly that was fluttering, like two petals detached by a gust of wind, brushed my hand, leaving a trace of very fine dust there.

"White butterfly," I said—the memory of the ballad inclined me to conversation with frail winged things—"don't hasten to flee: rather alight on this leaf—a flower would occupy you too much—and respond to a question that I have always wanted to address to you or one of your kin."

The butterfly settled on the leaf. "I'm listening," it said.

For why should it not have replied to me, since I had spoken to it?

"Frivolous lover of roses and lilies," I said, "where does the light powder come from that your wings shed while you flitter from one calyx to another, and which surely gave performers the idea off velvety waves. Yours are the only wings, butterfly, from which a scattered whiteness falls, like a dust."

"Curious person!" said the butterfly. But as it had the leisure, it did not disdain to inform me; I truly believe that one could learn many things that are not in books, and which scholars do not know, if one chatted more frequently with the insects of the woods and the fields, butterflies, moths, cicadas and ladybirds.

When red-haired Eve was born, at sixteen years—an age when the women of that time were not long delayed in having sufficient insistence—in the miraculous Eden swarming with life and youth, she remained ecstatic before so much magnificence, but no desire bit her heart. Before seeing her reflection in the mirror of a spring, she sensed that she was more beautiful than all the beauty that surrounded her, and as soon as she had looked at her image in the spring she took pity on beings and things.

Yes, the mane of the lion, with its quiver of flames, was superb in the light, but Eve's hair, spread out, was more luminously resplendent. That the sky was blue was possible, but her eyes were more exquisitely azure. Why would she be jealous of the swan, having that neck and those arms made of living snow; why would she be jealous of the creepers, having slower and more treacherous enlacements, why would she be jealous of the obscurity of the odorous underwood, knowing that she reserved in the mystery of her body profundities more tufted and more perfumed?

Proudly, she considered the new nature, saying "Doubtless it's very nice, but so what? Is that all?" And the game in which she took pleasure, still under a tree, was kissing the nails of her slender fingers, and laughing.

But one day, she saw a rose.

The rose was there, before her, scarcely pink, almost white, in its triumphant grace. It opened radiantly, like a flower that would rather be a star! It was as radiant and alive as a star that would rather be a woman! A passing tiger wept with tenderness while considering it.

Then Eve felt troubled. She understood that, for eternity, she had a rival, Beautiful as she was, the rose was no less beautiful. Perfume against perfume, smile against smile, floral flesh against womanly flesh, there would be an unremitting struggle until the end of time. In vain, amorous poets, in enthusiastic madrigals, would try to prove to their mistresses the defeat of the sovereign flower; Eve was under no illusion; the rose would always challenge her, magnificent and victorious; it would be the eternal humiliation of woman to be compared to her blooming rival.

A sadness of which one can have no idea took possession of her, to whom all other created things were submissive, whom only a single flower resisted. She no longer loved to mirror herself in the clarity of springs, to watch the swans playing, less white than her, on the celestial azure of lakes. Lying next to her husband, she sometimes dreamed bitterly, for entire nights, with her fists in her teeth, under the indifference of the stars; and she sometimes remained sitting under a tree for long hours, without kissing the pink and slender nail of her little finger.

Eventually, she resolved to destroy the flower that disputed with her the triumph of being the incomparable beauty. Oh, doubtless she knew full well that one dead rose was not the disappearance of roses forever; they would be reborn every spring, every summer, too beautiful, for the shame of less vermilion mouths. But at least Eve would be avenged for the first insult; she would not have tolerated, without reprisal, the victory of a rival.

She thought at first of ripping the enemy apart, of biting it, of trampling it underfoot, in the dust, among the pebbles, and then throwing it, utterly ragged, to the furious passing wind. Once, she had seen a vulture seize a skylark; that was how she would have liked to seize the rose. However, she decided on another torture. With dry grass she built a little pyre on the sand, lit it by dropping a glow-worm into it, and when the plants were in flames she plucked the flower and hurled it into the conflagration.

Oh, how the frail petals shivered and curled up, with plaintive crepitations! How sad and cruel it was, that roseate whiteness, those perfumes, that life, all that charm, burned! Finally, nothing any longer remained, on the light relenting furnace, but a little white dust—that was the ashes of the rose—and the woman, already ferocious, was content.

But the despair was great among the butterflies of Eden. The loved the rose that the woman hated. What! It was no more? They would no longer alight, quivering with delight, on the tremor of its petals; they would no longer brush, by extending their wings, the embalmed mystery of its heart? While the fatal work was accomplished, they had fluttered, bewildered, around the merciless executioner; Eve did not even see them, entirely given to her vengeance. Now she drew away, triumphant, and they gazed at the pale remains of the beloved, on the little heap of extinct grass.

At least they would keep of her that which they could take!

Very numerous, in tumult, together or one after another, they threw themselves on the precious relics, rolled in them, enveloped themselves in them...

And the fine flying powder that the wings of butterflies have scattered since that time is the ashes of the rose.

The Little Bird, the Pearl and the Rose

The little bird said: "I have no perfume, alas."

The pearl said: "Alas, I can't sing."

"What is cruel," said the rose, "is that I have neither the voice of a bird nor the pale gleam, with a tremulous orient, of a pearl."

I was passing by; I heard them, and I couldn't help feeling sorry for the melancholy of the rose, the pearl and the little bird.

I tried to console them. "It's necessary to be reasonable," I said to them. "One can't have everything. It's very enviable, already, little bird, to enchant the nocturnal silences with song; pearl, to be as clear and milky as a tear fallen from the distant eyes of the moon; and rose, to be as perfumed as the mouths of young women at the moment when the kiss obliges them to blossom."

Speaking in unison, the rose, the pearl and the little bird replied to me: "Only yesterday, we would have shared your opinion. Perfume, gleam and song, it seemed to us, were functions any one of which was sufficient to the pride of a created being, whatever it might be. But there was a strange adventure; not far from us, a young woman passed...

"who sang better than me," said the little bird,

"...was more luminous than me," said the pearl,

"...and was more odorous than me," said the rose,

and the three plaintive voices added: "with the consequence that our defeat is as bitter as possible; we were constrained to admire and love, grouped in a single person, the three charms of which one alone had been given to each of us."

I meditated, and said: "I see what must have happened. Marion has come this way. But try to forget an unfortunate moment, and quit your sadness. Being her friend, I'll obtain from her that she doesn't walk in your vicinity, and you'll never have to suffer such a humiliation again, since, of all living creatures, Marion is the only one who has perfume, song and gleam simultaneously."

A Quarrel With a Rose

While all the warmth of the day was like diffuse liquid gold around us, this rose, in this garden, said to me:

"Ah! Well, no, you're picking me too soon. Look, I've scarcely opened. It was only this morning that I emerged from the bud under the pallor of the dawn, and I still have a little dew on my petals. It's true that I'm no longer unaware of the delight of feeling my heart penetrated by the warmth of the summer; I'd try in vain to hide that, already, more than one hornet—I prefer hornets to bees, because I have good morals—sucked in with an agreeably brutal caress the sugar of my pistil. But then, so many joys are still reserved for me in this redness in which the quivering of wings abounds. How many butterflies—if you don't hasten too rapidly to pick me—would alight on me, in a frisson of desire, with which I might tremble, in spite of the scolding of my thorns, those duennas who don't know what they're talking about?

"Don't pick me, passer-by! Are there not other flowers in this perfumed enclosure? Look, there are hyacinths, carnations and jasmines; couldn't you find, while leaving me on my stem, the wherewithal to compose the most splendid and odorous of bouquets? And many other roses are also offered to you, who wouldn't complain about being picked, having already swooned under all the kisses that a calyx can expect. For they're old roses! But me, I'm a girl-flower, almost unopened; many hopes are permitted to me; I don't want to be an eglantine mummy in a Japanese vase, with too few memories. Let me intoxicate myself with the pleasures that are offered to me! Let me yawn for a long time to the caresses of butterflies, sunbeams and the passing wind; let me live until the dusk of my nuptial day."

I replied:

"Young rose, believed that my heart is softened beyond the possible by the lovely elegy with which you have charmed my ear; if it were permissible for me, I would withdraw the hand that is menacing you; but I have to choose for Coelie the most exquisite of the flowers born in this garden; nothing can prevent me from accomplishing my duty."

"Oh!" she said. "It's for Coelie that you want to pick me?"

"For Coelie," I replied.

"Is Coelie the young woman who was strolling in the crimson light a little while ago in a peignoir of muslin and lace so delectably aromal that all the dragonflies and all the breezes left us in order to follow the perfume of her moving skirt?"

"Yes."

"Is Coelie the young woman who delights the daylight with a smile in which all the gleams of summer are amorously posed?"

"Yes."

"Oh, in that case, pick me, pick me," she said. "I consent to it, I want it; and I won't regret anything, neither the quivering of wings, nor the passage of breaths of wind over my emotional calyx, provided that Coelie, two or three times, distracted and thinking about something else, deigns to place on my mouth, almost similar to the mouth of a woman, her lips, entirely similar to the lips of flowers!

Rose To Let

As I was walking in the garden on a bright summer morning, admiring the recent blossoming of a carnation here and a hyacinth there, I noted, among thorny branches, a very small leaf that advanced between the other leaves as if it wanted to attract the attention of passers-by; and behind it, very close by, there was a partly-open tea-rose. But the wind, in brushing the branch must have moved that sprig of verdure aside, and I was about to go away when I perceived, in the middle of the smooth and narrow surface, infinitely small symbols, very pale, scarcely visible. One might have thought that they were minuscule letters traced by the foot of an insect dipped in pollen or a little dust from a butterfly's wing.

It is probable that many people, in my place, would have had some embarrassment in deciphering what was written there; I had reason to praise myself, in that circumstance, for having long studied the language, almost imperceptible to the human ear, that the little creatures of flower gardens employ to talk between themselves, and the alphabet they use—the complaisant breeze inclining a branch of carrying away blade of grass—for the correspondence of one bush with another, or one clump and another. Not without difficulty, I spite of my habitude in such reading, I distinguished the words: *ROSE TO LET, presently*.

There was no possible doubt; that leaf was a notice! And it was for the partly-open calyx behind it that a tenant was desired.

I could not help being passably astonished, for the insects—not matter how much they are accused of flightiness and instability—rarely abandon the flowers that they have elected as an abode. It required a powerful motive for the inhabitant of that one to be resigned to ceding it.

Putting my eye close to the narrow opening of the rose I saw, in the depths, a ladybird that seemed to be prey to the most dolorous melancholy. Ordinarily, human eyes have difficulty telling the difference between one of the good God's little creatures devoured by cares and one rejoicing in existence, but I recognized immediately that that ladybird had as much about which to complain as possible, and while she uttered sighs that you would not have heard, but which cleaved my soul, and beat her wings feebly, poor thing, I said to her, with a compassionate curiosity:

"It's you, then, Mademoiselle who wants to rent out this half-closed flower?"

"It's me," she replied, "and one can affirm that there isn't a lodgment as pretty and comfortable in the entire garden Take a look! It's delicate, elegant, freshly floral; a delightful odor emanates continuously from all parts of it; and it's so well arranged, with silky little nooks everywhere, that two, three or even four could live here. This rose would suit very well a household of flea-beetles or tinder beetles with several children. Note that it will open further, with the consequence that it will be possible to see clearly, even by night because of the stars, without needing to have recourse to glow-worms, which are often very importunate and very expensive. As for water, there's dew on all the petals every morning and evening. But in truth, I think that I'm mad, and I'm wasting my time talking like this. The lodgings can't suit you, I can see that clearly; you're one of those gigantic living things who put our houses in their buttonholes, and whose brick and iron dwellings are as large as mountains."

"It's not for myself that I want to rent your rose, though," I replied. "There's an insect among my friends who is very discontented with his dwelling because of a bumble-bee in a nearby tulip who makes a strangely noisy and discordant music."

"Go fetch your friend, then," said the ladybird. "Provided that he's an honorable insect, tranquil and of good morals, and provided, above all, that he has no resemblance whatsoever to

212

the beautiful green and gold cantharides, who take pride in such a disreputable renown, I'll immediately cede my place to him. Anyway, I'm not asking for any rent. He won't have to worry about the charges that one ordinarily has to pay from dawn to midday, from midday to dusk and from disk to midnight—for our lives are ephemeral—and all I demand is that he maintains the rose that I'm leasing to him in perfect condition. Oh, she's so dear to me that I'd have been out of here a long time ago if I didn't dread leaving her defenseless, prey to the rudeness of the wind or the vagabond looting of hornets and bees."

"Oh, Ladybird," I said, "why are you so eager, then, to quit such agreeable lodgings?"

"Alas," she replied, "because I'm the most deplorable of the little creatures of the summer; because the one that I adored—the beautiful husband with the red wings—quit me in a squall, and because I'll die if I don't find him again. Oh, the minutes were so sweet when we flew together, amid the odor of blooming flowers, very close to one another, in a ray of sunlight, when, in our dear perfumed dwelling, we cadenced out amour to the somersaults of our colliding elytra! But how bitter was the moment when the wind carried him away, far away from me, perhaps irrevocably. Alas, what has become of him? Has the tempest broken him against some wall, or the trunk of an oak? The most frightful thing would be if he requested hospitality from one of the ladybirds devoid of modesty who lie in wait night and day for passers-by, placed on the highest petal of her ever-open flower. Oh, Monsieur, hasten to bring the tenant who will watch over my dwelling, in order that I can set forth in search of my lost friend!"

To tell the truth, while I drew away after promising to return soon, I was as perplexed as possible. I did not know any insect who was in need of lodgings. I knew faunids, whirligig beetles, cyprids and springtails, but they were houses, some in tulips and some in foxgloves; as for certain lanternflies among my friends who had no domicile, they were notorious

213

noctambulists that I would not have been able to recommend decently to the honest abandoned ladybird. They would have led a fine *vie en rose!* There would have been suppers in the conjugal corolla, and hesperides, unrestrained dances agitated by an orchestra of mosquitoes, that would have scandalized al the surrounding foliage with an inappropriate jigging of elytra.

No, I did not know what I could do to sustain the lie that my compassion and my curiosity had prompted, when, amid the moss, at the point where the tallest stem of a lily protruded, I saw a creature of the good God who was in a truly pitiful state. It was dragging a broken wing, poor thing! All that I could make out among its laments, when I had placed it on the back of my hand, was that it had been surprised in the lilies by a very irascible rival at the moment when it was palpitating over a little creature of a very noble family; and, beaten, bitten and torn, it had been thrown out of the royal flower without being given the leisure to fly away. Now it was a poor little being who was going to die.

Well, that was exactly the tenant that was required. I was going to accomplish two god deeds at the same time. The wounded individual—who was a male—that creature of the good God, would have a shelter in which to recover, and the sad wife could go in search of the vanished husband.

Oh, I was far from expecting the dramatic scene that brought tears to my eyes! Having returned to the rose to let, I had scarcely allowed the insect in such poor condition to slip between the petals than the ladybird hurled herself upon him and embraced him with her little wings quivering. She recognized him! She forgave the dear infidel!

Alas, her joy and mine were of short duration. The husband had died without knowing that she was there, living and loving, just as Romeo died before the awakening of Juliet! And the pitiable widow expired of sadness on the pretty pink cadaver.

Full of melancholy, I gazed at their defunct hymen. I thought about verses that would be their tender epitaph. Then a breeze passed, crying their mingled remains away amid the leaves and the thorns, into the distance.

Now the tea-rose is empty. One can still read on the notice: *ROSE TO LET, presently*. But no tenant offers himself, and there is silence and shadow, even in broad daylight, around the solitary flower. The butterflies avoid her; the bees do not collect pollen there, for it is said that the phantoms of the dead lovers still flutter invisibly over the deserted calyx, rejoining one another there on moonless nights. No one wants to lodge in the haunted rose.

The Avenged Leaves

Since the vine, finally flourishing again, now decorates the hills of Bourgogne and Guyenne with a beautiful abundance of clusters of grapes, it is permissible to reveal the veritable cause of the disease that corroded for such a long time the august plant to whom humans owe the laughter and the renewed vigor of kisses. Once, such a subject of discourse would only have darkened souls, because it would have made people think of uprooted stocks, unemployed hills and glasses full of strange red liquids invented by the lucrative malevolence of chemists. But now, after the festivals in which the true blood of grapes has flowed, we can strike the earth with a free foot. It is in the open air, in the plains and on the slopes, and no longer in shady laboratories that the vermilion or gilded vintages are finished off. The thyrsus of Iacchus is no longer next to the pestle of Monsieur Fleurant,[38] and we have drunkenness without intoxication.

So, learn, now that it is cured, why the vine was sick. Oh, how despicable the scientists are in their subtle and absurd hypotheses! Learn also how it was saved, by the adorable clemency of women.

By the clemency of women?

Assuredly. From whom could such a benefit have come but those who dispense the only sweetness in which one finds the strength to endure life and to hate death?

People who know something about the laws that regulate the universe are not unaware that the care of supervising the vegetal world—verdure, flowers and honeyed fruits— maintaining its good order and the equitable proportion of

---

[38] Fleurant is the apothecary featured in Molière's *Le Malade imaginaire* (1673).

efforts and salaries was confided by the initial Providence to a seraph whom the pots encountered more than once in the fields or the orchards, clad in cornflowers and ears of wheat, or dressed in snow and roses like a Norman apple tree.

One day, that seraph—many years have passed since that day—experienced, as he put the tip of his toe on the spring grass the most disagreeable surprise imaginable. How sad the flowers were, and the leaves especially, to the right and the left, before and behind him, from one horizon to the other! He had never seen a similar melancholy among the plants submissive to his empire. The roses were hanging down like dead lips. The forget-me-nots resembled blind eyes. The may-blossom was in mourning, like the virgins of countries where white is worn in mourning. And the foliage, of the tallest trees and shrubs, was twisted, shriveled and sometimes bristling, showing a despair mingled with anger. Alas, what a frightful April the earth would have that year, and what would the amorous think when they went forth, their hands united, in the hostile mystery that rendered the slopes sullen?

While the seraph, as perplexed as possible, was wondering what event had changed the amiable nature of calices and verdures in that manner, the little thorny leaf of an eglantine whispered: "Know the truth, Celestial Highness." She had just been chosen, unanimously, by the surrounding vegetation, to formulate the common complaints, because of the bold attitude she had and her propensity for stinging impertinence.

"What is it, then?" said the angel. "Speak."

She replied: "We leaves—the leaves of rose-bushes or elm trees, the little leaves with which the collarets of daisies are lined or the vast leaves of plane trees between which the nests of large birds swing—cannot tolerate any longer the injustice of which we are the victims; and since the flowers, as is natural, have taken our side, spring will retain the sullen expression of grim winter until we have been given satisfaction for our just resentments."

"Eh? What are you complaining about, leaves of the paths, the flower-bed and the woods?"

217

"Hear this," she continued. "We certainly have rare privileges. Several of us sway in the immensity of bright azures, and sometimes the plumes of passing swans fall upon them. Others know the delight of surrounding the marvelous rose. Others, humbler, know how pleasant it is to be brushed by the thin feet of gilded aphids and tony ladybirds. Others, picked with carnations or camellias, swoon in ballrooms between the divine breasts of women. But those pleasures, those prides, are at the price of the incomparable joy and glory that were accorded to one of our sisters, who has finally become a detested rival."

"Eh?" said the seraph. "Who is this hated sister?"

"The vine-leaf!" cried the eglantine leaf, in an eddy of the breeze. "Ah! Because we are distant in the forests or the gardens, you thought that we would never know about the criminal partiality of which you, the master of our destinies, have given proof with regard to that good-for nothing, that profligate, who rubs the grapes—that drunkard! But we have listened to what is murmured in the shade by poets, readers of little odes and elegies, we have heard the words of lovers coming from the cites on Sundays in summer, and we are no longer unaware of the function with which you have made our sister of the viny hills proud.[39]

"The beautiful pleasure of being cradled in the blue of vast skies and receiving the alms of winged snow that a swan allows to fall, or enveloping the exquisite rose, or being tickled by prowling insects; even delectable death in the cleavage of a waltzer, cannot be the supreme joy for a leaf smitten with the ideal. The perfect enchantment and the ineffable triumph are reserved for the vine leaf! She it is who veils the most intimate, the most sacred, the most essential treasure of feminine beauty; she it is who touches, who keeps for herself, beneath her swollen roundness, the quivering and tufted rose of the

---

[39] In English the leaf performing the function in question in paintings of Eve in Eden is generally known—inaccurately, in botanical terms—as a "fig-leaf."

most distant modesties. She is the charming obstacle, the adorable refusal, the symbol of closed virginity! And even if she is holed and torn, it does not matter, she is no less worthy of envy, since she appears at the green margin of the august nuptial wound!"

The speaker drew breath in a passing gust of wind, also angry; then, stiffening somewhat, she continued:

"We, the leaves of the hedges, the woods and the boscages, in accord on this point with all the flowers, have therefore resolved to maintain, from one end of the earth to the other, morose attitudes, by which the springs and the summers will be saddened, so long as the exquisite privilege that is refused to us has not been withdrawn from the vine leaf, and so long as she has not expiated, by means of a fall proportional to her unjust triumph, the glory and good fortune with which she has humiliated us."

Confronted with such an ultimatum, the seraph had to yield. Could he deprive April and July of the vibrant life of verdure and the smile of flowers? He sacrificed the vine leaf, and hence the vines themselves. A redoubtable scourge, the origin of which the scientists have not succeeded in discovering,[40] devastated the august plant to which humans owe the laughter and renewed vigor of the kiss.

That was, as everyone remembers, a time of dolorous proofs. There was still wine, alas, although there were no grapes. Anyone who drank anything other than spring water risked a prompt death. It was not rare to encounter on the

---

[40] The disastrous blight that affected French vines in the late 19th century is nowadays though to have been caused by an aphid of the genus *Phylloxera*, although some controversy lingers even today, and the blame was hotly contested at the time. The problem was solved in the 1870s when French growers began grafting their plants on to American root-stocks immune to the parasitism, and the industry recovered during the 1880s.

roads people who had rendered their souls because they had been thirsty. Fortunately, the god Amour soon observed what was disastrous about such a state of affairs; there was little love since the true blood of grapes no longer warmed hearts or brains. The welcome of tender retreats in the woods, the odor of profound foliage and the troubling fragrance of calices was not a sufficient compensation for the vanished energy of sincere wines, counselors of caresses and delicate violations.

After having conferred with the seraph supervisor of pathways and flower beds, the god Amour immediately imagined a means of remedying the evil. What was the vine leaf, in reality? A symbol of feminine modesty; an image of strict virtue. He therefore addressed himself to amorous young woman; he made them understand that if they deigned to renounce necklines that were too high, skirts that were too long and many other vain modesties, the leaves would have no reason henceforth to hold a grudge against the vine leaf, which would be nothing more than a silly and outdated metaphor.

Heaven! How much it cost our friends to resign themselves to such a neglect of their natural modesty! But it was necessary to come to the aid of humankind, thirsty for bloody grapes. They consented, because they are so good, to allow all the whiteness of the shoulder and the breast to be seen at fêtes. They consented, in delectable intimacies, to more complete unveilings. Then, since the leaf that had previously been envied jealously was no more than a leaf like any other, the verdure of the paths and forests permitted the reflourishing vine to decorate with a beautiful abundance of clusters the hills of Bourgogne and Guyenne. And you drink honest wines, comrade, because your mistress, last night, with one knee on the edge of the bed, with a little shake, allowed the fleeting chemise to slide over the calf, to be retained for an instant by the roundness of the heel, and then to fall entirely.

One of Three Flowers

Reader, your mistress is deceiving you.

Notice that I haven't said: "Your wife is deceiving you," firstly because, even in these frivolous pages, I like to remain respectful of conjugal honor, and also because I don't want to suppose you sufficiently devoid of common sense or abandoned to the gods to have committed the imbecilic crime of having yourself granted by law what is only precious if it is given by amour. Only free lips can kiss; a man who gets married evokes the idea of a man going to ask the mayor for permission to pick a rose. Furthermore, someone—the great Balzac, I think—formulated the axiom that: "It is unnecessary ever to have a wife or a journal; there are always imbeciles who will take charge of having them for you."

So, your mistress is deceiving you.

You protest! You affirm that I am displaying a strange impertinence. "Why would my friend be unfaithful to me? Am I not young, handsome, elegant and witty? Does she not have, every day, when she passes by on my arm, the delight of hearing the envious murmurs of other women? Only yesterday, after much delicate rhetoric, I proved to her several times that the concern of literary phrases does not deflect me from more serious duties; and has she not had around her neck, this morning, a necklace of pearls and sapphires that I gave her in order to thank her for having such white teeth and such blue eyes?"

Reader you have no need to tell me these things. I have never had any thought of putting in doubt the merits that adorn you. You are, rolled into one, Hylas and Hercules, Alcibiades and Gorgias, with a little more modernity. And by what right would you be reading this newspaper, for which good rhymers write, by what right would you be intoxicating yourself with ambrosia, if you were not a kind of young god? I will even add that I, mediocre as I know myself to be, would have disdained to offer you so many tales in which I strive to imitate Amarou, Apuleius and Théodore de Banville, if I did not judge you worthy of the love of all women—which implies the esteem of all poets.

But your mistress is deceiving you.

She adores you, since you are worthy of bring adored; I grant too, so inclined to concessions am I, that she is, by nature, as virtuous as she is amorous, and that she experiences intolerable remorse when she kisses with the most passionate stammers lips that are not yours. Oh my God, yes, the poor thing suffers from lying to you; you will never have any idea of the bitter pangs that accompany her treason, above all when she cannot help taking pleasure in it. The more agreeable her crime is, the more frightful it is to her. A martyr, that is what she is when she faints with intoxication. But in the end, she is deceiving you, deceiving you, deceiving you!

In any case, you cannot be excessively desolate, since a fault is less to each individual when it is common to all. Your misfortune, reader, is ours. You are deceived, as are we all; and all mistresses, in that regard, are like yours.

But let us beware of holding it against them.

If they are unfaithful—oh, how it costs them!—it is not their fault.

No, the fault is that of the Sultana Amalaide, who was walking one day, a little less than twenty thousand years ago, in the garden of the enchanter Jeschadour.

The sultana, while breathing in the fresh air, said to the enchanter: "It's certain that I feel inclined not to be as cruel to you in future as you have the right to reproach me for having been thus far. Apart from the fact that you have rendered yourself, thanks to your magical art, as handsome as the most handsome of young men, who resemble the most beautiful of young women—your beard, delightfully silky and blond has the troubling semblance for me, of appearing out of place on your chin—and apart from the fact that you know how to say things that would make a heart beat in a marble breast, you have made me gifts that do not leave me indifferent.

"It is to you that I owe the possession of a pearl that, when I blow upon it, becomes, in accordance with my desire, a star that I can put in my hair, or a sedan chair lifted by swans that fly toward the Milky Way. You have created for me an invisible nightingale that, with words more melodious than any birdsong, sings the praises eternally of the pale rosiness that flourishes on the nail of the big toe of my left foot, And once, while traversing a field of daisies, when, weary of all that whiteness, I manifested the desire to see another color—a little red, for example—you had the complaisance to have decapitated before me, in a single morning, a million young pages and servant girls, with the consequence that the entire earth, from, horizon to horizon, was as scarlet as a field of poppies.

"Such courtesies are made to touch a delicate soul, and I confess to you that, finally, you are not far from the supreme good fortune that your passion solicits. I even think that the day will not end without you having many thanks to address to me—if I can satisfy, thanks to you, one more caprice that has occurred to me."

"Oh, Madame," said Jeschadour, "of what would I not be capable in order to obtain the delights that would stream from your open robe as honey streams from a broken beehive? State your desire, Sultana, and whatever it is, I think it will be obeyed."

After a silence, Amalaide sighed.

"It's certain that the flowers of this garden where we're taking the air are very beautiful and delectably odorous; but alas, they're jasmines, tulips and hyacinths; they bloom in similar calices in almost all flower-beds; and if I pick that rose, another woman, coming after me, will also be able to pick a rose. I would like you to make flowers bloom that no other hand than mine will be able to detach from the stem, and which, once plucked, will never bloom again: flowers that will only live once, just long enough to charm my gaze and perfume my lips."

Jeschadour replied: "That, Madame, is a wish that it is very easy to grant, and I expected, in my expectant gratitude for the recompense that is promised to me, a more terrible request. Would you care to follow me behind this bush, higher than a wall? You will see three admirable flowers that human eyes have very rarely contemplated. You may choose one of them, and the one you have picked will never bloom again on earthy."

"What! Of the three, I can only pick one?"

"Alas, my power has limits."

"I shall be able to limit my desire, then. But hasten to conduct me to these marvelous blooms."

When she was in the presence of the three flowers, the Sultana Amalaide could not help confessing that she was dazzled, so radiant and superb was what she saw.

Emerging from a stir of leaves that resembled living emeralds, one of the calices, vast, proud and august, opened like a blossoming dawn, reminiscent of an enormous rose made of gold and snow.

"Oh!" said the Sultana. "What is the name of that flower?"

"Madame," replied Jeschadour, "its name is Beauty."

Another calyx, a poppy, palpitating and shifting as if it were being stirred by a storm, had the redness of the furnaces of the sun on the horizon that it is setting ablaze. It was charming and it was frightful, and on standing close to it, one experienced everywhere the horrible delight of a burn.

"Oh!" said the Sultans. "What is the name of that flower?"

"Madame," replied Jeschadour, "its name is Amour."

The third calyx was as severe and pale as a young girl clad in a white dress. It had the pure and slightly melancholy appearance of a lily made of grandeur and virtue.

"Oh!" said the Sultana. "What is the name of that flower?"

"Madame," replied Jeschadour, "its name is Fidelity."

Then, Amalaide pondered. Pensively, she said: "So, I can choose between these three flowers?"

"Yes, Sultana," said the mage.

"And if I pick the rose of gold and snow?"

"It will never bloom again."

"You mean that there will be no more beauty on earth?"

"There will, indeed, be no more."

"What! Will I be ugly myself?"

"Even you would be—but I would not love you any less."

"It's an experiment that I don't want to make, so I'll leave that flower on its stem."

She approached the second calyx. "And if I pick this poppy?" she asked.

"It will never bloom again."

"You mean that there will no longer be any amour in this world?"

"Even I would no longer love you. But you would not cease to be beautiful."

"Good! What pleasure would one have in being pretty for eyes that would never be able to be smitten? That's a flower that I shall certainly refrain from touching."

She leaned toward the third calyx.

"And if I pick this lily?"

"It will never bloom again."

"You mean that there will no longer be any fidelity in this world, that no woman henceforth will love her lover or her husband constantly?"

"Even you would betray the sworn oaths. But you would be no less beautiful and no less adored."

After reflecting, the Sultana Amalaide said, with a little laugh: "Aha! I think that between various evils, it is necessary to choose the least; and since my caprice urges me to pick one of the three flowers..."

She plucked the pure, slightly melancholy lily, the lily that was made of candor and virtue.

At first, Jeschadour approved of the choice, for that very evening, the Sultan was deceived as much as it is possible to be; but the enchanter showed less satisfaction when, three days later, Amalaide, still beautiful and still adored, quit his palace and his gardens, and the mage as well, to follow along the highways a young beggar clad in rags and sunlight, who had blown her a kiss as he passed by.

The Little Girl Who Knew Nothing and the Garden That Knows Everything

Berthile's fifteen years are entirely anxious. The little person is beginning to realize that one is not fifteen years old in the month of Aprilin in order to employ the hours solely in darning grandfather's socks next to the window, or sleeping in a little bed so narrow that even a dream could not lie down next to you. In the morning, scarcely awake, still in her chemise, when she considers in the mirror the exquisite creature that it is given to her to be, she suspects strongly that her eyes, her mouth and her small breasts, which are already lifting the fabric, and the other charms with which she is provided, ought not to remain useless to her. But of their employment, being so simple, she has no idea; and so, one afternoon, sitting by the open window, where she is singing to an old tune, she abandons both her needlework and her song; she is on the point of weeping, so troubled is her soul, when a green-gold scarab beetle lands and closes its wings in one of the clematis flowers in the casement.

THE SCARAB: Good day to you, dear Berthile.

BERTHILE: Oh, isn't that strange? A scarab beetle that talks!

THE SCARAB: There's nothing strange about that; don't humans talk?

BERTHILE: Yes indeed.

THE SCARAB: Well, then, why shouldn't insects also talk?

BERTHILE: You're right. Only it's not usual, and I was astonished at first.

THE SCARAB: Cease to be, my dear, and listen to me, if you please. I've come to get you out of difficulty.

BERTHILE: Oh, you did well to come.

THE SCARAB: You're anxious to know to what usage, which you don't anticipate being unpleasant, your April ought to be employed, now that you're fifteen years old?

BERTHILE: Can you tell me, insect that speaks so well?

THE SCARAB: No, but I can tell you who can inform you. Not far from here there's a garden whose flowers know everything that damsels who don't know anything don't know. Go into that flower garden, dear Berthile; interrogate the flowers that resemble the treasures that you have, and you'll come back very thoughtful, but very knowledgeable.

BERTHILE: Alas, I'd gladly go to that obliging garden, but grandfather, who is very malign, locks me in every time he goes out, and I'm a prisoner here until the evening.

THE SCARAB: What are you thinking? Do you suppose that a winged being—I thought you were simple, not stupid—would advise you to leave by the door like housewives going to market? Come here, dear Berthile; put the tip of your foot on one of my extended wings..."

BERTHILE: Ha ha!

THE SCARAB: What?

BERTHILE: Ha ha!

THE SCARAB: What does that mean?

BERTHILE: My feet are small, certainly...

THE SCARAB: To whom are you talking?

BERTHILE: What, you know that?

THE SCARAB: The other evening, prowling around the stone of your threshold, I was nearly crushed by a very heavy pressure.

BERTHILE: Pardon me, beautiful green-gold insect! I didn't see you.

THE SCARAB: Don't apologize. It's your grandfather who nearly flattened me under his sole. Anyway, I thought I might die of pleasure rather than fear, because I'd seen your foot, which is so small, so small!

BERTHILE: It's true that my foot is much smaller than that of my neighbor Madeline, but, dainty as it is, it wouldn't be able to stand in your wing, even open.

THE SCARAB: Try.

BERTHILE: Are you joking?

THE SCARAB: Try, I tell you. Climb on to the window sill, stick out your leg, and extend the foot. Marvelous. Move the muslins on your arm slightly, so that they're like wings in the air. Don't be afraid. I'm flying. We're going down, we're going down. There, we've arrived. Jump on to the road. Follow that path. It's after the third oak on the left that you'll find the garden that knows everything. Au revoir, my dear Berthile. Do you know that you aren't as heavy as a ladybird?

Berthile follows her path while the scarab flies away. He said: "After the third oak to the left." She hastens, having a great desire to know how the treasures of her fifteen years might be useful. Now the garden appears. It is so pretty, so bright, so perfumed, that she never thought one could see a garden so marvelous. "Perhaps it's because it's made of flowers to which I have a resemblance that it's so pretty?" she thinks. For, even when very innocent, one has one's petty pride. She pushes the golden gate—certainly the gate was gold; why would it have been a less precious metal?—and enters the main pathway, where all the flowers, inclining as if before a little queen, make her a double hedge of colors, perfumes and sunlit butterflies.

BERTHILE: Good day, flowers.

ALL THE FLOWERS: Good day, Flower.

BERTHILE: You know what brings me here?

ALL THE FLOWERS: We've been informed by one of our friends, a scarab

BERTHILE: Well, inform me.

ALL THE FLOWERS: How maladroit you are! Do you think we're going to respond in chorus, in a crowd, without preserving all the interest of the idyll that a poet hidden over there behind a lemon-balm bush is spying on delightedly? Interrogate one by one, child, the resemblances of the beauties that are in you.

BERTHILE: Cornflower?

THE CORNFLOWER: Berthile?

BERTHILE: You have the color of my eyes?

230

THE CORNFOWER: That is my pride, my darling.

BERTHILE: What is it necessary to do with my eyes, which resemble you, Cornflower?

THE CORNFLOWER: Tender gazes for a proud and handsome young man, gazes that await him, gazes that hope for him, gazes that adore him for having come.

BERTHILE: Thank you, Cornflower.

THE CORNFLOWER: Adieu, Berthile.

BERTHILE: Rose?

THE ROSE: Berthile?

BERTHILE: You have the color of my mouth?

THE ROSE: That is my glory, my darling.

BERTHILE: With my mouth, which resembles you, what is it necessary to do, Rose?

THE ROSE: Kisses for a proud and handsome young man, kisses that pretend to refuse themselves, kisses that give themselves, kisses that want, when they are obliged, when they are finally weary, not to be fatigued at all.

BERTHILE: Thank you, Rose.

THE ROSE: Adieu, Berthile.

BERTHILE: Liana?

THE LIANA: Berthile?

BERTHILE: You resemble my arms?

THE LIANA: Not sufficiently; and that is my sadness. But if I'm not as white as them, at least I'm as flexible as them.

BERTHILE: With my arms, which you would resemble if you were white, what is it necessary to do, Liana?

THE LIANA: Enlacements of the neck of a proud and handsome young man; enlacements that give the impression of not knowing why they are tightening, nor why they are loosening, and tightening again when scarcely loosened.

BERTHILE: Thank you, Liana.

THE LIANA: Adieu, Berthile.

BERTHILE: Viburnum?

THE VIBURNUM: Berthile?

BERTHILE: You're the sister of my breast, I believe?

THE VIBURNUM: Yes, for fresh candor, but an eglantine is flowering on your breast.

BERTHILE: With my breast, of which you are the sister, even though you lack an eglantine, what is it necessary to do, Viburnum?

THE VIBURNUM: Tender beats toward the ardent lips of a proud and handsome young man, and frissons after the bite, frissons that want even more bites!

BERTHILE: Thank you, Viburnum.

THE VIBURNUM: Adieu, Berthile.

BERTHILE: Golden Lily! Golden Lily! Golden Lily!

THE GOLDEN LILY: Why are you calling me three times, Berthile?

BERTHILE: Because I fear that you are a little deaf.

THE GOLDEN LILY: No, no. What do you want with me, child?

BERTHILE: I think that you have some resemblance...

THE GOLDEN LILY: Certainly, since you are as blonde as ears of wheat and saffron.

BERTHILE: Well, with the blonde lily that resembles you, what is it necessary to do, Golden Lily?

THE GOLDEN LILY: It is necessary, for a proud and handsome young man...but lean over a little toward my calyx, for there are things that those curious violets and daisies there in the moss ought not to hear.

BERTHILE: Oh!

THE GOLDEN LILY: It's this.

BERTHILE: What?

THE GOLDEN LILY: Nothing more terrible, I grant you,

BERTHILE: Can one not...?

THE GOLDEN LILY: No.

BERTHILE: However...?

THE GOLDEN LILY: One can't avoid it.

BERTHILE: Alas, Golden Lily!

THE GOLDEN LILY: You won't die of it, Berthile!

Now Berthile returns to her house. She is simultaneously less anxious and more troubled. She succeeds in getting back in without being seen, returns to her place, sews with mechanical fingers, and sings with a voice that does not know what it is singing. At supper, she is very distracted.
"What's the matter girl?"
"Nothing at all, grandfather."
Immediately after dessert, she goes back up to her room, sits down near the window and dreams under the dangling caress of the mad vines and clematis that traverse the blue of the sky and the gold of the stars.
Time passes. She is still dreaming. Night has fallen completely; sighing, Berthile stands up in order to close the window; soon she will go to sleep in the narrow little bed. But a frisson of wings, very light, causes a leaf to tremble.

THE SCARAB: Good evening to you, Berthile

BERTHILE: Oh! Good evening, pretty green-gold insect.

THE SCARAB: Have you been well informed by the flowers of the garden that knows everything?

BERTHILE: I thank you, and I have no complaint to make of them; they have even told me many more things that I desired to know. The Golden Lily, especially, revealed mysteries of which I had no idea and which are very frightening. But where is the advantage of being well-informed if one can make no use of the acquired knowledge? Alas, I have not yet encoun-

234

tered the proud and handsome young man about whom the Cornflower, the Rose, the Liana, the Viburnum and the lilial calyx spoke to me.

THE SCARAB: I think, Berthile, that he is here.

For that scarab, who was a very sly insect, and who had not sent her without reason to the educative flowers, has just mutated into a young man with a handsome face; and before Berthile has the time to be surprised by such a metamorphosis, it is necessary for her to confess that she is delighted, so rapidly does the lover devoid of wings, pushing her with caresses into the depths of the room, oblige the little girl who knew nothing to use the lessons given to her by the garden that knows everything.

The Wisdom of the Dragonfly

"Golden dragonfly?" said the blonde rose.

"What is it?" said the golden dragonfly.

"This," said the rose. "The pleasure that you obtain in posing on the edge of calices, I would like to know it too. Please give me your wings, in order that I can flutter over the flowers. In the meantime, you can take my place, entering the leaves on my stem, and as we're both gilded, no one will perceive the exchange."

"But will you return my wings to me?" said the dragonfly.

"Certainly," said the rose. "As soon as I have satisfied my desire to quiver over the pistils, I'll hasten to come back, and you can resume your flight."

"You swear it?"

"I swear it."

"Here are my wings, then, blonde rose."

"Thank you, golden dragonfly."

And while the insect suspended himself from the stem, the flower escaped amid the sunlight of the garden.

She took great pleasure in fluttering here and there, in alighting on a lily—scarcely, for lilies are so squeamish—and lingering for a long time over the fluffed-up carnations that do not refuse flying caresses. But, remembering the dragonfly, who was waiting and must be getting bored on the stem, she returned to her natal rose-bush.

"Here are your wings; let me resume my place."

But she did not obtain any response.

"Eh! Didn't you hear me, golden dragonfly?" she said.

"I can hear you," said the dragonfly, "but I no longer care for my wings. Since I've bloomed, immobile, so many wandering kisses have brushed and delighted me, without me going to any trouble, that I intend to remain a flower. Nothing is worth as much as the idleness of being loved."

The Dream of a Day in May

*While to their perverse works
Men run breathlessly...*
Théophile Gautier[41]

What prevented me from going to sleep, even though I had found, under a ray of sunlight on the Île de Croissy, a carpet of grass entirely suited to repose, with the root of an old elm tree, well padded with moss, for a pillow—was a warbler in a nearby bush, stubbornly twittering, so prettily that it was impossible for me not to sacrifice my desire for slumber and for silence to the pleasure of hearing it sing; and I only closed my eyes when it flew away, chased by a gust of wind.

With my eyes closed, did I go to sleep?

I dreamed, at least—but a dream so diaphanous with true clarity, so penetrable to the things of nature, that it was, in fact, rather than an incoherent and obscure dream, an illusion in which reality became enchanted without being abolished...

The wood was in fête: a marvelous wood, with roses on every branch, droplets of diamond and wings of gems on all the tips of the blades of grass, and joyous competitions of nets in all the verdant bushes. Pink, yellow and blue butterflies, fritillaries, meadow browns and melicertas, no longer knew where to alight, there were so many flowers in bloom. The joy of quivering ephemerae put an ardent dust into the diffuse gold of the sunlight. Flies, intoxicated by virtue of having gorged at stamens, were trumpeting their triumph. Hornets could be seen no longer able to fly, letting themselves fall into the grass like drunkards, so much perfume had they inhaled from calices. Sparrows were pecking wild cherries; nightin-

---

[41] The quotation is from Gautier's poem "Premier sourire de printemps."

gales were catching flying ants. Unstable dragonflies were shivering over the coolness of springs and the tickling of moist water-cress. Throughout the wood, summery as well as spring-like, amid the clement warmth and the benevolent zephyrs, spread the laughing, singing, reckless victory of living.

Abruptly, however, all the joy fell silent and was extinguished.

Why?

Because of the news that a messenger bullfinch, perched on a fir branch, brought.

It announced that it was no longer a time to laugh; that the angry bees were emerging from their hives in order to come to trouble the fête of the beautiful day. They were weary, he said, of being the ones who make the honey and do not eat it: an eternity of work without a salary! It was thus for the bees long before the verses of Virgil, but the laborers without recompense were finally in revolt. Yes, yes, they flew in the sunlight like the butterflies and settled on flowers like the ladybirds, but it was not for their own pleasure, it was for that of others, in order that the cells of their honeycomb, stolen from them so rapidly, would be more golden and more flavorsome.

Now their patience could no longer submit. They were demanding less labor and more joy. The perpetual enchantment in which the roses ecstasized undeservedly, having only taken the trouble to flower, was an insult to them. The butterflies had only to flutter, the little birds had the unique task of charming one another with their own songs. And since others were unjust to them, they would be terrible toward others. They had weapons, the bees! They were able to charge, to sting, to pierce, to ravage: good workers, but ferocious killers.

While the bullfinch was announcing that news, something redoubled the fear: black by virtue of being innumerable and compact, the entire population of bees, in an enormous swarm emerging from the hives, was advancing on the sunlit wood. What a battle there would be, alas, and how many lacerated flowers, insectile wings and avian feathers would litter the field of combat.

Anxiously, I said to two roses: "Have pity, please! At least let dread counsel you to justice. It is befitting, when the bees alight in your hearts, that you are gentle to them, and sometimes exchange a kiss to console and encourage them."

And I said to the butterflies: "It's true that you have no other care that to marvel at the carnations and hyacinth. Be equitable to the makers of honey! Don't begrudge them a share of the perfumes that are your delight."

And I said to the little birds: "As a poet, I love you, because you sing. However, you would be wrong not to be merciful, you who are cradled in the rhythmic indolence of the melodious branches, to those who labor, without songs, in the somber hive."

But a little eglantine, very ferocious, said: "Oh, the bees have utterly insupportable stings; I'd be glad if they were all killed."

And a libertine butterfly "Why should I share with evil insects the lovely odor of smitten flowers? It's high time that I was delivered from those importunate rivals."

And a nightingale, pensively: "What are you saying to me? I don't understand, nor do I want to understand; what is important to me is to listen to the memory of my song in the echoes."

The consequence was that the wood was not moved by all the complaints of the bees, and had no other care than to vanquish the rebellion of the laborious insects. The thorn-bushes extended their thorns for the defense of the flowery bushes. Spiders prepared ambushes. Warrior insects flew in battle order. The hornets raced around violently, sounding bellicose fanfares. Even the birds, launching forth from the branches, swooped upon the swarm that had emerged from the sad hives. And the latter retreated before numbers and strength, dispersed, and took refuge, vanquished but full of rage, in the somber honey-factories.

Then, in the marvelous wood, after the victory, the fête recommenced, more joyful and more luminous, with more roses on the branches, more dew and butterflies on the tips of the blades of grass, with more birdsong in the flowery bush-es—and there was a universal joy.

Lying on the moss with my head on the root of an old elm, however, I thought, in my dream penetrable to the reality of things, that the bees would come back, more redoubtable, furious and invincible, and I felt sorry for the roses, the butter-flies and the nightingales...

PART V: THE QUEST FOR THE IDEAL

The Pale Sister

She was the only daughter of the greatest king in Asia. As you can imagine, she lacked nothing that might make the happiness of a young princess. She lived in a pink jade palace traversed by sunlight; when she went from one room to another, languid and sustained by black servants, her beautiful bare feet sank into profound carpets that shod her with caresses; and at any hour of the day, invisible orchestras played her music that would have delighted the most delicate ears.

It goes without saying that she had in her caskets made of a single moonstone all the diamonds, all the rubies and all the sapphires of which the reckless ambition of a coquette might dream; it would have been possible to pave an entire city by scattering so many stones. Her clothes were very becoming; they employed the muslins of Srinagar, the supple wools of Kashmir, and the fine silks of Cherbassy and Ispahan.

What was appropriate above all, however, to maintain joy in the mind of the princess, were the marvelous gardens around her palace. No drop of rain ever fell from the eternally blue skies there; the rarest flowers bloomed there, magnificent and violent, swollen with sap, overheated by the golden summer, eventually inclining their calices, which wept balms. The ferocious beasts of the woods and the ravines—lions, tigers and panthers—were like seductive cats there, mewling with pleasure under the hand that stroked them; one suddenly saw , in the tapering of cactus bushes, the gentle shaking of manes and the monstrous smiles of gaping maws.

And over the wide open flowers, the beasts wandering or lying indolently in the warmth of moss and grass, the light of the sun was resplendent, with a furious magnificence. Everything was golden: the leaves, the calices, the pebbles of the pathways, and the fiery distances of the horizon.

The princess, however, gave no evidence that she was satisfied by so many splendors; she was discovered sunk in morose reveries; it was visible that she was bored and becoming pale, like a pink rose changing into a white rose. It was generally supposed that she had a mysterious desire, a secret chagrin. But what desire? What chagrin?

"My beloved daughter," said the old monarch, "why do you not reveal to me the worry that is haunting you? Do you not know that I am omnipotent, and that, in order to make you smile, I would accomplish the most difficult enterprises? If you do not have enough gems in your jewel-cases, say the word and I will go to conquer the realm of Golconda and that of Visapour, in order that you will never lack bracelets of carbuncles and coral necklaces.

"But perhaps it's that you desire to be married? Speak without dread; say the name of the man your heart elects, and I attest to Heaven that you will have him for a husband, whether he is the heir of the most glorious of sovereigns or the bastard of a woodcutter, who binds faggots while whistling tunes.

"No, it isn't marriage that preoccupies you? Perhaps you find that the golden solar radiance with which your gardens are flamboyant has insufficient brightness and not enough luminous warmth? If such is your thought, don't hide it from me; for, by means of hecatombs and temples build in honor of the gods. I will obtain, in order to make you smile, that they redouble the splendor of their sun!"

"Yes, there is something I lack, something I want. But what is it? I don't know. Oh, truly, I don't know, and I'm dying of a desire of whose object I'm ignorant."

"What!" said the king. "You don't have any idea?"

"None," she sighed. "No precise idea."

Then, her eyes vague, with the slow and distant voice of someone talking in a dream, she said: "I only believe that it's very white and pale, and distant, the unknown thing that I need, the mysterious thing whose absence is causing my despair..."

On the advice of her most devotee courtiers, the king decided to send his daughter traveling. Perhaps she would encounter, in some country nearby or far away, what she coveted with such bitter and uncertain desire. In any case, the surprises and the adventures of the roads might be able to distract her from her melancholy.

Never had a caravan been seen comparable in magnificence to the one formed for the voyage of the princess. Before an innumerable troop of camels, which carried the provisions and the baggage, among a thousand servants clad in silk or richly armed, some of whom played the kusser and the archviol in order to mark the rhythm of the march, eight white elephants trained to advance at an even pace set forth, bearing a vast carpeted floor and an entire house with several floors thereon.

Behind a window, with her forehead to the glass, the traveler watched the cities and the landscapes go by. Everywhere alas, everywhere, under the eternity of the burning azure, she saw dwellings gilded by the sunlight, oases gilded by the sunlight and the infinite sands and smoky gold of her horizon. Everywhere, the ground opened, as if ripped and bitten by the devastating sun. It was not worth the trouble of having quit the palace gardens if she were to rediscover, everywhere else, the implacable splendor of the perpetual summer.

Even when she abandoned the caravan in order to board a ship, the sun did not quit her, blazing and furious, making the immensity of the sea shine like golden silk, and causing the crests of the waves to glitter with scintillations. The princess sank increasingly, hopelessly, into her irremediable ennui.

However, a tempest carried the ship away, in spite of the skill of the captain and the zeal of the crew, it was tossed for more than a week by the rage of the water and the wind. At every moment they expected to see it sink into some abruptly opened gulf.

The princes alone was not frightened, for it costs those who have lost hope in life very little to die.

Finally, after the dawn of the eighth day, the tempest calmed down. In what region the ship was, even the captain could not have said with precision. It was probable that it had been driven a long way northwards, for it was the very pale light—phantasmal, one might have said—of a dead sun that rose over the waves and whitened them softly.

The princess gazed at that cold light, enveloped by it as if by an exquisite freshness. Then, suddenly, dazzled and ecstatic, extending her hand toward the nearby shore, she said: "Oh! On the slope of that mountain, under the dull and mild daylight, what is that vast, mysterious, unknown whiteness out there, which rises up and is lost in the pallid sky?"

One of the sailors replied: "That is snow, Madame."

"Snow! Snow! That's what I wanted," she said, "and it's you that I love, my sister."

Then, whatever anyone could do to turn her away from her design, she ordered a landfall.

She was the first to leap on to the pale shore, and to lie down on the snow, touching it with her open hands, kissing it with her lips, soon chilled. And after a start, she did not get up again. She remained lying in the whiteness, motionless and smiling, happier than any living being. She had died of kissing that snow, in the delight of a frisson.

The Three Drunkards

One day, three brothers were walking together along the same road, three young men as fortunate as possible, for they were the sons of King Mataquin, vanquished dethroned and killed the year before by a neighboring monarch. If it is frightful for poor children to be wandering without shelter from dawn to dusk and to sleep on cold nights under the overhanging roof of some barn, with a stone for a pillow, it seems even crueler to delicate lords who are in the habit of lodging in a marble palace with sumptuous furniture, and idling every morning until it is time for chocolate in soft feather beds behind curtains of gold satin and crimson velvet.

"It's too much!" cried the eldest, stamping his foot on the ground. "I can't endure such a life any longer."

"Nor me," said the second.

The youngest did not say a word; he was a silent child, who, without ever complaining, kept his eyes lowered by day toward the little flowers of the ravines, and raised them in the evening toward he little stars of the night. Even in the days when he had been a prince he had scarcely spoken, spending his time strolling under the trees of the park, thinking about no one knew what, listening to the nightingales; and sometimes, he took a little crystal flute from his pocket, with which he imitated the song of the birds—but the wicked people who had sacked the king's palace had stolen or broken the flute. He regretted it. Blond and frail, his pale face slightly blue-tinted, he resembled a little girl who has been ill for a long time and is convalescent.

"When I recall," said the eldest, "that we had all that glory and all that wealth..."

"When I recall," said the second, "the resplendent fêtes at which the princesses danced the pavane, bare-shouldered, and their feet shod in gold, visible when the brocade skirt was tucked up..."

"...Despair grips my heart and tears it."

"...Burning tears devour my eyes."

"Fortunately, I've imagined a means of forgetting our former felicity and our present distress."

"Oh? What means? Speak, quickly!"

"Do you not know that all memories, the sweetest as well as the bitterest, are drowned in forgetful intoxication? How many times I've envied the drunkards who beat the walls of villages! Let's imitate them, my bother. Follow me to that tavern from which the sound of colliding tankards is emerging."

"Eh? We don't have any money to pay our bill."

"I've found two pearls in the lining of my coat. Take this one, and I'll keep the other. They'll give us a few jugs of wine in exchange."

"So be it, I'll go with you. Only, it isn't on the lips of glasses that I want to get drunk; the tavern maidservants might be pretty; I'll drink forgetfulness from women's lips."

And they went away, without worrying about the silent child, who continued waking along the deserted road. So long as the daylight lasted, he gazed at the little flowers of the ravines.

What was he thinking about? The broken flute. And as soon as dusk fell, he raised his head in order to watch the stars come out.

It turned out that each of the pearls was very valuable; a Jewish merchant at a table in the tavern evaluated them, bought them, and paid a high price for them.

Then, his pockets full of good money, the eldest did not limit himself to drinking the inferior wine with which peasants devoid of delicacy were content. He went into towns and got drunk on the costliest wines. In his glass, filled as soon as it was emptied by the illustrious Johannisberg, the color of pale sunlight. Lacryma Cristi, like golden molten lava, Madeiras and Malmseys, honest Bordeaux, redoubtable Bourgognes and brutal Jurançons succeeded one another or mingled. He drank Falerno, Massico and Cecuba; he compared the wine of Chio with that of Cyprus, and Thalassitis, which it is necessary to put in the hold of a ship to cool, with Thalassene, which is only good when mingled with sea water. Tokay appeared to him to have some resemblance with Tenedos, and when he had emptied a few flagons of Romanee or Saint-Pourçain, or Garnache, or Genetin. or Lampasque, or Sabaillon, he did not disdain a few bottles of Champagne, because of the froth, which is amusing. The result was that it would have been difficult to find, even by searching hard, a drunkard as perfectly drunken as the eldest son of a king, and he staggered through the streets with neither a cloak nor a hat, howling songs.

For his part, the second son, almost rich after selling the pearl, had not stopped at the vulgar maidservants with bare arms and headscarves knotted around the neck who went from table to table, and later from bed to bed. In many towns he had many beautiful women. He gave himself the pleasure of ripping satin robes from which snowy roundness emerged and biting rosy mouths that melted under the teeth like ripe strawberries. An hour did not go by without a young woman saying to him: "I love you," for he showed generosity. Brunettes pleased him, and then blondes, and then redheads. He mixed them up, not knowing which to prefer. Enveloped by caresses, he resembled those Italian oaks that vines climb up, allowing their clusters of grapes to hang down. When less ardent, he made singular choices, hoping that Caffirines would render him a taste for Georgians, and that a mulatress would serve as a transition for his return to blondes. He maintained himself resolutely. He grouped in his cluttered chamber, night and day, more blonde-haired women than an adolescent has dreams. The result was it would have been difficult to find, even by searching hard, a lover more devoted to amour than the second son of a king. When he traversed the streets with his troop of amorous women, he was like the glorious Aretino followed by forty Aretines.

But neither the eldest nor the second son found, in the intoxication of wines or kisses, the entire forgetfulness of the glories of old and the lost kingdom; for one awakens from every joy, with a sad heart or a bad taste in the mouth; and they had morose tomorrows.

When they returned to the road, weary, exhausted and ruined, thinking with an even crueler bitterness about an even more distant good fortune, they were very surprised to see their younger brother at the foot of a flowering bush, beneath a flight of bees, who was smiling. He had a kind of ecstasy blossoming in his eyes and on his lips.

"What!" cried the eldest. "Have you ceased to suffer?"

The child replied: "Yes."

"What!" cried the second son. "You no longer know the anguish of old?"

The child replied: "No."

Then they asked: "What have you done, then, to forget the past, the present.. life?"

"I've done as you've done," he said. "I got drunk, and I'm still drunk; and I live in an infinite enchantment. It's not a matter now of dethroned kings and palaces ravaged by pillage and conflagration. What does it matter to me what was, what is and what will be? I've even lost the memory of the broken flute, because of the delectable intoxication that envelops me with dreams more brilliant than the halls of marble and gold, more beautiful than the fêtes in which bare-armed women passed by, and more melodious than the song of the nightingales in the trees of the park. And it's an incomparable intoxication from which I shall never wake."

"Oh! From the flames of what wine...?" said the eldest.

"Oh! From the sugar of what mouth...?" said the second son.

"...Has such joy come to you?" they asked in unison.

"From no wine and no mouth." And the child added: "Every morning, I drink drops of dew in a rose that flourished on the other side of the bank, and every evening, in a lily open to the azure, I drink a ray of starlight."

The Good Star

That evening—oh, how far way that hour is, how far away!—a star fell into the gutter.

She said to me: "Perhaps you think that I've descended for no reason from the marvelous azure above your obscure earth? What an error! I knew very well that you would pass along this street at the very moment of my fall; and if you wish, agitating my rays like the plumes of a wing, I'll take you away to the divine abodes of peace and light. Up there, high up and higher still, human realities don't exist. What you call the true has never saddened the eyes of the bright stars, but dreams are the familiar passers-by of the luminous routes."

I didn't hesitate; I replied: "Open your wings and carry me away, bird made of light."

Then the star lifted me up toward the land of the chimera and dreams, and since that time, I have never come back.

Avarice

Once, when I was very young, I was walking around a lawn when I saw a flower in the hedge so pretty that I had never seen one as charming. I picked it very quickly; it was an admirable eglantine. A lady who was passing by, who was not very beautiful, said to me: "Give me that flower. I beg you."

Certainly, I could have made a present of that discovered spring to a young woman, so blonde and blushing, with whom I had played innocent games the previous day, and whom I loved with all my heart. However, I replied: "Since you want this flower, Madame, here it is."

Once, when I was slightly less young, and poor, and sad, I was walking in the nocturnal streets of Paris when I saw near the gutter, fallen from some pocket, a shiny gold coin. I had been a long time since I had seen a gold coin! I picked it up very quickly; it was a guinea, which was worth a great deal of money. A young woman who was passing by, who was rather ugly, said to me: "Give me that gold coin, I beg you."

Certainly, I could have had a good meal with that discovered treasure, which was very necessary to me, or bought some verses, nicely printed, by an excellent poet. However, I replied: "Since you want this guinea, Madame, here it is."

Another time—young or old, rich or poor, I no longer remember—I was walking on the shore of the sea, all luminous with stars, when I saw a star fallen from the sky in the sand; it was not very radiant, alas, but it had fallen from such a height! I picked it up very quickly. Passing by, the most radiant of princesses—oh, how the royalty of her hair, in a crown, shone in the darkness, and how I would have adored her, that Highness!—said to me, by virtue of a caprice: "Give me that little star, I beg you."

Certainly, I could not make any usage of that celestial glimmer down here; the things of the heavens have no value on earth. However, I did not reply to the princess, and I kept the star.

The Louis d'Or, the Jewel and the Star

Between two paving-stones in the dirty, muddy street something bright gleamed on that December evening.

Poorly clad, his sordid hair beneath a furless hat, a little old man passed by, quite hideous and very amiable, obliging his wrinkles to the smile that a ferocious and benign money-lender has.

He perceived the gleaming object.

"One could believe," he said, "that it is a louis d'or."

But that passer-by was not one of those people who can be abused by appearances. It was to acquit his conscience, as they say, that he bent down to pick up the shiny thing. A louis d'or? Not at all; the glint of a pebble that had caught the light of a gas-jet.

The man who looked like a money-lender continued on his way, slightly chagrined not to have found a coin, but very proud of not having been duped.

A beautiful young woman came along who, for hours, in a little room in a restaurant where people pretend to drink and laugh, had seemed so crazy that she might have been mistaken for a fauness in a wood of vines on the last day of the grape-harvest. In reality, she was as placid and impassive as a cold stone over which melted ice is flowing.

She perceived the gleaming object.

"One could believe," she said, "that it is some precious jewel fallen there by chance."

But that passer-by was not one of those women who allows herself to be dazed by deceptive glimmers. It was in an already disillusioned manner that she bent down to pick up the luminous object in the mud. A fine gem? No way: the glint of a pebble that had caught the light of a gas-jet.

The beautiful girl who never got drunk continued on her way, slightly discontented at not having found an ear-ring or a ring, but quite satisfied at not having been mistaken.

Envious of the money-lender and in love with the vain lover, a poet had taken it into his head to roam in that street. He was a child, quite ridiculous, with long hair and eyes that gazed above all the walls, toward the horizons and beyond. It would have given him pleasure to have in his pocket the wads of bills that lenders at interest have at their disposal, because when one has a great deal of money one can make gifts of bracelets and flamboyant necklaces to the little flower-sellers of the cafés, and he coveted the beautiful young woman, drunk or not, because she had red lips like a made-up rose. But what he liked more than anything was the little icy silver gleam of a star, in the evening, on the edge of a cloud, like a pearl in the last swish of a gauzy robe.

He perceived the gleaming object between the paving stones.

"Ah!" he cried. "It's certainly a star that has fallen from the Milky Way into the street, in which is eternalized, after the fall, the stubborn clarities of Heaven and the flowery reminiscences of paradisal gardens."

He was one of those mortals devoid of common sense, quickly wonderstuck, who is always eager to believe in something radiant. Full of certainty, he bent down to pick up the glimmer. A star? Yes a star. As soon as he had it in his hand, the brightness of the pebble that had caught the light of a gas-jet was, indeed, a star, since he had believed that it was one. And the rays that were like the petals of a star in flowers that he had inserted in jewels by a skillful jeweler, in order to be able to offer beautiful presents to the only woman he loved, reserving the smallest part of the sidereal light, almost nothing, for himself—one is always egotistical, if only a little—in order to make for his forehead a little of the glory that the future would see from a distance.

The Key in the Sea

In a country by the sea, in those days—times so distant that the mot decrepit oaks of today were not even green acorns then—there were three brothers whose poverty would have moved tigers and rocks to compassion. Alas, it did not move either men or women.

Gerbert—he was the eldest, although he was only twenty years old—labored in a field full of stones, but that field could have been the most fertile in the world and he would have been no better off, for it belonged to a miserly and cruel peasant who paid very little and nourished very badly.

The second, named Amarin, was a fisher on the ocean in the service of a boat-owner who kept for himself all the fish spread out over the shingle and the seaweed from the teeming nets. He was paid even less and nourished even more poorly than Gerbert.

As for the youngest, sixteen years old, named Cyrille, he never consented to receive, either in the fields or on the water, the wages and the insults of a master; an instinct counseled him to wander freely in the solitudes, thinking about things, and he thought incessantly even he did not know exactly what things were. By profession he was a bird-catcher, of finches and wagtails, and he had invented very ingenious traps to catch those birds, but his ingenuity was no use to him because, as soon as he had caught them, he let them go, moved by their palpitating fear, with the result that he was even poorer than Gerbert and Amarin, for the people at the market would not buy his mercy for the birds, which, in any case, he would not have sold.

What redoubled the sorrows of the three brothers is that they had not been born in the condition in which they now found themselves. Those unfortunates were the sons of a king and a queen, but a very powerful enemy, after many victories, had conquered their patrimonial kingdom and killed their father and their mother; and having escaped, while very small, in the garments of paupers, those rags had become their true costumes permanently. What heart-rending discourses there were, every evening, after work, when they talked between themselves, regretting the ease of their childhood and deploring their present distress.

To tell the truth, Cyrille, even though he was the most wretched of the three, complained less than the other two. At times, thinking about things, he considered the horizon where the little stars vacillated; perhaps he saw them as silver wagtails and golden finches and, repenting of having caught them in his nets of azure, set them free in the dusk.

Now, outside the village church one Sunday, a charlatan arrived, clad in finery of all colors, who sounded his trumpet while the ears of two brightly caparisoned donkeys hitched to the caravan painted red and green went up and down, as if to say: "Well, let's go, come on, it's this way!" and they brayed as if they were trumpeting too. But the charlatan did not extol, as his peers usually did, some drug good for curing all maladies, and did not offer to replace rotting teeth with pearls fished up from the seas of India by sea-serpents rained for that exercise. What he offered for sale, in pompous harangues, when he took his trumpet out of his mouth, were three ebony caskets, closed but fitted with their keys, each of which contained an incomparable talisman.

Whoever bought one of those boxes would be before long, fortunate, glorious and superb among all the living.

"And you doubtless think that I sell these marvels very dear? No, Messieurs, I'm almost giving them away. If you have no gold, or silver, or copper, I'll content myself with some object, even of mediocre value. Come on, Messieurs, who wants to buy good fortune?"

Naturally, the villagers, a suspicious race, turned a deaf ear. How could anyone believe that one could acquire, for next to nothing, the most precious goods? The crowd, momentarily compact, dispersed with laughter and shrugs. Gerbert and

Amarin, prowling around the square, mocked no less than the other people, by Cyrille, pensively, said: "Who knows?" And he added: "Better to be always disappointed than never to believe. For myself, I think that we should buy the charlatan's caskets."

Often, although they made a show of not taking him seriously, his brothers followed his advice, so the three of them bargained for the boxes.

Gerbert obtained the first for a bunch of onions that he had stolen from his master's field.

Amarin paid for the second with a dab that was none too fresh, left on the shingle the day before by the carelessness of the boat-owner.

For the third, Cyrille gave a little sparrow fallen out of the nest, which, although he had held it with his hand open, had not escaped, because one of its wings was injured, and which he had kept under his rags in order to warm it up. But the charlatan had to swear that he would let the little bird fly away and that, if it were not healed, he would put it in the sunlight in a large cage with gilded bars with another sparrow, equally pretty, in order that it would not know the melancholy of twittering all alone.

A few weeks after that, there was talk, from the north to the south and the east to the west, of a king so considerable by the number of his subjects and so glorious by his fortunate wars that he was the envy of the greatest emperors of Europe and the most famous sultans of Asia.

It was Gerbert who had found all that power and all those victories in the casket bought with a bunch of onions. Whenever he was named, foreheads were lifted as if toward a clement god who might deign to smile, or lowered as if beneath a terrible god who was about to thunder. If he emerged from his palace, the prostrate multitudes gladly made a living carpet for his golden shoes; if he returned to his dwelling, a thousand courtiers, amid the joyful fury of clarions and the enthusiastic beating of drums, formed a long double hedge along the stairways of kneeling finery; and in the evenings, after the feasts in which servants clad in gold—who were princes who had solicited the honor of being his head waiters and cup-bearers—had served him on a silver platter the white meat of a Corsican fowl (for he did not have a large appetite) and poured Cape wine the color of burned topaz into a tiny glass (for he was not very thirsty) made of a veritable topaz, he scarcely slept under a brocade awning amid the amour of twenty young women from every country in the world, equal in beauty and yet different to such a degree that if they caressed him one after another, the first ecstasized him with a kiss that he only recognized after the twentieth.

But if Gerbert was the most powerful of monarchs, Amarin, in the same city, was the richest of merchants. He had found all treasures, and the art of trafficking them in order to increase them further, in the casket purchased with a none-too-fresh dab. His ships traversed the seas, and the seas brought him cargoes of rubies and chrysoprases, which, unloaded and heaped up, made piles so flamboyant that people thought they saw, when he opened his warehouses, conflagrations of crimson and gold. He also lent money at interest, which earned him a great deal of money. If he had wanted to buy the principalities of princes and the empires of emperors, and then sell them at a profit, nothing would have been easier for him, he possessed so much money in coffers as big as small hills, in the currency of all nations and the notes of all banks, and had such skill in commercial transactions.

You can well imagine that, rich as he was, he did not spend all his time adding up figures, inclined over a green book with a brass lock. He permitted himself distractions. A king by means of gold, as Gerbert was by means of the scepter and sword, he too knew the pride of walking over prostrate crowds, being adulated by kneeling parasites forming a hedge, and the joy by night of changing kisses.

To tell the truth, those two brothers divided the world between them, and they were the happiest mortals who had ever lived—with the result that, two or three years having passed, they began to suffer from ennui, to the point of yawning all day; and one of them would have given all his power, and the other all his opulence, for the possibility of a covetousness not yet assuaged. But what could they have desired, since they had everything, and more?

Neither the trumpets nor the drums diverted Gerbert from the melancholy into which he had fallen; it was all the same to him to walk over grateful napes and to pass between richly-clad hedges of courtiers, as he knew all kisses, various as they were. As for Amarin, you would have felt sorry for him if you had been able to see the bleak gaze with which he now considered the arrival of his ships laden with precious stones, It no longer gave him any pleasure to receive high interest on a sum lent to some poor devil, and more than once, bloated by wealth, he envied the flash of joy in the eye of a beggar after receiving alms of a liard.

They were both so unhappy that their thoughts finally turned toward their younger brother; they had not seen him for a long time. After the purchase of the caskets, they had left without worrying about him and without asking him where he was going. Doubtless Cyrille, too, had found triumphs and joys in the marvelous box; but like his elder brothers, he must, at present, be weary of his good fortune, suffering from no longer wanting anything, having possessed everything; and because satiety produces evil thoughts, they imagined that in the sight of another's ennui they would find some alleviation of their own.

Thus, they both set forth in search of their younger brother.

The earth is vast; many days went by before they arrived—hazard alone having served as their guide—in the land where Cyrille lived.

It was one morning in April when they perceived him. He was lying in the grass of a cliff overhanging the sea. One might have thought that he was asleep there, so tranquil;

finches and wagtails were fluttering above him, very close to him, in the sunlight.

What astonished the newcomers was that he was dressed in rags, as before. What! Had the charlatan cheated Cyrille, then? Had he given him a box without a talisman? At the sight of that poverty, a pride returned to them, in spite of the distastes they had known, one for his grandeur and the other for his opulence. They approached, with a nasty intention of triumph.

But they saw that Cyrille was not asleep, and in his half-closed eyes, raised toward the sky, there was such a perfect, ecstatic expression of delight that envy immediately rendered them their ennui. Yes, certainly, he was happier, happier than he had ever been, that young man clad in rags, who was enveloping the nascent daylight and the birds with bright and light caresses.

They, however, hid their disquiet regarding his happiness beneath a feigned pity.

"Oh, my God, I find you in a bad way, little brother!" said Gerbert.

"You're surely in a state appropriate to touch our hearts," said Amarin. "We'll certainly come to your aid."

"The casket hasn't give you any help, then?"

"You haven't found anything in it to extract you from your destitution?"

Without turning his gaze away from the celestial distances, Cyrille replied: "Oh, don't speak ill, my brothers, of the box I was given in exchange for an injured sparrow. For I owed to it, and still owe, and always will owe, infinite delights."

"What, then...?" asked Gerbert, jealously.

"...did it contain?" Amarin finished, seized by rage.

"I don't know," said Cyrille.

"You don't know..."

"...what there was inside?"

"How would I know, since I haven't opened it?"

His elder brothers looked at one another, believing him to be mad. But in a slow and soft speech, he said: "Oh, dear little box, you have given me something better than the real joys that you enclose, since, thanks to you, I have been able to dream about them. So vivid in being possible, but sweeter and more durable for not being true, I shall always have them, not having had them, and they will never disappoint, since you will always remain closed, my eternal future!

"Go, my brothers, go; return to your life, and leave me to meditate here, my eyes and my soul in the heavens, amid the daylight and the wings. There is no happiness that is worth as much as one's chimera, in an order not to be tempted to open the casket, I have thrown the key in the sea."

The Soul in the Corner of the Wood

One moonlit night in winter, in the time when I was a highway robber—and then, I gave no thought at all to the beautiful rhymes of the sonnets I made later—I saw a soul lying in the glass at the edge of a wood, a frail little soul which, all alone there, was asleep...yes, alas, there, oh, alas, there! And at first I turned away, for what had I to do with a soul? What I needed was some colporteur with a full sack, some farmer returning from the fair where he sold his chickens and his calves.

Not having eaten since the grouse that one of my friends, a poacher, had given me two days before, and which, being famished already, I had swallowed raw, feathers and all, with what suddenness I would have attacked the passer-by charged with coin! And if he had hesitated to surrender his money to me, I would have killed him without any remorse, thinking of the good meat and vulgar wine in the nearby inn, kept by a famous receiver. Certainly, I would not have had any remorse, having been hungry! A hundred times I had stolen, twenty times I had killed, and I had the placid conscience of a wolf or a child.

As for the little soul asleep there, it could not have been of any utility to me. I was about to go on my way when, involuntarily, I looked at it again. It seemed to me, so radiant was it in the moonlight, that it was entirely clad in diamonds and amethysts! To tell the truth, I had never had such fine stones; I learned later that those amethysts were Dreams and that the diamonds were Glories.

I launched myself forward, my hands outspread for rapine, and I grabbed the soul by the neck.

"Oh, don't strangle me!" it said, waking up with a start. "Anything that you want, I'll give you. I'll even give you, if you don't do me any harm, another diamond, which I don't have on me, but which I have within me, the purest and the most beautiful of all: Amour. Only be gentle with me; that's all I ask of you; and you'll see how resplendent and warm it is, the kohinoor that I reserve for whoever doesn't brutalize me."

But my rage was unleashed; I couldn't constrain myself; I strangled the soul, the little soul, and then I carried away the jewels in which it was clad.

Since that time I've become illustrious among men. I scarcely remember being a highway robber. Thanks to the Dreams I stole and the Glories that I usurped. I sang verses that the enthusiasm of crowds repeats in public celebrations. But the remorse that I did not know, once, after so many thefts and murders, is now tearing me apart! And what desolates me and sickens me above all, is that I don't have, and will never have, the other diamond, the purest, the most beautiful of all, which the soul didn't have on it, which was within it, and which it would have given me, if I hadn't killed the little soul at the corner of the wood.

The Cruel and Glorious Alms

It might be the case, however, that the irony of the Unknown is mistaken, and, thinking that it is humiliating humans, is uplifting them. Mystery, if it chances to play practical jokes on poets, has reason to fear that they might transform them into glorious sublimities.

On a night in August, resplendent with stars, the good rhymer Albert Glatigny, having climbed a long hill, sat down on a stone, out of breath, and very sad. The day, in the city, had been cruel to him. The editors had said: "Your verses? What would we do with them?" The beautiful young women had said: "Your amour? We don't want it." And the best of his friends, at dinner, had refused him two francs. Glatigny had gone into the country. He had sat down on a stone. He gazed at the dazzling sky, and he extended his hand toward divine charity.

"Eternal skies," he said, "Enormous skies, skies of splendor and clemency; since the earth has refused me, not only glory and amour, but bread, it's toward you that I'm raising my sights, from you that I'm begging. Gods, or God, it doesn't matter, let me have a sou, in order that I can buy a small loaf of bread."

Now, in eternity, Mystery resolved to play a joke on him. "Here," it said, "is a poet asking for a small coin. I could give it to him, but I'd rather play a trick on him."

And in response to a sign, a shooting star was detached from the sky and fell into the imploring hand, and burned it, and burned the arm as well, and made the shoulder sizzle.

Then Mystery burst out laughing. "Ha ha ha! He doesn't have the sou he wanted, and he's a pitiful state, and he'll die of hunger."

But Albert Glatigny, standing on the stone, raising the ember of his arm, cried, full of proud joy: "Yes I'm suffering! Yes, I'll die of hunger! But I've had a star in my hand!"

PART VI: FABLES, APOLOGUES AND ALLEGORIES

The Sacred Tree

Impelled over unknown seas by a wind that had never yet inflated sails, the ship of the Conqueror, after the tempests, the reefs and so many vague mirages, finally made landfall in a deserted country. There, the new nation that the prophets had announced was to be established triumphantly, and the leader descended on to the shore with his companions, armed with pikes and axes.

A forest loomed up before them, immense, inextricable and grim, in which beasts jealous of their solitude were roaring and hissing.

At that sight, many of the men recoiled.

"This land," they said, "is not propitious for the foundation of a city, and it is appropriate for us to set sail again in order to discover another."

But the Conqueror elected by Providence replied:

"It is here that the city must be built. Instead of roots, the foundations of habitations of the sons of Adam will plunge into the soil, and their roofs will rise higher than the highest foliage. A humane and fraternal race will increase and multiple where the snakes and tigers pullulate. Cut down the brushwood; fell the trees. To work, comrades!"

No one resisted that order. On the edge of the footrest, before the armed hands, there was a ripping of foliage, a cracking of branches, and the flight of frightened beats into the depths of the woods.

An ax attacked an oak.

It was a tree so tall and so majestically crowned that the men had never seen its like in their homeland. It dominated the entire forest, like the giant king of a dwarf people, and the eagles that circled its summit appeared no larger, seen from below, than songbirds over an eglantine.

At the first stroke of the ax, a grave voice spoke, emerging from the oak.

"Men come from afar, what fury is driving you to outrage my antiquity? A long time before the first-born wailed on the breast of the first woman, I stood up, opening the profundities of the earth with roots, tearing the clouds of the sky with branches, and the fall of my acorns has down around me the multitude of my race. Eternal witness of ephemeral things, I have seen deluges fall that have not carried me away, volcanoes erupt from the ground and reenter it; islands surge from the waves and sink again. Back, sacrileges! I am the immemorial ancestor, venerable to God himself."

The woodcutters interrupted their work, troubled by dread and gripped by religion. Before the august oak, similar to a paternal old man, the ax trembled like the arm of a parricide.

But the Conqueror said: "A man goes to the conclusion of his will, without lingering over vague respects. Oak, I shall sculpt from your braches the beams of my roof, as I would build, if it were necessary, the house that is my due with the bones of my ancestors."

Under the fury of efforts, the tree fell in a formidable din, bending, breaking and knocking over the plane trees and the elms; a lioness, caught by the fall of the trunk, unable to free herself, roared and writhed.

An ax attacked a birch.

It was a slender and graceful tree, which inclined, even in the absence of a breeze, as if gripped by fear or modesty, with a rustle of silver frissons.

Under the ax, a soft voice spoke, which emerged from the birch.

"Men come from afar, why are you doing me harm? Can you not see how delicate and fragile I am, and will you not take pity on me, so weak? Several of you have doubtless left at home, in their distant fatherland, a wife or a fiancée whose amour has followed them with the swallows that fly around the masts. Look! Look! Am I not as svelte as them? Have I not, in the tremor of my leaves, the dread that stirred them on the evening of the first kiss? Listen: you will recognize, in my sighs under the wind, her dear scattered voices. O lovers, O husbands, you will not be cruel enough to torture the tree that resembles the beloved!"

The woodcutters interrupted their work, troubled by a memory of amour. Before the pretty birch, in which the grace of young women lived, the ax trembled, as in the raised hand of a child asking for forgiveness.

But the Conqueror said: "A man goes to the conclusion of his will, without lingering over vain tenderness. Birch, I will break your weakness, which inconveniences me, as I would tear away from my neck, if necessary, the amorous caress that would slow me in my path."

Under a slight effort, the tree fell with a dying plaint. Bending, breaking and crushing the heather and the flowering herbs; a dragonfly, trapped beneath the fall of the trunk, unable to fly away, beat the air with its little wings.

A ax attacked a willow.

It was a melancholy tree, curbed over a dormant pool, allowing its branches to hang down, like the undone hair of a widow over a tomb.

Under the ax a sad voice spoke, which emerged from the willow.

"Men come from afar, will you no take pity on me, who weeps. Have you never wept yourselves and inclined, like me, over an eternal dolor? Have you not leaned over the bed in which a cherished child was dying, over the sepulcher in which a gray-haired mother had been laid? O fathers without children, orphan sons, spare me in the name of common mourning, and amid the solitude where the winds lament, let me weep into the dead water, leaf by leaf, forever."

The woodcutters interrupted their work, moved by the memory of the dead; before the desolate willow, which reminded them of the cemeteries of their homeland, the ax trembled like the arms of someone about to violate a sepulcher.

But the Conqueror said: "A man goes to the conclusion of his will, without lingering over vain despair. Willow, I will make useful flames with your branches and your leaves, without supplicant arms and your tears, as I would throw, if it were necessary, the planks of a coffin into the stove that cooks my food or the furnace of my forge."

Under a single effort, the tree fell with a sob, bending, breaking and overturning the nenuphars and pale lotuses of the pool; a flowery creeper, caught by the fall of the trunk, unable to free itself, was as pale as Ophelia retained by the hair.

In vain the other trees of the forest attempted to arrest the murderous axes by means of supplications. They all fell under the arms of the woodcutters, while the Conqueror saw in his mind the strength and the glory of the future nation. Finally, what had been an immense woodland, full of roars and hisses, was a plain where the city rose up. One single tree remained standing, which the last blow was about to fell.

A little bird, perched on a branch, said:

"What are you doing, men come from afar? I am the bird-poet of fresh spring mornings and warm summer nights. It is my custom to nest and sing in this tree. If you fell it, it will be necessary for me to take flight, and never again, never again, will anyone in this land hear me sing."

This time, the woodcutters with a disdainful laugh shrugged their shoulders, and the axes were raised.

But then the Conqueror said: "You who struck the august oak, the birch reminiscent of young women and the willow mourning the dead, leave that tree to that bird; it is sacred, since a voice sings therein. And a man would weaken under his task, devoid of joy and courage, if, in order to delight the soul and revive the heart, someone did not sometimes sing him a song."

Balbine's Heart

An old beggar, his empty sack over his shoulder, approached me as I was weeping, and said in a soft voice: "What are you doing here all alone on the edge of the forest, melancholy child, and why are your tears running over the violets and the moss, astonished by that warm dew?"

""Alas, good pauper," I replied, "what good would it do me to tell you the cause of my chagrin? You could not come to my aid; my dolor is not one of those that can be consoled."

"I know many things, having lived many days; when you have informed me of what afflicts you, my advice might not be as useless to you as you think."

"Learn, then, old beggar of the roads, that I am the son of a powerful monarch who has his kingdom not far from here, on the other side of the hill, and that I shall love until my dying day a young peasant girl, more beautiful than any princess, who comes to wash linen at the spring behind my father's palace.

"One morning last month, we met, Balbine and I—it was not by chance—on the edge of a wood, and the very place where I am weeping now. She sat down in the grass; I sat down next to her; and we talked about amour while the swallow fluttered and twittered around us. It would be impossible for me to say how happy I was; Balbine loved me as much as I love her; she permitted me to hold her frail and tremulous little hands in mine; during the confessions, her lips touched mine, with the result that our words, mingled when scarcely proffered, were like the song of two little birds pecking one another over the edges of two nests that were almost touching.

"Oh, how tender she was, and how clement her heart was to me! Time passed, however. As the sun became very hot, Balbine was thirsty, and asked me, pointing her finger at the leather bottle encrusted with precious stones that hung from

270

my waist, to go and fetch her a little water from the spring in the forest.

"It was cruel for me to quit my friend, but pleasant for me to obey her. I hastened through the braches, frightening wings and scratching myself on thorns, but, diligent as I was, my absence hasted no less than a quarter of an hour, for the spring is rather distant, out there among the rocks, and when I returned—oh, good pauper, good pauper, what a terrible thing!—I no longer saw Balbine. She had disappeared— perhaps disappeared forever, because, for two weeks, I have searched for her and called to her in vain.

"Such is my adventure, old beggar of the roads; that is why I am weeping unconsolably, and you can do nothing for me, unless you know what has become of the pretty peasant girl who came to wash linen behind my father's castle."

"I know exactly what happened," said the old man.

As I considered him attentively, already suspecting that he was a genius disguised as a pauper, such as one encounters frequently on the roads, he continued speaking.

"Lean the truth, melancholy prince. Scarcely had you left in order to go and fetch the water, than Balbine, a trifle weary, went to sleep in the grass. That was a great imprudence. Her breath, more odorous than any perfume, tempted the passing wind, and the wind took that breath.

"As she spoke in a dream, saying her name, a nightin-gale, with a flap of its wing, carried away the voice that she had on her lips.

"Two doves saw her snowy whiteness and, jealous, stole it from her.

"A pale eglantine that wanted to be pink charged two butterflies with going to steal and bring to her the redness en-closed in the child's mouth.

"The sun, which saw her asleep, recognized that she had hair more golden and brighter than all its radiance; in order to be more luminous at midday, it stole the gold of the hair lying loose in the moss.

271

"The sky thought: *the broad daylight will not last much longer; this evening, would I not be proud to have, amid my blue shadow, the stars that are slumbering beneath Balbine's eyelids?*

And, I know not how, the sky took possession of your friend's gaze. Then other beings and other things deprived her further, and in the end, when you returned from the forest carrying a little fresh water in the jewel-encrusted leather bottle, nothing any longer remained of Balbine on the deserted edge of the wood."

"My misfortune is as great as possible then," I cried, sobbing, "for I shall never be able to recover my beloved, scattered throughout nature."

But the old man said to me: "Nothing is impossible to those who love truly. Go, search, demand, implore, and obtain from the thieves that they restore the dispersed treasures. Every time you have recovered one of Balbine's charms, put it in this sack that I am giving you, and when it contains all the beauties for which you are weeping, empty it on the grass all at once. You will see, as herself, the young peasant girl who came to wash linen at the spring in the royal garden.

It would be difficult to imagine all the difficulties I had in making the authors of the larceny see reason.

The wind replied that, no longer having Balbine's exhalation in its breath, it would no longer think itself worthy to brush the mouths of young women or the calices of young roses.

"If her voice is taken back from me," the nightingale objected, "no one will listen to me in the silence of long summer nights."

The doves said: "We'll be like black crows if we no longer have the whiteness of snow."

And the eglantine said: "Fie! To become as pale as a faded cheek again!"

As for the sun, in order to hide from my entreaties, it made the decision to hide behind a cloud with the stolen gold, and the night, that day, fell much later than on other days because the sky was afraid that the stars it had stolen would be recognized.

But I did not allow myself to be discouraged, either by refusals or evasive responses; I ended up obtaining full and entire restitution, and I emptied on to the grass the sack full of Balbine.

I saw her again!

No, among all the words that humans pronounce, there is not one that is capable of expressing what were then my joy and my enchantment.

"Oh, dear treasure, more precious for having been lost," I cried falling to my knees, "it's true then, that you're here, that I'm contemplating you, that I'm touching you, that I can hear you! Come on, follow me, let's flee together toward solitudes so profound that no jealousy will be able to pursue us there, and I can possess you there entirely, without fear of the thieving wind or larcenous doves!"

But Balbine, with an astonished expression, said: "Who are you, who are speaking to me thus? I do not think that I have given you the right to use such language with me, and you would do well to address yourself to other young women, because, for myself, I do not have any desire to follow you into solitudes or anywhere else, and amour is no concern of mine."

Such was my dolor on hearing those words that I would certainly have thrown myself into a river that ran nearby if the old beggar of the roads, having emerged from a ditch, had not held me back and said:

"I see what it is. I forgot to tell you that Balbine's heart, like everything else, has been stolen from her."

"By whom? Tell me, please!"

"By a wolf that passed by, in search of adventure, and which was lured by the heart of the young girl, so tender, rosy and appetizing."

I scarcely waited for the pauper to finish in order to launch myself into the nearby forest that was haunted by wild beasts.

The moon illuminated a vast clearing; there, I saw many wolves, which were howling at the pale star. I ran to them and I said: "For pity's sake, if it is one of you who took it away, return my Balbine's heart to me."

And there was so much supplicant tenderness in my voice that those ferocious beasts could not help being moved.

"Wait, wait," growled an old wolf that had gray hairs in its tawny pelt. "I remember an adventure that has some resemblance to the one you mention. Is it not a matter of a young heart, fresh and pretty, alive, which was palpitating on the grass at the edge of the forest one morning, a few weeks ago?"

"Yes," I cried, breathless with hope. "Return it to me, good wolf!"

"Return it to you! In truth, I'd consent to that gladly, for your despair touches me. But what have I done with it, that heart?" the animal continued, pensively. "Oh, I remember; it seems so tender that I reserved it for my cubs' meal. They assured me that they had never eaten anything so delicate!"

Alas, I have not ceased to love Balbine since she has recovered the perfume of her breath and the song of her voice, the snow of her breast and the rose of her mouth, and her sunny hair and her starry eyes; but she rejects me, and does not want to hear me, so pretty and so cruel; and my torment will never end, since the wolves have eaten the dear little heart that she had.

Flowers and Precious Stones

"Do you, whom so many young men adore, beautiful and cruel child, not want to love?"

She replied: "Listen to a story."

There was once, a long time ago, a peasant who had a garden beside his cottage enclosed by walls.

A girl passing by said to him: "I'm going to a rendez-vous, good peasant, near the water, under the willow tree. Let me come into your garden, I beg you; I'll pick a hyacinth there, which I shall put in my hair, in order that my lover will find me prettier."

But the peasant shrugged his shoulders and refused flatly. "Go on your way, indiscreet person. You'll find enough flowers to adorn yourself on the slopes of ravines. I don't want anyone to touch my hyacinths."

She went away, very discontented.

Three schoolboys came along, burned by the sun and limping with fatigue, dusty from a long journey. They stopped, and one of them said: "Good peasant, we set forth early in the morning, as soon as the star under which we slept was extinguished, and, weary as we appear to be, we are even wearier; let us, I beg you, enter your garden; we'll repose there on the cool ground in the shade of a flowery bush, in order to recover the strength that will permit us to complete our journey."

But the peasant shrugged his shoulders and refused again. "Go on your way, vagabonds that you are; you'll find enough clearings in the woods where you can lie on the grass; I don't want anyone to lie down in the shade of my bushes."

They went away, dissatisfied.

And many other people asked for permission to enter the walled garden. A page wanted to interrogate the daisies in order to know whether the lady for whom he wept night and day would finally deign to smile at him. A genteel woman, very proud and clad in rose-red suite would have been curious to know whether the haughty tulips had airs as grand as her own. A mild drunkard accustomed to sing songs after drinking would have taken pleasure in shredding roses into his glass, in accordance with the precepts of poets. To all of them the peasant made surly responses, shrugging his shoulders.

The rumor of his obstinacy spread so far and wide in the realm that it reached the king's ears.

"Harness my carriage!"

And His Majesty had himself conducted, in great pomp, all the way to the poor hovel.

"Open the gate of your garden, my good man; I am doing you the honor of waiting to visit you."

The king certainly thought that the obstinacy of which he had heard mention would not hold out against his will, but in that he was mistaken.

"Sire, you have great parks in which the long robes of marquises trail in the golden sands of the pathways; go and walk there, if it pleases you to see flowers and trees."

"What! Wretch! It's thus that you reply to one of the greatest monarchs in the word? Do you not know that, if such were my pleasure, I could order that you be put to the torture, or have you executed in the cruelest fashion?"

"You can do that, Sire, and you can do many other things as well, but not enter into my garden with my good will."

Fortunately, the king was not a wicked man.

"I see that I can obtain nothing by threats; it's necessary for me to use another means. If you consent to open this gate to me, I'll give you as many fine gems as the largest of your lilies can hold."

"No thank you; its stem would break under the weight."

"I'll permit you to draw from my treasury with full hands."

"It isn't with florins of ducats that I like to have my hand full."

"I'll make you a prince and accord you my daughter in marriage."

"It isn't a princess that I love."

The result was that the king was obliged to return to his palace, as crestfallen as the girl and the schoolboys, the page, the genteel woman and the mild drunkard.

Then the peasant, left alone, went into his garden. Oh, the innumerable and delightful flowers! Peerless roses, more exquisite than women's mouths, were blooming everywhere; the whiteness of jasmines made sheets of aromatized snow, from which the crimson of poppies sprang forth here and there; between the lilac bushes, under the dangling wisteria, near the pompous dahlias, smiled in thousands, with a incomparable brightness, carnations, amaryllis, begonias and asphodels, as if all the greenhouses in paradise had shed their petals in that corner of the earth.

"Oh, my flowers, my dear flowers," said the rapturous peasant, "you are too beautiful to be delivered to the banal curiosity of passers-by, even if they are kings, and I alone, every summer, will be ecstasized by your colors and intoxicated by your perfumes!"

"The tale seemed pretty to me, so soft is your voice, but you haven't explained to me, beautiful and cruel child whom all the young men adore, why you don't want to love?"

She replied: "Listen to another story."

There was once, a long time ago, a gnome who lived in a grotto, in the depths of which, behind a rotating rock, there was a treasure. The treasure was not only ingots and gold coins, but gemstones, and talismans so precious that no fay had ever possessed the like.

A beggar, passing by, said to the gnome: "Good sir, it's more than two days since I've eaten, and I'm going almost naked in this chilly morning. Give me alms, I beg you, in order that I can buy bread in the nearby town and dress myself a little more warmly."

The gnome only replied with a burst of laughter, and sent the ragged man away.

A young man, out of breath from running, fell to his knees before the entrance to the grotto. "Good sir," he begged, "I shall have no other recourse but death if you don't help me. I love with the most ardent amour the daughter of a vavasour, who loves me no less; but her father, who is very miserly, judges me too poor to become his son-in-law. Oh, for pity's sake, give me some money—you, who are so rich, it would cost you so little? If not, I shall hang myself from that tree on the road, and the woman I love, heartbroken by my death, will throw herself into the river, in which her corpse will be found, pale and icy, among the water lilies and the sad nenuphars."

The gnome replied again with a burst of laughter and sent the amorous man away.

The latter hanged himself from the tree and the vavasour's daughter drowned herself in the river. The gnome refrained carefully from feeling any remorse.

A crowd, frightful to see, an entire population of the sick and the dying, precipitated toward the grotto, uttering lamentable clamors, for, because of the anger of a magician, there was a plague in the land.

"Sire, good Sire, extract us from peril, save us! We are suffering such pain that no one can have any idea of it, and all of us will be lying in the tomb within an hour; but if you give us a single one of your precious stones, which are talismans, we will recover health immediately, and instead of dragging ourselves over the stones, dying,, we shall dance and sing around fire of joy."

Among the crowd there were old men ready to render their souls, and young women whiter than the shrouds in which they would soon be clad; there were mothers who were almost lifeless kissing their expiring children tearfully.

The gnome uttered such bursts of laughter that those who heard them might have thought it the croaking an entire flock of crows, and he chased away the wretches who, too weak to regain their houses, all died on the highway.

Then, left alone, he went into the depths of the grotto and made the rock rotate. Oh, the innumerable and flamboyant precious stones! There were, in a formidable heap lavish with gleams, emeralds, chrysoprases, jacinths, amethysts, olivines, sapphires, rubies, diamonds, topazes, turquoises, tourmalines and girasols, the most beautiful of all gems; on might have thought that a summer sky had let its thousands of stars fall behind the rock.

"Oh, my treasure, my dear treasure! Radiance! Splendor! Dazzlement! You are too magnificent for me to deliver you to the covetousness of beggars or sacrifice you to the salvation of vile mortals, and I alone, until my eyes are blinded by them, will rejoice in your colors and be dazzled by your flames!"

"That tale, although a trifle sad, doesn't appear to me less pretty than the other, so soft is your voice. But once again, beautiful and cruel child, you haven't explained to me why you don't want to love."

She replied: "Listen to a story, the last one."

Once, in the dark, with my forehead on the pillow, caressed by the lace of the curtains, I was about to go to sleep. But it is necessary not to believe that the eyes of young women are extinguished behind close eyelids. No longer able to look outwards, they look inwards, and I saw within me—within my heart, within my soul—the most adorable spectacle: candor so fresh and blushing so tenderly, such white innocence, such delicate modesty, that none of the roses, lilies or jasmines behind the peasant's wall would have been comparable to them, and, at the same time, hopes so warm and tenderness so ardent that there were fewer flames in the gnome's grotto.

What flowers! What precious stones! What a garden I am, and what a treasure! Who, then, would be worthy to possess me? I know that I am too delightful and too precious not to be miserly with myself. Love, beg, sigh, weep—no matter! Even if, as in one of the tales, you were a king, and even if, as in the other, you were dragging yourself along the road, dying, you would not obtain from me the smallest rose, nor my least luminous opal. Oh, reign or die; I shrug my shoulders or I laugh, and I reserve intact all my enchantments, for the sole gaze of my closed eyes!

The Vanquished Shadow

Everyone in the world knew that a treasure was hidden in a certain room, which was the only one in an ancient chateau whose walls were still standing and whose ceiling had not collapsed. It was a treasure of inestimable value, consisting of pearls and precious stones, concealed under a flagstone or behind some pillar. Anyone who came to possess it would not only become richer than emperors and kings; he would also attain boundless happiness and limitless fame, for every one of the precious stones and the pearls was a magical object of irresistible power.

As you can imagine, there was certainly no shortage of people determined to lay their hands on that treasure. The people who lived in the neighboring town and those who lived in the surrounding countryside no longer devoted themselves to their business affairs or their work. They forgot to open their shops and they let the fields lie fallow; their one and only thought was to discover the hiding-place in that ancient room.

Indeed, people came from all the countries of the world to the ruins of the chateau; some on foot, others in stagecoaches or mounted on horses harnessed with gold. They all came: beggars and rich men, villains and gentlemen, poor women and princesses, all drawn by the prospect of an incomparable windfall. No one, however, was successful in this enterprise.

Why? Was the room sealed by a door so tightly shut or so solid that none had the power to open or penetrate it? By no means; it had no door at all, and the entrance was as large as the hallway of a palace. In that case, was one met upon the threshold by basilisks or dragons spitting fumes and flames? Not at all; no being or thing menaced the visitors, who could enter at will.

The only thing which prevented anyone from putting a hand upon the treasure was the fact that the room, whatever the hour or the season, was filled with an obscurity so black and so thick that the best eyes in the world could see nothing at all within it. There is no way to describe the intensity of the darkness which reigned there: the densest of other shadows, when compared to that one, appeared to have the transparency of dawn. The bright sun could hurl into that shadow its most luminous rays, but no light could ever insinuate itself, despite the vastness of the entrance, into the mysterious interior of the room. It was as if it were defended by a door of black diamond: impalpable, invisible, but utterly resistant to daylight.

Some of those who accepted the hazards implicit in entering the gloomy place subsequently said that it seemed that the pupils of their eyes had been plastered over by bitumen or pitch, but many had not come out back, having died of hunger before finding the opening.

By what means could one contrive to find, in that unparalleled darkness, a hidden treasure? Needless to say, all imaginable means of illuminating the room had been tried repeatedly. The people of the town had brought their lamps and torches, the peasants their sheaves of straw or corn, thoroughly dried-out and set vividly alight. The moment that such devices were brought to the opening, their flames were extinguished like sighs in a storm, even though no perceptible wind came out of the room. Bombs and shells had been hurled into it, and all manner of explosive devices; they would explode with an exceedingly loud noise, but without the least spark of light!

Emperors and princes, avid to possess the riches and the magical objects buried in the shadow, summoned their wise men, and said to them: "You will receive a share of the treasure if you manage to bring daylight to that room." The wise men did their utmost, inventing new combinations of oils and gases, which could burn even at the bottom of the sea. They rediscovered the secret of Greek Fire. They constructed an optical instrument whose barrel, containing a thousand lenses, could focus at a single point all the luminosity of the brightest noon.

All of this produced not the slightest effect; nothing was capable of bringing any pallor into that invincible darkness.

At that time there were in the land two poor children, a boy of sixteen years old and a girl of fifteen. They were handsome children, but they went about half-naked and in rags. They wandered about the roads, begging when there was anyone else about, collecting flowers when no one passed by—and they were better pleased to find a faded eglantine than to receive a newly-minted five centime piece.

You might have asked all the swallows who nested under the eaves, where the home of the children was, but they could not have told you, never having seen them enter or leave any house while they twittered with their heads outside their nests; the bare-foot urchins had neither home nor family. But in their turn, the swallows could remember very distinctly how they had brushed the children with their wings, morning, noon and night, out in the fields, or beside the streams, or in the golden greenery of the woods—everywhere, in fact, where there were buttercups which shone, dragonflies which hovered, sedge-warblers which sang.

Those vagabonds rejoiced in the mere fact of being alive. It was their pleasure to wander in deserted places, sunlit and flowery; the more they were by themselves, the more they felt part of everything. They had no troubles at all, except to find, in one village or another, a little bread which they might eat, some distance from the road, in the depths of some thicket, biting into the same crust until their teeth met in the middle.

All meals are exquisite to those who have a kiss for dessert, and if they had not the wherewithal to buy bread, they contented themselves with blackberries, or crabapples, which they disputed with the hedge-sparrows.

When they lay down to sleep without a roof over their heads they felt no sense of deprivation; what roof, be it a hovel or a palace, could be better than the crowns of the trees, or the

283

stars which studded the sky like sequins? And they had little to complain about because they were in rags, because, thanks to the holes in those tattered garments, they had no need to undress so that their bodies might come together.

It is true, of course, that it is not always spring or summer; that there are dull days in autumn and freezing nights in winter. December is the cruelest month; the snow is a cloak that does not prevent one from catching cold. Hunger comes whether or not there are berries on the brambles or apples on the trees to appease it; it is painful to have to go to sleep on an empty stomach, on hard ground, under leafless branches. But how can they suffer, those who love and are loved? I ask you, frankly, whether it is possible to be cold when one is enveloped by the flames of the heart, and whether one regrets having nothing to chew upon when one can put one's lips to an adored mouth?

Now it happened that while they were climbing a hill one warm afternoon, these two were overtaken by a great thunderstorm. There was a torrential downpour, interrupted by flashes of lightning and rolls of thunder. They took shelter under a tree, but they were given hardly any respite; the rain soon began to come through the canopy. They resolved to let it wet them—they were, after all, at liberty to shake their rags as the birds shook their feathers—but then they espied, close by, a large opening among the remains of a collapsed wall, heaped about with stones. They entered into the room where the eternal shadow reigned!

At first they were a little surprised by the darkness all around them. They alone, in all the land, did not know the story of the treasure hidden within the impenetrable shadow, being more attentive to the songs of thrushes than the chattering of wayfarers. But they were not afraid, because they were able to take one another by the hand.

They sat down on the flagstones within the chamber, huddling close together. They entwined their arms about one another, tenderly and happily.

"I love you!" said she.

"I love you," said he.

And then, because they had spoken that word—the sacred Word, which made the daylight and the heavens, that divine Word!—all the immensity of the room became suddenly more luminous than a plain of golden sand beneath the bright July sun!

Hearing their cries of astonishment, men and women flocked to the place in great numbers, for there were always people prowling nearby, in the hope that some accident of fate might liberate the treasure.

A great tumult grew up among that greedy crowd when its members beheld, through a crack in the wall, the scintillation and the radiance flamboyantly produced by glorious heaps of pearls and gemstones. With madly flaring eyes and grinding teeth, elbowing one another out of the way, falling over themselves in their urgency, they threw themselves forward.

They found within those walls such an abundance of wealth and so many magical objects that there was enough for everybody; many of those who were there that day became richer than emperors and more powerful than magicians.

The poor children who, in saying "I love you!" had dispersed the invincible shadows, were the only ones who did not think to demand a share of the treasure. They had another, sweeter treasure which was sufficient for their needs.

The storm having passed over, they resumed their journey across the countryside. A man passed by, and they asked him for five centimes.

"No!" said the man.

They did not complain. They smiled. They amused themselves by watching the sodden forest dry out beneath the re-emerged sun. The raindrops which dripped from the leaves were like jewels, and there were trembling pearls at the tip of every blade of grass.

Hygiene

When I arrived in the city toward which the hazard of reveries had conducted me, I could not help experiencing a great surprise, for it appeared to me that its only inhabitants were extraordinary aged old men. In the streets into which the smoke of factories fell back, on the thresholds of the soot-blackened houses, and at the windows, there was not one young face, but craniums that were bald if not white-haired, foreheads furrowed by wrinkles, lifeless eyes from which a dirty tear ran like the last drop of tallow from an extinct candle, toothless mouths with flaccid lips, and very long beads the color of trampled snow.

Shopkeepers who had difficulty standing behind their counters were measuring cloth or weighing gold powder with the tremulous hands of the moribund; sellers of old clothing, broken pots or worn-out shoes, leaning on the walls continually, so much were their legs buckling, were crying their wares in agonized voices. I saw one man leaning over a large book with brass corners; he was so weary that his head fell on to the folio at every minute, effacing with his nose or his chin the figures that he had traced there.

In a dilapidated hall where justice was being rendered, the judges and advocates were so old that some of them would certainly render their souls before the end of the trial. And, lamentably, none of those individuals displayed the serene, majestic, august beauty that decorates the old age of heroes and godlike thinkers with white hair, the ancestral beauty that constrains the most disrespectful adolescence to some veneration.

All I had around me was decrepitude and caducity, rendered even uglier by I know not what baseness. Al those centenarians must have occupied their days and used up their strength in sordid thoughts or vile employments. And in order for my ears not to be less offended than my eyes, coming from all directions—like the rising gurgle of an overflowing drain—was a continuous noise of inveterate asthma and ancient catarrh,

No, not for an hour, not for another moment, would I have remained in the morose city to which my dreams had taken me, if, just as I was about to flee, the most delightful spectacle that had ever marveled the gaze of a traveler had not suddenly appeared.

Beyond the shops, the tribunals and the factories, flourishing in sunlit daylight, was a wood of magnolias and large oleanders, where the chatter of springs enlivened the song of a thousand beautifully colored birds, which gave the impression of flying clusters of gems. There, on the mosses of the edge, in the more distant freshness of clearings, under the arbors of interlace creepers, young men were walking, so handsome that one cannot imagine anything similar, with their lovers no less young and no less beautiful, talking to them in low voices, lips near the neck, every word soon dying away in a kiss. How many happy couples under florid trees, and trains of brocade robes disappearing behind the thickness of bushes, into greater solitude and greater mystery!

Musical instrument were playing. Guided by that sweet sound, I approached a temple of pink marble. I saw adolescents playing the theorbo and the lute with a perfection of which one cannot have any idea; at the same time they were improvising verses, sonnets, rondeaux and ballads, which little pages on their knees were writing on sheets of Japanese paper. They were the most beautiful verses in the world.

Hidden behind a tree, I listened, having never heard anything as delightful, I listened for such a long time that dusk eventually fell in the wood of oleanders and magnolias: a dusk made of perfumes as if the shadow were the smoke of invisible censers. Then I thought that the adolescent lute-players and the lovers of both sexes would return to the houses of the city, but not at all. They headed, with me following, toward a palace of alabaster and gold, which had suddenly surged forth, as if by magic, and they went into an immense hall, decorated with statues and paintings, where a magnificent feast was served.

They sat down, ate from silver plates and drank from Venetian glass in which the light of chandeliers was opalescent. Each of the young men had a bare-shouldered young woman next to him, who sometime put her arms around his neck, with a sound of heavy satins sliding; and because of the good wines, because of the intoxication that emanated from beautiful living flesh, amid the splendors of marble and fabrics, beneath the streams of light, they had all joy in their eyes and all glory on their foreheads. But it was not their joy or their glory that I admired most. What made me ecstatic was their florescent and radiant youth, similar there to a vast blossoming of new roses set ablaze by a dawn awakening.

One of the guests perceived me and said to me: "Take your place among us. You will be such as we are if you are not unaware of the art of beautiful rhymes..."

"I have, at least, studied them," I said.

"...And if you love beautiful women."

"I love them all too much!" I exclaimed.

However, I hesitated to sit down. I thought about the sad old men, the sight of whom had frightened me a little while ago. Imbued with the honest advice that serious people never cease to lavish, I feared that so much caducity and decrepitude was the punishment of an existence devoted to frivolous art and the voracious kisses of beautiful women.

"Alas," I murmured, "I would like nothing better than to be similar to one of you, but will I not become, later, similar to one of your fathers?"

"Our fathers?"

"Yes, the old men I saw in the streets, in the shops, near the factories and in the hall of justice."

All the guests burst out laughing. "They aren't our fathers!"

"Your grandfathers," I said. "I ought to have guessed."

The bursts of laughter redoubled. "Oh, no—they're our sons!"

Their sons!

As I gave signs of the most perfect amazement, the one who had spoken first expressed himself in these terms:

"Once—I no longer know the months or the year for too many innumerable days have passed since that time—an immortal couple came to this land. They were the god of Poetry and the goddess of Amour. They taught us verses and the kiss. Since that time, forgetting all vulgar duties and all vain labor, hypocrisies, ambitions and lucre, we have lived, madly and furiously, in the intoxication of the lyre and lips. Without repose, without slumber, we have sung and we have loved.

"For beautiful rhythms and beautiful creatures, we have sacrificed, in hectic joy, everything that tempts imbecile humankind, without counting the minutes of our lives or the drops of our blood. We have been, and we are, the wisps of straw forever consumed and charmed by the double devouring brazier.

"Meanwhile, sons were born to us, sand we tried to transmit to them the teaching of the two immortals. The new races, alas, differed from the races of old; other cares absorbed them. Our sons, grave, methodical and precise, disdained rhymes and women. They shrugged their shoulders because we gave serenades at adored windows. They had factories built, installed counters, obtained employments. It pleased them to be laborious, rich and considered.

"Now they seem to be a hundred years old, those who still remember their cradles, while we, the centenarians are twenty! They, the sober and the placid, totter and cough, and are always ready to render their souls, while we, the enraged coveters of chimeras and delights, prodigal with all our being, are triumphant, robust, beautiful and happy in our unexhausted vigor. For youth is the miraculous bird that never ceases to flutter under the beautiful sun or the cherished stars, as long as it has the two sublime wings of poetry and amour!"

The Vielle Player

There was a merry evening feast in the main room of the inn. My God, the men who were there did not deprive themselves of anything. Haulers, colporteurs and farmers, sitting in front of white tablecloths, stuffed themselves with the most flavorsome victuals, sausages freshly grilled over embers of vine-braches, whole geese gilded by a crackling fire, tripe cooked three times in a little white wine, sharpened with verjuice; and they did not neglect to drink as much as they ate. As for any idea that they might end up running out of food or drunk, that could not occur to anyone, for the poultry removed from the spits was immediately replaced by others, and without repose, bare-armed maidservants came back up from the cellar laden with old dusty bottles. It was a veritable orgy of gluttony, such as had never been seen, and all those men at table, healthy, plump and happy, who had the wherewithal in their purses to pay the bill, displayed the roundness of their bellies and added to the cheerful light of the lamps and candles the redness of their illuminated faces.

While they continued to eat and drink, a young boy, thin, pale and as pretty as a sickly girl, clad in rags, with no hat and barefoot, came into the inn with a vielle on his back.[42] He was doubtless one of those little wandering musicians who go from town to town, showing in the main square a monkey in the uniform of a general. But this vagabond seemed more wretched than the majority of his peers. He did not even have

---

[42] Although the term *vielle* was originally applied to a Medieval stringed instrument ancestral to the violin, employed by troubadours, it was also applied from the late fifteenth century to a hurdy-gurdy, which produced sounds by means of a hand-cranked wheel; later versions were equipped with a keyboard. The instrument featured here is evidently of the latter type.

a monkey! His must have died of starvation or cold, in some roadside ditch, when the snow was falling on the trees devoid of flowers or fruits.

"What are you doing here, beggar?" demanded the inn-keeper.

"I would like to be served," the boy said, "a fat chicken, well roasted, and a bottle of the best wine in the cellar."

The innkeeper burst out laughing. "Do you have the money to pay for such a meal?"

"Alas, no. Money, I've never possessed, and if I had any, it would have fallen out through the holes in my rags."

"Get out of here, then, little wretch. And don't dare to set foot in my inn again."

The musician lowered his head and left the room. He was so weak, perhaps because of a long fast, that he could not drag himself as far as the road. He fell down on the steps of the perron and remained motionless.

In the inn, no one spared him a thought; it is not while one is eating that one spares a thought for those who are hungry. However, a few people, at the sound of music, put their noses to the window. The boy was playing the vielle, and when he had stopped playing, those who were watching him had good reason to be surprised, for there, on the steps of the inn. Even though there was no table before him, nor any sort of nourishment or beverage, he was making the gestures of someone eating and drinking, and saying, in a delighted voice: "Oh, how good it is! Oh, the delightful ambrosial honey! Oh, the incomparable nectar!" And the clicking of his greedy tongue was audible.

The king of that land had invited all the noblemen of the region to a feast, in order that the princess, his daughter, could make the choice between them of a husband worthy of her. The most famous gentlemen, counts, dukes and marquises, did not fail to come to the court in great pomp, for there had never been a young woman in any country as perfectly pretty as the princess; the dream of being her husband was the most beautiful that it was possible to form. You can imagine how re-splendent the feast was at which so many handsome noblemen were gathered, clad in the richest garments, and bedecked with jewelry!

While the king's daughter, sitting in a large crimson and gold armchair, was considering all those glorious suitors, not without disdain, something strange happened. A poor young boy, thin and pale but pretty, clad in rags, whom no one had seen enter, slipped into the crowd and arrived close to the gold and crimson chair.

There was a great scandal! Chamberlains hastened to ex-pel the intruder.

"What are you doing here, beggar?" the king demanded.

"I would like," said the boy, "the princes to be given to me in marriage."

The king burst out laughing. "Are you noble, as it is ap-propriate to be in order to aspire to such a marriage?"

"Alas, no. I never knew my mother or my father; it was a brave man, whose profession was robbing travelers in the woods, who found me, one morning in December, new-born, devoid of swaddling-clothes and shivering, on a heap of stones where I had been abandoned."

"Get out of here, little wretch, and never dare to set foot in my palace again!"

The child lowered his head and left the hall. But he drew away very slowly, perhaps because of his great amour for the king's daughter; having arrive on the terrace he sat down on the paving stones, amid the palm trees, the orange trees and the large flowering cacti.

As you can imagine, no one in the palace spared him a thought; it is not when one is seeking to obtain the love of an illustrious princess that one worries about an abject rival who has been dismissed.

However, a few little pages, at the sound of music, put their noses to the window. The boy was plating the vielle, and when he had stopped playing, those who were watching him had good reason to be surprised, for there, on the terrace, where no woman, young or old, was beside him, he was making the gestures of someone embracing with delight an adored individual, and saying, in a swooning voice: "Oh, how beautiful you are, my darling! A hundred times more beautiful than the king's daughter! Oh, how happy I am!" And the sound of hectic kisses was audible.

Now, the story of these adventures, and a few others almost similar, did not take long to circulate throughout the land. Most people thought that the young boy was a lunatic, but another idea occurred to others: perhaps the vielle was a talisman by means of which the musician obtained the realization of all his desires. He had been refused something to eat? He only had to play the vielle for a magnificent feast to be served before him. He was denied shelter? A few chords of the instrument transformed into a soft couch the stones of the road or the brambles of the wood. He was not given the young woman with whom he was smitten? Thanks to a little music, he saw himself surrounded by the prettiest women and the most famous princesses, who put kisses on his mouth.

Naturally, that opinion was born among those who conceived the desire to possess the omnipotent vielle. More than one took it into his head to follow the vagabond, in the hope of surprising him while asleep on the far side of some embankment and stealing his talisman.

Once, when the boy was asleep, unsuspectingly, on the moss of a clearing, three evil men—a rich peasant, a bourgeois from the town, and a lord of the court—slipped up to him and fled, taking away the vielle. As you can imagine, it was not long before they wanted to test its power.

"For myself," said one of the thieves, turning the handle, "I desire to regale myself with a young larded guinea-fowl, with truffles and pistachio nuts!"

But no served table emerged from the ground.

"For myself," said another, "I want to see a magnificent castle rise up with four towers, built in pink marble."

But no edifice surged forth from the ground.

"For myself," said the third, "I ask that the most beautiful young women in the world come to dance around me, showing their bare arms and naked breasts!"

But it is probable that the most beautiful young women in the world were otherwise occupied at that moment, for not one of them appeared.

The disappointment of the three wicked gentlemen is easily imaginable, and what redoubled it was a loud burst of laughter behind them. The boy, having woken up, had followed them, and was holding his sides while mocking them

"Go on, go, on, turn the handle, run your fingers over the keyboard, it won't do you any good!"

"What! Your vielle isn't a talisman, then?"

"Of course it's a talisman! But you won't get any advantage from it; its power depends on the tune one plays on it, and you'd have to be able to play it as well as me."

"We'll learn the music that it's necessary to play!"

"You'll never know it, villains that you are," said the child of the highways, "for it's the ingenuous song of the dream, which is only known, without their having learned it, to poor poets with pure hearts."

The Black Crystal

In the epoch, already distant, when rock crystal, blacker than the blackest night, had the opacity of charcoal...

An impatient reader might not let me say any more and swear that such an enormity is intolerable. "What? The luminous transparency through which one can see the stars, and which illuminates the gold of Tokay or Lacryma Christi so prettily, was once an obscure thing, resistant to light? That is the most ludicrous idea in the world; you can well imagine that we won't believe a word of it."

Nothing however, is more true. But since an affirmation might not be sufficient, I shall put off until another day the tale that I had intended to tell, and relate the pleasant circumstance in which rock crystal, blacker than charcoal, became as clear as diamond, which will prove that it was not always so.

The daughter of the King of Ormuz, who was the most beautiful princess in the world in the times when all the princesses were pretty—ugliness was only seen, in those days, in peasant cottages or the houses of merchants; all that, has changed, thank God!—was walking in the country one summer afternoon with a little page who was carrying her train.

She was so magnificently dressed in yellow satin, gilded muslin and all her jewelry, that you might have taken her for a ray of sunlight with the appearance of a damsel. But the little page did not waste time admiring the diamonds and the pearls, or the luminous fabrics. What occupied him was the slightly russet nape of the neck whose curls unrolled beneath the chignon of the princess, and the slender feet, clad in ermine, that he perceived momentarily beneath the skirt, lifted a little too high.

He sighed, with a sadness that would not have failed to move you, for he loved the daughter of the King of Ormuz as

295

tenderly as is possible, and it is cruel—agreeably too, but cruel—when one has an exceedingly smitten heart, to see a foot of which you will never know the leg, and a neck, with a down like a golden moss, where so many kisses that come to your lips will never find their nest. On hearing the poor child sigh, the roses of the road became suddenly melancholy.

A pigeon, under the mystery of the foliage, said to his dove: "There's a boy who had much to lament."

But the dove replied: "Hey! What are you thinking about, when I'm cooing?"

The princess was even nastier than that wood-pigeon. No, not nasty—indifferent. Did she spare a thought for the little page behind her, who was lamenting? At that moment, four crowned sovereigns had asked for her in marriage: the King of Mataquin, protected by the fays; the Emperor of Trebizond, who had built, in order for her o deign to enter it, a palace in which every column was made of a single ruby and every window of a single pearl; the Prince of Bagdad, who had in his gardens, on the stems of bushes, instead of roses and hyacinths, stars that genii went to collect for him every evening in the sky—if they had been collected the evening before he would have said: "Bah! They're faded!"—and the Rajah of Visapour, whose colossal throne was placed on the back of four white elephants, which had musical instruments in their trunks, from which sounds emerged so melodious that one might have thought that the huge beasts were full of little birds.

Which of the four suitors would she choose? It might also be the case that she would incline in favor of a very rich merchant who had brought back from his voyages Aladdin's lamp, Solomon's ring and a little pebble that was even more precious, for every time another stone was struck with it, sparks sprang forth, each of which immediately became fourteen thousand gold angelins.

As one can imagine, solicited by such lovers, the most beautiful of princesses was scarcely thinking about her little page. What would become of him, the one who was sighing?

Well, on the day of the wedding, he would carry the train, among the strewn flowers and fine gems.

She, still swollen with pride, and he, still sighing, arrived on the shore of a great lake, so blue, so pure and so diaphanous that one might have thought that the sky had allowed itself to fall upon the earth, and as she was weary, because of her long walk and the sun, the daughter of the King of Ormuz sat down on the sand, on the edge of the water, from which a freshness was emerging.

Later, the Emperor of Trebizond, who would not be the husband of the princess, having learned that she had reposed on that sand, sent men to take away, in gold baskets, as much of it as they could carry, and spread it on the staircase of his palace' it is since that time that the courtiers of the emperor only climb toward their master's throne walking on the banisters, because it would be very unbefitting even for illustrious people to put their feet on sand on which the princess had deigned to sit down in the midst of her inflated skirt.

Sitting there, she gazed at the beautiful cool lake, and the fantasy came to her to bathe in it. Since it resembled a sky, it was worthy of a star. Oh, what a beautiful, white star she would be, so softly radiant in her scattered hair, in that azure. But what made her hesitate was the presence of the page standing behind her. When one is a princess, one does not undress in front of such a petty individual, and in any case, as she had been well brought up, she would probably not have consented to undress even before a very great lord.

Send away the page? She had thought of that, but returning to the palace soon without being accompanied was an extremity reproved by etiquette. Perhaps she would have renounced bathing in the lake if she had not seen, not too far away, between the rocks, amid dangling ivy, a kind of great black block, the sight of which gave her an idea.

"Little page," she said, "I think that I shall bathe in this water, which is the most beautiful in the world. During that time, you will stand behind that block over there, which gives the impression of a wall of charcoal. Go, keep quiet, and don't budge.

"It will be done as you desire, Highness."

And he hid behind the black thickness, while the king's daughter began to take of her yellow satin skirt, all her jewelry, and her stockings—which she had a great deal of difficulty taking off, because they resisted, wanting to stay where they were, amorous of her lily-white legs and little pink feet.

It would be difficult to give an idea of the despair to which the page abandoned himself behind the dark wall. What! So close to him—he could hear the rustle of sliding fabrics—the princess was allowing the sight in broad daylight of her arms, her shoulders, and, little by little, her body of florid snow. A passing bird could gaze at a bosom as fresh and round as a double clump of may-blossom; a butterfly almost had the right—rendered innocent but its habitude of roses—to alight on one of the tips of the princess's breasts! And it was necessary for him, devoured by virtue of a foot glimpsed in the ermine footwear and a slightly russet nape beneath the chignon by the desire to see all of that adorable person, to remain behind that dark thickness, through which even the blaze of the sun would not have been visible.

Certainly, he knew that it was not made for him, the divine body of the princess, promised to emperors or kings. To kiss it, to touch it, were dreams that he had never permitted himself. But at least, since the opportunity had presented itself, might he not glimpse it, and share the joy of the daylight, the birds and the breeze, which were not kings or emperors either?

Oh, what a temptation not to remain behind the somber obstacle, to take a step, to extend his neck; but he was a very honest servant; he had promised to keep quiet and not to budge; he would keep his promise—with the consequence that finally, hearing a loud noise of disturbed water—oh! oh! completely naked! She was completely naked, alas!—he started to weep because of all the joy that he might have had, and would not have.

He had it, however, for, moved to pity, the great black block, which was a block of crystal, was gradually clarified, and became as luminous as diamond, more diaphanous than the lake itself. And later, the Rajah of Visapour, to whom the princess was married, was quite wrong to believe that he had been the first to see all the snow mingled with red roses and russet moss that the fall of the nuptial robe revealed.

It is true that the little page had not have the opportunity to laud himself for the consequences of that adventure; he died shortly thereafter, of regret of the treasures that had appeared to him, but did he not carry away beneath his closed eyelids the wherewithal to charm the dreams of the eternal slumber?

It was, therefore, by virtue of compassion for an amorous pain that the crystal, from the black that it was, became perfectly clear, and if I were obliged to take a lesson from this tale, I would advise you, young women, to be suspicious of the pity of things. They are less cruel than you; they aid us when your barbarity constrains us to cry for help. If the wicked child whose smile tortures me ever takes it into her head to get into a bath, one day when I am not too far away from her, let her beware. Let her not trust either the thickness of curtains or the opacity of doors and walls, for they might be moved by the anguish of my desire; the fabric, wood and plaster might become more transparent than the finest batistes, transparent to the point of allowing me to admire at leisure the mysterious intimacy of your charms, Mademoiselle, and even the little brown birthmark that you might have a little above the ankle.

Three Kinds of Good Fortune

Once—I was no more than sixteen years old—I encountered on the road a dainty child named Christine, who was walking alongside a hedge with the little steps of a hurrying bird. Why was she not flying, since she was in such haste? She certainly had wings, the little angel, hidden under the ratinelle of her dress., but it would have been necessary for her to take off her blouse, and, modest as she was, that is what she would never have consented to do in the open air. Trotting along, she was making the greatest possible diligence, not pausing to pick the clumps of may-blossom on which ladybirds put red dewdrops here and there, to listen to the chirping of quarreling hedge-sparrows, or to gaze and the quivering sparkle of dragonflies over the clear water. The spring must have been quite humiliated to see her traversing it in that way, without paying any heed to it.

"Well, here you are, my dear Christine," I said to her. "Where are you running to so rapidly, far from the little house where your grandmother is singing an old tune while spinning flax as white as snow on her spinning-wheel?"

At first, she hesitated to respond to me. There are confessions one dare not make to people passing by; finally, blushing, and lowering her eyes, the lashes of which were reflected on her cheek in little shadow fans, she said: "I'm going to met my lover, He's waiting for me in the aspen wood that you can see over there, to the right of the road."

"Oh, how right you are!" I exclaimed. "There are a great many young women who, in your place, would still be playing with their dolls or worrying about teaching their little sister to read. That's an agreeable diversion and an interesting occupation! Or they're busy with household chores, helping their mother and the servants dust the furniture, arrange the faience in the crockery cupboard, or patch underwear—excellent means of reddening the hands and breaking the fingernails.

"No, no, what it's appropriate to do, when one is young and pretty, is to offer one's lips to the person who desires them. It wouldn't be pleasant to live if it weren't pleasant to love. Give your heart, your dreams and al the mysterious charm of your blossoming adolescence, in a single bunch of fortunate flowers. Know that the mouth is made for kissing, as the rose is made for the caress of smitten bees; even when cruel, amour is the incomparable ecstasy; and after the joy of a smile, there is none more delectable than that of weeping. Go, go, my dear Christine, run quickly, faster still, toward the only sweetness and the only bitterness that make being born and not dying worthwhile."

But, undoubtedly, Christine had no need to be encouraged to tenderness, for, no longer listening to me, she was already far away, out there near the aspen wood, which I saw her enter with the dart of a swallow falling into a trap.

I made haste and approached. Behind the dense stir of grass and branches, I could not see anyone, but I heard—the birds had fallen silent in the attentive breeze—the sound of a kiss, and another kiss, and I wished my darling Christine a beautiful and long amour.

Another time—I still remembered, but already vaguely, the time when I was young—I encountered at a fête the beautiful Lady Christine traversing the hall of a palace with the arrogant stride of an empress who does not deign to smile.

She scarcely resembled, now, the little girl who was trotting so rapidly alongside the spring hedge. Less pretty, she was more beautiful, in the gleam of fabrics and the splendor of jewels; one could not have said whether the flamboyance that enveloped her was made by the light of the chandeliers or the amour of all the eyes fixed upon her. For the handsomest of princes, all the ambassadors and all the courtiers, only accorded attention to Christine; it was easy to see that the least smitten of them would have died of joy merely for the glory of kissing, on his knees, the cluster of golden ribbons she had on her ermine slippers.

But she paid no heed to so many amours and so much respect. Indifferently, she traversed the ecstatic groups. She did not even see, near the door, a little page who was looking at her, swooning languorously.

"Well, here you are, my dear Christine," I said. "Where are you going, then, with that pride, without compassion for the crowd that surrounds you and accompanies you with such ardent desires?

She did not reply to me immediately, considering me with disdain; you might have thought that she did not recognize me, the beautiful lady; finally, superb, speaking with the slowness that a spring certain of pouring out diamonds and pearls would put into its droplets, she said: "I'm going to meet the king; he's waiting for me in the gallery where the portraits of his ancestors are hanging; it's today that he ought to offer me, along with the title of marquise, all the booty of gold and precious stones that he obtained recently in his battles against the Rajah of Srinagar."

"Oh, how right you are!" I exclaimed. "There are many women who, in your place, would have stayed at home preparing soup for their husbands or washing dirt off their children. That's a noble employment of time and concerns befitting an intelligent person! Or, sensing reveries of the heart, they'd be softened by the murmurs of those princes, those ambassadors and all those courtiers ready to die of amour; perhaps they would go so far as to console with a tear the poor little page swooning between the golden braid of the curtains. No, no, the frenzied desire for glory and riches is the only one worthy of occupying the soul. What is important is to be saluted by the tremulous veneration of the people, to live in a house of marble and mosaics as august as a temple, to have inexhaustible wealth in one's drawers and coffers. Go, go, my dear Christine, go to meet the king, and you're very humble to be content with the title of marquise and the mediocre treasure of a rajah."

But Christine had not wasted time listening to me; she was already far away, in the vestibule paved with jade and malachite; and I saw her disappear through a tall door, the curtains of which fell back.

I had followed her and I approached the curtains; through the thickness of their majestic pleats I could not see anything, but I heard, in the fearful silence that falls in the dwellings of kings, the rustle and further rustle of a heap of gold and precious stones, and I wished my darling Christine a long and glorious opulence!

I encountered her one last time—I was even less young, almost aging, sadly. It was in an autumn dusk, on the wide flat road between a double row of elms with russet leaves. She had been laid, her face uncovered—as is the custom in that land—on a black litter that four men were carrying, and she was very pale because she was dead. Behind her extended the cortege of relatives, friends and mourners, who were lamenting under their long veils. And the sky, made of a single gray cloud, the black fields moistened by a slow rain, and the trees with scarce, rattling leaves, were all melancholy, on that delicate autumn afternoon, But she, being dead, did not see either the desolation of people or that of things; she had no sadness.

"Well, here you are, my dear Christine," I said to her. "Where are you going, then, with this morose pomp, far from your house, far from the city, far from life?"

I thought I was speaking in vain; it is infrequent for the dead who have scarcely gone to sleep to respond to people who are passing; however, without a quiver of the eyelids, without a movement of her lips, in a voice that was barely a breath, she said: "I'm going to my grave. It has been dug in the little cemetery you see over there, to the right of the road."

"Oh how right you are!" I exclaimed. "It's this time, it's this time that you're right. You've finally received the sweetest of kisses, the one that closes the lips forever, and Death is a king who gives you the incomparable treasure, the silent treasure of peace and forgetfulness. Let them hasten, the gravediggers, to lay you down in the soft and profound tomb, and let them throw over you a great deal, a great deal, of earth, in order that you will never again hear the vain murmur of things and the even vainer tumult of human beings."

I followed her. I did not weep.

Through the somber verdure of pines and the light tearfulness of willows, having remained to one side, I did not see the funereal bed descend into the grave; but I heard—amid the silence that rises from sepulchers—the repeated sound of the earth, falling in spadefuls, and I wished my darling Christine a long and good slumber.

Imperial Patience

Once, as the Emperor of Trebizond—he was a very calm monarch who meditated for a long time before acting, never rendering a decree or giving an order without having reflected at length, and who would not have allowed himself to be carried away by anger or impatience for anything in the world—was walking in the country with his twelve chamberlains he perceived a very ugly peasant on the road whose appearance was as disagreeable to him as possible.

Master of himself, as it was his custom to be, he cried, while making noble gestures: "Someone fetch my four executioners! Let them bring all their axes, all their woe blocks and all their instruments of torture. For it's truly intolerable that a man as hideous as that one dares to show himself to my gaze. To punish him for having offended my eyes, I want to make him perish under the worst tortures."

Knowing the forbearance of the master and what little danger there was in not obeying him very rapidly, the chamberlains raced away to look for the executioners.

While awaiting the return of his servants, the emperor was so placed that he spent the time biting the bark of a young birch tree until he broke his teeth on it. But while he was giving evident signs in that fashion of his patient humor, the peasant had gone on his way and now there was a little shepherdess on the road, so fresh and so dainty that one might have thought her an eglantine changed into a young woman by the power of some fay.

The emperor was so slow to make resolutions that he hesitated for more than three minutes before deciding to marry the passing shepherdess, and the chamberlains, followed by the executioners, had come back.

"It's truly extraordinary," he cried in a tranquil wrath, "that you always act recklessly, without giving yourself time to think about things. What need do I have of these executioners, these axes, these blocks of wood and all these instruments of torture? Go fetch me the twelve high priests who are lodged in my palace, and let them come in full dress to bless my union with that shepherdess, who will be the Empress of Trebizond."

The chamberlains rushed off in search of the pontiffs.

In the emperor's place, what would a man incapable of dominating his passions have done then? He would have seized, embraced, and carried off into some solitude the little shepherdess similar to an eglantine changed into a young woman. But while the executioners, who had stayed there and, not knowing how the use the time, were sharpening their axes on a big stone, he limited himself to knocking the girl down in the long grass that bordered the road.

He had scarcely finished raping her for the fourth time when the chamberlains and the high priests appeared, and he was irritated to such a point by seeing them in tumult, all out of breath for having been running—for he detested nothing more than disorder and precipitation—that he ordered that those over-zealous servants be put to death; but he enjoined the executioners to proceed methodically, with a sage slowness, warning them that they would be responsible before his cold justice if they employed less than ten minutes cutting off the heads of the twelve chamberlains and the twelve high priests.

Metempsychoses

Once, when we were talking about forms in which we have lived in past centuries—for everyone who has a little memory can recall their anterior existences—I asked the one who was my sole joy and my unique concern: "Do you remember, my most dear, having been loved in the distant past, when you were not yet the prettiest of present beauties?"

"Certainly I was loved," she said. "When I went up to the Ceramicus, clad and coiffed in accordance with the latest fashion, the richest and handsomest young men turned away from their route in order to compliment me on my costume and offer me golden ear-rings in exchange for a glance or the promise of a kiss, or the gems that Lydian slaves were carrying on crimson cushions behind them.

"Later, in Rome, it was for me, an impudent and magnificent courtesan, that lubricious red-clad cardinals killed one another in the streets after mass, or in the cloisters after supper. And once—for a hundred years is only a minute in the eternity of the migration of souls—I was such a beautiful woman in Porcherons,[43] and very virtuous as well, that the most noble gentlemen, amused by the rebuffs with which I responded to their enticements, made a glory of showing on their cheek the mark of my five fingers!

"I think I have also been, in another time, the very austere spouse of a Calvinist pastor who said to me, in adoration; "There are saints, however, since you exist!" and the fiancée of a lieutenant of hussars, who got himself killed in battle because, on the day he went on campaign, I refused him the rose of my corsage!"

---

[43] Porcherons was an ancient hamlet north-east of Paris where taverns accumulated in the eighteenth century and where the aristocracy went slumming.

I was quite satisfied, not without some jealousy, to learn that my friend, in all the hours of the past, had had the where-withal to please.

"And," I asked her, slightly anxiously, "do you remember having loved in the lives of old."

"Certainly I remember having loved," she said. "The queen of a barbaric country, I fought at the head of my army the men of the Occident who came to steal the treasures amassed under our desert tents; but after the victory I pierced my breast with an exceedingly sharp blade because one of my favorite young warriors had died in the battle. Clad in furs in my subterranean hut, I adored a handsome Greenlander, a hunter of narwhal and walrus. In my bedroom, as a marquise, I flirted, not without tenderness, with an abbé as fresh as a young damsel and a comte made up like an opera singer. In the time when I was known as Doña Leonor, I tore, lacerated and strangled with my two pink hands, which were all red, my rival Dolores in the bed of Don Paez. I've been a little grisette waiting for her lover and singing a song under the flowers dangling from hr skylight, and I've also been a frail bride, blushing all over and my heart hammering, in the nuptial chamber that my husband was about to enter."

That she had loved so many times annoyed me slightly. At least it proved the tenderness of her heart, persistent through the ages. I adopted the expression of someone who was very content.

"And do you remember," I asked her—oh, how anxious I was, this time—"having been, in those vanished days..."

"What?"

"Faithful?"

She reflected, and thought about it for a long time. Finally, she said: "No, I don't remember that."

That statement, as you can imagine, desolated me cruelly. How can one believe in the present constancy of a person who has not been constant at any time?

But my despair was not of long duration, for she threw her arms around my neck and said: "No, no, I have no memory of being faithful, but I'll remember it in my future existences!"

The Good Excuse

Let the beautiful young women who are reading these se-
rous lines not take immediate exception to the apparent impertinence of the words that I am going to write, but for the time
it takes to pass a powder-puff over a cheek, let them accord
me a benign attention; for, I swear that, far from wanting to
offend their natural modesty, my unique objective, in spite of
the contrary semblances, is to furnish a very valuable excuse
for certain infractions by which they frequently and so involuntarily belie the prefect virtue that is, as everyone knows,
their very essence.

Doubtless it cannot be denied: the most ingenuous damsels and the most honest ladies behave in many circumstances
as if the latter were not honest at all and the former not in the
least ingenuous; in order to specify only one case, experience
demonstrates that jealous skirts—I mean, with the skirts, the
underskirts of white silk or white muslin, and nainsook chemises more diaphanous than the air, and bloomers even more
transparent—hold the various charms they veil less securely
than the tunic of Nessus clung to the shoulders of Hercules.
(By the way, some people insinuate that the only reason that
Deianira did not use that tunic herself is perhaps because no
one would have been able to take it off her.)

It is incontestable that, from the month of June onwards,
one sees dispersing between the branches with the morning
mists many light undergarments poorly retained by complaisant resistances; in the same way that one could, in any season, contemplate in the penumbra of boudoirs or the better
alcoves, many pale fallen fabrics that have renounced being
obstacles.

Yes, that is certain: young women—and old ones too,
alas—appear to have, even in the hours when people are not
asleep, a strange propensity to be undressed by lovers full of

zeal. One might think, in verity, that they only get dressed in order to get undressed!

Given that point, ill-intentioned people, or those not up to date with things, do not fail to draw consequences unfortunate for the renown of the most irreproachable individuals; people go so far as to suppose that, if they allow their intimate veils to fall or fly away, it is because they experience some pleasure in being embraced, naked, by reckless arms. For what do people take them? It is all right for us, being men, to be vulgar, to covet the quiver of flesh under flesh, but they are very far from yielding to such desires, and if, sometimes, they show themselves as deprived of a modest envelope as a lily devoid of leaves or a turtle-dove devoid of plumes, it is because, victims of a fatal law, they cannot do otherwise.

What law? And imposed by whom? I shall reveal that, in order to reestablish the honor of so many young women unjustly suspected of lustful condescension.

In very ancient times, snow did not only fall during the cold days of winter. Whether it was spring, summer or autumn, it extended over the summits, the woods and the gardens, and did not melt even in the ardent sunlight, mingled with the Alpine polemoniums, the lemon trees of the slopes and the jasmines of the flower-beds. Delighted with so much snow and so many snowy calices, which were like mirrors for them, doves fluttered over that twin candor; and just as the snow did not melt, the pale flowers never ceased to flourish, not the pale birds to soar.

The result was that everywhere, for the deceit of the eyes and the fingers, there was an exquisite whiteness; a quivering tuft was mistaken for a wing; people thinking they were picking lilies made bouquets of snowflakes. Think how pretty the earth was in those days, and how fortunate poet-lovers were to find on every plain and every branch the resemblance of their lovers' foreheads. It seems that the modesty of the first Eves was spread all over the world; wherever one put one's lips, one kissed the albescence of a virgin breast.

311

But humans weary of the most charming spectacles and the most adorable delights. Soon the living of that ancient epoch ceased to take pleasure in the white splendor that was always the same; for the vision of a single slightly pink eglantine they would have given all the snow, all the lilial flowers and all the doves; and they resolved o make the ennui known and to carry their complaints to the One who had established and maintained the universal whiteness.

Now, in those distant days, so close to the first hour, the Lord God, who had not yet been importuned by so many pestering prayers and lying vows, felt very inclined to grant supplications. He welcomed the human ambassador and, because he knows everything, deduced what it was about as soon as the first words.

"If I understand you rightly," he said, "You want the snow to melt not long after it has fallen?"

"Yes, Lord, in order to see the green grass of the fields."

"And he jasmines, the lilies and the lemon-blossom to fade not long after flowering?"

"Yes, Lord, in order to pick, in the same location, forget-me-nots, buttercups and peonies."

"And for the doves, soon after alighting, to fly away?"

"Yes, Lord, in order to admire, in their stead, jays, green woodpeckers and birds of paradise."

"Well," said the divine Complaisance, "it shall be as you desire; return to the sphere of which I have made you the gift; henceforth the whitenesses will only remain temporarily where they have had the custom of always remaining."

What God promised was accomplished without delay. Al the colors of the terrestrial surface appeared returned to the enchanted eyes of humans. If it snowed, the flakes vanished quickly, allowing the sun to illuminate the emerald of the meadows; if lilies or jasmines opened, they withered quickly, replaced by poppies or bloody roses; when a dove perched somewhere, it fled after a few palpitations of its wings before the flamboyant flight of a thousand birds with wings like gemstones.

Naturally, it was young women, most of all who were ecstatic before such brilliant diversities. But they did not take long to perceive that those changes were not without some damage to the honest renown that they had already acquired in ancient times, for the Lord God, whose universal thought did not worry about the detail of things, had said: "The whitenesses will only last for a moment," and now, the underskirts of white silk or white muslin, and the chemises of nainsook more diaphanous than the air, and the bloomers even more transparent, were scarcely fastened before disappearing,

It would, therefore, be a flagrant injustice to render ladies and damsels responsible for the sometime strange precipitation with which, for the delight of our eyes and the ecstasy of our lips, they disperse their most intimate garments. Instead of criticism, they merit compassion, alas. It costs them, no longer to have them those veils; they would have liked to keep them, hermetically closed, but what can they do? It is necessary for them to obey a providential law; they undress—oh, with what dolorous resignation!—because God has willed it; and it is their blushing despair to think that such a necessity, which is so painful for them, will be perpetuated for as long as the snow melts not long after it has fallen, and lilies fade not long after opening, and doves fly away almost as soon as they have settled.

Complicity

"Sleep!" he said,

She went to sleep.

Thus far, nothing but the utterly banal.

Recent experiments in magnetism and hypnotism have informed us that a virile gaze on feminine eyes, or an expertly progressive application of the hand above the knee is sufficient to oblige the best endowed subjects to sleep and obedience. As for myself, it has happened to me, in encounters whose frequency has the wherewithal to make me proud, to oblige docile individuals, by means if the insistent and reiterated passes that give rise to a kind of catalepsy, not to refuse that which they might doubtless have accorded me in a state of perfect wakefulness. But I have offered them an excuse to their accommodating modesty: it was not their fault. The utility of science!

Valentin is not a man to attempt such mediocre experiments. If he had asked Mademoiselle Anatoline Meyer, that exquisite, slightly plump actress, no less illustrious on the banks of the Neva than those of the Seine, to sit down in that armchair with her head tilted back; if he had consented to adopt, in spite of what she had of the romantic and superannuated, the dominating attitude of a spell-casting mage, it was in order to show us, in the studio where we had supped, phenomena of an entirely new and quite extraordinary order. We hoped for prodigies.

The women were afraid. Jo, who was there, said to Lo, whose neckline was too low: "What if the desire took her to bite you?"

"Good!" said Lo. "Where would the miracle be? You're a somnambulist, then?"

But those frivolous words were scarcely whispered in a profound, almost religious silence. We waited, full of an agreeable anxiety. What was about to happen?

Valentin had placed a finger on each closed eye, from which the fireworks of a mad gaze had previously erupted; while awakening the idea of an Urbain Grandier in a dinner jacket, he had something of the appearance of someone trying to prevent the cork emerging from a bottle of champagne.

He said, professorially: "Mesdames et Messieurs, it is not without reason that, in order to convince you of the importance of magnetic phenomena, I have chosen, among so many young persons perhaps more agreeably nervous, Mademoiselle Anatoline Meyer of the Théâtre des Nouveautés. She is as beautiful as a swan and as stupid as a goose. Whatever she does, in the somnolence into which I shall plunge her, you will take pleasure in seeing her do, for is there a gesture, even modest, that the beauty of the arm does not excuse? And if she should happen to pronounce a word that is not a confession of the most irremediable stupidity, you will all be obliged to recognize and proclaim that she is not in her normal state.

"You have before you, Mesdames et Messieurs, the most extraordinary example of what can be produced, in our civilization, by the whiteness of the skin aided by the perfect nullity of intelligence. Anatoline Meyer, I do not hesitate to declare, is an astonishing person. She has seven or eight carriages and twenty horses in four stables; all dresses and all diamonds are for her; even though she has never had any kind of voice—she does not even sing out of tune; silence alone, with a perfume of roses, emerges from her mouth—it is for her that all the Lecocqs write all the operettas, for her that Russians come from Saint Petersburg, Austrians from Vienna, Rajahs from India and Franc-Comtois from Besançon; it is of her, because of newspapers that one reads in secret, that the dreams of provincial schoolboys who might be scholars or poets one day, are full.

"In brief, she is the seductive, opulent, famous individual whom everyone obeys, and the sole apparent reason for that charm, that wealth and that glory is a little snow in orange roundness in the gap of a corsage.

"Messieurs et Mesdames, I do not contest that there is an appreciable pleasure, whatever the sex of the lips might be, in kissing the quivering swell of a celebrated breast, but in the end, in the present case, I believe it possible to think that there is some disproportion between the victories of Anatoline Meyer and the whiteness that earns them for her; the plump gracility of her bust, aided by the genius of corset-makers, does not sufficiently explain the fact that the eldest son— sixty-five years old—of a northern king wanted to persuade her to accept his imminent crown. In order to vanquish princes and marquises, all men and all women, she must have some talisman, some mysterious means; and if I have put her to sleep, if I have reduced her to a state of responding with entire frankness, and even with an intelligence that is not habitual to her, to the questions that it will please you to address to her, it is in the hope that she will reveal the secret that had made her the richest and most celebrated of women who are not virtu- ous."

Twenty voices, in a pretty tumult, cried: "Yes, yes! Inter- rogate her! Let her reveal the secret of her triumph to us!"

For there were large number of young women there de- void of prejudice and determined to any concession, who were very curious to know how one maddens the Highnesses who come from abroad to the extent of the offer of a crown, or even its resemblance in Brazilian diamonds.

"Speak!" said Valentin.

Anatoline Meyer, her eyes closed, asked the sleep- inducing mage, in a very humble tone: "Truly, you're ordering me to reply?"

"Yes."

"I'll reply, then." Then she adopted a pensive expression. "But shall I speak fully clad, or stark naked? It seems to me that it would suffice, to satisfy all curiosities and legitimate all my conquests, to display the white candor, flourishing with roses, of my skin, which has been greatly admired in all the imperial and royal courts of Europe."

"Are we little negroes, then?" cried Jo, justly offended, with the white effrontery of all her offered cleavage. "It's quite certain that if it were sufficient, to reign over Paris and the world, to be exquisitely pretty with all batiste removed, all those of us who are here would have nothing to envy you, and your secret would be that of Madame Polchinelle, supposing that Madame Polchinelle were as beautiful as Venus Aphrodite and the ugliest of us. But no, we are led to believe that, in order to reduce the proudest courages to their knees, you have a mysterious, personal means that is unknown to us, and we are taking advantage of the somnolence to which you are reduced to demand the revelation of that mystery from you."

"Alas!" moaned Anatoline, resistant.

"Speak!" said Valentin

"Alas!" she moaned, again.

"Speak!" cried, from the heart, the amorous women devoid of prejudice and determined to any concession, in the studio where we had supped.

"You shall have the truth, then!" said the young woman as beautiful as a swan and as stupid as a goose.

An lucidly, explaining for the first time, under the magnetic influence, things of which she had never dreamed while awake, she spoke, proffering terrible confessions.

"What ensures that I am adored is that I never sleep with any of those who love me, and I never sleep even with someone who doesn't love me. Why? I don't know. I didn't set out expressly to be what I am—someone who hates kissing. The mouth is for eating and drinking. I've heard it said, in operetta couplets, that men and women peck one another like birds in a cage. It's possible. I don't know. I don't want to know. It doesn't concern me. I have no idea of what is called pleasure, abandonment, and many other words you say; I don't understand them. For myself, at night, I have only one desire, which is that he goes away. Who? The man that is there, the man that is pestering me. And when he has gone, I sleep, I sleep well.

317

"I've always been as I am now. My mother, a concierge and nurse, said to me because I was crying on the staircase when the valets de chambre pinched me: 'It'll be necessary to put you in a convent; it's your vocation; you're an angel.' She said that angrily; she was mistaken, I'm not an angel. No, I'm a woman whom *that* annoys. What? You know very well. Perhaps I'm a virgin, but I'm not sure; since it's necessary to be frank, I don't believe so. No, I don't believe so, because, after all, there are abrupt men, and then, by chance, by night, while sleeping...does one know, in the morning? In sum, I suppose I don't make more of a chore of it than the first time. Yes, that's it. After several. But I never wanted to do it again. Mama said to me: 'You're losing your future.' She let anyone in, the old lady! It's necessary to believe that she only sat up with imbeciles, who knew nothing, or who posed, like hanged men.

"The real truth, you hear, little ones"—and at that moment the voice of Anatoline Meyer became grandiose, like that of a prophet—"is that I became—well, there's also the theater, the stage, and breasts that pop out—I became the desire of everyone, yes, everyone, when it was confirmed that I didn't experience in any fashion the desire to love anyone who loved me. What charms men is that they bore me, and I want to throw them out when they become sleepy. That's my secret.

"You're much mistaken, my comrades, in thinking that your lovers are grateful to you for the pleasure you've had. Most often, it exhausts them. For myself, it embarrasses me. Hence my fortune, and all the celebrity that I have around me. To be pretty is nothing; there are plenty prettier than me; but, to be as cold as yesterday's soup, that's what's important and what gives them pleasure, since they don't need to wear themselves out having me in order to have the right to say that they've had me. I don't contradict them; I'm a good girl. I'm content that they boast, since it spares me from helping them not to lie.

"My idleness—what luck!—is the accomplice of their weakness. It's the marriage of not wanting with not being able. Well matched unions: no union at all. And they're de-

318

lighted. And I sleep alone. That doesn't prevent—quite the contrary, for they're cunning—my passing for a diabolical woman who has no chill in the eye or anywhere else; a dash of the pencil under the eye, you see, flatters a lover at breakfast before the friends. But fundamentally, the most amorous of all those who adore me play two hundred thousand francs a semester for the right never to love me and to say to my coachman, when I've rung at the door or my town house: 'Home, quickly!'

"In any case, I'm honest. What I do, I don't do by virtue of a system. No, I'm like that naively and naturally. But now, asleep, in the darkness where I can see clearly, I'm explaining the cause of my strength and my triumph. Since men are no longer men, they need women who aren't women. They love me because I'm not amorous; they want to sleep with me because I don't want to sleep with them. In this bleak modern life in which true love is failing, I'm a resistance that authorizes retreat; at least, with me they aren't humiliated. We understand one another well enough to say to one another: 'Until tomorrow!' them being unable to do any more and me yawning.

"Now, follow my example, become illustrious rich and idolized by the same means. The prince who wanted to marry me, who would perhaps have put me, not in a bed, but on a throne—who knows?—has been obliged, since becoming king, to have his wife produce an heir with the aid of two or three colossal and magnificent domestics.

"But all that is something that I would never have told you if I hadn't been put to sleep by Valentin the hypnotizer, in the presence of Jo and Lo, in a studio where we've drunk champagne."

The Mildness of the Monster

In the days when knights made a game out of vanquishing winged tarasques and dragons vomiting flames, the rumor spread throughout the earth that in a lair beside the sea lived a mysterious being more redoubtable than the most savage beasts. What sort of living creature it was no one could say, since, of all those who had dared to penetrate into its abode, none had emerged again.

To tell the truth, you would never have suspected, on considering the entrance to the grotto, the peril that there was in risking passing over the threshold, for branches were hanging down from the rock that were always in flower, skimmed by fluttering birds and buzzing bees, and from the interior came, not the sound of clicking jaws or the grating of claws being sharpened on stone, amid the reek of slaughter, but the warmth of perfumed breezes, and the sounds of a delightful distant music that was like the voice of a marvelous bird.

Woe betide the imprudent traveler who, charmed by the illusions of the flowers and the song, attempted the adventure of confronting the unknown monster! After a silence traversed by tender plants, the people who passed by heard loud screams, the screams of someone being torn apart and devoured by a tiger. The traveler never saw again the clear blue air of the day; undoubtedly, the soil of the lair, like that of a frightful charnel-house, was entirely strewn with bones whitening in the gloom.

Now, in those days, there were three men equally famous, for different reasons, among all men. They were: the Emperor of Srinagar, who reigned over twenty peoples, and whose pompous majesty in his crimson and gold robe was such that the most arrogant potentates bowed down before him filled with religion and fear; the merchant Sebahim, the creditor of all the kings in the world, who never had a shipwreck in transporting between nations the precious objects of his trade, and who possessed mines of gold and precious stones in various countries where workmen more innumerable than the ants of the roads were employed; and the knight Alfanor, in his armor that resounded itself like the impact of two armies, who was so tall when he was on horseback that he could brush the summits of the tallest oaks with his crown and who, in order to liberate enchanted princess, had choked between his arms a hundred giants as tall and broad as towers in the debris of fallen keeps.

Those three men, when they heard mention of the monster that lived in a lair beside the sea, where ruffled in their vanity; they resolved to vanquish the formidable unknown being, and they arrived on the same day, followed by a multitude, in front of the flowery entrance where the birds were fluttering amid the buzzing of bees.

When they had drawn lots in order to decide which of the three would have the honor of attempting the adventure first, the Emperor, whom fortune had designated, advanced toward the grotto magnificently.

A melodious voice was coming from the obscure depths. He shrugged his shoulders and said: "Futile cunning! You are terrible, being that I have come to confront, but what strength and what pride will not bow down, seized by respect, before my sublime majesty?"

And he went in, holding his scepter aloft.

After a few minutes, a terrible clamor was heard, the clamor of a dying god! The monster had accomplished its customary work; the entire multitude, knees trembling, feared and admired the being which showed so little veneration with regard to emperors.

The merchant Sebahim, in his turn, marched toward the threshold of the lair. The treacherous voice that emerged from the mysterious darkness was even sweeter. He shrugged his shoulders and said: "Vain stratagem! You are ferocious, being that I have come to challenge, but what violence and what

321

rage cannot be appeased, changed into humble and avid supplication, before my scintillating wealth?"

And he went in, carrying in his arms, wide open, a coffer luminous with diamonds and carbuncles.

It was after very few minutes the desperate appeal of a dying man resounded. Once again, the monster had triumphed. The fear of the crowd was increased by the keenest surprise. What was it, then, the creature that gave such a rude welcome to bearers of precious stones?

Thirdly, the knight Alfanor advanced. No words can give any idea of the tenderness with which the distant voice was appealing in the darkness. He shrugged his shoulder. "Mediocre trickery! You are formidable, being that I have come to brave. But I have hugged lions against my breast and those lions have suddenly ceased to roar. I have walked, like a reaper amid the scythed wheat, amid the cadavers of enormous wyverns with extinct maws. What courage would dare to insult my valor? And what claws, even those of a devil accustomed to vanquish archangels, would not be blunted against the ever-unbreached steel of my armor?"

And he went in, holding his lance aloft.

In even less time than it had required to dispose of the emperor and the merchant, the monster reckoned with the knight Alfanor. When they had heard, amid the sonorous fall of weapons, the scream of the dying warrior, the multitudinous spectators, mad with fear, turned their backs and started running, in a hectic tumult, like an army in panic.

But several of them retraced their steps, because someone called them back, saying: "Wait, I beg you. Those who went into the lair doubtless did not know what it was necessary to do in order to subjugate the monster, and I want to attempt the proof too.

Frightened as they were, the people who had retraced their steps could not help laughing.

The man who wanted to combat the vanquisher of the three most famous men on earth was a little shepherd, an adolescent who looked like a girl. Oh, how far he was from having glory, wealth and strength! He did not even have decent clothes, clad entirely in rags; a gust of wind could have knocked him down. He was often encountered in the pathways of the woods, singing songs in a soft voice—singular, plaintive songs that no one understood—and picking violets in the moss, which he assembled into bouquets. More than once, the master of the farm where he was in service had been obliged to beat him because it often happened that the little idler did not bring the flock back at the customary hour, fully occupied as he was in hazing at the first stars appearing and twinkling in the sky. And he always had a tenderness in his eyes, which caused people to make fun of him.

"Ha ha!" said the people. "That's funny, in truth. You'll succeed, you, where the most majestic of emperors, the richest of merchants and the bravest of knights have failed?"

He did not reply. He went into the grotto without a scepter, without any rich offering, and without a weapon; except that, from the flowery branches where the little birds and the bees were flying, he had picked a very small rose.

Truly, people ceased laughing; they felt sorry for him. Poor child! What madness had drawn him? Soon they would hear the scream, the frightful cry of death.

No, what they heard, on the contrary, ever sweeter, was the delightful music—but now it seemed to be made by two mingled voices. And the astonishment increased from one minute to the next, in an attentive silence.

It became similar to the stupor that people experience before the most unusual of prodigies when the shepherd reappeared under the florescences of the entrance, safe and sound, and radiant, clasping in his arms a young woman clad in silk and sunlight, so beautiful that there could not have been any princess on earth as beautiful as her. And that exquisite creature was looking at him, humble and blushing, with eyes shining with tenderness and delight.

Then, the conquering child said to the ecstatic crowd: "This is the monster that lived in the lair beside the sea. It is, in fact, the most formidable of creatures, since it is a woman.

But a woman, atrocious and devouring, who could not be sub-jugated by majesty, wealth or strength, is easily defeated, even by a little shepherd, when one knows how to capture her. It is sufficient to talk to her about amour, with a sincere heart, while offering her a flower."

The Well-Merited Absolution

One alone of the three confessed sins would have sufficed for the sinner to be consigned to the tortures of Hell—
with the consequence that the honest director of conscience
remained silent, and did not know what to resolve when,
through the trellis, rose to his nostrils, insensible in any case to
such delights, an invisible dust of rice powder and an intimacy
of hair and the culpable pepper of a dash of sandalwood,
and—as you have said, divine master—yet another odor; for,
in the excess of her religion, so breathless had repentance left
her, Francine de Luciol, kneeling, bewildered, shifting her
forehead in her veil like a bird rubbing self with dust, had unfastened the top of her corsage. In the confessional there was a
little of the nudity that had so terribly aggravated the last and
worst of the three sins.

The priest finally emerged from his fearful reverie, and
because he brought back some mercy from his consultation of
the eternal clemency, he said, albeit angrily: "What! Is that
possible, my girl? You, born of an illustrious family and married to a gentleman whose ancestors fought and died—not all
of them, but some of them, at least—for the august cause of
the Church," (Francine dared not interrupt to object that Monsieur de Luciol, gouty ten months in twelve, less handsome
than the most hideous ape, was almost as old as the ancestors
of whom he was so proud) "you, who ought to give an example of perfect virtue, have abandoned yourself to such weaknesses. Last month, on a warm morning," (Francine thought:
Oh yes, so warm, there was a storm in the air!) "you permitted
a mouth that was not the mouth of your husband to pose on
your lips?"

"Alas," said the penitent, like a swallow beneath a soar-
ing vulture.

"A few hours later, in your boudoir, at dusk," (Francine thought: *So why had the chambermaid forgotten to bring the lamps?*) "you did not call for help when an adulterous hand slid beneath the satin of your corset?"

"Alas, alas!" said the penitent, curbed like the grass of the fields under the threat if the wind that is about to roar.

"Finally, on a July night, while everyone was sleeping innocently in your château in Normandy," (*Oh, innocently!* thought Francine. *I definitely heard doors closing in the first floor corridor after furtive entries that pretended to have mistaken the bedroom!*) "you welcomed between sheets already disordered by the restless impatience of waiting, a man, perhaps unclad," (*Oh no*, thought Francine, *a silk chemise, perfumed with iris!*) "a man with whom you were not united by the holy bonds of matrimony!"

"Alas, alas, alas!" said the penitent, entirely similar to a birch tree struck by lightning.

"And doubtless, in each of these three sins, you took some pleasure?"

"Oh, more pleasure than I can say!" she confessed, in her devout consternation. She even added, weakly: "In the last, especially."

Then the priest exclaimed: "Wretch!" But he calmed down. "Give thanks," he went on, "to the adorable Redeemer, who only opens the gates of Gehenna regretfully! Frightful, and unworthy of pardon as your three sins are, unless redeemed, a means of avoiding the vats of ever-boiling oil and the eternal embers is offered to you, poor soul!"

She raised her forehead, in the intoxication of possible salvation. "A means?" she sighed.

"Yes. Listen. Absolution might perhaps not be refused to you if you submit to the penance that a celestial inspiration counsels me to impose on you. Three times, in culpable joys, you have offended Heaven. Well then, by three sacrifices, three martyrdoms as abundant in torments as your sins were in enchantments, expiate those sins! And when you are summoned to the sacred tribunal, exculpated of the triple pleasure thanks to a triple suffering, perhaps you will not be refused the pardon that opens to tender souls the hidden door by means of which the likes of Mary Magdalen and Thaïs enter Paradise!"

To tell the truth, Francine de Luciol, when she had quit the church of Saint-Philippe de Roule, felt as perplexed as possible. She had experienced, because of the kiss of the lips, because of the hand beneath the satin corset, because of the embrace in the bed, under the caressant plush, so much delight that she despaired of ever imagining tortures as cruel as those delights had been exquisite.

To be admitted, clad in coarse fabric, to some hospital or field hospital, to lean over the pale lips of the moribund, to allow herself to be brushed by the gratitude of the sick with bleeding wounds, to console gasping death-throes with quasi-maternal embraces, would certainly be meritorious actions, but how much less the horror of resigning herself to that would be than the ecstasy felt in the sins that they had to redeem!

For—it was necessary not to say the contrary—the lover thanks to whom she was plunged in such an awkward perplexity had a fashion of inhaling the breath of a person, and caressing silky flesh beneath silky cloth, and slipping between vainly resistant sheets, that rendered equivalence in torments to the pleasures he gave almost impossible. Oh, how easily she would have expiated their common joy if he had been less lovable!

However, not to be pardoned, not to be absolved, she, who, before marrying Monsieur de Luciol, gouty ten months out of twelve, less handsome than the most hideous of apes and as old as his oldest ancestors—a husband sufficiently horrible in other ways—had been so renowned in the convent for her ingenuous piety and her fidelity in ornamenting the little altar of the Virgin with white eglantines, who had, for three years—O admirable virtue!—resisted the tender urgency of the man who had finally vanquished her, was truly something impossible! She could not and did not want to renounce Paradise, even for amour; and it was necessary for her to imagine some frightful and salutary expiation.

For long days she searched, searched and searched again, so much that finally, with a gleam in her eyes, like the martyrs who accepted the frightful agonies of the, circus, she cried: "I've found it!"

It was a Holy Saturday, before midday, when she dared to present herself at the tribunal of penitence. Clad in black, with an august melancholy in her garments, the pallor of her face and her entire attitude, she traversed the church, waited for her turn in the confessional, knelt before the trellis the perfumes traversed, and, although very humble, she manifested the beautiful pride of someone who has just accomplished heroic exploits in the interest of her salvation and in honor of the Church.

The priest said: "It's you, my daughter?"

"Yes, me," said Francine de Luciol, "and I've merited that you open for me, with a gesture of benediction, the door through which the likes of Mary Magdalen and Thaïs enter Paradise."

"Good," he said.

"Did I not have to obtain pardon for my triple sin by punishments as great as the pleasure the sin had given me had been?"

"Undoubtedly."

"Well, the pleasure of my lips on lips I have expiated in a kiss."

"What?" said the honest director of conscience.

"The acquiescence of my breast to a friction beneath the satin, I have also expiated by means of the acceptance of a hand in my corsage."

"Oh!" said the confessor.

"And for the delight of a tender body alongside mine beneath caressant plush, I have punished myself by not closing my alcove at night."

"Mercy!" said the priest. And he added: "What! You think to redeem your sins with similar sins! You dare to boast of the renewal of your crimes!"

But the penitent, with a proud smile, said: "Don't hasten to condemn me Father; rather prepare yourself to absolve my former sins with admiration. For the man to whom, in recent days, I have not refused my mouth, my breast or my bed is..."

"Is?"

"My husband," she said.

The Dolor of the Sea

"Yes, Madame, naked, stark naked, that is what is meant by nude."

"Oh, Monsieur, what are you daring to say?"

"I am daring to say, Madame"—Baronne de Caldelis and Monsieur de Marciac were conversing that morning on the shore of the Norman sea among a hundred Parisiennes sitting in their quivering summer dresses under the mauve, gray, green and pink umbrellas that were made to undulate around them like waves of silk by a wind so bright and ardent that one might have taken it from the breath of the sun—"that if I were, like you, a woman and the most beautiful of all, I would not hesitate for a moment before these profound blue waves to take off my crepes, muslins and most intimate lace. Then, without recourse to the stupid and ugly decency of bathing costumes, I would march triumphantly, veiled only by the air, the daylight and a modest blush, toward the great wave with the sheen of azure and gold that swells beneath the sky, and I would enter the sea, nude."

"That is certainly the most impertinent of advice! In addition to the fact that the natural modesty of well-born people would be more alarmed that one can say, can you imagine, Monsieur, the abominable scandal that it would occasion if it were obeyed?"

"I can imagine it, Madame. At the sight of your beauty, fully revealed, there would be, among the men, thousands of "oh ohs" and even more "eh ehs." Behind the umbrellas lowered in a recoil of folding chairs, the women of your society would turn away, and the ladies of the bourgeoisie who have come from Rouen or Evreux would flee, bewildered, toward the casino, carrying their children. It might even be the case that the gendarmes would arrive; a brigadier would doubtless put his excessively fortunate hand brutally on the slender and curvaceous shoulder over which the damp hair was gliding in golden streams."

"That would, you will agree, be a fine adventure!"

"A very fine adventure indeed," said Monsieur de Marciac solemnly, "for you, serene and gloriously imperturbable, would be able to respond to the insulting admirations, the sniggers, the angry modesties and the armed force: 'Know that, at the risk of being criticized by dull minds, I am fulfilling at this moment the noblest of duties.'"

"The noblest of duties? You're mad, I think."

"As Periander of Corinth and Thales of Miletus! And if you do not understand me, it is because you were not initiated into matters of Mythology in the convent of the Ursuline ladies."

While she looked at him, astonished, Monsieur de Marciac, who was something of a poet that day, as is befitting at the edge of the sea, went on, not without a certain grandiloquence:

"Do you know why the mysterious and dolorous sea laments perpetually on the sand, sobs on the shingle, and moans and howls over the rocks? Perhaps you think that she is suffering from being bounded by the strands and cliffs, being broken against sharp reefs and islands, and being tortured by black hurricanes and lightning? What an error is yours! If the sea has been desolate, with neither repose nor silence, for so many centuries, it is because the ingrate Cypris emerged one day from her waves and has never returned there.

"By means of her presence, the Immortal with the brown eyes, who bears a crown of violets on her golden hair, enchants humans and gods, causes the birds of the woods to sing and charms the atrocious beasts; she passes by, and roses bloom. But if the earth and the sky possess her, she refuses herself, cruelly, to the maternal waters. The sea contains exquisite pearls and marvelous flora, and the splendid gold of somber galleons, but she no longer has her Anadyomene! And she weeps, she cries; her waves writhe in despair and, becoming malevolent, erode coasts, dismantle ships and roll pale cadavers. O deplorable oceans, how your fate has the where-withal to touch hearts, even the least sensible! For the goddess who follows the Desires and the Games is firmly resolved not to return to the tenebrous abysms, and you will suffer eternally, unless..."

"Unless what?"

"Unless," said Monsieur de Marciac, "in a sublime surge of mercy, the most radiant of women, substituting for the most radiant of goddesses, renders to the widowed waves the delight of touching, caressing and embracing perfect beauty!"

"Oh! Is it necessary to go as far as drowning oneself?"

"No, no, I don't think so. The waves will be clement to whoever is charitable to them."

The baronne laughed under the umbrella whose guipure put a perforated vacillating shadow over her cheek.

"Go on," she said. "I don't want to begrudge you any longer an impertinence that is a madrigal. But know full well that even if I believed your tale, it seems to me that the sea wouldn't have as much to lament as you say. Many women bathe in her, many pretty women! She has found many petty Cyprises."

"Yes, some satisfactions are accorded to her, here and there, and that is why she sighs, on occasion, with less desolation. But how imperfect they are, the most charming! In any case, they never fail to put on, blue, black or violet, the atrocious, hideous bathing costume, and the waves are demanding lovers who experience little pleasure in only being able to kiss through fabric the snow and rose of flesh. You, Madame, who have—for I would swear to it!—a flawless splendor, should have the sublime courage to undress without hypocrisy! Enter, nude, into the moving azure from which Aphrodite was born, and, thanks to you, there will be no more shipwrecks or drownings—the ocean without dolor will be without anger—and thanks to you, the laments on the sand, the sobs on the shingle and the howls between the rocks will fall silent, and the earth and sky will marvel on hearing endlessly, beneath the sun and the stars, the appeased and rapturous sea laughing and singing delightedly.

After a silence that might have been slightly mocking, Madame de Caldelis said: "In truth, your counsel no longer appears to me so extravagant. It's certain that there would be some glory in sacrificing oneself for the happiness of the bitter gulf. In any case, it goes without saying that it would not be indispensable to bathe, so scantly veiled, before a very numerous crowd?"

"Oh, not indispensable at all."

"Good."

"It would, however, require a witness."

"A witness?"

"Yes, to affirm to the rest of humankind the magnificent devotion of the most beautiful of women."

"But only one."

"Only one, certainly."

"Who would be...?"

"Who would be...," repeated Monsieur de Marciac, moving closer, a warmth in her eyelids.

"You, for example?"

"Yes, yes, me!" he stammered.

"Very well. It's just a matter of reaching an understanding. And the thing could take place, could it not, after dark?"

"Of course. In the evening, on a solitary beach."

"Even later?"

"So be it. By night, if you wish."

"That's it: in darkness, very thick, very obscure, very black."

"Oh, as black as you please!"

"Well, I don't say no," murmured Baronne de Caldelis, after another silence.

"Madame! Madame! Heaven!"

"But," she finished, laughing madly and taking the arm of her husband, who was coming out of the casino, "there are only nights as dark as that in the worst months of winter, and then, Monsieur, the sea is too cold to bathe in it!"

The Impossible Resurrection

Like everyone else, I had heard mention of the extraordinary charlatan recently arrived from America in seven or eight steamships—for three ships would not have been enough to transport the glory of such a man. What! Could he cure the most obstinate invalids with an imposition of hands, or breathing on his forehead, or, more classically, by means of some panacea? You judge him poorly. It would be a fine thing if he had limited his art to such mediocre results; Sganarelle could have done as much with a piece of cheese. No, it was not malady that he cured, that traverser of the seas, it was death. It was averred—one only had to read the fourth page of any newspaper—that he could resuscitate for you a person dead for several thousand years in less time than a assassin endowed with some experience takes to dispatch a man to the other side of the Styx.

To tell the truth, the announcement of such a power, agreeable to so many desirous living persons—oh, my God, why?—to revive after ordinary decease, had not failed to produce some anxiety in the subterranean world of catacombs and necropolises. For there are dead persons who would not care at all to recommence the insipidity of existence, and you do not take the trouble to lodge a bullet in one's head or to swallow a glass of strychnine—which tastes nasty—in order for your valet de chambre to wake you up a few days later, saying: "Here are Monsieur's newspapers" or "Monsieur knows that he is expected for lunch today by Mademoiselle Constance Chaput?" And it is no more amusing if it is Mademoiselle Rose Mousson.

But the majority of human beings, smitten with their rag, would welcome the discovery of the American empiric with an enthusiastic acclamation, and I confess that I, myself—I was in love at the time with the prettiest and most implacable

of Parisiennes—did not learn without contentment that henceforth, in return for a certain sum, although one only paid after
the resurrection, one could bring back to life the most inveterate dead.

Not alone, but in company with my darling, I went to see
the prodigious scientist. The house where he was residing, in
the city center, astonished me with a pompous profusion of
marble of all colors. Nothing was more natural, however, than
all the alabasters and sarrancolins, since that dwelling, dis-
mantled stone by stone in order that it could be transported by
land or by sea, was made of all the crypts and all the mausolea
that the resurrected, very satisfied to be out of them, had offered to their evoker as a sign of gratitude. As for the vestibule
and the apartments, they were hung with fabrics that must
have been shrouds and funeral draperies, but which, dyed red,
blue or green, were resplendent with so many precious stones
in the form of calices and leaves that they were as joyous as a
hedge in the month of April.

When I was introduced into the consulting room—my
darling remained behind the door, sitting on a bronze throne
encrusted with rubies, the offering of an imperial resurrection—the glorious charlatan was half-lying in a coffin, of
which the art of upholstery, lavishing silks and lace, had made
the most adorable of chaises-longues.

I bowed, not without respect, and said:

"Inclined as I am by habit to dream of admitting all miracles, and although the assiduous reading of five or six poets
has accustomed me to many other miracles greater than the
lifting of the slab of a tomb by a sleeper weary of being
dead—such as, for example, a metaphor both vague and precise, and new, in a strophe of four incomparable correct and
perfect lines, without any appearance of correction or perfection—I confess that I have not welcomed without some incre-
dulity the news of the power that is claimed to be conferred on
you."

Nonchalantly, he replied: "Oh, if only you had come a
few moments earlier, I would have had the pleasure of intro-

ducing you to the delightful and bloody queen who, in the intimacy of gardens tremulous in the moonlight, took pleasure in being named the Dove with the Iron Beak.[44]

"What! You have brought the winged daughter of Derceto out of her immemorial sepulcher?"

"My God, yes! It seemed tedious to have breakfast alone this morning; I resurrected that royal and divine person. What historians say about her had always counseled me with a desire to know her. She was a little surprised, at first, by our fashion of sitting down to eat; the forks, especially, made her laugh. But she quickly took her part in our modernity and, a little drunk on Tokay, she told me things that are quite unknown regarding her son Ninyas; it appears that he testified all the regard for her that one could expect.[45]

"And after dessert, you sent the exile back to her tomb?"

"No; she'll return this evening; I had the carriage harnessed for her and she has gone to take a turn round the Bois."

"That's admirable!"

---

[44] The fictitious Assyrian queen Semiramis, or Shamiram (the author renders it elsewhere as Chamiram) is featured or cited by this appellation in other stories by Mendès. Semiramis is credited in some accounts with being the daughter of a goddess, named Derceto by Clesias, but better known as Atargatis or Atarateh, who was probably transmuted into the more famous Astarte or Astaroth. George Whyte-Melville's novel *Sarchedon: A Legend of the Great Queen* (1871), with which Mendès might well have been familiar, alleges that she wore a amulet on her breast representing a dove in the forms of an arrow,

[45] Some versions of the legend of Semiramis alleges that Ninyas, once imprisoned by his mother for masquerading as her, plotted with the palace eunuchs to depose her, and that she considered him to be an ingrate, although she still left her kingdom to him.

"Oh, that's very little. Yesterday evening, Petronius and I dined together, and as I have a cook who took care of the service..."

"Lucullus?" I said, rather foolishly.

"Bah! Lucullus didn't understand anything about cuisine. A usurped reputation! My cook had the glory of reducing to the most frightful gastritis a satrap of Archaelis, so subtle in what concerns the delicate mysteries of the table that he said one day, after having sucked the egg of a pink grouse through hole made by a golden needle..."

"Pink?"

"There are pink grouse in Cappadocia.""

"I'm delighted to hear it."

"...That he said one day..."

"Yes, while sucking the egg of a pink grouse."

"...'Certainly, the bird that laid this egg had slept, the day before laying it, in plants greatly warmed by the sun—clover rather than Lucerne—not far from a wild vine on which a thrush had perched, not for very long, before fleeing before the flight of a plover.' Information was sought, and the satrap was correct."

"He was a clever man!"

"His cook was even better than him. He gave us good cheer yesterday, and Petronius was consoled with regard to Trimalchio."

"I'll wager that," I said, smiling, "put in a good humor by an exquisite meal, you had thoughts after the ginger and the sugared wine of which an austere morality might not have approved...?"

"Ha ha! That's quite possible; Petronius says things that that might incline the most serious minds to tender frivolities."

"And you only had to proffer a word or a gesture to avail yourselves the most beautiful lovers of all countries and all ages?"

"As you say."

"Which then did Petronius prefer, among all of them?"

"Petronius?"

"Yes."

"Hmm! Hmm!"

"Well?"

"Petronius..."

"Oh! Yes, I understand; let's pass on. Those Romans were extraordinary. What about you?"

"I had hesitations, precisely because of my omnipotence."

"Yes: the embarrassment of choice."

"Let's see, speak frankly, in my place, among all those who were beautiful, which would you select?"

"Oh, me...," I said.

"Cleopatra?"

"On no pretext! She had, according to what historians relate who don't merit any credence,[46] a deplorable mania for putting to death, the day after the caress, the handsome slaves that she welcomed in her arms."

"You criticize her for those peccadilloes?"

"Let's make a distinction. I don't reproach her at all for the death of her lovers. I criticize her for having made them die by iron or poison when she could have done it, so delightfully for them and for herself, with a few kisses more."

"Aspasia?"

"Oh, Monsieur, she occupied herself with politics."

"Laïs?"

"A nice enough girl, but I'm always suspicious of the taste of Aristippus. Then again, I confess that I would refrain from going back so far, from sepulcher to sepulcher, in the eternal succession of amorous women. In your place—I say in your place, because the only one I would have desired for myself isn't dead, at least, not entirely—is Manon, whom I would have taken on my knees at dessert."

"Manon?"

"Lescaut."

---

[46] The author probably has in mind his former mentor and ex-father-in-law, Théophile Gautier.

338

"That's admirable," cried the illustrious charlatan, "for it's precisely with the mistress of the Chevalier des Grieux that I was drinking champagne until the hour when the windows were tinted with the rosy color of her lips."

Such a conformity of tastes was bound to give birth to a certain sympathy between the resuscitator and me. I no longer hesitated to explain to him what service I awaited from his marvelous science.

I said, in a melancholy tone: "Let's leave this idle chatter. Since it is given to you to reanimate the most ancient cadavers—I have no doubt, I know, I believe!—will you deign, in my favor, would you deign to exercise your power on the person who is dearer to me than any woman has ever been to any man?"

"Very gladly," she said. "But your friend is dead, then?"

"Rather in Heaven," I replied. "It isn't that she has ceased to live, it's only her heart. She speaks, she walks, she eats, she drinks, she sleeps, she wakes up, and nothing about her seems similar to something that is no more—but her heart is dead, dead, dead...deader than the most ancient buried corpse."

He smiled, very benevolently.

"Such cases," he said, "are not as rare as people think, and, always very easily, I have forced the resurrection of hearts that a premature death has reduced to no longer beating, and no longer loving. Bring me your friend; I will cure her of the insensibility that is desolating you."

"She's here, in the vestibule of your palace."

"Well, have her come in."

She came in. So pretty and so young, she had a mouth so tender and eyes so radiant that one would have been able to believe that her heart was. in fact, dead. Oh, the delectable coffin of a stubborn decease!

Immediately, the scientist ausculated my darling. He had the smiling expression of a practitioner sure of his affair. But then he ceased to smile. He ausculated her, and ausculated her again, while I considered her, full of anguish. He went very pale; he shook his head; and finally, he turned round sadly."

"There's nothing to be done," he said.

Then a fury took hold of me.

"You are a usurper of renown," I said, "an abuser of credulous souls. You haven't breakfasted with Semiramis, or dined with Petronius, and Manon has never sat on your knees. Ha ha! Behold the great sorcerer, the admirable mage, who can't even revive a woman's heart!"

Without anger, he said: "You're insulting me unjustly, poor lover disappointed in your last hope. I've evoked from their tombs more of the dead than there are stars in the sky in the month of August, and by means of my science I've reanimated the divine beats in thousands of breasts. But I only awaken the dead. I can do nothing with regard to your mistress's heart, because it was never alive."

The Miraculous Catch

All white, with his white cat purring around him, Gilles is fishing, with his line in the water.

For fish? No, for planets.

For Gillette had said to him: "If you bring me a basket full of stars, I'll permit you to kiss my lips."

First, he thought about casting his line into the sky, but the sky is very high, and he resigned himself to fishing in the river for the reflections of stars.

A bite!

It is Venus that has bitten. He reels her in and puts her in his basket. He casts his line again. Mars, Mercury, Neptune and Jupiter bite in turn. The basket must be full now; Gilles thinks that he has the right to go to Gillette and demand the promised recompense.

Followed by his cat, which is purring, he arrives, with his basket on his arm.

"What are you bringing me there?" she says.

"The reflections," he says, "of the stars that you wanted."

"Good! It's the stars themselves that I wanted. Since you're only offering me the vain resemblance, you'll only have the image of my lips in the mirror. Come on, come on, in this glass in which I'm reflected, kiss my mouth; I grant you that."

Giles is extremely disconcerted. But then, anything is better than nothing at all. For want of the true lips, he is about content himself with their rosy image, when Gillette, whose finger has lifted the lid of the wicker basket says: "But your basket is empty!" And, furiously, she turns away from the mirror, in which Gilles, if he had put a kiss there, would only have kissed the absence of a smile.

Where are they, then, the reflections of the stars fished out of the water?

The cat has eaten them.

The Bad Clock

"Aiee! Grandmama! Aiee!" said Jocelyne.

"What's the matter with you, then, my darling?"

"Aiee! Aiee! Aiee!"

"But what is it?"

"Aiee! Aiee! Aiee!"

"Are you feeling ill?"

"Aiee! It's because I'm dying, Grandmama."

"Good! You're joking, I think. You're as fresh as an early morning rosebud that has barely opened. Why would you die, pray?"

"Because the hour has chimed, Grandmama."

"That's a fine reason to die. The hour chimes twenty-four times a day without anyone thinking of rendering their soul."

"Oh, Grandmama, there are hours and hours. Midday has just chimed on the big clock in the downstairs room; that's the moment when I ought to see the friend that I love amorously coming, and since he hasn't come, defunct or infidel, I have nothing more to do than die."

And, in fact, she died immediately, letting her dainty head, in which the pink roses of her cheeks became white roses, fall on to the window sill, while a snow-white butterfly emerged from her half-closed mouth, like a little winged lily, and flew away through the casement. That was Jocelyne's soul.

To describe the despair of the frightened grandmother, who dropped the distaff with which she was spinning, would be quite impossible. Tearfully, she embraced and kissed the dear dead girl, or went back and forth in the room, tearing out her gray hair in handfuls, stammering in her sobs: "Alas, alas! Now she is no more, the darling who was so lovely. She had no peer for lulling my afternoon nap with songs, and when she

342

took me for a walk in the orchard, I thought, with my hand on her shoulder, that I was leaning on a walking lilac bush, so flowery and perfumed was she."

The old woman was so sad that, in the fatigue of her dolor, she finally fell on to the floor, half-fainting, no longer paying any heed to anything—with the result that she did not see the snowy butterfly return through the window, alight on the mouth of the dead girl, slip between her teeth and disappear like an insect penetrating a flower.

"Hee hee! Grandmama! Hee hee!" said Jocelyne.

"Miracle! You aren't dead any longer then, my darling?"

"Hee hee hee!"

"And why are you laughing like that in coming back to life?"

"Hee hee!"

"But what is it?"

"Hee hee hee!"

"Can it be that you have some great joy?"

"Hee hee! It's because the big clock in the downstairs room doesn't know what it's chiming! My soul, which was flying to paradise, passed close to the bell tower; it looked at the time on the church clock; it's only quarter to twelve, Grandmother! The friend I love amorously is neither dead nor infidel, and he's running along the path where we swore to love one another forever, and he'll kiss my returned soul between my lips!"

The Rose Mass and the Black Mass

Jo, Lo and Zo, and you too, Lila, and you, Colette, come, little beauties who are greatly culpable, and prepare—don't smile, please, because your smiles are so pretty—to be subjected to great reprimands. It's time for me, in my turn, to tell you your fate. Precisely because I've had the weakness, for a long time, not to hate the subtlety of your mingled graces and perfumes, I feel obliged to a particular severity—a natural compensation for an overly inveterate indulgence. Fear, strange criminals, the violent equity of a judge who was almost your accomplice, and don't be surprised when, in a little while, I inflict some frightful penalty on you, as a punishment for your sins; such as, for example, going three hours without running a powder-puff over your cheek, which sometimes still blushes with the regret of modesty or the dread—the dread only, since we know full well that in the end, the torture will not be realized—that if, by some mischance, your neckline, broken in the effort of a waltz, suddenly ceases to hide breasts denuded of analogy with the firmness of fresh snow, from which two pale faded roses emerge.

So, come here.

Truly, I've learned fine things! To think that I've read, in recent days, all over the place, that it's you, yes, you alone, Jo, Lo and you, Zo, my favorite—futile Brunhilde, alas, of a frivolous Wotan!—who have caused all the evil that there is in modern amour. If frightful ambushers of virginal innocence attack and break frightened girls, as the frail trunk of a birch tree is knocked down by a blow of the knee, leaving them torn on the bed of a suburban inn; if pure young women succumb, sobbing and bleeding, like angels devoured by a she-wolf; if the pale inmates are not sleeping, two by two, in convent dormitories; if the bellies of brides, instead of the sacred stigmata of maternity, show the bites of infecund kisses; if conjugal

344

beds are empty of wives, gasping in feminine alcoves; if, everywhere, lovers are lamenting because of their lovers ravished—oh, so ravished!—by female lovers; if some obscene old lady similar to the vagabond bitches of Horace and Martial demands of the redness of a near murder the illusion of her atrophied sexual parts; if only morphine, calming and redoubling remorse, consoles and dilapidates and kills those possessed by the demon Mephistophela; if, in spite of the advertisement that the austere and bleak novel gives, which is, certainly, the most mediocre but also the most desolating, of books;[47] if, in spite of the novel in which a mother no longer dares to kiss her daughter, a woman transgresses to the point of going beyond the pardon the eternal law imposes on humankind; if the infamous dream abolishes and mocks the august bestial instinct, august, in fact, for being bestial; if, finally, for the glory of Hell and the defeat of the divine Charity that disconcerts the irremediable, accomplishes the prophecy of the melancholy poet:

The woman shall have Sodom and the man shall have Gomorrah
  And, casting far away an irritated glance,
  The two sexes will die, each on its side;[48]

It is your fault, little ones, it is because of you, Jo, Lo, Zo, and you are the examples and counselors of universal perversity."
  Then:
  "Yes," said Lo.

---

[47] The reference is to Mendès' novel *Méphistophéla* (1890), in which the eponymous demon possesses the female protagonist with uncontrollable lesbian lust.

[48] The lines are slightly misquoted (the terms Sodom and Gomorrah being reversed) from Alfred de Vigny's poem "La Colère de Samson," included in the posthumous collection *Les Destinées* (1863).

"Of course," said Jo.

"So what?" said Zo.

Then all three of them roared with laughter, and Lo, laughing closer to my lips, said: "You're too silly! Truly, if you hadn't invented us, I'd think you were a fool, so absurd is it to pay any heed to the reprobation of those who seek, in the libertine futility of a few pages, the excuse for their immemorial vices. That's a fine story! It's because I've sighed tenderly, not too far from a mouth sister to my mouth, and because you, tenderly moved, have annotated the melody of our sighs, that the frenzied and premeditated rut of a few monstrous creatures torments the innocence of virgins and the placidity of serene wives? It's because the three of us have laughed that lovers and husbands weep, because we are the exquisite simulators of a desire we don't have...for no, we don't have it...!"

"No," said Jo, hesitantly.

"No!" said Zo, more resolutely.

"...It's because we imitate in harmonies of phrases almost similar to verses, in the elegance of rhythms, the cooing of Cytherean doves, doves without wood-pigeons, that amour without a male lover soils with its villainies and bites with its exasperated angers, ingenuous lips and venerable breasts? You're joking, I think, and the innocents are us."

"Certainly," said Jo.

"Undoubtedly," said Zo.

Slightly troubled, I went on: "However, you can't affirm that you're irreproachable. It's certain that, in more than one of my tales, you have not dissimulated sentiments that have the wherewithal to alarm a somewhat austere morality."

But Lo, very literate: "Under the great myrtles where roses mingle, Erinnys, one hot summer evening inhaled from the lips of Amymone perfumes sweeter than those of roses and myrtles."[49]

---

[49] This reference is enigmatic, but presumably symbolic; Amymone was a Danaid whose name means "blameless," on whom Poseidon fathered a child after rescuing her from a sa-

346

Jo, no less savant: "On the festival bed at the feasts of the Good Goddess,[50] beautiful patriciennes rarely disdained the recumbent vicinity of a friend initiated in the tender rites, and the most charming of young men was only admitted to those mysteries clad in a woman's robe.

Zo, even more erudite: "In a temple in Sicily, not far from the mountain that vomits lava, where the possibility of punishment seethes, the only devotees admitted to kneel before the Venus of flesh-colored marble were those who paid the priestesses a tithe, and that tithe was a long caress."

The Lo said: "At the Château de Signe, in the times when Lady Clermonde presides over the contests of amour, Bernard de Ventadour nearly died of pain because he saw, in the hair of Alaïs de Roquemarine, a woodland flower that his darling Alcyone, served by so much virile amour, had refused him."[51]

Zo, thirdly, said: "Since the king's favorites only accorded a distracted glance to the emotion of young breasts lifting the silk and lace, the Marquise de Romans thought it sage not to refuse the lips of Madame de Belleval the pride of observing that emotion, scarcely appeased by a kiss than strangely revived."[52]

---

tyr. Erinnys is the archetype of the wrathful Furies, who exacted vengeance on perjurers and evildoers

[50] The Roman goddess Bona Dea.

[51] Bernard de Ventadour is the French version of the name of the famous twelfth-century troubadour Bernadet de Ventadorn, whose works helped to establish and from the notion of "courtly love." The other names are fictitious.

[52] The king in question is Louis XV; the episode in question is not recorded in orthodox histories, but might be derived from one of the many scurrilously slanderous fictitious accounts of the decadence of his court published in the eighteenth century. The "Monsieur de Fronsac" cited in the next paragraph is presumably the Duc de Richelieu who was notorious in that court.

Lo went on: "It wasn't a sadness for the Lady of the court and the prostitute invited to supper in the house in the faubourg where Monsieur de Fronsac was late in arriving, for, in the little room with the lovely paintings, sitting before the narrow table where the rosy spice of strange preserves was bleeding diaphanously in the plates; the champagne soon advised them of a hundred follies by which the melancholy of waiting is consoled."

Then all three of them, in mingled loquacity: "And later, many girls-with-golden-eyes kissed violet eyes and forget-me-not eyes, which were very unexpected under virile eyelids, and so Théodore de Maupin, in a single night, had two nuptial nights![53] And no longer in books but in life, so many young women knew that a fragrance warmed on the lips of young women where no memory of cigars or alcohol lingered!"

And they concluded: "With the consequence, pusillanimous poet. That it is as immemorial as it is recent, of old and before no less than of today, the sin for which we are accused of setting the example! Turtle-doves with united beaks are sufficient to educate demoiselles walking in pairs in woodland pathways during the month of vacations."

Increasingly perplexed, I murmured: "It's nevertheless true that you do me little honor in the world, and it wouldn't be without reason that I'd regret having invented you. I grant that you are imitators and not initiators, but no matter; it would have been decent not to regulate yourselves on such unfortunate models, and the sin of others does not exculpate yours."

Lo, approved by Jo and Zo, cried: "First of all, that sin, we have never admitted that we were inclined to it. Who, then, would dare to claim that we have committed it? In what page of your work have you rendered us culpable of it? Well, reread yourself, I beg you, if you dare to brave the boredom; you

---

[53] The eponymous heroine of Théophile Gautier's *Mademoiselle de Maupin* (1835) calls herself Théodore when disguised as a man.

won't find a line in which a single one or our smiles swooned, definitively, in an averred kiss. You are, in reality, a remarkably moral storyteller.

"Even if it were true that we imitated Erinnys enlacing Amymone under the myrtles mingled with roses, or the prostitute and the Lady of the court supping in Monsieur de Fronsac's little house, we still wouldn't have any resemblance to execrable devourers of virgins and wives. They are the violent, the furious, the hideous; we are the tender, the sprightly, the pretty. Their desire, made of lust and anger, would frighten ours, made of reveries and idleness. It isn't our smile that informs their rictus! Our scarcely-sharpened fingernails have nothing in common with their acerbic claws. They go to the Black Mass, we go to the Rose Mass.

"We are very different even from the heroic and formidable damned women made illustrious by the great Baudelaire! Go on, you're calumniating yourself, or making yourself believe it, poet of delicate dreams! In your most hazardous inventions you never lose the memory of the fleeting grace of nymphs disappearing between the quivering of willows, nor that of the marquises, all lace and perfumes, who lay on Crébillon's sofa, letting their foot hang down, denuded of the fallen slipper!

"Well, since so many odious lunatics are so intent on taking us for models, let them imitate us, who do indeed offer them an example: the pretty folly of our laughter, almost ingenuous in spite of a certain slyness, and the childishness of our perversities, and the bright dream of our eyes, and the fresh rosiness of our lips, which no bitter kiss has paled!"

The Song of the Mark

Jo said: "Sometimes, at night, I suffer from ennui."

"At a ball?" asked Lo.

"At supper?" asked Zo.

But Jo, elegiac, said: "In bed."

"No!"

"Bah!"

Jo affirmed: "Yes, at night, between the closed malines of the alcove, I sometimes suffer from ennui. I can understand your surprise, darlings, and with that astonishment is mingled, I'm sure, a secret scorn for the young men who, not without difficulty, sometimes obtain the task fulfilling next to me, from the lighting of the night-light to the renascent dawn, the functions whose first effect ought to be precisely that of banishing all morose languor. Oh, don't think too badly of those who only succeed insufficiently in diverting me; the only person culpable of my yawns on the pillow—which are pretty besides, teeth of rice between strawberry lips—is me."

"You're calumniating yourself," said Lo.

"Grace for the grace that separates you from the Idalian Graces!" said Zo.

"You can't know, sister of the roses of which bees never weary...," said Lo.

"Bees!" cried Jo, interrupting. "Fie!"

"Pardon me!" said Lo, blushing. "I meant to say butterflies."

"Good!"

"You can't know," Lo went on, "the lassitude of the divine Kiss. The truth is that, like us, you have to lament the deplorable mediocrity of lovers, which resigns us, after so many vain experiments, to the conviction of being unable to substitute triumphant competitors for then, for, not only has the colossal race of the Heraclides disappeared forever from the earth..."

"Alas!" said Zo.

"Not only are they no more, those grandsons of Zeus, who obtained from the sublime ancestor the endless redoubling of thunderclaps with the intrepid jet of incessant lightnings..."

"Alas!" said Zo.

"But even those we admit give us, by means of delicate and subtle artifices—fireworks instead of lightning—the illusion of formidable and glorious thunderbolts, avoiding the concluded pact in ignorance or idleness calculated to disconcert persons resolved to perfect annihilation."

"Alas!" said Zo.

But Jo, solemn, said: "No, I tell you, it's not in the oft-failing valor of young men or in their lack of skill that it's appropriate to seek the cause of my nocturnal melancholy, nor in my long habituation to the most supreme delights that a lover can invent and realize. I'm desolate, at the hour of culpable caresses, because I deplore and reprove them, because I regret the ingenuous charms of puerile amours."

"Eh?"

"What?"

"Yes. And I think that I wouldn't fail to die of sadness before every dawn if I didn't have, in order to deflect me from spleen, the song..."

"The song?"

"What song?"

"The song of the mark!"

She did not give them time to believe that it was a mediocre play on words.[54] She continued right away: "Little Lo, litle Zo, certainly, at a point in your bodies daintier than the doll offered as a baptismal gift to the daughter of the Queen of

---

[54] It is a play on words in French because of the similarity between "le chant du signe" [the song of the mark] and "le chant du cygne" [swan song].

Chrysanthemums by the smallest of the fays of Japan, you hide—not always, but after all, one is sometimes dressed—one of those exquisite imperfections of the skin, a flaw and not a flaw, a blackness and not a blackness, or a pinkness almost not pink, with, sometimes, the tip of a single little curly hair?"

"Personally," said Lo, "it's the imperceptible resemblance of a mulberry that I have..."

"Where?" asked Jo.

"On the left breast. Not above it or below it, but near the point at which the snowy hill inclines toward the snowy valley."

"Ah?"

"Yes."

"As for me," said Zo, "it's a tiny, very tiny scarlet pebble that I have..."

"Where?" asked Jo.

"At the projection of the right hip; and one might think it were a fragment of praline, left there by teeth crunching bonbons."

"Ah?"

"Yes."

But Jo: "Mine," she said, "is a violet that I have, mysteriously flowered, and that violet, when I get bored at night, immediately starts to sing."

"It sings?"

"It sings?"

"So delightfully that, in my ennui, my soul is quite ecstatic."

Neither Lo not Zo, accustomed to enchantments, was a person to be astonished by so little. They did not have the idea for a moment of denying the singing floret. But what did it sing? They were curious about that.

Interrogated, Jo replied: "This is what it sings, the violet I have, heard by me alone:

"Child, child! They weren't true, then, the oaths sworn behind the little house, in the garden pathway illuminated by

352

glow-worms, while the grandparents were paying whist in the dining-room by the light of the ceiling lamp?

"He took you by the hand, he held you by the waist, he told you that he would graduate next year and afterwards would be an advocate and a député, glorious and rich, and that he'd marry you and you'd be happy. But in the meantime, he asked for your lips.

"Child, child! They weren't true, then, the oaths sworn behind the little house, in the garden pathway illuminated by glow-worms, while the grandparents were paying whist in the dining-room by the light of the ceiling lamp?

"He asked for your lips, and you refused them. You swore to him to wait for him; but since he loved you, since you loved him too, what need did he have for a kiss? A kiss doesn't prove anything, and isn't worth as much as a sincere word.

"Child, child! They weren't true, then, the oaths sworn behind the little house, in the garden pathway illuminated by glow-worms, while the grandparents were paying whist in the dining-room by the light of the ceiling lamp?

"He kissed you anyway. You weren't married at all; and you didn't deny him the confession of the pleasure that his lips had, quivering, at the point where he put them. Your ease even repeated the previous promises, and you were as happy as possible, under the stars, in the company of the little cousin on vacation.

"Child, child! They weren't true, then, the oaths sworn behind the little house, in the garden pathway illuminated by glow-worms, while the grandparents were paying whist in the dining-room by the light of the ceiling lamp?"

"Damn!" said Lo.

"Damn!" said Zo.

"That's a singularly loquacious mark."

"And you take pleasure in hearing it?"

"How could I not take pleasure, amid the monotony, in sum, of savant caresses, in remembering first amours, such sincere, such chaste amours, remembering the candid kiss that enchanted my entire soul..."

"The entire soul?" asked Lo.

"The entire soul?" asked Zo.

"Oh, the entire soul," said Jo.

The other two smiled.

"The mulberry that I have isn't so talkative," said Lo,

"The praline that I have isn't so prolix," said Zo.

"That's because your birthmarks are natural imperfections, albeit so exquisite, of our dainty little bodies, while the violet with which I'm flowered, and which speaks and sings and reminds me of the pure ecstasies of childish tenderness, is the mark, persisting in a gentle blueness—as sometimes happens—of the candid kiss that I didn't avoid."

"Good!" said Lo.

"That explains everything," said Zo.

But, pensively:

"The singing mark...," said one.

"Where do you hide it, then?" said the other.

Oh, how Jo blushed as soon as those words were spoken! And it was scarcely in a murmur that she stammered her head turned away: "Heavens, how cruel it is to interrogate me like that! Don't you know that it's in the moss of the woods that violets flourish?"

The Blood of a Swallow

They were innumerable, the people who, in those times—what times? It does not matter, all times are as good as one another in which roses bloom and the mouths of women are more odorous than the roses—made the pilgrimage to an old female hermit, the inhabitant of a cave in the side of a mountain, who sold the blood of swallows. She was so old that the most ancient crows could not remember having seen her young; the twice centenarian oak said in the Dodonian murmur of its branches: "I believe that she was a little less than seventy years old when, the daughter of a woodcutter, she brushed with her naked foot, already desiccated, the green acorn that I still was."

Ancestral as she was, however, and in addition, very ugly when she appeared in the threshold of the cave in which she lived in austere devotion with an infinitely pretty great-granddaughter that she had, people still brought her presents of every sort: things to eat, things to drink, furs in order to be warm in winter, muslins to make herself beautiful in summer—her, beautiful! ha ha ha!—and gold, which was buried at the feet of trees, and precious medals, and also, in sculpted ivory boxes similar to all little reliquaries, relics recommendable by virtue of the twenty miracles they performed.

Why was she accorded such largesse? Because, in exchange, she offered two drops, or three, or four, almost red—yes, red—of the blood of a swallow in a kind of pink lily, speckled with gold, which she picked, she said, in the nearby rocks, and which was a striking resemblance.

A resemblance? To what? I cannot say. But what is certain is that the drops of swallow blood operated veritable prodigies.

Unfortunately it was not every day that the old lady consented to hand them out, in a pink lily speckled with gold.

Many people came from the most distant lands, to whom she responded: "Come back next week," or: "Come back next month," and if anyone cried: "Eh! Why not satisfy us right away?" she replied: "It's because the swallow from which the blood for your salvation drips has flown away, and won't be back until the day I've told you."

Infrequent as the presence of the swallow was, however—five or six days a month—the drops of blood were so efficacious that they compensated, with the rapidity of the cures they obtained, for the rarity of the treatment. The effects were truly extraordinary.

Decrepit old men had been seen, who no longer had any teeth, or eyes, or anything that it is appropriate to have in order to be an acceptable husband, suddenly mutated, by means of a pink tear finally drunk, into vigorous fiancés made impatient by the retardation of the wedding to the point of rape.

Sexagenarian ladies recovered, in less than the blink of an eye, the charms that had once rendered them so pleasant.

For having drunk that swallow's blood, cowards were also seen to become brave, the ugly to become handsome, and imbeciles to equal the glorious poets whose strophes enchant souls.

As soon as the pretty blood of the bird had been applied to the lips, poor little children near to dying in cradles that already resembled little coffins often recovered vitality and smiles. Young women who, unhealthy and meek, bewailed not daring to love under the falling autumn leaves, knotted arms as vigorous as they were tender around the neck of their friend.

In sum, all the living were full of health, strength and beauty because of the seller of swallow's blood in gilded lilies, who lived with her infinitely pretty great-granddaughter in the cave in the side of the mountain.

One day, however, a singer of tender songs passed along the road, handsome to behold, even lovelier to hear, who, when he mirrored himself in springs, rendered the reflection of the leaning jasmines jealous because he was so white, and when he replied with a ballad to their roulades, rendered the nightingales jealous, he sang so agreeably.

As he went past the cave, the old lady said to him: "Hey, you, traveler with a handsome face, don't you want to buy a few drops of swallow's blood? It has never been as bright and as salutary as it is at the present moment," for she was very miserly, and understood her métier.

He said: "No, thank you; I'm young and good humored, and have no need of the drugs people sell."

But beyond the old lady's shoulder, he saw the eyes of the young girl—the child's name as Fideline—and he stopped.

"Nevertheless," he said, "I'll gladly accept the hospitality of your cavern, and as a testimony of gratitude, I'll sing before slumber songs so beautiful that the surrounding silence will swoon and the sky will open all its stars wide, like golden ears."

To tell the truth, sometime after that, there was a great sadness, at first in the neighboring region and then throughout the earth. It was in vain that the old, the sick and the sad came in pilgrimage to the cavern; they did not obtain the customary cures, even on the days previously indicated. The old woman said to them, not without the air of someone who is not content: "Go away, I beg you. The pink lily, speckled with gold, has not creased to flourish, and I even think that it is blooming better than it has ever done, but the bright blood of the swallow no longer drips there in rosy tears. Take your present away, which I cannot accept without dishonesty, since the exquisite panacea with which I comforted you has dried up, like a spring burned by the sun."

And the distress was as desolating as possible. Nothing was seen on the roads but people in tears, saying: "Alas, I shall never recover youth!" or "Alas, I shall never be loved by the one I adore!" or "Alas, I shall always have this wooden leg!" or "Alas, without the hope of ever opening them again, I feel my blind eyes closing," for the bright blood of the swallow had dried up.

In the evenings, however in pathways in the woods bordered by eglantines like little white stars that lit up on the bushes, and in the luminous clearings, and in the profound shadows where the mysterious moss is so soft, the great-granddaughter of the old hermit walked hand in hand with the handsome singer of ballads, who, since the day when he had entered it, had not quit the grotto again, doubtless finding himself very comfortable there.

Were they married, the girl and the balladeer? Not if you mean by the word "marriage" the legitimate union of persons, which a priest has blessed, but married in fact if, in order to be believed to be, it is sufficient in your thought that there are no longer any kisses except the ones two people give to one another, and they will get marred later, when they find the time. But they were happy, mingling their fingers and mingling their gazes in the enchantment of the spring evening; I wish such a delightful hymen to the most married of people. They did not even lack the hope of a blond and pink being, boy or girl, who, not in a few days but after many months, would revive their love, in being the living evidence of it.

And the lover clasped to his heart, more tenderly, the soon-to-be maternal, but as if still virginal, lover, being so young and so white. And nothing troubled their happiness in the perfumes and the rapture of the shadows—no, nothing, it being irrelevant to them that the entire world was suffering, lamenting and weeping because there was no more swallow's blood in the golden lily.

What Makes Life Worthwhile

There was a very knowledgeable man who, by virtue of reading old books and conversing by night with mandrakes blossomed at the foot of gallows, had become a great sorcerer. Destiny obeyed him to the point that he could, if he pleased, realize the wishes of the most ambitious dreamers, and it was child's play for him to enable the dead to emerge from beneath sepulchral slabs.

In a nocturnal cemetery he went from tomb to tomb, offering life to the dead.

Rap rap!

"Who's knocking?"

"One who resuscitates."

"Oh, let him be welcome."

And the cadavers resumed life, returning to the upheavals, the sorrows and the treasons. Humans are so stupid, even after the last sigh, that none of them refuse to resume dolorous existence.

But it is in vain, to begin with, that the very knowledgeable man raps on the stone that, in the most overgrown part of the cemetery, shelters under a willow silvery in the moonlight, for there reposes a dead man more clear-sighted than the others, having been a poet while he was alive.

"Hey, sleeper, can't you hear me?"

No response.

"Has the earth filled your ears to the point that you can't hear, or have the worms eaten your tongue to the point that you can't respond?"

Still silence.

The sorcerer, gripped by anger, knocks so violently on the tomb that the dead man, losing patience, gets annoyed.

"Eh! Can't one rest in peace, even in the supreme bed? Go on your way, sorcerer, I beg you, and don't trouble my slumber any longer."

"You don't want to see the sky full of stars again, then, and the flowery woods, and the red roses of gardens?"

"Heaven preserve me from ever seeing them again! I've wept under the impassive stars, I've wept in the flowery woods, and I've wept because of lying mouths similar to the roses of gardens."

"You don't want to revive because you've suffered. So be it. But what if I were to offer you as many joys as you've known sorrows?"

"There are no joys on earth; on earth there is nothing but despair."

"What if I were to give you, whom insulting scorn followed through the streets like a gang of guttersnipes following a masque, the glory of being a triumphant monarch sitting on a golden throne, or a radiant charmer of souls who leads the enthusiasm of crowds to the Capitol?"

"Let me sleep. The glory of kings or the glory of singers is not even a noise in the thunderous din of the infinite universe."

"What if I were to offer you, whom only poverty visited in some hovel under the rooftops, wealth, all the gold and precious stones that fill the coffers of fabulous bankers who exchange ruby mines for diamond mines?"

"Let me sleep. The wealth of fantastic sellers of metals and stones isn't worth any more than the alms fallen into the bowl of a beggar on the highway, even if those alms are in false coin."

"What if I were to offer you an honest and tranquil hearth, where one warms one's feet in the evening, while children play around the table that is not yet cleared?"

"The blaze of the hearth is a traitor that sets fire to the house."

"What if I were to give you a pure and grave wife, a good housekeeper all day long who, when you come back home, welcomes you by giving you her forehead to kiss, almost sororally or maternally, with her soul in her pure eyes?"

"The good housekeeper lets the stew burn, there's an odor of adultery in her kiss, and her soul in her pure eyes lies like a devil in a font."

"Well, you're demanding! I can see that, in order to convince you to revive, it's necessary to give you the most exquisite felicity that is permitted to a man under heaven. Reinflate your lungs with air, stand up, shrug off your shroud, lift the slab and walk; follow me, and I'll take you, close to a village, to a wooded path full of eglantines not yet in flower, where the ingenuous fiancée of puerile amours is waiting for you, her heart beating with an unknown desire, her lips never yet opened to kisses. Come, follow me and you shall know the incomparable delight of plucking the hesitation of the first avowal from virgin lips."

"Let me sleep, I tell you. The ingénue in the wooded path soiled by the slime of slugs and stinking with the ordure of beasts that prowl and couple there would bring me, along with a heart haunted by the fantasy of being a lady of the town, a mouth bitten a hundred times over by an ox-drover or a farm laborer."

Then the resuscitator cannot find anything more to offer the obstinate dead man, and already, not without some humiliation, he is about to leave the cemetery when a thought occurs to him. He retraces his steps quickly and leans over the indocile tomb.

"Monsieur Sleeper," he says, in a low voice, "In an outlying district of the city, behind Venetian blinds traversed by the soft light of a lamp, I know a girl, not pretty and not young, but who has in her favor that she is not virtuous, and as she is detestable to honest bourgeois and austere mothers of families, she occupies her lucrative insomnias in stubborn experiments; she has invented, if one can believe her renown, a kiss—a strange kiss, a novel kiss, which, by virtue of the acerbity of the bite or the exasperated indolence of the kiss, is quite capable of reducing to extreme breathlessness, suddenly or gradually—in accordance with the desire one manifests—the man least sensible to the subtle incitements of the most adroit courtesans. And, stubborn dead man, if you wish, I will take you to that subtle individual."

Then, well-advised, the buried poet cried: "Why didn't you say so sooner?"

And, resuscitated willingly, he ran through the deserted streets, breathless already, toward the house denounces by a Venetian blind traversed by a soft light, toward the house where a obscene prostitute, spiced with ginger and sweating all over with a musky sweat, mocks and surpasses, by means of a rare kiss, the glory of being Charlemagne or Petrarch and the wealth of sellers of priceless jewels, and the peaceful hearth, the wife and the virgin.

Madeleine's Amours

I. The Name of Everything

Once, when I was weeping—it was under the desolate caress of a willow near the pool of Ville-d'Avray—a passer-by interrogated me:

"Listen, man who is weeping, and tell me what your pain is?"

"My pain," I replied, "is named Madeleine."

The passer-by said, not without mocking slightly: "That's very funny. I never heard mention of such a chagrin. There is treason, there is perjury, there is abandonment, there is mourning, but I don't know that a pain exists that has the name you cite."

"Alas, Monsieur," I replied, "for me, lying amour, false oaths, a solitary bed and defunct dreams are Madeleine."

Once, when I was laughing—it was in the arbor of a tavern on the Île de Croissy—a passer-by interrogated me:

"Listen, man who is laughing, and tell me what your joy is?"

"My joy," I replied, "is named Madeleine.

The passer-by said, in a mocking fashion: "That's quite absurd! I never heard mention of such a delight. There is the kiss, there is glory, there is the hope of amour, there is the forgetfulness of life, but I don't think a joy exists that has the name you cite."

"Oh, Madame," I replied, "for me, the moist softness of lips, triumph over the greatest, the hope of sincere tenderness and the divine Lethe are Madeleine."

Once, when I was being grilled—it was on a very ardent grill in a red corner of Purgatory—a devil interrogated me:

"Listen, sinner who is being grilled, and tell me what your evil is?"

"My evil," I replied, "is named Madeleine.

The devil said, after shrugging his shoulders: "That's perfectly stupid. I never heard of any such torture. There are vats of boiling oil, there are skewers of red hot steel, there is sulfur and there is naphtha, but I don't believe an evil exists that has the name you cite."

"Alas, devil," I replied, "for me, what burns, what transpierces, what chokes and what consumes is Madeleine."

Once, when I was ecstatic—it was on the fourth step of the Throne, in the august splendor of Paradise, a seraph integrated me:

"Listen, elect who is ecstatic, and tell me what your delight is?"

"My delight," I replied, "is named Madeleine."

The seraph said, not without an irony in which mercy was mingled: "That's well worthy of someone who was a man. Never, in Heaven, has there been any question of such an enchantment. There is the mystical bread, there is the liquor fermented from the starry vine, there is the music of the spheres, and there is God himself, but I affirm that no delight exists that has the name you cite."

"Oh, handsome seraph," I replied, "for me, the adorable host and the astral wine and the celestial music and the unique divinity is Madeleine."

II. The Breath Lost and Found

"Alas!" I sighed.
"What's the matter?" asked Madeleine.
"Oh, it's a strange misfortune."
"Say what, I beg you."

"It's that, just now, in our bed of amour, while your clement lips, O Made, O Leine, O Madeleine, were parted toward mine, a bee from the garden, bumping into the window, distracted me with its slight sound, and I allowed your breath to exhale without collecting it in my mouth."

"So what?"

"That's the disaster I'm bemoaning. That breath, which was destined for me, that breath more precious than the perfume of a flower that would be a ruby, more intoxicating than the fresh warmth of lemon-balm plants in spring, I didn't breathe in, and it has flown away, and is lost, and perhaps I shall never ecstasize myself with it."

"But yes, yes!" said Madeleine. "The red carnation from which it emanated has not faded, and you can now savor the odor again, if you lean over a little."

"It wouldn't be the breath of a little while ago. It wouldn't be the breath that, like an imbecile, I allowed to escape, and I need to find it."

With that, I leapt out of bed and started prowling around the room. Where could my friend's breath have alighted? On the poppy of that Japanese cup? No, the poppy had the natural coldness of faience. On the hyacinth buried in the diaphanous shroud of a partly-open crystal casket? Amid the decorations of the Japanese screen? Or the guipure flowers of the flounce of the bed-curtains? Alas, no; I do not recognize the dear perfume there, nor there, nor there, nor elsewhere; and the adored perfume does not enchant my lips.

Then Madeleine, seeing my chagrin, said: "Oh well, learn the truth. While you drew away from my lips, distracted, the bee that had bumped into the window came in through the poorly-closed shutter and, rapidly passing by, stole from me the breath that was destined for you."

"And did it fly away?"

"Certainly. It's in the garden."

"Oh, God! So now, taking nectar from the roses, the lilies, the jasmines and the jonquils, it has left your dear tender aroma there, and in order that the breeze doesn't carry it away, it's necessary that I go and pick all the flowers in the flower-bed."

I did as I had said. I ran outside, scarcely dressed—we had neighbors with modestly closed Venetian blinds—into the blooming garden, and I picked the jonquils, the jasmines, the lilies and the roses. But the breeze had been quicker than me; I didn't recognize in the calices the exquisite fragrance of Madeleine's lips.

Where had it gone? Where had the wind dispersed it?

"The breeze whispered: "Poor man! It is, indeed, me who took it and carried it away. But I've already returned from Tiflis, where the bulbul is dying of amour for the ingrate blossoming rose, and as I brushed, out there in Asian Russia, a stream that as flowing toward the sands, you'll have difficulty recovering Madeleine's breath in the babble of the waves with which I mingled it.

I didn't hesitate. I departed for Tiflis. When I arrived there, the bulbul, a nightingale indulgent to poets, was kind enough to indicate to me, with an inclination of the beak, the stream into which the breeze had put my friend's perfume.

On my knees, bending my spine and lowering my head, I drank from the palm of my hand a little of the flowing and fleeing water; I did not find the odor of the adored mouth there.

"The fact is," said a very small wave, babbling and laughing, "that the little waves received it a long time ago, and it went with them, gliding into the distance, toward uncertainty, toward the unknown, out there, far away, where I'm following it."

"I'll follow you, then!" I cried.

As rapidly as the little wave of the babbling stream, I launched forth, without knowing where, running after a breath. But what was my desolation! Suddenly, the streaming water sank into the sand and disappeared, and was no more.

Don't think that I lost courage! With my fingernails, furiously, I dug into the soft soil, and I kept digging, along the damp line left by the flowing water; and suddenly, I fell, the sand collapsing, into a crypt painted with pink ibises and green crocodiles, where, over the hermetically closed mouth of a mummy, the last drop of the stream was weeping.

I leaned over and sucked it in, that drop, and I drank therein all the divine aroma of Madeleine's mouth!

I had reconquered the lost breath; I had on my lips the delectable exhalation of the adored lips.

Triumphant, I returned toward the bedroom, toward the chamber of amour where Madeleine, while waiting for me, had doubtless gone to sleep.

She was there in fact so pretty, oh, so pretty, more adorable than she had ever been, but she was not asleep.

Gloriously, I told her the whole story of my travels across the world. I told her about the bee, the flowers, the breeze, the stream, and the mouth of the mummy where, with an inhalation, I had finally rediscovered the vanished breath. I did not speak without pride. I had dared such strange enterprises, I had completed such difficult voyages; that was well worth her thanking me and being kind.

But, furiously, she said: "Leave me, Monsieur, and refrain from ever appearing again to my eyes. For it is necessary to reserve one's lips for the person one loves, and I could never love a man who deceived me—with a mummy!"

III. Wickedness Punished

One evening when I went to Madeleine's residence—the residence of the much-beloved Madeleine—I had, I don't know why, a soul as wicked as possible.

At the corner of the street I saw a merchant in his shop counting cash. I had no need of money, being, since the heritage of my uncle, the Maharajah, richer than the most opulent kings in the world, but it irritated me to hear that merchant counting all that sonorous coin. I went in, I pushed the man away, and I fled, taking his treasure with me, which I threw into the mouth of a drain a little further on.

In one of the gardens of an outlying district, a nightingale was singing delectably in the high crown of a tree. I had no motive for conceiving any envy since, being a poet, I was able to sing a hundred times better than all the birds of gardens and woods, but it irritated me that the nightingale was modulating so tenderly. I climbed up between the branches, I seized it, and I squeezed its neck, not enough to strangle it but enough to stifle permanently the voice in its little throat; and the tree mourned, devoid of song forever.

Having arrived in the country I saw a young Bohemian lying on the rim of an embankment, gazing recklessly at the stars. I had no reason to be jealous of him, for, bearing within me the soul of Orpheus and of Simonides, I could contemplate infinite constellated skies with my eyes closed, but it irritated me to see that poet so charmed by nocturnal gleams. Approaching him with a sharp stone in each hand, I put out his eyes, so that he would lose the joy of admiring the beautiful sky.

Then I felt less cruel, because I saw the lamp shining in the much-beloved Madeleine's window.

As soon as I was beside her I said: "Oh, let me kiss the flaming gold of your dear hair!"

But Madeleine was no longer blonde, and it was gray hair that she had.

"Oh, speak to me; your voice is the enchantment in which my entire being swoons."

But Madeleine did not pronounce a word, and by means of signs, she made me understand that she was mute.

"Oh, look at me; your eyes are brighter and more celestial than the highest sidereal gleams."

But Madeleine turned dead eyes toward me, and I understood that she was blind.

As I was desolate, in a frightened surprise, a tiny fay, occupied in leaping from petal to petal in a bouquet in a Japanese vase, said: "Only blame yourself for what has happened. Because of the crimes that you've committed in your unmotivated wickedness, Madeleine has lost the three charms that made your delight; she will only recover them if you repair your faults."

"I'll repair them," I said.

I ran back to the Bohemian poet lying on the embankment.

"Since I've extinguished your gaze, I'll give you my vision of infinite and splendid spaces."

Running more rapidly, I reached the tree in the suburban garden where the nightingale was no longer singing.

"Since I've silenced your song, I'll give you my art of gathering the sounds of the sacred word in incomparable rhymes."

Running out of breath, I reached the merchant's shop.

"Since I've stolen your gold, I'll give you in exchange all the prodigious heritage of my uncle, the Maharajah."

Those justices done, I went back to the residence of my much-beloved Madeleine. Heaven! The little fay had given me good advice. My mistress had recovered her sight (O irises of lapis lazuli, in which golden flecks sparkle that resemble the dust of stars) since I had rendered the sky to the poet; she had recovered her voice (O ineffable echo of paradisal concerts) since the nightingale was singing my poems on its branch; and she had recovered the gold of her hair, since the merchant was able to count my prodigious riches in his shop. Ecstatic, I advanced toward her on my knees, and I adored her, and already I was dying of intoxication in thinking about the delights that would soon be mine...

But Madeleine shrugged her shoulders.

"What are you doing here? It's others that I shall enchant with my reconquered charms, and I think you'd better be off as soon as possible; after all, what do you expect me to do with a lover who can no longer see the stars, who is no longer a poet, and who isn't even a millionaire?"

IV. Contradiction... Up to a Point

"Come here!"
She went away.
"Go away!"
She came back.
"Look at me!"
She turned away.
"Don't look at me!"
She burned me with a fixed stare.
"Speak to me!"
She fell silent.
"Shut up!"
She sang.
"Kiss me!"
She refused me her lips.
"Take your mouth away."
She ecstasized my with a hundred kisses.

Then I understood how she was inclined to do the exact opposite of what was asked of her, and I resolved to take advantage of her propensity for disobedience to obtain all imaginable delights.

But she doubtless perceived the trap in which I wanted to catch her, for the other morning, after I had said to her: "Oh, be unfaithful to me, I implore you," she deceived me seven or eight times before midnight.

V. When She Passes By

The skylark said: "I heard a skylark."

"Well, yes," said a passing cloud, slightly roseate in the dawn, "it's your own song you heard."

"No," said he bird, "it wasn't my song."

The violet said: "I smelled the perfume of a violet."

"Well, yes," said the tufted moss mingled with little strawberries, "it's your own perfume that you respired."

"No," said the flower, "it wasn't my perfume."

The ruby said: "I've seen the redness of a ruby."

"Well, yes," said the ermine of a cardinal's cloak that was trailing over the steps of the church, "it's your own color that you saw."

"No," said the ruby, "it wasn't my color."

Then the skylark, the violet and the ruby said: "That's very strange; it's inexplicable that there was the song of a skylark, which wasn't a skylark, the perfume of a violet, which wasn't a violet, and the redness of a ruby, which wasn't a crimson cloak."

But I said: "What's astonishing about that? Under the roseate dawn cloud, in the moss mingled with strawberries and on the steps of the church, Madeleine passed by, singing, perfumed and with such red lips!"

VI. The Impatient

As I was going to see Madeleine, the darling who has a little of the fay in her, I saw a flower-stall at the corner of the Rue Blanche, where there were so many flowers that one might have thought that all of spring was piled on a stall. But what astonished me was not that all the eglantines, all the orange-blossom and all the violets were there, in a single heap; it was the perfume they exhaled, sweeter, purer and lighter than any perfume of a calyx had ever been.

My nostrils charmed, I said: "That's very strange. It seems to me that I'm inhaling the scattered aroma of Madeleine's lips."

But I added "What a crazy thought! Madeleine is at home, her mouth half-closed, awaiting my kiss; I'm very foolish to waste time like this smelling flowers."

And I went on my way.

As I approached Madeleine's residence I passed the house in the Boulevard Haussmann where the famous gypsy flute-player who has been the admiration of all Paris for two years lodges. And indeed, sitting on his window-sill, his legs dangling toward the street—for he is a trifle eccentric and carefree—he was playing the flue for the pleasure of passers-by. Oh, the plated well, the exotic virtuoso. He truly captured in a roulade or a trill an entire choir of nightingales and warblers; I truly believe that he would have astonished Luscignole herself.[55] But what surprised me was not that all that diverse birdsong was emerging from a single flute, it was that a melody was mingled with it more exquisitely troubling than any melody of the flute.

My ears ecstasized, I said: "That's quite extraordinary! It seems to that I can hear Madeleine's voice scattered in that music.

But I added: "What an absurd idea! Madeleine is at home, singing at the piano, in the expectation of my delight, in a little while, the reverie of Elsa leaning over her balcony or the miraculous plaintive phrase of Fricka amid the distress of the gods. I'm very foolish to waste time like this listening to a flute.

And I went on my way.

As I was on the point of arriving at Madeleine's residence, I saw, on the corner of the Rue de Miromesnil, behind the display-window of an illustrious seller of paintings, an ancient canvas by some forgotten master, in which a Madonna was more delightfully pretty than the most hyperphysical visions of poets. But what astonished me was not that there were, in a single smile, all graces, all enchantments and all paradises; it was that a virginal candor blossomed there, so infinitely celestial, that even the baby Jesus did not have.

---

[55] Luscignole is the eponymous heroine of Mendès tragic novella, published in 1892.

My heart enraptured, I said: "That's very singular! It seems to me that I can see the innocence of Madeleine in that pure visage."

But I added: "What an extravagant imagination! Madeleine is at home, with all her miraculous ingenuousness, not without the hope of losing a little of it; I'm very foolish to waste time like this admiring a picture."

And I went on my way.

But when I arrived at Madeleine's residence—that of the darling who has a little of the fay in her—I was very angry. She was not waiting for me; she was not in the dear bedroom where the sunlight often traverses the closed Venetian blinds and the moonlight the open window—for the sun is indiscreet and brutal, but the moon has such a tender gaze—interested in our faithful kisses.

Impatient by nature, I did not hesitate to break with my fist the two Japanese vases that ornamented the mantelpiece, to stave in with my heel the harpsichord that wept dolorously, and to break with my shoulder two or three Venetian mirrors the vacuity of which reminded me, with its ironic void, of the absence of my beloved. I was in the process of crushing and pulverizing a third Saxe figurine between my wrathful fingers when Madeleine opened the door and appeared, smiling.

"Where have you been, traitress?" I cried

"Oh, don't scold me, my love" she said. "Impatient to see you, I didn't want to wait for you to come into this room, and I went to meet you."

"To meet me?"

"Well, yes."

"Where, pray?"

"Various places," she said, "and don't hold it against me that I didn't join you sooner, for—since I have a little of the fay in me—I needed a little time, in coming back, to reassemble the perfumes that I added a little while ago to those of the flowers in the stall, and the voice that I put into the song of the flute, and my candor, mingled with the innocence of the Madonna behind the window of the merchant of paintings."

VII. The Obstinate Name

That day, in order to be certain that her name, the name of Madeleine, execrated and adored, would not follow me everywhere, would not haunt my soul and my heart for ever more, I proceeded somewhat after the fashion of a murderer who divides the body of a victim into three sections and hides them at a great distance from one another.

I departed for Srinagar, a sufficiently distant city. There, on the tremulous leaf of a rose-bush, I traced the syllable *Ma* with a golden needle.

Then I went to Tromso, a city nowhere near my customary domicile. There, on a leaf of belladonna, on the edge of an icy pond, I traced the syllable *de* with a silver needle.

Finally, I departed for San Francisco, where one doesn't arrive without traveling for a few days. There, on the leaf of a magnolia, I traced the syllable *leine* with a diamond needle.

Then I came back, not without losing many days along the route, to my Parisian house, where I found my affairs, abandoned for so long, in a very poor state. But no matter! At least I was liberated from the name, the execrated and adored name. And, lying in my bed, I went to sleep very content.

But who, then, opened my window to breezes that were coming from far away? For when I awoke, I saw on my heart, come from Srinagar, Tromso and San Francisco, three joined leaves, on which I read the name Madeleine.

VIII. Two Birds, A Single Nest

Because Madeleine was slightly indisposed, I nearly went mad with pain.

"Come on," she said, "Don't be so alarmed, and learn the cause of my suffering, which won't last long, in any case, and will end in very pleasant delights."

She reflected, and said: "Once, I had a heart."

"Alas," I said. "What did you do with it?"

"Nothing at all," she said, "but now I have two of them."

"Two hearts, all to yourself?"

"Well, yes," she said. "Mine and yours. Are you going to complain because I've put your heart beside mine, directly beneath one of my breasts, the one whose rosy tip is dearer to your lips and teeth?"

"Oh, I have no complaint to make," I admitted.

"You're quite right. Now, having those two hearts within me, it sometimes happens that one of them, jealous, cruel and excessive—that's yours, Monsieur—picks a quarrel with the other, which isn't always as resigned as it needs to be. Hence the battles, which can't help but be cruel in the breast of a young woman."

"Alas, Madeleine."

"But don't judge me too unfortunate, I beg you, for often, also, those two hearts are in accord to such a degree that it truly seems to me that they only make one, and I know unparalleled delights in sensing our double life mingling and fusing and swooning within me."

IX. The Impossible Presents

I said to Madeleine: "When you no longer love me, give me, without saying anything, a rose devoid of petals, and I'll understand that it's time for me to die."

"Right!" she said. "If I cease to love you, I'll give you a rose devoid of petals."

But I added: "It might be that, carelessly, you'll give me a rose devoid of petals one day, without thinking any evil. Add to the sad present of the flower a dead dove, and I'll understand that it's time for me to die."

"I agree with that," she said. "If I cease to love you, I'll give you, at the same time as the sad rose, a dead dove."

But I said: "I fear that, frivolous as you are, you might take it into your head one day to give me, without thinking any evil, a rose devoid of petals and a dead dove. I want to avoid the cruel misunderstandings of hazard, and, in order that I can be quite sure of my disaster before succumbing to it, deign, when you no longer love me, to give me, with the withered rose and the deceased dove, an extinct ray of sunlight."

"I consent to that gladly," she said. "If I cease to love you, I'll give you, at the same time as the pale flower and the inert bird, a ray of sunlight, similarly dead."

For days, I lived in the anguish of receiving the sinister presents. But since this morning, I'm as happy as one can be on this earth, for in the best-informed newspapers I read that, by virtue of a new decree of the celestial Providences, roses will never fade again, doves will never die and the crepuscular sun will never be extinguished again on the western horizon.

X. Alms Recompensed

I encountered a beggar who asked me for alms; I gave him all the gold—very little—that I had in my pocket.

I encountered a fool who wanted to be glorious; I gave him my dreams, my exquisite subtleties and my art of finding new rhymes.

I encountered a general who was going to fight a battle; I gave him a plan of campaign, thanks to which he triumphed over his enemies.

I encountered a writer of newspaper articles anxious about an imminent deadline; I gave him all the news that I had invented over dessert at lunch, while the newsvendors were hawking the morning newspapers on the boulevard.

I encountered a coward who was about to be beaten; I gave him my imperturbable composure, my vivacity in the attack and my briskness in the riposte.

I encountered an impious man; I gave him my eternal belief in gods in whom human reverie is eternalized.

I encountered a wretched millionaire who had never loved, although all the beautiful women in the world had offered him their hair and their breasts; I gave him the tenderness of which my heart is made.

Then, denuded, I went to visit Madeleine.

In order to recompense me for my charities, she permitted me to kiss her on the lips; and on her mouth, in the odors moistness of her mouth, I recovered—centupled treasures—wealth, talent, strategy, wit, courage, faith and amour.

XI. The Imbecile Assassin

An assassin, with a blow of a hammer, drove a nail into my temple.

But I didn't die.

"It's very little," I said, "an iron spike in the head! If you want me to die, you'll need to think of a more violent implement."

He went away. He came back. He had in his right hand an enormous sledgehammer for killing cattle, with which he gave me five heavy blows on the back of my neck.

But I didn't die.

"A fine thing!" I said. "You're strangely mistaken if you think I'm going to render my soul under your abattoir instrument. I advise you, if you want me to expire, to have recourse to more subtle means."

"Just wait!" he said.

He went away. He came back. He put under my nose a little phial, the liquid in which was due to the combined arts of all the Locustas and all the Brinvilliers.

But I didn't die.

"How stupid you are!" I said. "Do you think that I will cease to live so easily because of a treacherous perfume? Even

if you used sharp knives, *aqua tofana*,[56] the bright droplet that
a rattlesnake conceals in its fangs, the blade of the guillotine
and explosive shells, I'd continue to exist nevertheless, having
a resistant life. Invent some other crime."

"Just wait!" he said.

But he didn't budge. He was, as they say, at the end of
his tether, and he looked quite pitiful.

Then I felt sorry for him.

"Oh, poor assassin," I said, "is it necessary to teach you
your trade? Send for Madeleine. Let her pass by without smiling at me, or smiling at someone else, and I'll die right away!"

XII. The Brambles and Her Amour

I saw a butterfly that was utterly pitiful; it had wings so
torn and so perforated that one might have taken them for lace
bitten by my teeth on Madeleine's breasts.

"Butterfly," I said, "you are, in truth, in a very pitiful
state; I've never encountered a butterfly in such a bad way. To
what adventure, if you please, do you owe such a disaster?"

"Alas," he said, "It's because, fluttering carelessly, I let
myself fall into brambles, the cruel stings of which I felt."

"You fate," I said, "certainly warrants compassion. But
think, at least, that thorns and brambles have always harmed
butterflies. What would you say, then, and how much reason
would you have to be astonished if, in brushing the smooth
calices of flowers, you were lacerated as my heart has been by
the tender amour of Madeleine?"

---

[56] *Aqua tofana* was a liquid poison used in Italy, reputedly
concocted by the infamous Giulia Tofana, a follower of the
profession of the similarly infamous Locusta, who was executed in Rome 1659, not long before the Marchioness de
Brinvilliers was executed in Paris, although the evidence
against the latter was very dubious.

XIII. The Snowflake

"What I want," she said, "is a snowflake,"

"Well," I said, "Consider, you to whom I am as submissive as a leaf and the powder flying from a butterfly's wing are to the wind, that for many days the meadows and the branches have been green, and the May sun is gilding the warmed waves of the river. One no longer sees any hivernal whiteness in gardens, or in the woods, or on the hills. Please, desire something else as the price of the kiss that the humblest of your lovers is imploring on his knees."

"What I want," she said, "is a snowflake."

"Would it please you to have a river of black diamonds in which the radiance of the inferno ignites, or an enormous sapphire in which all the blue of the sky is contained, or a ruby so red, so delectably red, that it would resemble a drop of the flesh of your lips? Would you consent to accept, in order to put it in your hair—in exchange for the kiss so long coveted— a star stolen, in a Japanese temple, from the celestial diadem of Ten-Sio-Dai-Tsin; or, in order to make earrings of them, two splinters of moonstone, one of which is on sale for a hundred thousand francs in the Hindu jewelers in the Rue de la Paix?"

"What I want," she said, "is a snowflake."

"Would you like a castle in Scotland, on the edge of a loch over which, by night. phantoms of queens dream, their shrouds gliding over the nenuphars? Would you prefer the house in the Champs-Élysées that Monsieur de Rothschild thought too dear? Would you like me to harness to your mail-coach, on the day of the Grand Prix, six Circassian horses more beautiful than those that pull the Tsar's carriage?"

"What I want," she said, "is a snowflake."

Then I understood that she would not let go. And since it was impossible for me to live any longer without having obtained the ineffable kiss, I departed for the distant Alps. Alas,

379

in the valleys and on the mountain slopes, it was not snowing; everywhere there was dazzling, burning sunlight. I risked the most perilous ascensions, but even on the highest summits, it was no snowing. Yes, undoubtedly, there was snow beneath my feet, but it did not consist of flakes, and it was necessary not to think of dealing slyly with the desire of the adored.

For ten days, without shelter, almost without nourishment, I waited under the implacable sunlit azure. Finally—O joy! O triumph!—on the morning of the eleventh day, it snowed, and I carried away a snowflake in the hollow ice that I had disposed to receive it; thank Heaven, it did not melt during the return journey.

Victorious, I cried: "You are obeyed, Madame, and I have merited the kiss.

Then she said: "Good! What is that, pray?"

"It's a snowflake."

"Undoubtedly, undoubtedly. I don't say no. It is, indeed, snow. But it's white."

"Well?"

"What I wanted," she said, "was pink snow."

XIV. The Excessively Hot Abode

A very disquieting devil—the one who ignites in the loins of men and women the inextinguishable conflagration of lust—was prowling the world in order to tempt feeble humans. All day long he amused himself, because of a hundred adventures, but in the evenings he found himself strangely discomfited because, having finally acquired the habit of sleeping in vats of boiling oil, or on hot grills and amid all the furnaces of Hell, the beds down here, even the most ardent, seemed to him to be strangely icy, and he was very much afraid of catching a cold.

He asked me for advice.

"What should I do?" he said.

"Take shelter," I said, "in an enormous bowl of punch, always alight, into which flaming red alcohol is always being poured."

He thought the advice good. But the next day, on emerging from the bowl, he said, pulling a face: "Very lukewarm,"

The, I advised him: "Sleep in the crater of some Vesuvius, among the bubbling lava and the spurting flames."

He approved of that idea, but the next day, having descended from the volcano—I think it was Hecla—he said to me: "I was numb with cold!"

And he had shivered all night.

Damn! I thought.

Taking pity on him, I really did not know what to imagine in order for him to be able to sleep at his ease, when I was struck by inspiration.

"Devil," I said, "you'll sleep this evening in the tender heart, the very loving heart, the very ardent heart, of my darling Madeleine."

He hesitated. Doubtless, such hospitality is not one of those that one refuses, but what likelihood is there of a woman's heart being less cold than flaming alcohol and flaming craters? However, he resigned himself to attempting the adventure when night fell. And scarcely had he entered the dear heart that I adore—him, the devil accustomed to all the vats, grills and furnaces of Hell—than he leapt out, howling: "Help! Help! It's too hot! I'm burning!"

XV. The Atrocious Name

I asked that melancholy poet, once illustrious but now forgotten: "Why when still young, did you cease to make verses? Was the love of beautiful chimeras extinguished within you? Had the branch of your dream on which the beautiful images flourished in clusters, with the double rose of rhymes, dried up forever?"

The melancholy poet replied to me: "No, I had not lost the noble enthusiasm, not the intense creative energy, but I ceased to write, and will never write again, because of the accursed Name."

"What name do you mean?" I asked.

"The Name of the hundred times treacherous and infidel woman who was my ephemeral joy and who will be my eternal torment, the name of the woman I hate as much as I adored her. That Name, proffered or written, is the disaster of everything that is pure, everything that is good, and everything that is beautiful. It suffices, like a horrible magic word, to extinguish the stars, to wither the lilies, to cause the rose of the modesty of the august cheeks of virgins to fade. I no longer want, and cannot any longer, make the abominable Name heard"

Well," I said, "What obliges you to sing it? Forget the vile perjurer. Sing the amour of others, sing the glory of heroes, and the loyal beauty of the sky and the sea."

"Alas, alas, I cannot," he said, sobbing, "for the atrocious charm of the Name does not reside only in the name entire; it disperses, without diminishing, in each of the signs that form it, with the consequence that there are hardly any words that I can write, and the holiest, the most chaste, the most sublime speech—the praise of an elect or a fiancée, or the glories of a redeemer—would only signify ignominy and abjection, because of a single letter."

The Voyage Before Dinner

On the fourth floor of the beautiful new house, in the vast waxed-walnut dining room, illuminated by the suspended radiance of two brass lamps and a dozen candles, the guests have already taken their places. Around the table white with damasked linen and bright silverware there are, with their wives or daughters, two notaries, an advocate, a retired silk-merchant, an architect and an inspector of finances.

The master of the house, the host, Monsieur Gauron-Delesmes, a notable tradesman and deputy Maire, hastens to re-fold his half-opened napkin and says: "I beg your pardon, but I cannot resist going to make, before the soup, a little excursion to the other side of the world." He adds, smiling: "I'll bring back a few exotic flowers for the ladies, depend on it."

"In fact," says Madame Gauron-Delesmes, "it's a habit that my husband has adopted for some time. He can't dine in a good humor unless he has made a little excursion to the far side of the world."

"Excellent habit," says one of the notaries.

"There's nothing like exercise...," says the retired silk merchant.

"...to give you an appetite," the inspector of finances finishes.

"Don't worry," adds Monsieur Gauron-Delesmes. "I won't be long. You'll see me return before the tureen is brought in."

"Take your time, take your time, my dear Monsieur," says the architect.

The chair in which the master of the house is sitting has already sunk into the floor toward the room below. Monsieur Gauron-Delesmes traverses, from top to bottom, a very elegant, very luminous mahogany dining-room in which a dozen people are already commencing dinner.

"Oh, my dear neighbor," said Monsieur Gauron-Delesmes, "forgive me for disturbing you like this."

"It's no trouble, dear neighbor, no trouble! We're accustomed to your little visits. Bon voyage."

"Thank you, thank you!"

"Bon voyage."

On the second floor, the voyager traverses another dining room, where the lamps are not yet lit. The butler, who is caressing the chambermaid, cries: "He's annoying, that fellow, coming through the ceiling like that without knocking!"

On the first floor there is a dining room full of trinkets and little decorations, and rose cameos above the doors. Three beautiful young women, who, if one can judge by their attire, composed for each of them of a sleeveless chemise, have just got up or are about to go to bed, are sucking crayfish between bottles of Moët in their seals, coated with white foam.

"Oh, say, stop for a moment, Monsieur. Have a glass of champagne. Are you in a hurry today"

"I have people to dinner today, I fear; I only just have time to take a little trip to the other side of the world."

"Go, go—another time. Tomorrow?"

"Tomorrow, it's agreed."

Monsieur Gauron-Delesmes traverses, from top to bottom, a hairdresser's boutique.

"A twist of the curling tongs, Monsieur? A shave?"

"No, no, another time."

He disappears, he sinks, he sinks; he sees, in the penumbra extending from the ventilation shaft, the barrels in the cellar and the neatly-arrange bottles. His chair is nearly stopped by the enormous pipes of the drains. He descends.

Here is the black earth, veined with gray and white, like the interior of an enormous truffle; and colossal tree roots are like frightening black boas, which, sated, are no long roving.

Splash! Monsieur Gauron-Delesmes, seated in his chair plunges into a subterranean lake, over which immense flaccid wings take flight, which are the bats of the interior night.

He sees, like furnaces stirred by invisible pokers, molten deposits of diamonds, beryls, sapphires and chrysoprases.

He traverses the moving, mixed, rolling conflagration that is the center, the belly, of the world.

He finds himself in darkness again. He sees other subterranean lakes, other giant rots, parts from bottom to top, stinking darkness, aspires light, fresh air, rises through long grass and finds himself in a hostelry of pink lacquer and porcelain, where three or four Chinamen are taking tea, punctuating with their fans the lines of verse that they are murmuring in the shrill voices of little birds.

"Oh! It's Monsieur Gauron-Delesmes."

"Bonjour, Monsieur Gauron-Delesmes."

"You're very late!"

"We weren't expecting you any longer."

"It's because I have people to dinner."

"A cup of tea?"

"No, a cup of rice wine instead; it's an excellent aperitif."

"Serve Monsieur Gauron-Delesmes a cup of rice wine."

"Oh, it's excellent. Hey, little flower-seller, let me buy your most beautiful flowers. But I have to get back; the soup will soon be served."

"Go, go, don't worry! Until tomorrow!"

The chair sinks again, through the entire earth; he sees again the darkness, the intestinal conflagration of the globe, the ocean of chrysoprases, sapphires, beryls and diamonds, the enormous bats of the subterranean pools, the colossal boas that are roots, the tunnels of drains, the neatly-arranged bottles and barrels of cellars, the hairdresser's boutique, the gilded dining room in which the three beautiful young women are no longer wearing any chemises at all, the as-yet-unlit dining room where it is now the chambermaid that is caressing the butler, the elegant and luminous dining room—

"Aha! it's the neighbor! Have you had a pleasant voyage, neighbor?"

"A very pleasant voyage, thank you."

—and here he is in front of his table, in his chair, among his guests.

"Excuse me, I'm a little late."

"Oh no!"

"No!"

"Yes indeed," said Madame Gauron-Delesmes. "You've taken more than ten minutes. Look, the soup-tureen has been bought in."

"Yes," remarks one of the notaries, laughing, "but the soup's still fuming."

"Let this obtain my pardon," says Monsieur Gauron-Delesmes, and he hands two Chinese rhododendrons to the notaries' wives, a scarlet cactus to the advocate's daughter, a Nagasaki carnation to the sister of the retired silk-merchant and a lily from the Mountains of the Moon to the wife of the inspector of finances.

All that is very simple; what would astonish the bourgeois would be if it were otherwise, for the Chimera is in society.

The Plurality of Habitable Worlds; Or, The Anthropophages

Scaramouche offered several members of the Institut—astronomers by profession—an informal supper. If anyone is astonished that the hospitality of such a character, even more insipid than passable, diabolical in his attire and manner, was accepted by such respectable scientists, it is because they have forgotten that the Night willingly dresses as Scaramouche,[57] and nothing is more natural than that intimacy between the nocturnal Abyss and the Telescope. In any case, the astronomers, amid the noise of forks, under the splendor of four candelabra illuminating the glassware and porcelain, and the tablecloth strewn with flowers, writhed with laughter—they were already drunk, albeit respectably—because someone, a reporter who happened to be there, had insinuated that the worlds of the sky were doubtless inhabited by beings similar to terrestrial humans.

"Ha ha!"

"Ho ho!"

"Hee hee!"

"Hi hi!"

"The planes inhabited!"

"Men on the moon!"

"It's necessary to be Cyrano de Bergerac..."

"...or Fontenelle..."

"...or Shakespeare..."

"...or Hugo..."

"...or Camille Flammarion..."

"...to believe in such nonsense!"

---

[57] The character Scaramouche, in the classic *commedia dell'arte*, usually dressed entirely in black.

They were writhing, increasingly drunk; for Scaramouche when he invites the Institut to supper, does things well.

One of the scientists, a practical man, said: "Let's leave these follies. Let's occupy ourselves with the dishes that we're eating. I don't know what ingredients they're made with—no, truly, I don't know—but they're perfectly exquisite, and this is a feast as delectable as it is mysterious."

The others howled:

"Delectable!"

"Mysterious!"

"There's a taste of grouse."

"Or trout."

"Pardon! Mountain bear in brine with a hint of garlic."

"Or frog sprinkled with saffron."

But everyone agreed that they had never eaten anything more flavorsome.

Then, tranquilly, Scaramouche said: "What you are eating, Messieurs, is Human! And I think that if you search carefully in the sauce, you won't fail to find a few small bones revelatory of the kind of meat you've been eating with so much satisfaction."

The writhing and he laughter redoubled.

But Scaramouche, said, imperturbably: "If I'm not the Night herself, I'm her cook. The immense blue vault is a transparent frying-pan, on which I fried, holding it by the Milky Way, which is its handle, Venus, Mars, Mercury, Jupiter, Neptune and all the stars, on the stove of the eternal Sun. The comets, which have the form of a cruet, pour flamboyant oil; every red bolide is a grain of Cayenne pepper, and the wind of infinite space has the function of a bellows that activates the fire under the frying-pan—with the consequence that it's the sky, cooked to perfection, that I've served you for supper. Not all the sky; the planets, being tough, remained in the cooker; but the little parasites of the heavenly bodies—I mean the living beings of the firmament—have sizzled in the sauce, and you've nourished yourself on your celestial resemblances."

At the same time, with a long black leg that raked the whole table, Scaramouche tipped over, broke and extinguished the candelabra; and in the darkness, while he roared with laughter, the dead-drunk scientists, sickened and frightened by the execrable feast, vomited parcels of cutlets, backs, fillets, ribs and fry of Mars, Mercury, Saturn and the divine flesh of Venus, which is golden in the blue of beautiful skies.

A Scene in the Hall

To François Coppée,
in remembrance of an old poem.[58]

In the theater of a music hall there was a very famous juggler.

A clown scintillating with spangles, he juggled with gilded walls, knives of damascened steel, and torches of blazing resin.

Or, in a frock-coat and a top hat, not too far too the right or left, an irreproachable gentleman, he juggled with his cigar, his monocle and the roof of the house, received twenty hundred-sou silver coins, one by one in his fob pocket, which one of his heels had kicked up in the form of five louis d'or, and made the droplets of an invisible water jet turn into pearls on a swirling umbrella.

The crowd acclaimed the very famous juggler, who never missed a single one of his tricks; he seemed to be very proud of the enthusiasm of the crowd.

But one evening, as a clown scintillating with spangles, he dropped a ball, and a knife, and a resin torch; then, as a gentleman, he was unable to prevent the monocle and the cigar being crushed by one of the roof beams; all the silver coins rolled on the floor, and from the umbrella, which was spinning too slowly, the pearls of the water jet scattered like the spillage of a necklace of drops of water.

---

[58] Mendès helped launch François Coppée's career by introducing him to the Parnassians, including Charles Leconte de Lisle and Théodore Banville, in 1866, but by 1904 they had drifted far apart as Coppée had become involved with far right-wing politics.

The crowd was astonished to see the juggler, who had never missed a single one of his tricks, miss them all; he seemed very saddened by the astonishment of the crowd.

He approached the front of the stage and said: "Excuse me. It isn't my fault. I'll tell you what happened. It isn't my fault. Every day, before noon, I work. I exercise, as they say in our profession, in order to remain worthy of your applause. This morning, while exercising—it was in the garden of the house where I live—I threw up, as usual, a little sold gold orange, in real gold, with signs on it, that I've had for a very long time, forever. It's like a fairy tale, the story of that little orange of real gold. It was fund in my cradle before the first sleep that I had there. That was what gave me the idea of becoming a juggler, and in order to exercise, I've always made use of it. But today, I threw it up so high, so high, that I waited in vain, with my palm open, for it to come down again. Had some large bird, passing overhead, caught it and carried it away? Had it been caught in the clouds above the azure? It didn't come down again. It didn't fall back. I no longer have the little orange of real gold. That's why I've missed all my tricks, I beg your pardon."

And the juggler sobbed violently between his shaking hands.

The crowd did not understand at all. Open-mouthed, its members waited, but they did not understand. Were they to laugh, or to get annoyed, as one does when one doesn't understand? What prevented them from getting annoyed or laughing is that they could see very well that the admirable juggler, now a wretched juggler, was weeping sincerely, that his grief was real, like the little orange.

Now, in a box, between the hats, like rose- and tulip-bushes full of birds of paradise, four beautiful young women, intoxicated by having drunk, at lunch, the blood of their bitten lips, the hair of a very famous poet loomed up. Everyone knew him, not by virtue of having read him, but by virtue of having seen his photograph in the shops of frame-sellers. Whispers went through the stalls.

"It's him!"

"Do you recognize him!"

"Him!"

"Do you know him?"

"What does he want?"

"Why has he stood up?"

"Perhaps he knows why the juggler is weeping?"

He did know, in fact. He shouted over the hats of roses, tulips and wings: "I understand! And I'll be understood by that desperate clown! All the tricks he did, I did them too, and like him, I never missed. A scintillating improviser of spangles, I juggled with gilded rhythms, with damascened rhymes, with flamboyant images; or, an irreproachable artiste, I charmed the multitude by means of the fantasies of the chimera, sublimities coined in the play of poems, the impossible scanned in vibrant strophes; and you applauded me.

"But once, I was exercising with the dream, with the dream in real gold, which, by a magnificent and cruel providence, had been put in my cradle before I had first gone to sleep there, and I threw it up so high, so high, that, my mind agape, I waited in vain for it to come back. Had an angel, having recognized it, seized it and taken it away to the original heavens? Had it vanished, vanished among the fraternal mysteries of infinity? It hasn't come back; it will never come back. I no longer have the dear dream in real gold. That's why, for such a long time, I've missed all my tricks. I beg your pardon."

And at the same time as the juggler, the poet sobbed between his shaking hands.

The crowd, perhaps moved, did not know what to think, or do.

But from the orchestra stalls, a critic said: "This is an affair, damn it! Don't you see, public, that they're making fun of you? All this was prepared. It's nothing but, after the spectacle on the stage, a scene in the hall. It's a joke, public, it's a joke!"

Then the whole crowd laughed. Disposed to sympathize, it laughed. The critic was right! And it laughed.

Can they exist, jugglers who weep, and poets who weep, because they have thrown something that is true gold too high? They cannot exist, inasmuch as there is no longer anything that is true gold. And what proved to everyone that the critic was right is that, soon, the curtain closed, and then reopened, and two clowns appeared on the stage of the Music Hall, one a dwarf and the other a giant—who, being, in fact, the juggler and the poet, slapped one another in the belly with enormous sonorous paddles, sprayed one another with soda siphons and collapsed with rubber legs on the round balloons of their behinds, while the luminous balloons of their skulls were popped by a blow from a hammer.

The Collector of Dream-Ends

One evening, in the street of a large city, I saw, from a distance, and then close up, a man coming toward me who seemed very old—a pink, cheerful head, snowy with white hair—and very small, seeming even smaller because he was bending down, sometimes less and sometimes more, as if to look at, and to pick up, things on the pavement along his route. And he made the gesture of putting the things he picked up in his pockets.

What things? I could not see either color or form in the hands that went from the pavement to the pockets. One might have thought that he was taking possession of empty air, of nothing. But at each invisible discovery, he appeared very satisfied, his face grimacing like that of an ape chewing a sugary fig.

I said to him: "Are you not, Monsieur, afflicted by madness, or at least mania? It's impossible for me to comprehend the motive for your incessant conduct."

He blinked.

"Do you believe that you would have understood, if it had not been explained to you, why Christopher Columbus opened his palms, which did not carry worlds, on the edge of the sea, toward the infinity of the Ocean? Neither mad nor manic, I am in the process, such as you see me, Monsieur, of assembling everything that it necessary for me to ornament the inside of the tomb that I am having built for me."

"Eh?" I said. "What interest do you have—supposing that you could find the wherewithal—to ornament the interior of your sepulcher? The buried no longer have a gaze."

"The buried who are dead. Although buried, I shall not be defunct. I picked up immortality a year ago, on a heap of rags and broken bottles."

"Immortality?"

394

"The same. I see by your bewildered expression that you continue not to understand. And, a little pressed for time—today's harvest is not yet very abundant—I don't have the leisure to inform you in detail. However, as I think you have a honest face, and you give the impression of someone who does not have enough money to ornament his sepulcher sumptuously, I don't see any inconvenience in revealing my secret to you. Here, take this little key; it's that of my crypt."

"It's gold!"

"You've seen that? You must be—I suspected as much—an itinerant poet. You can take it without scruple; it seems to be gold, it's made of hope; I have a similar one, made of illusion. Now, listen to me carefully. In four days, on Wednesday evening, at eight forty-five I shall render the last sigh, as they say..."

"How can you know that?"

"I picked up divination toward the end of last spring, behind a boundary-marker. So, on Wednesday evening, at eight forty-five, it will seem that I'm rendering my soul. I shall carefully refrain from rendering it. It's so precious to me, so divine! Twenty-four hours later, my body will be taken to be buried. It will be necessary to retain myself, in order not to laugh at the undertakers. I won't go on. I'm in a hurry. Come to the cemetery on Friday evening. You'll recognize my crypt easily. It's in the first pathway to the right, between the tombstone of a little girl died at the age of five and the slab of an old man who died at ninety. I wanted to be buried between two infancies. Open the door with the key made of hope, go down four or five steps, and then I'll inform you of things that will interest you."

He went away, bending down, straightening up and bending down again, drawing further and further away, and disappeared. Because he had said strange things to me, I was beginning to be convinced that he was not madman or a maniac. Real madmen have too little imagination; ordinary human folly, alas, is nothing but exasperated stupidity. I promised myself to be prompt at the rendezvous that he had fixed.

In fact, I did not fail to go there. The following Friday, a little after nightfall, I emerged from behind the sepulcher—I had hidden there while the people who were able to leave left the cemetery—and very easily, in the twilight between daylight and starlight, I found, in the first path to the right, between a tombstone and a slab, the little old man's mausoleum. I opened the door, by means of the key, made of gold or hope, and went down four steps. It was very dark.

I didn't feel any malaise, however, at penetrating into the darkness of the tomb, into death. Death had haunted me for so long that I had become accustomed to it; it had even installed itself within me, and as I bore it within me, I experienced a certain pleasure of vengeance, in turning the tables. Death might be afraid of the anxiety of life...was it frightened? But in all the blackness, two little gleams lit up; I divined that they were eyes.

"There you are!" said the little man.

"Yes, here I am," I said. "How have you been able to break the boards, or lift the lid, of your coffin?"

"It's because I found strength and patience last year," he said, "behind the wall of a bunker. But let's not dwell on trivia. Look around you, Monsieur Passer-by, around me! Look, contemplate, be dazzled! Isn't it resplendent, the tomb that I've decorated for the enchantment of my eternal wakefulness?"

"Not to lie, Monsieur Dead Man," I replied. "I can't see anything, apart from your eyes, but the opacity of darkness."

"Yes, yes! Your eyes, which divined the golden hope of the key, still have need of light to see the infinite splendors. So be it. Do you smoke?"

"Not at the moment."

"I was asking whether you smoke habitually."

"Of course."

"Then you have a box of matches on you?"

"Yes, Monsieur."

"Light a match, then. Only one! For the neighboring dead, alerted by the glimmer, might break through the walls of

396

earth and rejoice in my treasures. I'm slightly selfish, like all collectors."

As soon as the match flared, I uttered a cry, so much was I enveloped—dawns, red noons, milky ways in the dazzling pure night—by all the prodigious blossoming of the entire dream in lily-diamond, in crimson flashes, in enormous snow-roses.

The match went out. There was no longer anything but darkness. But my host, in his tomb, said:

"You've seen! You've seen! Listen, now, and understand. The people who walk in the city sometimes lose their handkerchief, their cane, or their purse. They go to the lost property office, and they lament, if the objects they're reclaiming can't be returned. The insensates! They lose, continually, things a thousand times more precious, which they never think of reclaiming.

"Not only are fine minds full of august and exquisite chimeras, which they drop, but even mediocre souls, vile souls, often bear dreams within them, noble dreams, that slip away, and which they don't regret. There is no coward who isn't traversed sometimes by the hope of a courageous act. There is no slut who isn't haunted, sometimes, by a desire for innocence. There is even no writer of vaudevilles who cannot conceive, momentarily, the ambition to survive in some immortal work.

"The base living, however, who have lost such grandeurs, don't think of searching for them; they even forget that they had them, however briefly. If there were a bureau of lost sublimities, they would refrain from going there to reclaim them. The imbecile life, and their own imbecility, obliges them to the Fact, and does not even permit them the memory any longer of the adorable and fugitive unreal. But for sixty years I've been walking the streets where all men pass, and patiently, ardently, always bending over the apparently-filthy pavement, a rag-collector of ideas, I've picked up beauty, amour and glory. Thanks to the faith that had fallen out of the haversack of a missionary in a railway station where emigrants were asleep. I've made light! And now, for ever and ever, for my infinite delight, which has no need of paradise, the walls of my sepulcher are ornamented with every human ideal."

The Opinion of the Image

Under the redness extended by the dawn over the rags on their backs, the two laborers, pickaxes over their shoulders, go up the street that is almost a road, with ruts softened into mud by the morning dew, toward the ridge from the top of which they will be able to see the entire city, where they earn their living with their picks. They bend over, their backs red, they groan, they climb, they reach the summit; they consider the enormous city, shadow and light, night, gaslight and dawn together, sleep and awakening, and they hear the profound and tenebrous muted rumble of humankind, like the mingled belches of consciences that are digesting poorly.

One of the two laborers brandishes his pick and says: "We've been hired to demolish a building; another will be put in its place, similar to the first. That's not serious. What it's necessary to demolish with this pickax isn't one house, it's all the houses, which won't be rebuilt as they were built; it's palaces, courthouses and churches!" Pointing to his implement and the city in turn, the demolisher added: "This will overturn that."

The other workman shrugged his shoulders. "Litterateur!" he said. "Me, I earn three francs ten sous a day."

They went down toward the city, toward the work. It seemed that, the red of the dawn having followed them, they left behind them something like a slippery caress of blood. The road-sweepers swept it away, with the more obscure mud.

The two workmen went past a church. Behind the gates there was an image of Christ, in gilded bronze, leaning forward.

The image said to one of the laborers: "Why are you worried about the three francs ten sous of your daily salary?"

And to the other, it said: "Since you want to demolish, demolish. Don't delay. Act quickly. Oh, man, in truth, I tell you this: I won't defend myself against your pickax, for final-ly, my crucified arms are weary of their eternal effort toward the universal benediction, and humans ought to have removed the nails from my palms if they wanted to be blessed. You, workman, laborer, brute, attack me with blows of the pick, demolish me; I've had enough of my futile example of re-demptive resignation, and perhaps, in my debris, there're will be fragments of salvation that desperate little children can pick up."

But the two workmen had not heard. They went to the work-site, as they did every morning.

No one knows what might happen on another day.

The Smoke-Merchant

The man in question, who was not mad, alas, but who would dearly have liked to be, learned that there was great poverty in a very distant country—in the direction, I think, of the Rose River, carrier of pale ruby sand—and that it would need no less than a million to help so many paupers. Charitable, although not mad, he said to himself: *That million I certainly don't have, but I could easily procure it by selling what I keep in this little tarred canvas bag.*

With that, he put on his overcoat and picked up his staff, and went to the city in order to sell what he had in the bag.

Having entered the city he did not take long to see, between the cathedral and the imperial palace, a vast and sumptuous store, which bore a sign saying: *Sale and purchase of all kinds of merchandise.* In addition, doubtless to inspire confidence in person who wanted to dispose of precious objects, enormous piles of coins and bowls overflowing with gemstones were sparkling amid the obligatory wads of banknotes behind windows illuminated by rich sunlight.

The man who was not mad said to himself: *I'll doubtless be able to do business here*, and he went into the opulent store.

Scarcely had he crossed the threshold than he perceived the Businessman. He was a person of tall stature, who—something rather rare among men of his estate, was wearing a cardinalesque crimson robe in a priestly manner, and an iron imperial crown encrusted with diamonds in the manner of stars. But he advanced with an eager haste.

"What can I do for your service Monsieur? New stock has arrived very recently."

"I've come to sell, not to buy."

"Good. What do you desire to sell?"

"What there is in this tarred canvas bag. But I warn you that I want a rather high price for it—at least a million."

"A million, so be it, if the thing is worth four times as much, for it's necessary to make a small profit, isn't it? But open the bag, I beg you, in order that I can see the merchandise."

"Eh? If I open the bag, there'll no longer be anything in it."

Then the man who would dearly have liked to be mad explained things. In the home of his parents, who were poor inhabitants of an outlying district, he had been brought up in company with a cat whose greatest pleasure was to prowl on the roofs night and day; they had prowled on the roofs together. And he had been smitten with smoke: the pretty smoke, the sad smoke and the light smoke, sometime mingled with sparks, that emerged from the houses through the chimneys. Down below, in each dwelling, in the bedroom of each dwelling, souls were dreaming, hoping, loving and suffering, and it was the dreams, the hopes, the amours and the suffering of souls, all the respiration of souls, that was rising towards infinite space. And for many years he had passed the time, as one catches clouds of butterflies in a butterfly net, catching the smoke of souls in a pouch of tarred canvas. And that was what there was in the bag.

The man who was not mad had not yet finished when the Businessman writhed with laughter and said "Ha ha ha! That's funny merchandise that I'm being offered. What can I—who, as well as managing this shop, am a cardinal of the cathedral to the left and the Emperor of the palace to the right—do with, or take any account of, human hopes and suffering? A million! I think you've lost your mind. Go on, Monsieur, get out. Not half a liard."

Then the man who would dearly have liked to be mad left, very discomfited.

Was that true? Had human hope and anguish no value? Perhaps he had been wrong to spend tome collecting them in a tarred canvas pouch, as one catches butterflies.

He was very sad, being charitable, because of so much distant poverty—women, old men, girls and many other people—who would not be helped.

As he came to sit down, a little weary, outside the door of a small tavern, from which music was emerging, a strangely pale and thin young man, who was wearing a stained frock-coat without a waistcoat, with a white rose in the buttonhole, said to him: "Monsieur, you seem chagrined; and, not very joyful myself, for I'm the poet who lodges at the Famine Hotel, I feel inclined to pity for you."

"Alas, Monsieur," said the other, "you can't do anything for me. The Businessman-Cardinal-Emperor has refused to conclude the bargain." And he told him the whole story.

The strangely pale and thin young man said "Rejoice, Monsieur. I'll buy what there is in the little bag."

The man who would dearly have liked to be mad but wasn't shook his head and replied: "Firstly, you wouldn't know what to do with the smoke of souls; secondly, you don't have the million necessary to come to the aid of the poor people I mentioned to you."

"No, I don't have the million, and I'm poorer than Albert Gratigny, who was singularly poor, even though he was much richer than Rothschild; but don't worry about anything. Sell me the dreams, the hopes, the amours and suffering of humans that you collected from the chimneys of dwellings, and give me credit for an hour. With the smoke of souls I'll make a song, which I'll give you in payment: a song so sweet, so sad and so beautiful that it will console all the poor people on the banks of the Rose River that carries sands of pale rubies—and all the other countries in the world."

The Vain Exchange of Two Souls

One of the dreams came, in the night, from a long way away; the other came, in the night, from even further away.

Dreams? Yes, but only near to being dreams; which is to say that they didn't yet have the impalpable body that they would soon take on in the sleep of the humans to whom they were destined by the mysterious will that consoles, on earth, the good who are unhappy, and also punishes the happy who are bad: the pleasant dreams that are a foretaste of Paradise, and the nightmares that are an apprenticeship for Hell.

One of the dreams was all pink, with the wings of a sylph. The other was black, with the wings of a crow.

They met, and looked at one another.

The pink dream said: "How somber you are! How terrible you are! Into what sleeping soul are you going to bring fear and disaster?"

The black dream replied: "I'm going to bring disaster and fear into the sleep of a atrocious old man, charged with crimes, in order that, while sleeping he'll expiate and wake up with his hair standing on end. But how bright you are! How charming you are! Into what sleeping soul are you going to bring charm and happy adventure?"

"I'm going to bring happy adventure and charm into the sleep of a young girl who hasn't thought, all day, about the young gallant who gazed, during mass, at the thin golden down on the nape of the neck, in order that while asleep, she'll smile and wake up with eyes of dawn and marvel."

Even all black, one can have pity.

"Rosy dream?"

"Somber dream?"

"Would you like to trade assignments?"

"What do you mean?"

"He's very desolate, since I've been haunting him for so many nights, the atrocious old man charged with crimes. You who console, go into his sleep, which I go into that of the sinless young woman."

"But she'll suffer unjustly, poor thing!"

"But he'll suffer a little less, the poor fellow."

"What will the eternal justice think whose servants we are?"

"The eternal justice is benevolent, and will doubtless approve of a little rare joy, in a desperate man, being purchased with a little anxiety for once, on the part of a happy young woman.

The trade was agreed. They changed course.

What marvelous beauties the sleeping soul of the atrocious old man saw that night! It seemed to him that he was walking, with the bare feet of a child, in a meadow full of flowers and dew.

What sad spectacles the pure young woman saw that night! It seemed to her that, while walking with soles reddened by infernal pyres over the points of knives, she saw the grimaces of the infinite population of the damned.

But he woke up with his hair standing on end! He remembered the beautiful dream as a frightful nightmare.

And she woke up with eyes of dawn and marvel. She remembered the bad dream as a delightful vision.

For one is what one is. Neither realities not chimeras can change anything. Souls are urns in which everything becomes what they are. Ink would become white in an alabaster vase. Honey would become bitter in a cup of quassia amara. If the good God could be mistaken, and, by mistake, elected a criminal and damned an innocent, the criminal would find Gehenna in Paradise, and the innocent would have Heaven in Hell.

The Best Alms

The young man was walking in the cemetery. He was a poet who had a great deal of talent, who had a very noble soul. He truly had a very elevated and very ingenuous soul—not without some ridicule, as befits simple people—and a talent that would have hesitated to affirm its self-confidence, by virtue of the detestation of and scorn for everything. Oh, the dear charming heart! You could have made him swoon in delight by reading him a poem by Léon Dierx.

He was walking in the cemetery because of the solitude, the bright sunlight, the space vaster than anywhere else, and the dream that he had in proximity with the dead. It seems, if one is very young, that one is giving the dead, from tomb to tomb—begging-bowls, those tombs—petty alms of life. And the young poet, in his lofty and fervent enthusiasms, venerated the tombstones of illustrious poets, and his chimera trumpeted glories silently before the sepulchers of heroes.

Then he wept because of the very small slab of a little girl, where there were florets, and, unexpectedly, a book opened—the wind was riffling through the pages—tremulously, one page dog-eared, as if someone, who had been reading that book with the dead girl before she died, had brought it there, in order to say that he would never read any further...

He wept, the poet without hatred. But something disquieted him. For some time, already, he had been followed by a tall lady, elegant under her veils—whether she was pretty it was impossible to tell, because of the thickness of the long crepes—who made him signs, as if in approval, when he inclined before a sepulcher of an illustrious poet or a hero, and complimented him, by a semblance of wiping away tears through the veil, when he took pity on a young woman who had died before so many promised kisses.

The tall lady even approached the amiable child poet suddenly, and put something in his hand, saying: "That's for you! It's for you! Oh, you deserve it! Keep it, make use of it." And she vanished.

Slightly astonished, the young visitor of the cemetery drew away, without opening his hand, as if in some dread. He went out, remarked to the right of the gate an old beggar who was always seen there, who must have been very old if he had been only fifty when he installed himself there for the first time.

"Monsieur," asked the poet, "do you know the tall lady dressed in black who is walking in the cemetery?"

"I believe I do know her. That's Madame Death. It's been days, months, years, that I've known her. I was employed by an undertaker for many years before becoming a cemetery beggar. She's not a very amiable lady, but she's very serious. She comes almost every morning, sometimes here, sometimes there, especially in spring. It appears that she adores the odor of tombs in April, as other people love the perfume of the first roses.

"She comes to see how things are going in her domain, so I'm told. And she makes gifts to people in passing, without seeming to make much of it. Some say that she gives them prizes, in accordance with the way they comport themselves in the midst of the tombs. She gives a little girl, who has come to mourn her little friends, a communion floret, an orange blossom to the amicable widower of a dead bride, and a branch of golden laurel to an old soldier who can only any longer extend a single living arm to a cadaver who also lacks a arm, the other having been carried away by the same machine-gun burst. And you, what has she given you?"

"This," said the poet, and opened his hand.

In his hand he had a very small flower, withered, skimpy, sad and also terrible.

The cemetery beggar who had been an undertaker until he was fifty stood up, wonderstruck, and then bowed respectfully.

"Oh!" he said. "Well, you've had a stroke of luck. You only have to put that flower in your mouth to die instantly. It's the poison-flower. It's only the fourth time that Madame Death has made such a gift. And you know, it's necessary not to publish it in the newspapers, because everyone would come!"

CLASSIC FRENCH FANTASY

Marie-Catherine d'Aulnoy. *Tales of the Fays* (2 vols.)'
Honoré de Balzac. *The Last Fay*
Gabrielle-Suzanne Barbot de Villeneuve. *The Naiads / Beauty and The Beast*
Chevalier de Béthune. *The World of Mercury*
Jean Carrère. *The End of Atlantis*
Charlotte-Rose Caumont de La Force. *The Land of Delights*
Comte de Caylus. *The Impossible Enchantment*
Félicien Champsaur. *Pharaoh's Wife*
Jacques Collin de Plancy. *Voyage to the Center of the Earth*
Gaston Danville. *The Perfume of Lust*
Comtesse D.L. *The Tyranny of the Fays Abolished*
Marie-Antoinette Fagnan. *The Enchanter's Mirror*
Paul Féval. *Anne of the Isles*
Charles de Fieux. *Lamékis*
Judith Gautier. *Isoline and the Serpent-Flower*
Nathalie Henneberg. *The Green Gods*
Gustave Kahn. *The Tale of Gold and Silence*
Edmond Haraucourt. *Dieudonat*
Nathalie Henneberg. *The Green Gods*
Françoise Le Marchand. *Florine and Boca*
Marie-Jeanne L'Héritier de Villandon. *The Robe of Sincerity*
André Lichtenberger. *The Centaurs; The Children of the Crab*
J-M. & Randy Lofficier (eds.). *The French Fantasy Treasury* (3 vols.)
Charles Lomon & P.-B. Gheuzi. *The Last Days of Atlantis*
Maurice Magre. *The Marvelous Story of Claire d'Amour; The Call of the Beast; Priscilla of Alexandria; The Angel of Lust; The Mystery of the Tiger; The Poison of Goa; Lucifer; The Blood of Toulouse; The Albigensian Treasure; Jean de Fodoas; Melusine; The Brothers of the Virgin Gold*
Marie-Madeleine de Lubert. *Princess Camion*.
Camille Mauclair. *The Virgin Orient*

Hippolyte Mettais. *Paris Before the Deluge*
Victor-Emile Michelet. *Superhuman Tales*
Henriette-Julie de Murat. *The Palace of Vengeance*
Charles Nodier. *Trilby / The Crumb Fairy*
Edgar Quinet. *The Enchanter Merlin*
Henri de Régnier. *A Surfeit of Mirrors*
Nicolas-Edmé Restif de la Bretonne. *The Fay Ouroucoucou* (2 vols.)
J.-H. Rosny Aîné. *Pan's Flute*
Marie-Anne de Roumier-Robert. *The Voyage of Lord Seaton to the Seven Planets*
Nicolas Ségur. *Penelope's Secret*
Brian Stableford (ed.). *Funestine; The Queen of the Fays; The Origin of the Fays; Tales of Enchantment and Disenchantment*
Kurt Steiner. *Ortog*
Charles-François Tiphaigne de La Roche. *Amilec / Giphantie*
Simon Tyssot de Patot. *The Strange Voyages of Jacques Massé and Pierre de Mésange*
Philippe Ward & Sylvie Miller. *The Song of Montségur*

www.ingramcontent.com/pod-product-compliance
Lightning Source LLC
Chambersburg PA
CBHW030932020726
47498CB00001B/208